# Oh wh
## tangled web...

By Pamela Hill

Published by Juliana Publishing

Book cover design and print by
Hillside Printing Services

Published by Juliana Publishing

Copyright © Pamela Hill 2009

British Library Cataloguing in Publication Data.
A catalogue record for this book is available
from the British Library.

All the characters in this book are fictitious
and any resemblance to actual persons living or
dead is purely coincidental

Juliana Publishing
Highview Lodge
Oulder Hill Drive
Rochdale
OL11 5LB


Printed and bound in Great Britain by Hillside
Printing Services, Rochdale Tel: 01706 711872
www.hillsidegroup.co.uk

IBSN 978-0-9559047-2-1

Oh what a tangled web...

Casting a fleeting glance at the dismal overcast sky, Robyn Ainsley stepped up her pace as she made her way towards the bus stop. Large spots of rain were beginning to merge on the flagstones, indicative of yet another blustery shower and adding to the many that had already fallen throughout the day.

She certainly wouldn't use *that* garage again! She was furious with the car mechanic who had assured her the repair would be, to use his words, *all done and dusted* by three-thirty. It was blatantly obvious he had allowed another customer to jump the queue and to further compound matters, the ill-mannered man hadn't even bothered to pick up the telephone to advise her it wouldn't be ready for collection that day. Had she not made a last-minute call to check, she would have trailed all the way to the garage by public transport for nothing. People were becoming so rude and inconsiderate nowadays, she grumbled to herself, at the same time covering her head with her scarf as the rain began to fall heavily.

She turned and peered up the road but there was still no sign of the bus.

Suddenly there was a flash of lightening, instantly followed by a loud clap of thunder that continued to rumble for a few seconds until the heavens opened, when swirling torrents of water flooded the gutters above overflowing drains incapable of handling the ever increasing flow.

Quickly, she stepped into a shop doorway to seek shelter from the sudden cloudburst, where instantly she was joined by several others who crammed into the confined area, while further pedestrians hurried past in the hope of finding cover.

Feeling nauseous and lethargic, she hoped the bus would arrive soon. The IVF treatment she had been undergoing of late had certainly taken its toll on her general health, causing her to feel anxious and very emotional.

Though she desperately wanted a child, following three unsuccessful IVF attempts, she had discussed her mental state with her husband David but he had emphatically demanded that she persevere with the treatment until she became pregnant. She felt angry and humiliated as she recalled his words, believing he should at least have shown a little consideration for her feelings. He had also reacted insensitively to her suggestion that maybe it was time to consider a suitable alternative such as adoption. To that he had countered irately that he didn't want to adopt....that he wanted his own child and had stormed from the room, leaving Robyn with some concerns about the stability of their marriage.

There was now a further matter of concern. David had become quite irritable of late and had taken to staying late at the office, often arriving home in the early hours and on some days, hardly a word passed his lips, yet throughout the first three years of their marriage they had been inseparable and very much in love. Things had slowly started to change around five years ago, in nineteen-ninety-two when Robyn was twenty-one, at which time David had suggested they should try to start a family. Although she had done her utmost to convince him there was plenty of time ahead to have children, he had nevertheless been very persuasive until she shared his views and she was equally disappointed when, two years later, she still hadn't conceived.

David's two elder sisters had each given birth to a son during those two years and good-natured quips from David's family members that it'd be their turn next had provoked a caustic response each time.

David and Robyn had both undergone extensive clinical tests and were already in the early stages of IVF treatment when his first nephew was born.

From the outset, he had insisted the IVF treatment remain a secret from his family. He didn't want his brothers-in-law scorning his virility, especially as it was *her* fault, he had told her in no uncertain terms.

His foolish remark had caused a heated argument and Robyn had been quick to retaliate by reminding him that it *wasn't* her fault, as she related what they had been told at the clinic where tests had revealed no cause for her failure to conceive. Although they were both fit and healthy, for certain couples it just didn't happen, they had been told and there was no obvious clinical explanation.

Robyn didn't feel well enough to undergo the IVF treatment for a fourth session. She'd had more than her fair share of ill-health for weeks; also there was the ensuing mental anguish each time the treatment failed. David was growing more and more paranoid about their childlessness and Robyn firmly believed his obsession could ultimately destroy them if they couldn't come to terms with the repetitive failures. Although she could understand his disappointment, what *she* suffered each time the treatment failed far outweighed *his* pain, physically as well as mentally.

Robyn checked her watch. She had been standing at the bus stop for almost twenty minutes since the heavy downpour had ceased and everyone else had decided to walk apart from three or four disgruntled people who still remained in the queue.

Shortly afterwards, the bus appeared in sight but as it approached the stop it was packed to the door and the driver sped past without stopping.

Robyn was furious as it was starting to rain again and she decided to return to the office to call a taxi. She felt cold and shivery and had experienced more than enough frustration for one day.

Her business partner Abbie Stewart, who was also her best friend, looked up in surprise when Robyn hurried into the office. 'Why have you come back? What's wrong?' she queried as Robyn slammed her shoulder bag and briefcase down on her desk, at the same time expelling a bad-tempered sigh.

'After the day I've had today, I could scream. I've waited more than twenty minutes for a bus and then it arrived full and drove right past the stop, so I'm calling a taxi,' she said, bursting into tears. 'I hate that inconsiderate grease monkey. It's all his fault.'

'Hey, come on....let me make you a cup of coffee and I'll give you a lift home. I intended to leave in a few minutes and it's not much out of my way to go via your place,' Abbie remarked calmly in an effort to placate her. 'I know how demoralised you feel at the moment but you'll overcome all these problems in time. More to the point, I've nothing in particular to rush home for, so if David isn't there by the time we arrive, I'll stay until you're feeling more settled. How does that sound?'

'Abbie, you are such a good friend to me. I don't know how I would have survived for these past few months without your support. I've decided to talk to David again about the fertility treatment. I honestly don't think I can face another session, coupled with the likelihood of another failure. It's very traumatic and it's not the end of the world if I can't become pregnant. We should be able to work through this. Other couples do so why should we be different?'

'Is David still as eager as he was to continue with the treatment?' Abbie asked.

'*Eager*, did you say? The word is *obsessional* as he feels it's a slur on his manhood. We've had quite a few squabbles about it. He scarcely acknowledges me anymore and he's rarely home before midnight.'

'I'm sorry Robyn. I didn't realise things were that difficult,' Abbie said compassionately, handing her the mug of hot coffee. 'The two of you have always appeared so compatible.'

'We were until we embarked on the treatment but that has put a terrible strain on our marriage. Don't get me wrong, I still love David very much and I'm sure he still loves me but he's become very moody and I can't get through to him at times. Last night, for instance, he turned up with a bouquet of flowers and he was very loving, yet other times, he doesn't even look at me. I've tried very hard to get him to open up to me but he won't make the effort and he leaves the room if I persist. I know that if I refuse to continue with the treatment he'll be furious and at the moment, the way I feel, I need David's support, not his contempt. He blames me for not giving him a baby and it's not fair.'

'Just try to put it to the back of your mind. These things have a way of working themselves out over a period of time. Try to relax and when you've drunk your coffee I'll drive you home. I'll also take you to the garage in the morning to collect your car. Don't forget you've had a rotten day today.'

'You're joking! How could I possibly forget that? I'm thankful that you're such a star, in fact I don't know what I'd have done without your support over recent months. You're the only person I can confide in. David would go mad though if he found out that you knew about our problems.'

Abbie took hold of her hand caringly. 'You know you can discuss anything with me and I'd never tell a soul.'

'David's not home! Still, that's no surprise,' Robyn remarked derisively when Abbie turned her car into the drive. 'I can't remember the last time he arrived home before me.'

As Robyn entered the house, Abbie looked back when she heard two car doors being closed nearby. Robyn had heard nothing and she proceeded to turn off the alarm. A policeman and policewoman were heading towards the drive and Abbie viewed them

6

with curiosity as they approached the house.

'Good evening. Are you Mrs. Ainsley?' the male officer enquired with a solemn expression.

Abbie was perturbed. 'No, she's just gone inside. Is there a problem?'

The female officer then contributed by displaying what Abbie could easily interpret as a disingenuous smile. 'Are you a relative?'

'No, I'm just her friend. Please tell me....is something wrong?'

'We need to speak directly to Mrs. Ainsley but it might be better if you were present,' she replied in a dour tone.

'Is somebody there?' Robyn called. 'Who are you talking to? Is it David?'

When she saw the uniformed officers, she halted and looking concerned asked, 'Can I help you?'

The female officer spoke again. 'Mrs. Ainsley?'

'Yes....er....why are you here?'

'May we step inside for a moment or two, to have a word with you?' the policeman said politely.

'I'm sorry, please do. I'm not generally so rude. I was just surprised to see two uniformed officers at my door,' Robyn said apologetically, showing them into the lounge.

Abbie sat facing them and looked on attentively.

'Please sit down Mrs. Ainsley. This might take a little while,' the policewoman advised with another forced smile that Abbie immediately recognised as a preamble to bad news.

Robyn crossed the room, sat down on the settee and stared questioningly at the two officers.

7

The female officer began by clearing her throat. 'Could you confirm that your husband is Mr. David Ainsley?'

Robyn was shocked. 'Yes, but why are you here? What's wrong?' she asked in a tone of utter panic.

Ignoring her question she continued, 'First of all, can you tell me where your husband is please?'

'Er....he'll still be at the office,' she said, glancing at her watch. 'He's been working late recently.'

'Does your husband drive a silver Mercedes with this registration number?' she asked, pointing to an entry in her notebook.

'Yes he does....but I don't understand. Has it been stolen or something?'

'I'm afraid our information is somewhat sketchy at the moment but I can tell you that Mr. Ainsley's Mercedes was involved in an accident earlier today on the M6 motorway. There were two people in the car....a man and a woman and we....'

'Then it must have been stolen,' she interrupted. 'David was in the office this afternoon. I spoke to him earlier, around two o'clock. He told me he'd be late home tonight and he promised to call me again when he was ready for leaving.'

The officer shuffled her feet uncomfortably. 'Mrs. Ainsley, I'm so sorry but we have reason to believe your husband was the driver of the Mercedes in the accident. The police at the scene removed his wallet and driving licence from his jacket pocket.'

Robyn was bewildered. 'I can't understand what you're telling me. How on earth could he have been on a motorway when I'd been talking to him at the

8

office? There's got to be some mistake. It couldn't possibly have been David. Anyway, he would have called to let me know if he had to go anywhere. He always does if he has to go out of town. Did he say he was my husband?'

'Mrs. Ainsley, I'm afraid there isn't any easy way to tell you this. The driver and his female passenger both died at the scene a short time ago,' she told her compassionately. 'We received radio notification as we were waiting for you to return home. We are so sorry.'

'Oh my God....that's *terrible*! Their families must be absolutely devastated,' she responded, appearing loath to accept what the officer was telling her.

'We are as sure as we can be at this point that the driver *was* Mr. Ainsley and that his passenger was a work colleague. The local police are trying to piece together what happened,' she stated and turning her attention to Abbie, who was silent and ashen-faced, she continued, 'Do you think you could make your friend a cup of sweet tea please? She's obviously in shock and I need her to understand what I'm telling her.'

She jumped up instantly. 'Of course.'

Robyn stood up and picked up the telephone. 'I'll call David and he might be able to throw some light on what's happened. Maybe he knows now that his car was stolen,' she stated, dialling his number. She waited a few seconds for him to answer. 'It's gone onto voicemail. Isn't that typical? I'll try him again later. There has to be some simple explanation for all this.'

9

The policewoman took hold of Robyn's hand but made no comment. She was an experienced Family Liaison Counsellor who had seen victims in denial many times. No one wanted to believe such terrible news and Robyn's cavalier attitude demonstrated to the officer how traumatised she was. People reacted unpredictably in such circumstances. The majority would break down instantly, while some grieved in a quiet and self-disciplined manner but Robyn fitted neither category and victims in denial were always the most difficult to console and counsel.

When Abbie returned with the mug of hot tea and handed it to Robyn, without a word she took it from her and continued to stare blankly ahead.

The male officer arose and addressing Abbie said, 'WPC Davies will stay here as long as is necessary but I'll be on my way now. There's nothing further I can do or say at the moment other than to express my sincerest regret. Are you able to stay for a while with your friend?'

'Yes, of course. Are you absolutely certain it was Robyn's husband in the car? Is there no possibility it could have been someone else?' she queried once they were out of audible range.

'I can only say we're as sure as we can be until a formal identification has been conducted but it will have to be delayed until your friend is well enough to be taken to the mortuary. WPC Davies will make the necessary arrangements. Once again, I'm deeply sorry for Mrs. Ainsley's tragic loss.'

'Thank you. I'll be sure to convey your very kind words to her,' Abbie responded with a sigh. 'I don't suppose there was any indication of where the two of them were heading?'

'No....and I don't want to make any presumptions at this stage. I can tell you there was luggage in the car belonging to both of them but there could be an innocent and justifiable explanation, if for example, they were attending a training course together.'

'I think you and I know that's highly improbable. Had that been the case his wife would have known about it.'

'Well, as I just told you, I don't wish to speculate about that. Besides, it isn't relevant to our enquiry about the accident which, early indications suggest, wasn't caused by Mr. Ainsley but as it's still under investigation, I can't comment further. I am merely the bearer of the tragic news. Mrs. Ainsley can rely on our support team to do all they can to help ease her pain.'

As Abbie closed the door, she stood silently for a few moments before returning to the lounge. WPC Davies smiled half-heartedly and as Abbie focused her attention on Robyn, who merely stared ahead in silence, gripping her mug of tea, she was aware that this was only the tip of the iceberg.

For some time, the three of them sat quietly until Robyn finally remarked in a hushed voice, 'What if it turns out to be true?'

'I think you have to accept that it *is* true,' Abbie replied caringly. 'I'm so sorry Robyn and I'll stay with you as long as you need me. You must try to be strong and I'll be here with you every step of the way, I promise.'

Robyn took hold of her hand, 'You believe them don't you?' she said with tears welling in her eyes. 'David really is dead isn't he?'

At that moment when the realisation dawned, she burst into tears and wept uncontrollably.

As Abbie looked on helplessly, the policewoman moved across and sat down beside Robyn. Putting an arm around her shoulder she whispered in a calm and reassuring voice, 'That's fine Mrs. Ainsley. Let it out. You've cleared the first hurdle now.'

'I'll make us a hot drink,' Abbie volunteered and when she returned with some sandwiches and three mugs of tea, Robyn was resting on the settee with her eyes closed and the policewoman was talking to her comfortingly.

'Has she any family nearby?' WPC Davies asked.

'Yes, her mother lives close I believe and she has a younger sister but she works in America. They'll need to be told and then there's David's family too. I don't suppose anyone's notified them?'

'No, not yet though that needs to be done sooner rather than later.'

Robyn stirred and slowly opened her eyes.

'Hi,' Abbie said. 'How are you feeling now?'

'I feel as if I'm standing on the outside of a circle looking in. I can't take it in because nothing makes any sense. I keep going over everything in my mind and I can't understand why David would have been on the motorway nor can I think who the passenger could have been in his car,' she told the officer.

'I am informed she was a work colleague of your husband's. As the investigation is outside our area, our information is rather limited. My priority was to notify you of the accident but later, we'll be able to tell you more. Your husband's family has to be told and I'm sure you have family members of your own to advise. Would you like me to make any calls for you or if you prefer, I could ask a colleague to visit your husband's parents or other family?'

'No thanks. *I* want to tell David's mother. It's not going to be easy but I think I should be the one who breaks the tragic news to her, in fact I'll do it now.'

'Are you sure you're up to it?'

'Needs must! I'll make the call from my bedroom if you don't mind. I'd rather be alone.'

Robyn stood up, took a deep breath and made her way upstairs.

She stared at the phone tentatively before dialling the number and when his mother answered, she felt a shiver run down her spine. 'Hi mum, it's Robyn,' she announced, attempting to speak confidently.

'Hello dear. It's nice to hear from you. We've just had our tea and dad's taking his usual nap. Are you both alright?'

There was a prolonged intermission before Robyn replied and in a broken tearful voice she spluttered, 'No mum. I have some terrible news. David's been involved in a car accident. The police are here now. There's no easy way to say this. They're telling me he's been killed.'

There was total silence as Mary Ainsley digested the news until suddenly she gave a piercing scream and cried, 'Oh no, that can't be true. Please tell me it's not true Robyn....I'm begging you....please tell me it's not true and that it's all a terrible mistake. I have to know it's a mistake. Please Robyn, put me out of my misery and....'

'It *is* true,' Robyn interrupted broken-heartedly. 'I couldn't believe it either when the police turned up. I'm so sorry mum. I realise it's dreadful news to tell you over the phone but I didn't want a policeman to come knocking on your door. I had to let you know. Everything just keeps going round and round in my head. Are you going to be alright?'

'Oh Robyn! What am I going to do? I don't know how I'm going to tell his dad. My sweet David. I'll never see him again. I'll never get over this as long as I live. Where is he and how did it happen? David was such a careful driver. He never took chances,' she sobbed bitterly.

'I don't know where he is mum. The local police don't appear to have very much information. All I know is that he was out of town when the accident occurred. My work colleague, Abbie, just happened to drive me home as my car's in for repair so she's here with me. I don't know what else to say to you. We're all going to miss David. I don't know what I'm going to do without him and I'm sorry to be the one who had to tell you. Everyone loved him.'

'Leave me to my thoughts dear. I have to tell dad and the rest of the family but I don't know how I'm going to do it. I'll call you very soon. I simply can't believe this. You take care of yourself. I know how much you and David meant to each other and so I can understand your pain too. We all have to try to be strong now,' she said quietly.

Robyn reflected pensively on the forgoing events, her head resting in her hands while trying to regain her composure. Her body was shaking from head to toe. She could well imagine her in-laws' suffering and the many tears that would be shed by the rest of David's family who would be totally devastated by the tragic news. No mother should ever have to out-live her child she cried inwardly while wiping her hand over her tear-stained face.

Robyn was on the verge of returning downstairs as Abbie entered the bedroom.

'Have you called David's mum?' she asked.

'Yes and it was probably the worst thing I've ever had to do in my life,' she said heaving a huge sigh. 'I keep telling myself there must be some mistake. I still don't understand why David would have been on the motorway. None of it makes any sense. He'd have told me had he been going anywhere.'

'Maybe something cropped up at the last minute that he needed to attend to,' Abbie prevaricated in a vain attempt to pacify Robyn, though from the brief discussion that had taken place between her and the policeman, it appeared that something more sinister would provide the ultimate explanation and she had her own thoughts as to what that might be.

'I don't know what I'm going to do Abbie. I keep thinking I'll wake up and discover it's all a dreadful nightmare. My whole life is about to change and I don't know if I can face the future without David. There are so many things going through my mind at the moment, I can't think clearly.' As she stood up to go downstairs, she hesitated. 'What's that there?'

she said, walking to her side of the bed, where she picked up an envelope bearing her name in David's handwriting.

She tore open the envelope and began to read the letter but her expressionless face gave nothing away as she turned over to the final page. At the end and without a word, she folded the letter and handed it to Abbie who took it from her in silence.

Before Abbie even read David's words, she knew what she would discover. 'Do you want me to read it?' she asked and when Robyn nodded, she opened the letter with quivering fingers. She could almost hear David's voice saying the words he had written.

*My dearest Robyn,*

*This is the most difficult decision I have ever had to make in my whole life. You are part of my being, and I firmly believed we would always be together. There is no way to soften the blow, so I must come straight to the point and say that I'm leaving. There is no blame on you Robyn. It is entirely of my own making. I have recently found myself in a situation I could never have envisaged in a million years. I've done a fair amount of soul-searching over the past few weeks and I've kept out of your way as much as possible to try to avoid a bitter confrontation. You see, I didn't even have the moral fibre to talk to you face to face, because, knowing you as I do, I knew you would do everything in your power to keep us together and you would probably have succeeded. In spite of what you think about me now, I love you more than anyone or anything in the world and this is the last thing I wanted to happen.*

*We have encountered so many problems with the IVF treatment. In addition to the disappointments, I am fully aware of the effect that the treatment has had on your health, physically and emotionally and I could sense that you didn't want to continue down this road any longer. I was so obsessed with having a child of my own that I selfishly assumed the IVF would go on till we were successful and I apologise for my lack of thought for your feelings.*

*Some months ago, I confided in Leanne at work. She was very supportive and a willing listener. We often went for a drink after work and she displayed a genuine interest in the progress we were making, hopeful we would succeed. It was not our intention to have an affair, in fact I can't recall how it began. I wanted a diversion, never a marital complication, and I never meant to hurt you darling. You are the only woman I've ever loved.*

*Two months ago, I tried to end the liaison. I told Leanne that I couldn't see her again, that I'd never wanted an affair with another woman. She seemed to accept what I said but two or three days later she asked to see me after work about an urgent matter when she then informed me she was pregnant.*

*I was so traumatised to learn that I had fathered a child, something I had always yearned for though with you Robyn, not with Leanne.*

*I am fond of Leanne. She is a caring and sincere woman but I don't love her and I doubt I ever will. Nevertheless, I have to think of my child. I couldn't turn my back on an innocent child and even if you had been willing to forgive my indiscretion, I would*

17

*still have wanted access to my child. My concern is wholly for you, for the torment it could cause were you to see me with my child when you might never have a child of your own and I could never put you through that Robyn, so the only dignified way out of this horrible nightmare is for me to leave you to get on with your life. I'm sorry darling. I love you more than you'll ever know and by losing you, I'll suffer for my deceit and weakness for the remainder of my life.*

*I've transferred sufficient funds to our joint bank account to more than cover the mortgage payments for the foreseeable future and I'll continue to top up the account periodically if you leave it open. Additionally, I have recently taken out a Life Insurance Policy naming you as the sole beneficiary to protect you for the future.*

*I sincerely hope that someday, you will find it in your heart to forgive me and that you will soon find somebody with whom you can share a blissful and rewarding life. It's what you deserve darling and I truly wish you well.*

*With deepest love,*

*David xxx*

Abbie returned the letter to her with tears flowing from her eyes and for a moment or two she couldn't speak. Robyn's life had been totally destroyed and there was nothing she could do to ease her pain. 'I don't know what to say to you. This is so tragic. It's cost *two people* their lives.'

'Wrong Abbie; *three* lives have been lost due to David's affair with that woman and that's discounting mine,' she corrected her soberly. 'Don't forget, David's unborn baby died too, the baby he wanted so much and that I couldn't give him.'

'Are you going to show his letter to the police?'

'I don't know that I should. It's not relevant to the enquiry about the accident. To be honest, I'm torn between keeping quiet about the letter to protect my in-laws from the truth or alternatively, bringing the matter into the open, but I can't win either way can I? I'm damned if I do and I'm equally damned if I don't as it's bound to come out that David was with another woman. The policeman told us there was a female passenger in his car.'

'There was luggage in the car belonging to both of them Robyn. The policeman mentioned that just as he was leaving so it seems they were going away together, which means it won't be a secret for much longer. Furthermore, if nobody hears your version of events, David's family might think that you were the cause of the failure of your marriage. People are always looking for somebody to blame and blood's thicker than water. Perhaps you ought to show the letter to the policewoman. That way, you're being open and honest from the outset. David clearly says that you're blameless and I for one think you have enough to contend with without having to face false accusations from anyone else. You have nothing at all to reproach yourself for and I know for sure that David would never have wanted any blame to fall on you. He wasn't a bad husband. He simply loved you too much to stay with you as he didn't wish to cause you any further distress. That letter says it all.

In your position, I'd be inclined to show his letter to the policewoman.'

Robyn sighed heavily. 'I'll do as you say. Since I've nothing to hide, I've nothing to gain by being secretive. Besides, there's nothing left in life worth caring about now I've lost David,' she sobbed.

Filled with deep compassion for her friend, Abbie held her in her arms and sobbed too.

When they went downstairs, Robyn disclosed that she had found a letter from David, advising he was leaving her.

Before showing the letter to the policewoman, she explained about the IVF treatment and the stress it had placed on their marriage.

She listened sensitively, allowing her to continue uninterrupted and then she took David's letter from her and read it carefully.

'I'll need to take this letter with me,' she told her. 'It's a vital piece of evidence that could be regarded as relevant to Mr. Ainsley's state of mind when he left.'

'May I see it again please?' Abbie said and when the officer passed it to her, she read it through again quickly before enquiring, 'Will you be calling here again tomorrow?'

'Yes, I'll be here when Mrs. Ainsley has had time to get some rest.'

'In that case, you can collect the letter tomorrow.'

'Oh no; I really ought to take it now because....'

'I said *tomorrow*!' she told her demonstratively. She didn't have to show you David's letter. I want to make a copy first and if, as you say, it might be a vital piece of evidence, she might need to seek legal counsel to protect her own interests.'

'From what?' the policewoman enquired.

'I've no idea but I'm taking no chances. You can have it tomorrow and if you would call me first to let me know what time you're coming, I'll be here. Here's my card. Use the mobile number please.'

An uncomfortable silence followed, during which Abbie gave some thought to a reference in the letter regarding a recent Policy that David had purchased.

As an Insurance Broker, she had a vast experience of Insurance Companies who would try a variety of scams to worm their way out of paying a claim and Robyn would need all the help she could get. David had legitimately provided for her future and Abbie was damned if she would stand by and allow Robyn to be denied what was rightfully hers. Abbie had all the right connections in the legal profession and she was owed a few favours for the amount of work she channelled their way so she would call in one of the favours owed first thing in the morning.

'You ought to rest now Robyn,' Abbie suggested. 'You've been feeling under the weather all day. I'll stay here tonight so you won't be alone.'

'That's a splendid idea,' the policewoman agreed, relieved to be joining in the conversation once more following the uncomfortable silence. 'You've had a very taxing day.'

'Would you like me to call your mother?' Abbie asked.

'Good Lord! I'd forgotten about her. I'd be very grateful if you would. I can't face another traumatic phone call. Would you tell her I'm resting and that I'll give her a call tomorrow?'

'If you're sure you can manage, I'll be on my way now,' the policewoman commented. 'I'll just radio through for someone to collect me. I'll see you both tomorrow and please don't read anything untoward into what I said earlier. I merely meant that it would explain why Mr. Ainsley was on the M6. It ties up a few loose ends for the investigating officer when he is trying to piece everything together. My transport will be here shortly so I'll wait outside.'

'As you wish,' Abbie replied with a forced smile. 'Goodnight.'

After the officer had left, Abbie turned to Robyn and said, 'Be careful what you tell the police. You were right to show her David's letter. That proves you've nothing to hide but just remember they're a suspicious lot. Don't let them harass you and above all, don't let them put words in your mouth.'

'I don't know what you mean. What could I have to hide? I didn't know about the other woman until I read David's letter.'

'Of course you didn't. I'm merely saying choose your words carefully and if anybody even *suggests* you were having marital problems, deny that. You admit to nothing....right?'

'Well we weren't! We were just stressed because of the repeated IVF failures but it was nothing we couldn't have worked out.'

'*We* both know that but you are very vulnerable at the moment; in fact I want to be there when you're being interviewed. If I'm not about, tell them you'll only answer their questions in the presence of your legal representative. That's very important.'

'I don't understand what's bothering you.'

'There's nothing bothering me. David loved you very much. Don't ever forget that. He believed he was doing the right thing by leaving. David didn't want you to suffer because of his infidelity. In his own way, he was trying to put things right and his death was due to a tragic accident. That's the point I'm trying to make. I'll speak to your mum now and then you can get some sleep.'

'Huh!' she grunted. 'There's little chance of that. Don't mention David's letter to mum will you? I'd hate anybody to think badly of him besides which I haven't made up my mind yet whether or not to tell the families about it.'

Robyn's mother was shaken and distressed at the disclosure and wanted to speak to her daughter but Abbie persuaded her to wait until the following day when Robyn would have had some time to rest and collect her thoughts.

Abbie settled down for the night on the sofa after escorting Robyn to her room and ensuring she was comfortable. She had worrying thoughts regarding the forthcoming investigation. As David's letter had been undated, Abbie was wise enough to know that the police and the Life Insurance Company would have a field day with that, were they to suspect that Robyn had found his letter earlier.

Despite feeling restless, Abbie managed to snatch a few hours of sleep. On the two or three occasions she crept upstairs to check on Robyn, she found her sleeping soundly and was still asleep when she took her a mug of tea and a slice of toast at nine o'clock in the morning.

She shook her gently and handed her the steaming mug. 'Drink this,' she said. 'It might make you feel better. You should try to eat a bit of something too. I've made you a slice of toast.'

Robyn sat up and took a tiny sip of her tea. 'I still can't believe it,' she remarked with an audible sigh. 'My darling David. I can't stop thinking about him. I don't feel the least bit angry over his involvement with that girl and I do believe he wanted to end the relationship. Try as I might, I can't feel compassion for her though. She knew David was a married man and she knew the difficulties we were experiencing. I see her as a cunning and sly opportunist who went out of her way to take advantage of David's state of mind and his vulnerability. Granted, the girl didn't deserve to be killed; no one deserves that....but she was master or ought I to say mistress of her chosen destiny and I won't waste my emotions on her. My grief is for David who was my soul-mate. Never in a million years would he have deceived me without encouragement and now, thanks to her, I've lost the love of my life forever.'

'For want of repeating myself, David loved *you*,' Abbie remarked compassionately. 'It will take quite some time but eventually you'll come to terms with your loss, believe me. Time is a great healer. Could you manage the slice of toast do you think? You've eaten nothing since we got back yesterday. You'll make yourself ill if you don't eat.'

'No thanks. I might have something later. I can't even work up enough enthusiasm to get out of bed, never mind eat. I didn't sleep too well.'

'Then stay where you are. There's nothing to get up for. Try and get some sleep. Listen, will you be alright for a couple of hours if I slip home for some things? I may as well stay here over the weekend as sit at home twiddling my thumbs. I'm sure I can be of some use here.'

For the first time since her arrival home the previous evening Robyn smiled. 'I'd really appreciate that if you're sure you can spare the time. I can talk to you and I feel so weepy at the moment.'

'I'm sure you do but we'll work our way through this together. I won't be very long. I want to make a photocopy of David's letter while I'm out. Should the police contact you, tell them to call later when I'm back. I'll definitely be back by twelve.'

Once home, Abbie packed her overnight bag and made a quick call to her friend Gerald Dunne, who was a legal wizard. She acquainted him with details of the accident and outlined how Robyn had found David's letter. After advising him of the content, he said she had acted wisely when persuading Robyn to show the letter to the police, though he too was concerned that the letter could give rise to questions regarding Robyn's knowledge of the extra-marital affair. Gerald was satisfied however that any such investigation would be likely to lead nowhere.

'The police have a duty to perform,' he explained. 'They must explore all avenues and particularly any suspicion of foul play. If there's any suggestion that a criminal act might have been committed, it's their duty to investigate that thoroughly in the interest of justice.'

'But no crime *was* committed,' Abbie told him. 'I was there when she found the letter.'

'I'm not suggesting for a moment that there *was* any crime but let's imagine your friend knew of the affair because she had found that letter earlier. They could have quarrelled and she could have tampered with his car when she found out he was leaving her that day. It would have been easy to plant the letter where she could find it in the presence of a witness. You said that she left work and returned some time later because she couldn't catch a bus. That period of time provides opportunity and she definitely had motive. As I explained, the police have a job to do. That's all I'm saying. I'm not suggesting she's done anything wrong but they will most certainly need to question her.'

'That's ridiculous Gerald! Robyn would *never* do anything to hurt David. She loved him.'

'Yes and did she love him enough to prevent him from running off with another woman? I'm trying to demonstrate how a skilful interrogator can make everything look the opposite of what it actually is. Let me ask another question and I'll play the part of the skilful interrogator. *Miss Stewart, would you tell me exactly how long Mrs. Ainsley had been absent from the office when she unexpectedly returned?'*

'I couldn't say exactly. I was busy at the time she left but she said she'd been waiting for the bus for more than twenty minutes and so with a ten minute walk each way, she'd have been away for forty-five minutes or so I guess.'

'*You guess?*' he said loudly and guffawed. '*What you mean is that you have no idea of the duration of Mrs. Ainsley's absence....right Miss Stewart? Mrs. Ainsley informed* **you** *how long she'd been waiting at the bus stop. That's what you said, didn't you, so it is quite possible, is it not, that your friend could have been absent for a much longer period of time? Maybe she was missing for an hour or more? Isn't that right Miss Stewart? In fact Mrs. Ainsley might have been missing long enough to take a taxi to her husband's place of work, tamper with his car, then take a taxi back to the office Miss Stewart, because you don't know how long she was absent, do you? Returning to the letter, you stated that Mrs. Ainsley went upstairs some time earlier to call her mother-in-law....and yet there was a telephone by her side downstairs that she could have used and despite the fact she was in the bedroom for some considerable time, she didn't notice the letter until you appeared. Doesn't that seem rather convenient to you? Does it not also seem rather convenient that on the very day Mr. Ainsley was leaving the matrimonial home, Mrs. Ainsley had booked in her car for a repair, my point being that you would offer to take her home and thus be present at the time she discovered her husband's letter?*'

'But she only returned to the office because it was raining hard and the bus was full.'

'*Do you know that to be true Miss Stewart? Did you actually see the bus speed past the bus stop or*

27

*is it not in fact true that Mrs. Ainsley **told** you that the bus was full when she returned to the office to create her alibi that you would readily support?'*

'This is awful, Gerald. Do you think Robyn might have to undergo such a grilling?'

'If there were any independent witnesses willing to confirm that Mr. Ainsley was an innocent victim of the accident, then she might not be questioned at all but the mere fact that her husband was about to leave her could raise suspicion. I don't want you to cause undue concern but she should be informed to say nothing that could possibly make her a suspect. I should see her as soon as possible. I'm pretty sure I owe you a favour.'

'Actually, you owe me several, Gerald!'

'Okay, several,' he conceded with a short burst of laughter. 'Try not to worry....at the end of the day, the police have to prove the case and their enquiries might well be clear-cut. It's the Insurance Company that concerns me. If the deceased had only recently acquired the Policy, they'll probe diligently into the causal factors of his death. Do you happen to know what type of Policy he purchased?'

'No, I don't have that information I'm afraid and I doubt that Robyn would know either but then it's not a subject he would have discussed with his wife if he intended leaving her.'

'Clearly not but if Mr. Ainsley had added what is termed a 'Rider' to his Policy, providing accidental death cover, we could be looking at a very lengthy process before the claim is met.'

'Why, what difference would that make?'

'That's what used to be called Double Indemnity cover. The Company would be liable to pay double the face value. We could be talking about a colossal sum of money but it's better that we don't speculate until we know. It might be an idea for Mrs. Ainsley to have a look for any paperwork about the Policy. Let me know if she finds anything and I can make some telephone enquiries. You keep a photocopy of the letter and hand the original to the police. If they want any information, I need to be there when she's answering any questions so be sure to give them my number please and they can call me. Has she been invited to attend a formal identification yet?'

'No but I think the police may arrange it today. Is it alright to go ahead with that?'

'Yes, that shouldn't present a problem. It's very unlikely they'll ask her any questions until later.'

'Right, well thanks for all your advice Gerald. I'll be in touch soon.'

Abbie made a photocopy of David's letter before returning to Robyn's, where she found her relaxing on the sofa in her night-attire.

'Oh, you've decided to get up! That's good. Are you feeling any better?' she enquired as she walked in the room.

Robyn turned to face her with swollen bloodshot eyes. 'No, not really. I can't stop crying. I just keep thinking how it's such a waste of a young life. I'm not denying we had our problems but most couples have problems don't they? There were no issues we couldn't have resolved had we made the time to sit down quietly and discuss everything in a civilised manner. We were very happy. We loved each other very much.'

'I know you did. Have you had breakfast?' Abbie asked, changing the subject.

'No, I was about to make myself some toast when mum telephoned me. She wanted to come round but I put her off and then WPC Davies rang to enquire how I was feeling today as they want me to identify David's body. She's picking me up at three o'clock and she'll bring me back afterwards. I contacted the garage as well. There'll be someone there until two o'clock, so I'll pick up my car if you could run me there please.'

'Let's have a slice of toast and a drink first. We'll be back in plenty of time for the policewoman.'

'I'll attend to it. You take your bag up and use the second room on the left. The bathroom is next door. I can't imagine why I was so inhospitable last night when you agreed to stay here with me. I didn't even provide you with a bed to sleep in!'

'Don't talk so stupid. You and I both know why. Besides, I was perfectly alright on the sofa; in fact I had quite a decent night's sleep, considering everything that had transpired.'

After collecting the car, they drove straight back to Robyn's house to await the arrival of WPC Davies.

Robyn was visibly trembling as she climbed into the police car. 'I don't think I can do this,' she told Abbie. 'I've thought of nothing else since the police contacted me. I don't want to see David's smashed-up body. I'd prefer to remember him just as he was, with a lovely kind smile. I do hope he didn't suffer and that it was over quickly.'

Abbie sighed understandingly and held her hand. 'You have to identify him. It needs to be someone reliable who knew him well. Just try to be positive. There might not be any visible injuries. If you want, I'll come in with you too and then you won't have to face doing it alone.'

Robyn exhaled audibly. 'Oh, would you? Thanks. I'd appreciate it if you did.'

As they walked up the seemingly endless corridor with the WPC Davies, Robyn was close to tears and when they were directed into the cold clinical room where David's body lay, Abbie held Robyn's hand, gripping it firmly.

The female attendant lowered the sheet, revealing David's face.

Displaying no sign of emotion, she looked at him for some time before nodding her head.

'Can you confirm that this is David Ainsley?' the police officer asked sensitively.

'Yes,' she said in a hushed voice before bursting into tears.

All previous hopes that it was a dreadful mistake were dashed as she leaned towards him and kissed his lips gently. 'I love you so much sweetheart,' she whispered tearfully.

'Would you like a few moments alone with your husband?' she asked.

'Yes, if that's alright.'

'We'll wait for you in the corridor. You just take as long as you need.'

The others left the room and Robyn stood silently beside David. He looked so peaceful, she thought. It struck her as strange that there were no noticeable injuries and yet he was dead. She was thankful that his face had not been impaired in any way. He was a very handsome man, just as much so with his now pallid complexion and she loved him so deeply. She stroked his hair gently and kissed his lips one more time before saying goodbye and leaving the room.

WPC Davies led her away, inviting her to have a seat while she went to make her a cup of tea. 'I am deeply sorry for your tragic loss, Mrs. Ainsley,' she told her compassionately.

While awaiting her return, Robyn remarked, 'He looked so peaceful and there was no sign of injury. He just appeared to be sleeping.'

Abbie squeezed her hand and smiled caringly.

When WPC Davies returned with the tea, Abbie gave her David's letter and asked if there had been any progress with their investigation.

She informed Abbie that a witness report alleged that the accident, involving several other vehicles in addition to the Mercedes, had been caused by a van driver who had pulled out to overtake a car.

There were other witnesses to interview however, she advised, and until every statement was to hand, the investigation was still ongoing. She gave Abbie her assurance that Robyn would be informed of all further developments.

'Did you make a copy of this letter?' she enquired and when Abbie nodded, she turned to Robyn. 'Can you tell me when you first came across this letter?'

'You already know that. I found it last night when I went upstairs to use the phone. As soon as I came down, I showed it to you.'

'So you're saying you never saw the letter before last night?'

'*Asked and answered*!' Abbie snapped furiously. 'We'd like to be taken home now please and I take exception to your distasteful questions at a time like this, bearing in mind I was led to believe you were a qualified family counsellor. Mrs. Ainsley has just identified her husband's body for God's sake! Are you totally without feeling and compassion? Hasn't she suffered enough?'

'Er....yes of course. I'm extremely sorry. I'll take you home at once,' she stated looking embarrassed. 'Please accept my since apology.'

During the journey, WPC Davies remained silent but directed a cursory smile at Abbie as she stepped from the car.

Handing the policewoman a sheet of paper, Abbie remarked abruptly, 'Be sure to call this number and make suitable arrangements with Mr. Gerald Dunne before asking further questions. Mrs. Ainsley won't be seeing you again without proper representation. Is that clear?'

She awaited no answer and slammed the car door shut, following Robyn up the path as the police car sped away.

'What was all that about?' Robyn asked.

'It's that bloody policewoman! She wound me up. She's so rude and insensitive. Fancy her asking you such questions after what you'd just been through! I think it's absolutely atrocious. I feel like reporting her....anyway, enough about her for the time being. When I was at home earlier, I contacted a colleague of mine and made arrangements for you to see him. He's a solicitor; he's very approachable and he will help you answer any questions posed by the police. He's going to arrange an appointment to see you as soon as possible so forget about the police for now. There's nothing whatsoever to be concerned about. Trust me.'

'I've searched through all David's stuff in the study but I can't find anything. I've even looked through all the files on his PC and there's no mention of any Insurance Company. There might be more papers in his briefcase but I expect the police will have taken that away as it would have been in the car. I haven't a clue where else to look.'

'Perhaps David arranged it at the office then. If he had wanted to withhold the information from you, it would have been the obvious place to do it,' Abbie advised. 'You might find it advantageous were you to collect David's belongings from his office and I would recommend you do that as soon as possible. I'd better have a quick word with Gerald first as we wouldn't want the police to believe we were trying to remove any evidence.'

'Evidence of what? What do you mean by that?'

'Oh nothing! It's just a figure of speech, that's all. We were open and honest about David's letter and we don't want the police believing you can't wait to get your hands on the Insurance payout. That could raise suspicion, so I'd rather clear that with Gerald first. That's what I meant.'

'Let me make this absolutely clear. I don't give a damn about the Insurance money! My only concern is to ascertain when and with whom David took out the Policy because that would give me some idea of when he hatched his plan to leave me.'

'Wouldn't there be some indication on your bank statements that a Direct Debit had been set up if he were making regular payments?'

'I haven't a clue. I didn't get involved in financial matters. As an accountant, David dealt with all that. I might need to go online to check. I think we only received bank statements twice yearly but I'm sure I can bring up our details. David explained it to me once. I can't believe you're encouraging me to do devious things like this when he's only just died.'

'Robyn, there's nothing at all devious about what you're doing. You're just trying to find information for Gerald.'

Despite her best efforts, Robyn was unable to find anything online. There was no mention of a Direct Debit to any Insurance Company but there had been two substantial transfers into the joint bank account during the previous month, which Abbie concluded were the sums David had referred to in his letter as funds to help pay the mortgage.

When Abbie called Gerald, she discovered he had already been contacted by the local police who had informed him a Post Mortem examination had been ordered. 'It's routine in traffic accident deaths,' he stated. 'The results will be passed to the Coroner's

35

Office and after due consideration, a decision will be made whether to hold an Inquest.'

Abbie described her earlier altercation with WPC Davies and Gerald laughed. 'I'd have liked to have witnessed that. Good for you,' he replied. 'I'm very surprised that the policewoman referred to the van driver's involvement though, particularly as there's an ongoing investigation. I'll just make a quick note of that and you keep a record of anything else you happen to hear, though I doubt anyone will contact Mrs. Ainsley. I made it abundantly clear that in her present state of mind, she must not be interviewed without my presence. Returning to the matter of the bank accounts, it's feasible that Mr. Ainsley opened a recent account in his own name and the monetary transactions to the existing joint account more than likely originated from there. It might be a good idea if Mrs. Ainsley were to remove her late husband's effects from his office without delay. Furthermore, if she's aware how to access any personal files on his computer, that could provide vital information. I'd be interested to learn which Insurance Company her husband used and in particular when the Policy was purchased.'

'I'll make sure Robyn attends to that first thing on Monday. Many thanks for your help Gerald and if you think of anything else, please get in touch.'

'Is everything alright?' Robyn questioned with a look of concern as Abbie replaced the receiver.

'Everything's proceeding normally. Gerald heard from the police and a Post Mortem examination is being arranged. We'll know soon if there's going to be an Inquest. Gerald would like you to collect all David's property from his office on Monday. I'll be there to help you carry it. He also suggested that the information he needs might be on his computer at the office. Do you happen to know the password he used at work?'

'I know his password here but I don't know if it's the same at the office. It was never discussed. You don't envisage when you're merrily plodding along with your day to day routine that anything like this is going to occur and so you're not prepared for the dreadful problems generated when something does happen. It's been an absolute nightmare up to now and I'm starting to wonder if it's ever going to end.'

Reassuringly she stated, 'Of course it is and we'll get through it together. We'll simply take each day as it comes. You can't be expected to feel any other way at such a tragic time. Will you be seeing any of your family today?'

'Mum's calling round later. I did try very hard to dissuade her but I couldn't put her off any longer, so if you want to go out I'll understand.'

'No, I'll stay here unless you want me to clear off for an hour or so.'

'No, I'd prefer you didn't. She won't stay as long if you're here and I couldn't face an all-night vigil with mum.'

'You really ought to telephone a Funeral Director. He won't be able to do anything until David's body is released but he'll be able to make the preliminary arrangements and prepare press notices. If you like, I'll sort that out if you tell me who you'll be using.'

Robyn grunted with frustration. 'Do you see what I mean? I've never even thought about the Funeral. I'll talk to mum about it tonight. She might know of someone you can call. I haven't a clue about things like that. How about we have a drink and I'll make a sandwich? I need a change of topic as I'll have to go over it all again when mum turns up and I'm at screaming pitch already.'

Following a tearful reunion with her mother, Robyn settled down and related the limited information she had obtained from the police, deliberately omitting to mention the presence of the female passenger in David's car or the letter he had written to her. There would be time enough to determine what she ought to do about that when the information was about to be made public.

Her mother was very supportive and when asked, she suggested the name of a Funeral Director with whom she'd had some previous dealings and who had been both sympathetic and efficient.

'We used him when your Uncle Arthur died,' she advised her. 'He was ever so kind and considerate. He attended to every detail including the notices in the newspaper and he....'

Frostily, Robyn cut in, 'That's what he's paid to do isn't he?' and then, realising how ungrateful she sounded, she apologised. 'I'm sorry, I'm very edgy. I can't bring myself to think of David's funeral. It's going to be absolutely unbearable.'

'I do understand what you're going through love. Don't forget I went through it when your dad died and I had both you and Bryony to take care of too, but you'll find the strength to cope. I know I did. I don't suppose you've been in touch with your sister yet?'

'No, I haven't but I might give her a call later. It's just that I get very distressed each time I have to go through it all.'

While they were talking, Abbie left them alone to afford them a little privacy while she telephoned the Undertaker who readily assured her he would liaise with the police and inform Mrs. Ainsley as soon as he had any information to impart. Once the Coroner released the body, nothing else stood in their way, he explained and he expected to hear something by Monday or Tuesday at the very latest. 'Please pass on my condolences at this very sad time,' he added.

'Right, I've left it with the Undertaker,' she told Robyn. 'He was most sympathetic. He'll attend to everything and when he contacts you, he'll need to know whether David is to be buried or cremated.'

At that, she burst into tears. 'I'd never given that a moment's thought. It wasn't a subject we'd ever discussed and I've no idea what David would have wanted.'

'Then why not discuss it with his mother and see what she thinks if you have no fixed opinion?'

'You're right. He was her son and she might have a preference. I was going to call her later so I'll talk to her about it then. I have a few people to contact as soon as I feel up to it.'

For a few hours, they exchanged reminiscences of better times and Robyn was relieved when the time came for her mother to leave. She was tired and her eyes were steaming from the tears she had shed.

The reality of David's tragic accident was firmly embedded in her mind as she climbed into bed. 'Oh David, you don't know what grief you've caused. I miss you so much,' she cried aloud and she brought to mind her mother's familiar saying, penned by Sir Walter Scott....'*Oh, what a tangled web we weave, when first we practice to deceive.*'

When uttering those emotive words, little did she realise how often she would be made to repeat them in the coming months.


There were many telephone calls from family and friends the next day offering help and support and there was an unexpected call from David's business partner, Roy Stanton, who'd called to speak to him.

Roy was astounded to learn that David had been killed in a road accident and was equally shocked to learn that Leanne had been killed too. He couldn't understand why the two of them had been together and was horrified by Robyn's revelation that there had been a physical relationship between David and Leanne.

'I had no idea at all that David and Leanne were seeing each other and I can't begin to describe how sorry I am for your tragic loss Robyn,' he expressed with genuine feeling and sympathy. 'I can't believe that I didn't know something like that was going on right under my nose. I'm shocked Robyn and I'll do everything in my power to help you cope with your terrible ordeal.'

'I can't believe it either. I keep thinking I'll wake up and find it's a bad dream. I didn't even *suspect* David was seeing another woman but then the wife is always the last to find out isn't she? I had no idea at all and David gave nothing away. Actually, there is something you could help me with Roy if it's not too much trouble. I need to pick up David's belongings from the office tomorrow morning, so can you arrange to have everything boxed and ready for me please? I couldn't face having to clear his desk with everyone watching and I also need to know whether you have the password he used for his computer. I believe he kept some personal banking information at the office and I need to access funds. I also have to notify the bank about his death.' Throughout, she attempted to appear composed, while in reality, she was choking on her words as she fought to restrain her tears.

'We both kept our passwords in sealed envelopes in the safe in case of any emergency, so that's not a problem. I'll make sure the envelope is here for you tomorrow and if you'd copy what you need onto a disk, any personal information can be deleted from his computer and if you advise me of his password when you've finished, I'll then be able to access the information I need relating to David's clients. This is such a terrible state of affairs.'

Robyn heaved a sigh of relief that a further hurdle was about to be crossed. 'I'll try to be there around ten o'clock then if that's alright.'

'That's perfect and I'll have everything ready for you. I can't begin to express my regret and I speak for Julia too and for all the staff who I'm sure will be as equally distraught as I am. David was a well-liked young man who will be sorely missed and if there's anything more I can do to help, anything at all, then please....'

'Thanks for everything Roy,' she interrupted. 'I'll see you in the morning.'

2

'Please Robyn; will you listen? I'm just thinking of you. You really do need a change of environment,' Abbie argued. 'Let's clear off for an hour or two, if only for a bit of fresh air. We can get something to eat while we're out. It'll do you a power of good.'

She wouldn't be swayed. 'No, *you* listen; I don't *want* to go out. I don't *want* to go anywhere. I'm an absolute wreck and I'm not hungry,' she snapped, running her fingers through her tangled hair.

'*Well I am*! All I've eaten in two days is a couple of ham sandwiches and three paltry slices of toast. I'm absolutely starving!'

Eventually, Abbie twisted her arm and when they returned late afternoon, Robyn felt much better. She had enjoyed a hearty lunch despite her earlier belief that she wasn't hungry.

'You've got to look after yourself,' Abbie advised her. 'You'll make yourself poorly if you don't eat properly. I've decided to stay here until Wednesday to help you through the early days and I'll be there to support you at the office tomorrow. It's going to be difficult facing David's work colleagues who'll just have been given the news. They'll be distraught too and will undoubtedly want to express their condolences but we'll get through it together.'

'I'm pleased you're here Abbie. I'll make it up to you when I've sorted myself out. I realise I'm not the easiest of people to get on with at the moment but that doesn't mean I don't appreciate everything you're doing for me. I'm very grateful to you.'

'Don't talk daft! You'd do it for me wouldn't you if our roles were reversed?'

Demonstratively she replied, 'Of course I would.'

'Right, not another word then. Why don't we see if there's anything worth watching on TV? It might just help to take your mind off things a little.'

She expelled an audible sigh. 'I doubt that but we can give it a try.'

As they settled down with a mug of coffee, Abbie was pleased to see Robyn show signs of relaxation for the first time. With mixed feelings of sympathy for her friend and uneasy concern at what might lay ahead, Abbie stared ahead edgily until her thoughts were suddenly interrupted when Gerald telephoned.

'Hi Abbie, I've called you several times but your mobile was switched off. Is everything alright?'

'Yes, everything's fine thanks. I persuaded Robyn to have a couple of hours' break away from here, so we've been out for lunch. I switched my phone off because I wanted peace and quiet in the restaurant. A lot of my friends tend to call me on a Sunday and I couldn't be bothered talking to them. Is something wrong?'

'Not at all. I have a slot free at eleven o'clock in the morning and I think I should see Mrs. Ainsley as soon as possible. Would that be convenient?'

'That should tie in nicely. We're going to David's office at ten but I'm sure we'll be done by eleven.'

'That's fine then. I'm afraid there has been, shall I say, a *development* and at this stage, I don't know whether or how it will affect the decision regarding a Coroner's Inquest.'

'What's that?' Abbie questioned, trying to choose her words carefully as Robyn was in earshot.

'Not one word to *anyone* and I do mean *anyone*!' he insisted in a harsh whisper.

'I won't Gerald. Tell me.'

'I'm not supposed to know about this....suffice to say I have connections. Post Mortem examinations were carried out yesterday on Mr. Ainsley and his female passenger and someone is telling lies. That woman was definitely *not* pregnant!'

Abbie was aghast. 'And there's no likelihood of a mistake?'

'None whatsoever, so either she was lying or Mr. Ainsley was when he wrote the letter to his wife. In my opinion, that woman's unquestionably the odds on favourite. Knowing how devious women can be to get what they want, I'm damn sure I'm right.'

'That's a very sexist remark Gerald.'

'Yes well, without going into detail, let's attribute it to personal and bitter experiences and just leave it at that,' he said sharply.

Abbie spent a very restless night as she repeatedly recalled Gerald's revelation. She had been sworn to secrecy and for that she was thankful as she had no desire to be the bearer of the dreadful tidings. Only one explanation *was* possible, that Leanne had used deception to take David away from his wife. What a scheming bitch, she concluded before her thoughts turned to Robyn who had lost the love of her life as a consequence of Leanne's despicable actions. Was there no depth to which that woman wouldn't stoop

45

to achieve her goal and what had it achieved? They were both dead thanks to her underhand plan.

Abbie was in no doubt that at a later date, Leanne would have deceived David still further by claiming to have suffered a miscarriage in the hope he would then stay with her but more importantly, how would Robyn react when she learned the truth?

Abbie went downstairs early before Robyn awoke and sat by the window, viewing the lush undulating countryside that extended further than the eye could see. This was a popular area of Cheshire and Abbie recalled how excited Robyn had been when she and David had first viewed that house. Situated in a tree lined avenue, each house was built on a huge plot. The well designed and staggered layout afforded all the properties outstanding and uninterrupted views. It was early spring and newborn lambs were clearly visible from the lounge window. Robyn, who loved animals, had wanted to buy a farmhouse and fill the land with livestock but David had failed to display any such enthusiasm and so she had been obliged to abandon her dream, she had told Abbie.

Abbie picked up a large wedding photograph that held pride of place on a hexagonal table beside the fireplace. They had been married for eight years but neither one of them had aged. David had developed a more distinguished appearance in recent years and small silvery patches, visible at his temples, merely served to complement his dashing good looks.

Robyn, on the other hand, had hardly changed at all. Her thick dark glossy hair that framed her oval face was at all times beautifully groomed. Her high cheek bones and her large expressive eyes were the envy of Abbie. She was a stunning, beautiful young woman who could have worked as a photographic or fashion model with her definitive good looks and her shapely figure. She also had poise and a vibrant personality....undeniably a woman to turn heads.

David had lost no time in making himself known to her when they had first met at a party and within a few months, they were married. Although Robyn had fully intended going to University, once David had entered her life, nothing else mattered, she told Abbie when she first started to work for her almost eight years ago. Since then, they had become close friends and around six years ago, they had formed a partnership, with Robyn assuming responsibility for the management side of the growing business.

Abbie, three years her senior was at the time in an on-off rocky relationship with one of her clients but when it had continued without direction for several years, she became disenchanted with his inability to commit to a permanent relationship and ended it. At that point she started to enjoy a more varied social life. The nature of her work brought her in contact with people from all walks of life and as word went round that she was a free agent, she was never short of invitations although she silently envied Robyn's stable and loving relationship with David, wishing *she* could find the right guy with whom to share her life. At the age of twenty-nine, she was becoming more than a little worried that her body clock was ticking away. It was also a distressing thought that she might never find true love.

Abbie wondered what surprises might be revealed at David's office. She checked her watch and it was almost nine o'clock. With a busy and nerve-racking few hours ahead of them she was very worried for Robyn and particularly so should Gerald opt to disclose the findings about Leanne as such devastating news would be very upsetting for her friend.

With Gerald still in her thoughts, she reflected on their earlier conversation, wondering what on earth could have given cause for him to have made such a caustic remark about women. Though he had given little away, he had nevertheless made it abundantly clear that his observations were due to personal and bitter experience.

There was a tense and grave atmosphere when they entered David's office. His partner Roy jumped up immediately and throwing his arms around Robyn, he offered his condolences once again as the office junior, Tracy, looked up at Robyn and smiled with compassion as tears coursed down her cheeks. The remaining staff, too shocked to speak, just glanced at her and looked away.

Recognising an awkward silence Roy announced, 'I think I've managed to find everything. If there's anything else I'll call you first and then I'll drop it off at your house. I've been through all his drawers. David is going to be missed so much by everybody. Have the police given you any further information about the accident?'

'No, no one's been in touch for the past couple of days but I expect to hear something today,' Robyn advised him. 'There were many witness statements to take so I expect it'll take time.'

'I've found David's password,' he stated, passing her the sealed envelope. 'Tracy will make you some coffee and I'll keep out of the way unless you need me. Just let me know if you can't find what you're looking for and I'll see if I can help.'

'Thank you Roy. I'd better make a start as I have another appointment in an hour.'

As she scrolled through the many files on David's computer, most related to business clients and she searched through various other locations to find any personal data but came up with nothing.

She sighed with frustration. 'Will you have a look Abbie? Maybe you'll spot the name of an Insurance Company. I don't want to miss it if it's there.'

Abbie paid close attention as Robyn ran through the seemingly endless list of files and then suddenly she called, 'Stop! I think that might be what we're looking for. Click on that file.'

Robyn selected and opened it to find details of the sought after Policy purchased by David.

'Right, send it to disk,' Abbie told her.

She groaned, 'I'm absolutely useless at this. Will you do it for me please?'

Abbie changed places and copied the information. She was also able to find David's bank details and copied that information to disk too. She checked for any further relevant files but there was nothing else of a personal nature. Having copied all the pertinent information, she deleted the two files and closed the system down.

'I think that's all we need for now,' Abbie said to Roy as Tracy appeared with coffee and biscuits.

'Thank you Tracy,' Robyn said with a warm and friendly smile at which point Tracy burst into tears, unable to contain her grief a moment longer.

'I'm very sorry,' she blubbered. 'Mr Ainsley was such a kind man. Everybody here thought such a lot about him. We're all going to miss him very much. We can hardly believe it's true.'

Robyn was overcome and blinked the tears from her eyes, aware that the rest of the staff had stopped working and were watching her.

Roy jumped up and intervened right away, taking control of the situation. 'Yes, thank you Tracy. We don't want to upset Mrs. Ainsley now, do we?'

In his earlier revelations to his staff, Roy had not divulged Robyn's exposé about Leanne and David though he felt sure that they would have quickly put two and two together when he had made known the finer points of their tragic deaths and his thoughts were later confirmed when, on the occasions he had reason to leave the office, he returned to a forum of surreptitious whispers that halted the instant he set foot in the room.

Tracy bolted from the room without another word following her boss's intervention.

When they had drunk their coffee, Abbie glanced at her watch. 'I think we should be on our way. We mustn't be late for our meeting at eleven. Gerald's a very busy man.'

Roy approached as Robyn arose and with another huge sigh, hugged her silently.

She smiled at him cordially. 'I believe I've found everything I need now but should you come across anything else of a private nature, would you let me know please?'

'Of course and if you need anything....anything at all, please call me. Julia sends her love and deepest sympathy. We are both so shocked.'

'I know. Thanks for everything you've done Roy. Here's David's password and I've deleted both the files I've copied. I'll nip to the loo before we leave. Bye everyone.'

There was a weak response from the office girls who were still far too traumatised to enter into any meaningful conversation with her.

As she entered the ladies' room, she was met by Tracy who had hurried in earlier to dry her tearful face and fix her make-up.

'I'm so sorry Mrs. Ainsley. I didn't mean to upset you. I can't imagine how you must be feeling. That scheming cow never left Mr. Ainsley alone. There she was, all over him, chucking herself at him. It's all her fault. She was constantly shouting her mouth off and bragging about how he fancied her and he didn't you know. She reckoned to be concerned for him because *you* couldn't give him a baby. Oh yes, Leanne told everyone in the office about that but I don't think Mr. Stanton knew or he'd have sacked her for sure if he'd heard her tittle-tattling like that. Mr. Stanton wouldn't have put up with that had he known. When she came to work one morning, soon after Mr. Ainsley told her he couldn't see her any-more she stood there in front of us, cackling like an old witch and she swore she'd get him back again, no matter what it took. *She'd* no intentions of losing a brilliant catch like that, she said. Those were her exact words Mrs. Ainsley and we were all disgusted with her. Three days later she flounced in, grinning all over her smug face, she was, telling us it was all back on again. She never did tell us what she'd had to do to change his mind and none of us knew they were planning on going away together. Oh yes, she kept that quiet. Not one word did she breathe about that but as it turned out Leanne got her just desserts, that I should say such a horrible thing. We were all shocked and horrified to hear about what happened. Everybody really liked your husband Mrs. Ainsley. He was a lovely man.'

'Yes, he was Tracy,' Robyn sighed.

'I'm sorry, I shouldn't have run off at the mouth like that but we're so angry about what's happened. It's her fault and that's what I wanted you to know so I'm sorry if you think I've spoken out of turn. I just thought you ought to know how we all felt.'

'Don't worry. You haven't spoken out of turn and you've certainly helped me to understand and piece certain things together, so thank you for letting me know Tracy.'

'Well, I'd better get back or I'll be in big trouble with Mr. Stanton.'

When Tracy left, Robyn sat down and holding her head in her hands she emitted a desperate sigh.

'David loved *you*. Don't forget that,' Abbie said reassuringly, knowing Robyn would be devastated by Tracy's revelations.

'I know but don't you see how it goes from bad to worse? In addition to everything else I've suffered, everyone in the office knows about all our personal issues. How humiliating is that to be advised by the office junior that I couldn't give David a child? It's so soul-destroying, having your dirty linen washed in public.'

'Hang on a minute! *She* never said that. She was just repeating to you what Leanne had said. I know it must seem like the end of the world right now but things will start to get better soon. Let's collect the boxes and get out of here.'

'Let me tell you something. I have a deep nagging suspicion that Leanne was never pregnant at all, if Tracy's account is to be believed. It sounds as if she deliberately trapped David when he tried to end the relationship. Well, if that was the plan, she certainly achieved her goal in taking him away from me,' she remarked sorrowfully.

'Tell Gerald what she said. It could be important,' Abbie said without confirming her suspicions.

En route to his office, Robyn asked, 'What does Gerald actually do?'

'He graduated in business law but now his work covers a vast field. He's very well qualified in most areas of law and he's also very knowledgeable. He likes fair play and he does more than his fair share of pro bono work when he feels passionate enough about his client though that obviously enhances his reputation. Gerald's very well respected in the legal profession and he earns megabucks! He's dedicated to his work and derives a great deal of satisfaction from facing almost insurmountable challenges that most solicitors wouldn't touch with a bargepole. He is an unusual kind of guy. He's never been married and I would imagine he'd be around thirty-eight to forty years old.'

'Have *you* been out with him?'

'Heavens no, but I would jump at the chance of a date with Gerald. Unfortunately, I merely exist on the end of a telephone.'

'So you've never met?'

'Oh yes, we've met several times but he's never given me a second look.'

'I'm rather nervous about our meeting. I cringe at the very thought of solicitors.'

Abbie laughed. 'You'll be fine. He's a really nice guy with a pleasant manner. I haven't seen him for two or three years but we have a chat occasionally on the phone about punters. I send him disgruntled clients who are unhappy with the way they've been treated by their Insurance Companies and he never fails to resolve their issues satisfactorily. That's the reason he owes me a favour and he didn't hesitate to offer his help when I spoke to him about you. He is definitely the best you could get.'

In her mind's eye, Robyn had an image of a staid, short, stockily-built, wavy-haired and bespectacled bachelor, dressed in a three piece old-fashioned suit smelling of mothballs.

As she walked into Gerald's smart modern office, she was taken aback when he practically leapt from his chair and rushed towards her, shaking her hand firmly.

'Happy to make your acquaintance Mrs. Ainsley, although I regret it couldn't have been under more agreeable circumstances,' he stated kindly. 'First of all may I offer my deepest sympathy for your tragic loss. Please....be seated. I'm Gerald Dunne.'

'Thank you,' she answered demurely, eyeing him closely from head to toe with more than a modicum of amusement, despite the sobriety of the occasion. The picture she had foreseen in her mind could not have been further from the truth, for towering over her at a height of at least six feet three inches, was unquestionably the most striking and distinguished man she'd ever met. 'Please....call me Robyn. I feel ill-at-ease with formality.'

'Me too!' he replied with a broad smile that lit up his face. Addressing Abbie, he remarked, 'It's good to see you again. I reckon it must be about er....'

'Two years at least,' she interrupted.

'Right, two years,' he stated in acquiescence as he kissed her on both cheeks. 'Well, you've certainly blossomed since I last saw you. You're absolutely stunning. Forgive my asking....but has that slippery cad made an honest woman of you yet?'

'Actually, I dumped the slippery cad a while ago,' she responded with a twinkle in her eye and in the knowledge that Gerald would be very embarrassed by his former remark.

'I'm so sorry Abbie. I was being frivolous. Had I been aware of that fact, I would never have....'

'Forget it Gerald. It's water under the bridge. It's been over for ages. I was merely marking time with him until someone half-decent turned up.'

'That's a shame....so I've missed the boat again?' he questioned jokingly. 'That's the story of my life I'm afraid. I'm always too late.'

'Not at all Gerald....not at all! I'm footloose and fancy-free at the moment so over to you!' she said with a provocative grin.

For several uncomfortable seconds, he attempted to construct a fitting response and when none was forthcoming she laughed. 'Well, there's a first time for everything and it's the first time I've known *you* be stuck for words.'

'Come to think of it, I can't remember a previous occasion either!' he answered with a reticent smile, 'but we have matters to attend to here,' and turning to Robyn he quickly changed the subject by asking whether there had been any further developments in the enquiry as Abbie smugly congratulated herself at her having brought the mighty Gerald to ground by causing more than a tinge of colour to appear in his cheeks.

'I haven't heard anything from the police yet but I called at David's office earlier today to collect his things. Obviously, I haven't had time to look in any of the boxes yet but I did manage to gain access to his computer and I copied some files onto this disk. You'll find his bank details and the information you requested about the Insurance Policy. I haven't read the Policy so I don't know what David bought but I deleted the file from his computer to ensure nobody else would be able to access anything of a personal nature.'

'So is this the only copy?' he asked.

'Yes, and I'm entrusting it to you,' Robyn replied with a smile.

'I'll read it later and I'll call the Company as soon as I can. Would you sign this authorisation form so I can fax it to them? They'll provide no information at all without your consent. Thanks,' he said as she handed it back to him.

Robyn took the bit between her teeth and spoke in a hushed voice. 'There's a further matter of concern to me and as you're aware of the content of David's letter I would like to bring it to your attention. It is my very strong belief that the female passenger in David's car wasn't pregnant after all.'

Gerald shuffled uncomfortably in his seat, at the same time casting a disparaging look at Abbie who merely raised her eyebrows defensively. 'And why would you believe that?' he asked.

'When I went to collect David's things, Tracy the office junior, made a point of informing me, though sympathetically, of certain facts. Apparently it was common knowledge that David and that girl Leanne were involved and Tracy further advised that when David ended the relationship, Leanne swore to get him back. It seems rather convenient to me that she should find she was pregnant a couple of days later, though I don't believe Tracy was aware of Leanne's alleged pregnancy or I'm quite sure she would have disclosed that as well. She didn't withhold anything else she knew.'

'How did it make you feel?' he enquired, leaning back in his chair, his eyes searching her face for the truth.

'Sick to my stomach and cheated! Losing David to some woman who was having his child was bad enough but the thought of losing the man I love to a scheming tramp who tricked him with nothing but a pack of lies is totally unbearable.'

He sighed heavily before continuing, 'When the medical findings of the Post Mortem examination are recorded, they will show whether or not she was pregnant. Should there be an Inquest, if the Coroner rules that the two cases should be heard in tandem, then you must be prepared for any such disclosure, so my question to you is, would you want to know the truth?'

She nodded her head. 'Yes, I have to know or I'll spend the rest of my life wondering. I need to know in order that I may lay my thoughts on the matter to rest. There's no doubt that David believed her or he would never have left me. He stated very clearly in his letter that he wouldn't abandon his child but that he didn't love Leanne.'

'If that's the case, then I think you should know sooner, rather than later. I wasn't going to mention it at this stage but as you've raised the issue, I can confirm that she was definitely *not* pregnant.'

'I knew it,' she said before bursting into tears and Abbie immediately jumped up and took her in her arms to console her.

'I'm sorry,' Gerald said, 'and because the source of my information isn't official, may I ask that you keep it to yourself please for the time being? Have you remembered to bring your husband's letter with you?'

'I've got it,' Abbie said, handing it to Gerald who read it swiftly.

'I don't see how anybody could suggest anything untoward by reading those words. His feelings for you are quite clear and though the letter isn't dated, no inference whatsoever could be drawn from that, other than, when he was writing it, he hadn't made up his mind when he was leaving. Abbie mentioned that you found the letter on the bed when you went upstairs to make a telephone call?'

'Yes, I went upstairs to call David's mother.'

'So, why did you decide *not* to make the call from the downstairs telephone?'

'Because I knew she'd be extremely distressed as I was. Abbie and the policewoman were there and I wanted some privacy.'

'And you didn't see your husband's letter as you first entered the bedroom?'

'No, because I walked round the bed to the other side....David's side, to use the telephone and when I sat on the bed to make the call, I had my back to the pillow where the letter had been left. As David was more likely to receive work related calls at unsocial hours, the telephone was kept at his side of the bed and as the letter had been left on *my* pillow, I only spotted it as I was about to leave the room.'

'Had you already called Abbie to the bedroom by then?'

'I didn't call her. She came up to check on me as she knew I'd be very upset after talking to David's mother. Am I missing something? Is there a reason for all these questions?'

'Not at all; I'm just trying to arrange a sequence of events in my mind. Have you mentioned David's letter to anyone else?'

'I showed it to WPC Davies that's all.'

'So you haven't mentioned it to David's family or to yours?'

'No....I didn't want to upset his mother more than was necessary. It was bad enough having to tell her her son was dead. I didn't want to call again after I found the letter. David's mother is quite an elderly lady who doesn't enjoy the best of health. She has angina, but having said that, I'm certain everything will come out eventually.'

'Not necessarily. Coroners don't generally make a point of reading out personal letters, unless such a letter is vital to the findings of a cause of death and in those cases, a brief mention of a suicide note, for example, would usually suffice where the deceased had clearly taken his own life. The Coroner would pay due regard to relatives' feelings where possible. The police investigation should provide additional information as their enquiries proceed but I still feel they'll want to interview you and you'll need to tell them what you've told me. I shall be present and if they ask any questions I deem inappropriate, I will advise you not to answer but don't worry. As I see it, there's nothing for you to be concerned about. I am correct in my assumption, am I not, that you'd no inkling that David was associating with another woman?'

'None at all. He had been quiet and morose but I believed that to be due to the repeated IVF failures.

He never once mentioned Leanne's name and I was unaware he'd discussed the treatment with anybody other than me but it seems he'd discussed all of our personal issues with that woman, who in turn, had disclosed everything to the girls at work, according to the office junior, although apparently, she hadn't mentioned she was pregnant, which as we all know now, she wasn't.'

'Can I just return to something before I forget to mention it?' Abbie interposed. 'Regarding the letter that David left on the bed, when I arrived upstairs, I was standing in front of Robyn as I was talking to her so I would have been facing the bed and I didn't notice the letter either. We were so shocked by the tragic news we'd just received that everything else paled into insignificance. Until we were leaving the room, neither of us saw that letter....that's the point I'm trying to make.'

'I'll make a quick note of that. Thanks Abbie.' He looked up at them and smiled. 'I'm about finished now, so if there are any questions you'd like to ask, please go ahead.'

He paused for a few moments before continuing. 'Right, here's my business card and you'll find my home number written on the reverse. If you need to talk to me at any time, give me a call. I'll probably receive some information during the next few days and we'll take it from there. Meanwhile, I'll have a look what's on this disk and I'll let you know when I've spoken with the Insurance Company. I'll guide you through everything. For now, try to concentrate on coming to terms with your grief and remember, please don't answer any questions if I'm not there. That includes anyone from the Insurance Company who definitely won't be happy at having to pay out on a Policy only recently acquired. Be sure to refer them to me immediately should they make contact by telephone and forward all correspondence to me. I'll deal with everything as soon as the official findings are to hand.'

'Thanks for your help Gerald. It means so much to have you in our corner,' Abbie said. 'And don't forget what I told you, that I'm footloose and fancy free now!' she added on a shrill hoot of laughter.

Gerald threw back his head and laughed heartily. 'Why not get straight to the point and say what you mean? I can't be doing with people who beat about the bush,' he said with a twinkle in his eye. 'Alright Abbie, you've twisted my arm. How about we have dinner one evening? I'll take you to an exceptionally good restaurant I'm sure you'll enjoy.'

She flashed a broad grin. 'Thank you Gerald. I'll look forward to that. I was beginning to think you'd never ask!'

'I didn't! *You* did,' he responded with a diffident smile. 'I'll call you to arrange a convenient evening Abbie. It's been a pleasure to meet you Robyn.'

'Thank you for everything and goodbye,' she said as she took one last look at the man who was every girl's fantasy. Out of earshot, she said, 'Hang on to him Abbie! He's an absolute dish!'

'I fully intend to,' she responded with a confident smile. 'I can't believe my luck….a night out on the town with Gerald Dunne. Wow!'

Abbie barely spoke as they made their way home. Her thoughts had been provisionally diverted from Robyn's troubles to what might lay ahead. Gerald Oliver Dunne....or 'GOD', as he was known in the legal fraternity by those who knew of his relentless approach to what he truly believed was justice, had invited her to dinner. That was definitely something to look forward to. Within his tough exterior there had to be a soft spot somewhere and she was hell-bent on finding it. Yes, Gerald had been a bachelor far too long!

They hadn't been home more than a few minutes when Gerald telephoned Robyn. After checking the information on the disk, and following a telephone conversation with the Insurance Company, he was happy to advise that a Rider *had* been added to the original policy four weeks ago. He informed Robyn that the face value of the Policy was half a million pounds in the event of David's death which meant, in the event of accidental death, the face value was doubled to a million. 'I think we might have quite a battle on our hands but you should try not to worry. For every clause they find to deny payment, I'll be sure to find *two* to make them pay. It might take a little while but you *will* receive your money. Whatever else David might have done, he certainly left you very well provided for. I realise of course that no amount of money is recompense for your tragic loss. Nonetheless, his concern for your future needs will make your life a little easier to bear.'

'Thank you Gerald. I was concerned I would have to sell the house when I learned about his death but he'd taken care of that too. He really was a decent man. He was simply misguided when he chose the wrong person in whom to confide. I'll be sure to let you know about anything that arises at this end and I do appreciate your call. Thanks for all your help.'

As she replaced the receiver, Abbie looked up and asked, 'What's up? You look dazed. Has there been a further development?'

'That's putting it mildly! Yes, there has....David's Insurance Policy is worth a million pounds! There *was* a Rider. What do I want with a million pounds? I'd rather be penniless, living from hand to mouth with David. All the money in the world could never compensate for what I've lost,' she sighed as tears flooded from her eyes.

There were no further developments on Monday or Tuesday but Wednesday, when the telephone rang at ten o'clock, Robyn guessed it would be Gerald.

He greeted her warmly and made enquiries about her general health before informing her he had been contacted by the police.

'They'd like to take a statement from you. Could you meet me down at the Station in about an hour? I have a free slot then and we could have a spot of lunch afterwards, if that's alright, while we catch up with any developments. There's nothing else in my diary until after two-thirty. The interview is nothing to worry about, simply a formality so we shouldn't be there more than half an hour.'

'I'll be there by eleven. The sooner it's over, the better, as far as I'm concerned. I've arranged to see

David's mother later today but that can wait if I'm not back in time. I've decided to show her David's letter. It's constantly on my mind that some way or other she'll find out that David was leaving me for another woman and then she'll be wondering why I kept it quiet. I'm sure she'll be well enough to deal with it now. The fact that Leanne wasn't pregnant caused me to change my mind as it shifts the blame from me to Leanne for David's death.'

'I don't understand your reasoning. You weren't to blame for any part of it Robyn.'

'You and I both know that but his mother might have believed I had driven her son into the arms of another woman. If I tell her everything face to face, she can judge me when she's heard the facts. That's very important to me. I need her to know about the IVF treatment I've had over the past two years and how the repeated failures affected both of us.'

'I do agree. It never helps to conceal the truth and you could add that you've left it until now to spare her feelings. Wait for me in reception at the Station if you arrive first and speak to no one. I'll see you shortly.'

Robyn arrived moments after Gerald had booked them in and they were quickly escorted to a private interview room by two male investigative officers previously unknown to Robyn.

Following brief introductions, one of the officers offered his condolences on behalf of both of them before informing Robyn that certain questions of a routine nature needed to be put to her.

'Is my client to be cautioned first?' Gerald asked.

'No Sir, that won't be necessary,' the officer said. 'We just need your client to clarify a few points at this stage.'

The majority of the questions related to David's letter and followed the original line of questioning by WPC Davies about how and when the letter had been found.

Without intervention by Gerald, she answered the questions honestly. A follow-up question however, astounded her when the more senior officer asked, 'When did you first suspect that your husband was having an affair Mrs. Ainsley?'

Defensively she responded, 'I *never* suspected my husband was having an affair! There was nothing at all about David's behaviour to suggest or raise any suspicion that he was involved with anyone.'

'You're saying you didn't find it suspicious when your husband repeatedly arrived home in the early hours?'

'My client's reply answered *both* your questions,' Gerald intervened. 'Don't answer that Robyn.'

'Then I'll rephrase my last question. At any time, did you speak to your husband about his late arrival home from the office?'

'No, because he had already explained to me that he was very busy at work and I believed him.'

'Didn't you advise WPC Davies you were having marital problems at the time?'

'No, I told her that we had encountered stress and difficulties because of the failed IVF treatment. It's very traumatic when the treatment continually fails. It crossed my mind that David might be staying late at the office because he wanted to avoid discussing the issues with me. He was aware that I didn't want the treatment to continue as it made me feel ill.'

'With hindsight, do you not think you were naïve in your belief that your husband was working late?'

Irritably Gerald declared, 'Alright, that's enough! My client is not required to answer questions about hindsight. We can all be wise after the event and so if you've finished we'll be on our way.'

'There's just one final question before you leave. I understand Mr. Ainsley recently acquired a rather large Insurance Policy, with you named as the sole beneficiary and providing double the cover should he die from accidental cause.'

Gerald intervened again. 'If you'd like to rephrase that statement as a question and get to the point, my client will be happy to answer it.'

The officer clearly embarrassed, cleared his throat and asked, 'When did you first become aware that your husband had taken out a rather large Insurance Policy on his life Mrs. Ainsley?'

'Two days ago....Monday.'

'Monday did you say? According to the contents of your husband's letter, you were aware last Friday that he had recently insured his life. Is that not so?' he asked with a supercilious smile.

'To repeat your own words, officer, I didn't know it was *rather large* until Monday.'

'So you're telling me your husband didn't discuss such an important matter with you before he bought the Policy?'

'Correct.'

'And you didn't come across any correspondence relating to it?'

'None whatsoever. Until I found David's letter I knew nothing about it and now if I may, I'd like to ask *you* a question, officer?'

'Be my guest!' he remarked with a derisive leer.

'If my husband had wanted me to know about the Insurance Policy, would he not have bought it from the Broker where I am a partner? After all, for such a hefty premium, a comparably hefty commission would have been received by the Broker and I can assure you that David, as a very shrewd accountant, would have wanted to negotiate his cut for putting the business our way! Do you not agree, officer?'

'I think we'll be on our way,' Gerald interrupted. 'I don't somehow think the police officer will deign to answer that question. Is that everything?' he said looking pointedly at the officer. 'I'm hungry.'

Feeling humiliated, he cleared his throat noisily. 'Would you mind waiting for a minute please?' He stood up and left the room with the other officer.

'You had me a bit worried there,' Gerald laughed. 'I wondered what the hell you were going to ask.'

'He was getting on my nerves! I've done nothing wrong yet I'm being treated like a criminal. I'm the innocent party here and I've just lost my husband. I can do without his contemptuous remarks.'

'I know it's tough but you have to remember they have a difficult job to do. Hopefully, we'll be away from here shortly.'

No sooner had he uttered the words than the door was thrust open and a more senior officer, instantly recognised by Gerald, entered the room. He greeted them both with a warm smile. 'It's nice to see you again Gerald. How's life been treating you of late? Are you keeping busy?'

'Oh you know how it is. I can't grumble George. I'm still managing to earn a crust,' he responded on a short burst of laughter. 'This is my client, Robyn Ainsley.'

'I'm pleased to meet you Mrs. Ainsley and I'm so sorry about your loss. It's tragic when a young man loses his life and in such circumstances,' he stated caringly.

'And what circumstances would those be then?' Gerald asked casually.

'Well, as you've probably gathered, the cause of the accident has now been investigated by the local police and I've been notified that a young man has been charged and remanded on two separate counts of causing death by dangerous driving. He'll appear in court later today. Off the record, several reliable witnesses have come forward and each provided a written statement that Mr. Ainsley was blameless in the accident. The van driver has admitted he didn't see Mr. Ainsley's car as he pulled over to overtake the vehicle in front of him. It may well have been that Mr. Ainsley's car was in his blind spot but unfortunately, the young man had been drinking and was marginally over the legal limit. He'll appear in court for a preliminary hearing and further charges might follow as other vehicles were also involved. The facts have now been referred to the Coroner's Office and I expect an Inquest will be opened and adjourned anytime soon. Once I'm made aware that the Coroner has released Mr. Ainsley's body, you'll be able to go ahead with the funeral arrangements. That could possibly be later today. Would you like me to call you when I know something, Gerald?'

'Please do. The sooner Mrs. Ainsley can begin to move forward, the sooner she can begin to get her life back on track. I'm obliged to you George,' he said, shaking his hand vigorously. 'I take it there'll be no further questioning of my client?'

'Our enquiries are now complete and I apologise for any anxiety this may have caused Mrs. Ainsley. Occasionally, we have to do things we're not proud of,' he made known, turning to face Robyn.

'Nice to have seen you again George. Right come on Robyn. Let's find somewhere for lunch,' Gerald said as he led her away. 'There's a place not too far up the road that serves pretty decent pub grub.'

'Sounds great. I believe my appetite has suddenly returned now that lot's over and done with.'

'And don't forget it helps the Insurance claim. I'll seek an interim award when I get back to the office. Meanwhile, let's enjoy lunch and try to forget about everything else for an hour or so.'

'If only it were that easy but I suppose I have to think of it as another hurdle I've crossed,' she said desolately.

'There you are....one G and T with ice and lemon,' Gerald stated, placing her drink on the table. 'Have you chosen what you'd like to eat yet? If you need any help, I can certainly recommend the steak pie.'

'Would you believe I fancy fish and chips? How sad is that when there's such a varied menu? It's a while since I've ordered that anywhere.'

'Same here. We'll make that two then, so I'll just nip back to the bar and place the order.'

As Robyn watched him hurry away she chuckled inwardly at her former preconceived image of him. He wasn't at all stuffy or imperious. He was a very pleasant and agreeable man who had put her at ease instantly but there was no doubt in her mind that he was more than capable of standing his corner in the courtroom and giving much more than he got.

He returned and took his seat, then after taking a sip of his drink remarked, 'Er....would you mind if I had a word with you about something....something unconnected with the enquiry that is? Do you think Abbie was....er....on the level about going on a date with me?'

'Yes, of course she was. Why do you ask?'

'I wanted to be absolutely sure before calling her. Our paths frequently cross because of the nature of our work and so I wouldn't want to embarrass her, were she merely being frivolous.'

'Believe me, she was serious. She thinks you're a great guy,' Robyn disclosed and he looked smugly gratified by her reply.

At that point the waitress arrived with their food, bringing that topic of conversation to an abrupt halt.

'Mmm, that looks very appetising,' Gerald stated. 'I'm glad I followed your lead now. Enjoy!'

'I fully intend to. That looks delicious and look at the size of the fish!' Robyn said hungrily.

'So, returning to what we were discussing, Abbie is a gregarious young woman. I admire her attitude of mind and her exuberant persona and I've thought of her quite a lot since our recent meeting,' Gerald readily admitted. 'I wish I'd known sooner that she was available.'

'Well, you know now. You're not involved with anyone are you? Sorry....it's none of my business. I have a big mouth and I shouldn't have asked such a question.'

'No it's fine really. I'm not involved with anyone. I meant, had I known, I would have approached her sooner,' he explained. When she giggled, he looked puzzled. 'What? Come on....share the joke.'

'As I recall Gerald, it was Abbie who approached you and somewhat undiplomatically.'

'Well, I suppose if I'm relying on the letter of the law....'

'Which you do....'

'Which I do....so I have to concede.'

'Can I ask you a very personal question Gerald?'

'That sounds ominous!' he chuckled.

'Not really. I'm just curious as to why you never married. If that's an awkward question, then you're allowed to take the Fifth Amendment,' she advised with an optimistic smile. 'So what's it to be then? Are you spilling the beans or taking the Fifth?'

'I was engaged several years ago but while I was studying for the Bar, my fiancée was studying other men if you get my drift. I was the last person to find out and I was something of a laughing stock among my so-called friends, some of whom were actually seeing her at the time we were making the wedding plans. It dented my pride somewhat to discover that I'd been so short-sighted. I'd earned the reputation of always having my finger on the pulse, yet I was too stupid to see what was going on right under my nose. That unfortunate episode not only cost me a part of my reputation, it also destroyed my trust in women and I vowed I'd never let anything like that happen to me again. You've heard the saying, *once bitten twice shy*?'

'In other words, you're scared of making another commitment in case it goes wrong again?'

'I suppose I am,' he admitted.

'Gerald, you can't give up on life because of one misadventure. It sounds to me like you had a lucky escape. There's something else in life besides work. You need to get a life outside the courtroom. Take Abbie out and see where it leads. She's a great girl and *she* wouldn't hurt you; it's not in her nature. If it transpires that you're not well-matched, no harm will have been done but if you don't try, you don't buy, as the familiar saying goes....or words to that effect,' Robyn laughed. 'I had eight fantastic years with David and I'd do it all over again without any hesitation....even knowing what I know now.'

'I thought *I* was supposed to support *you* through *your* difficulties Robyn?'

'There's no legislation I'm aware of, stipulating I can't reciprocate where there's a need.'

'I can't say I've come across any but I might look it up when I return to the office, which reminds me, I have an appointment in forty-five minutes so I'll have to leave shortly. Would you like another drink before I go?'

'No, I'm driving and I've had more than enough of the police! So are you going to call Abbie?'

'It's clear you won't leave me alone until I do, so yes I am! I've enjoyed our lunch very much Robyn and the conversation has been quite....invigorating. I'll call her this evening. I promise.'

'Make sure you do and once again, many thanks for everything Gerald.'

'No, it's I who should be thanking you. It's done me a power of good to confide in someone. Yes, I must say I'm looking forward to a nice evening out with Abbie. It'll be a most enjoyable diversion. I'll be in touch soon Robyn.'

Later that evening, Abbie called Robyn. Excitedly she shrieked, 'You'll never guess who's just called me.'

'Er...let me try! Could it possibly have been your friend Gerald?'

'How on earth did you know that?'

'Call it women's intuition! I'm so happy for you. Where's he taking you?'

'It's somewhere in Chester. I'm a wreck. I've got the collywobbles and I haven't a clue what to wear. I really wanted to make a good impression!'

'Calm down. You'll find something suitable and from what I've seen of your extensive wardrobe, he *will* be impressed. Don't forget, you have to report every minute detail to me afterwards.'

On a piercing cackle of laughter she remarked, 'I won't promise I'll tell you *everything*.'

'Listen….a word of advice. Don't rush him. He's a cautious guy!'

'Why do you say that?'

'He needed a heavy push when you propositioned him so let it flow at his pace for the first few dates until he feels comfortable. That's all I'm saying.'

'You appear to have Gerald summed up after only five minutes in his office.'

'Trust me. I do know what I'm talking about,' she replied without further comment.

'Have you heard anything more from the police?'

'Yes, their enquiries are complete. The van driver has been arrested and charged. He'd been drinking. There's going to be a Coroner's Inquest but it won't take place until after the Criminal Proceedings are completed in Crown Court according to Gerald and it's merely a formality, a paper exercise.'

'Have you spoken to Gerald today?'

'Yes, he called me earlier,' she answered with a half-truth.

'So am I to assume then that my name featured in your conversation?'

'You may assume whatever you choose. My lips are sealed,' she answered in a supercilious tone.

'Thanks Robyn. You're brilliant. I owe you one.'

'You owe me nothing after everything you've had to do for me. We take care of each other, right?'

Abbie laughed. 'Right!'

The next morning, Robyn received a call from the Funeral Director, advising that arrangements could proceed with the funeral, once she had obtained the necessary certification from the Registry office.

The funeral had been provisionally arranged for the following Tuesday and further to a brief though tearful discussion with David's mother, Robyn had contacted the Funeral Director to advise it was to be a burial.

Early indications suggested there would be many mourners in attendance to pay their final respects to him. The Rose and Crown, where Robyn and David had regularly popped in for a pub lunch, offered to provide two private rooms for anybody wishing to attend after the funeral. Having an extensive menu, catering to everyone's taste, it was the ideal venue, providing an easy solution to the catering needs for numbers that could not be precisely calculated.

Robyn dreaded the day she would have to say her fond and final farewell to David.

She had not yet disclosed the existence of David's letter to their respective families and was aware that she must address the matter without further delay. There would be some mourners in attendance who were acquainted with Leanne too and the likelihood existed for someone with a loose tongue like Tracy, to make an ill-conceived comment to a member of David's family.

Robyn decided there was no time like the present and grabbing her bag and car key, made her way to her in-laws' house first.

Clutching David's letter in her quivering hand she earnestly awaited her mother-in-law's return from the kitchen, where she had gone to make her a cup of tea and when she sat down, rather than hand the letter to her without any introductory preamble, she began by describing the various problems they had encountered with the fertility treatment.

'Well, that's come as a shock. I had no idea there was a problem,' she remarked, looking astonished. 'David never mentioned anything to us about that.'

'He was embarrassed about it mum. He believed it made him less of a man but it was neither David's fault, nor mine for that matter. It was simply one of those unfortunate things that can happen with some couples. David took it very badly and he refused to talk about it with anybody in the family but I found out recently that he'd discussed it with a woman at the office....a woman named Leanne.'

At that point, Robyn broke down and cried, 'This is so difficult for me to explain mum. I loved David very much and he loved me just as much but he was depressed and unwittingly, he became *involved*, if you understand what I'm saying, with the woman at work. He never meant for it to happen and he tried to end the relationship as he didn't want anything to jeopardise our marriage. I need you to know that I don't blame David. He was under a lot of pressure. When the police were with me, I found this letter in our bedroom. I didn't mention it to you earlier as it didn't seem right to burden you with added distress when you had just lost your son. I've never judged him and I don't want you to judge him either, but I *do* want you to read this letter,' she said, handing it to her. 'Please don't think badly of him. That's the last thing I want.'

Robyn looked on compassionately as the elderly lady tried to unfold the letter with some difficulty, hampered by her arthritic fingers. 'Here, let me help you,' she offered.

Mary Ainsley blinked rapidly to contain her tears, at the same time reaching into her apron pocket for her handkerchief that she dabbed repeatedly against her nose as she digested the heart-felt words written by her son. It took her several minutes to finish the letter and after reading it in silence, she returned it to her daughter-in-law. 'I don't know what to say to you Robyn,' she murmured almost inaudibly, with tears streaming down her face.

'I know mum and you don't have to say anything. I'm not angry with David and I would have spared your feelings had it been possible but unfortunately the woman referred to in the letter was with him in the car....and she died too.'

'And the baby,' she acknowledged rhetorically.

'According to my information, there never was a baby. That evil-minded woman was determined to have David and she invented the baby to hang on to him when he tried to end the relationship. She knew how much it meant to him to father a child and she used that knowledge to her advantage by claiming to be pregnant, aware that he would never abandon his child. I received my information from one of the girls in David's office,' she told her, not wishing to divulge that Gerald had furnished the confirmation.

'David was a foolish lad but he didn't deserve to die. He worshipped you,' Mary spluttered tearfully.

'I know he did Mum. He made a silly mistake and I would have forgiven him, in fact I *have* forgiven him. He just needed a confidante and he made a bad choice. She took advantage of his vulnerability and now we've all lost David because of her,' she wept. 'I think it right that the family should be told about this and I'm sure they'll all understand that David's intentions were honourable towards the woman he believed was carrying his child and that he truly felt it was in my best interest to leave me.'

'You're such a good girl Robyn. How can you be so compassionate after what's happened?'

'Because I know he never wanted to hurt me. He was trapped and he wanted to protect me.'

'The coming months will be very stressful and I'd like you to know we'll help you any way possible. You brought so much happiness into David's short life and his father and I will always be very grateful so anything we can do for you, we will. That's what David would have wanted.'

'David always wanted what was best for me and if he'd been open and honest about that woman, we would have worked it out somehow. Now I have to spend the rest of my life without him.'

'You're just a young woman Robyn and none of us knows what the future holds in store. I know for sure that David wouldn't have wanted you to throw your life away; in fact, he released you when he left with that woman. There's already been one wasted life. Please don't make it two,' she begged her with tears filling her eyes.

'I can't bring myself to even think of the future. I suppose I might feel different given time. It's early days yet. Right, I'd best be off to see mum now; she doesn't know anything about David's letter yet and she has to be told too but I wanted to show it to you first.'

'Give her our fondest regards. We'll be seeing her next week at the funeral,' she wept, holding Robyn in her arms. 'I'm sorry for all your troubles and for David's wrongdoings. I think you're a brave young woman. Take care of yourself my dear.'

The modest church at the Cemetery was packed to capacity and despite Robyn's clear instructions that the service was to be a celebration of David's short life, it was nonetheless a most traumatic occasion. The Minister delivered his words with respect and sympathy though not omitting to include one or two amusing anecdotal stories of past experiences with David, alluding to happier times when they used to play cricket together on the local team.

Most former and present team members were in attendance as were all staff members from David's office, together with many of his old school friends and former teachers who had read about his tragic accident in the local newspaper. Family members, friends, neighbours and dozens of his clients made up the number to exceed a hundred and Robyn was totally overwhelmed by the huge turnout.

Following the burial, she spoke briefly to many of David's associates and friends prior to making her way to the Rose and Crown for lunch and a much-needed drink. Although everybody had been invited to attend for lunch, many simply opted to pay their final respects and leave the family members to their thoughts.

Gerald attended with Abbie to offer some moral support and Abbie likewise rallied round to enable Robyn to cope with a traumatic day. Though Robyn had been dreading the day, she found it less testing than expected. The Funeral Director had been most professional and had been of great help and support in lessening her pain.

Gerald and Abbie took her home and stayed with her for a while.

'It was a dignified, moving service, a service I'll never forget,' Abbie commented as she and Gerald prepared to leave. 'I heard several people making a similar comment. The balance was just right. It was respectful to David's memory without being overly morbid; in fact I'd go as far as to say it was exactly what David would have wanted.'

Robyn reflected on Abbie's words as she watched them drive away. A funeral of any kind would have been the last thing David would have wanted. Until a few short months ago, he had been full of life and joy and now he was gone from her life forever. She would never again see his happy smiling face, nor would she ever hold him in her arms again.

Tears that had been but a blink away now scalded her bloodshot eyes as they coursed uncontrollably down her face and as she closed the door and turned to face the stark empty room, she felt she had also closed the door on a significant chapter of her life.

As the tears continued to flow she wondered what the future held in store and whether she would ever find peace and happiness again without her beloved David, the love of her life.

3

'I've just popped in to pay the bill,' Robyn advised the receptionist at the Funeral Parlour, handing her a gift-wrapped box of assorted chocolates, together with a card on which she had written a message of appreciation for everyone's kindness.

The receptionist thanked her warmly. 'I hope you soon start to feel a lot better,' she told Robyn. 'It's a difficult time when you're trying to come to terms with everything.'

'I'm doing alright I guess,' she replied, hurrying to close her bag in order to escape the smell of fresh flowers that revived such painful memories. Thanks again for everything.'

As she returned to her car, she passed by a Travel Agency where she stopped to peer in the window. It had been more than a year since she and David had taken a holiday. So often had they talked about the possibility of visiting New York where her younger sister Bryony lived but during the time Robyn had been receiving the fertility treatment, she hadn't felt like travelling too far away from home. Bryony had repeatedly begged them to visit but Robyn had been adamant. Some days she had felt so weary that she could barely drive to the office, so what would have been the point in going all the way to New York if she hadn't the stamina to enjoy it once she got there she had argued with David who had finally relented in his efforts to persuade her.

She had spoken to Bryony on the telephone a few times following David's death and also the evening prior to the funeral that sadly, she had been unable to attend. They enjoyed a lengthy conversation during which she again pleaded with Robyn to visit.

'You'd love it here and the change would do you a world of good! Please come,' she reiterated for the umpteenth time.

Only when Robyn promised to think about it did Bryony drop the subject.

Bryony was employed by the Foreign Office and spent little time in England. She had been posted all over the world and at the age of twenty-four, lived life to the full, enjoying her generous income with barely a cent to spare at the end of the month. With an enormous circle of friends, she loved New York and was truly captivated by the United States, much more so than by any other country she'd been sent to in recent years. Flights to other states were cheap and plentiful with an abundance of last minute bargains and she had taken advantage of the give-away flight prices when visiting New England in the fall and Las Vegas in the springtime.

Perhaps a holiday would help her come to terms with recent events, Robyn contemplated as she read the spring bargains on offer but the vast majority of the ones displayed were to places she would never consider visiting alone, until a cruise on the QE2 to New York with the option of a three-day stop-over caught her eye. That would provide the opportunity to spend a little time with Bryony.

She had always envisaged a leisurely cruise as a wonderful experience but David, a devotee of beach holidays, had displayed little enthusiasm for such a holiday in the belief it would feel too cramped and claustrophobic.

It's a ridiculous idea to even be thinking about a holiday, Robyn said to herself as she returned to her car. What would people say were she to book such a trip only days after her husband's funeral?

Despite those reservations, the prospect of seeing Bryony still appealed to her. They hadn't seen each other for eighteen months and a complete change of environment might just make her emptiness a little easier to bear.

She checked her watch. It was eleven o'clock and she decided to spend half an hour with Abbie who would be taking her lunch break around noon. After calling at the sandwich shop, she walked the rest of the way to the office.

Abbie looked up and beamed at her. 'I'm glad to see you're out and about. Where've you been?'

'Nowhere exciting I can assure you. I've just been to pay the Funeral Director and thought as I was out that I'd pop in to hear how your evening went with Gerald. I'd have asked yesterday but my powers of concentration have been sadly lacking.'

Abbie looked guilty. 'I wanted to call you the day after but with David's funeral drawing close, it just didn't seem the right thing to do….to be telling you how I was full of the joys of spring when you were having such a rotten time.'

'Don't be daft. Come on, out with it. I'm dying to know what's happened,' she asked eagerly. 'Did he rise to your expectations? Are you going to see him again?'

'Hang on a minute! One question at a time!' she laughed. 'To start with, he took me to a magnificent restaurant. It was obviously one of his old haunts as everyone knew him and fussed around him all night and the food was unbelievable. I'm sure, because of who he is, that we received special treatment. The portions were *enormous* and it was very expensive.'

'These weren't!' Robyn interrupted, throwing her a packet of chicken sandwiches. '*I've* bought your lunch so you'll have to rough it today. Carry on! I can't wait to hear the juicy bits!' she exclaimed in anticipation of what was to come.

'It was such a perfect evening,' she made known without elaboration as she nibbled on her sandwich and stared into space nostalgically. 'These chicken sandwiches are really nice. Did you buy them down town?'

'No, I didn't. I bought them at the usual place and I haven't traipsed all the way down here to discuss chicken sandwiches *so get on with it,*' she shrieked impatiently. 'I want to hear every little detail about what happened on your date and *afterwards.*'

'I've already told you,' Abbie taunted. 'We had a really good time.'

'Doing *what*?' she questioned, close to screaming pitch.

'Talking et cetera,' she said impassively, avoiding her eye.

'What does *et cetera* mean?' she squealed.

Abbie sighed dolefully. 'Well....we didn't end up in the bedroom if that's what you're waiting to hear so if it is, you've had a wasted journey.'

Robyn howled with laughter. 'There's no cause to sound so disappointed. It's early days yet. I'm sure you will when the time's right.'

'Well, it certainly didn't happen on Saturday,' she grunted, then with a broad sassy grin added, 'but he certainly rose to the occasion on Sunday, in fact he stayed the night!'

'*Terrific*!' Robyn shrieked.

'He's absolutely fantastic! When I think of all the years I wasted with that other useless plonker....'

Robyn sighed. 'He's a true gentleman, there's no denying that. I was hoping things would work out for you. I found him to be a really special guy when we went to lunch the other day.'

She was stunned. 'Er....excuse me....but when did *you* go for lunch with Gerald? He never mentioned to me that he'd taken you out to lunch.'

'Oops! I've put my big foot in it now haven't I? I suppose I'd best come clean before you jump to the wrong conclusion. I had to attend the police station to make a statement, so I met Gerald and after that he took me up the road for lunch. He wanted to talk about you. He needed reassuring that you really did want to go on a date with him and that you weren't just being frivolous so I made it very clear that you were absolutely crazy mad passionate about him!'

With a look of horror she exclaimed, '*You didn't say that*!'

Robyn howled with laughter at Abbie's astounded response. 'No I didn't....well not in so many words, but I did assure him you were serious; then I just let nature take its course!'

She smiled with relief. 'Thanks for that Robyn. I really appreciate it.'

'Actually, we had quite an interesting discussion. Has he told you about his former fiancée?'

'No, I didn't know Gerald had ever been engaged so come on, dish the dirt.'

'Apparently, she was sleeping around behind his back....*and* some of the guys were mates of his. Can you believe that? He was demented when he found out and it dented his pride as well. Gerald feels very insecure and that's the reason he's still a bachelor if you ask me. Like I said, don't rush him Abbie. He's a really nice bloke so look after him.'

'I intend to. He's the best guy I've ever been out with. He's good fun; he's handsome; he's wealthy and he's very caring. What more could a girl want?'

'Yes well, you're probably the best *girl* Gerald's ever had. You're very caring too. Look how you've helped me through all my troubles.'

She giggled like a schoolgirl. 'He rang just before you arrived. He certainly appears smitten.'

'And so do you,' she laughed.

'It's good to see you laugh again Robyn. Are you feeling a little better?'

She sighed audibly. 'I take each day as it comes. I hate being in the house alone because there are so many memories of David. It's so depressing.'

'I can imagine....well no I can't. It must be awful. I wish I could do something to help.'

'Well actually you can....you can give me a bit of advice.' She proceeded to tell her about the cruise, displayed in the Travel Agent's window and shared her concerns about what other people would say or think were she to take such a holiday so soon after David's death. 'I'd love to visit Bryony but half of me cries out that it'd be disrespectful to his memory and the other half says I should take a break to pull myself together. After all, it's not as if I'm planning a rave-up is it? I'd be visiting my sister and a cruise would be a nice relaxing way of getting there. What do you think Abbie? I'd like you to be honest with me. Do *you* think it's too early?'

'First of all, forget everybody else. You didn't ask for any of this to happen and the only people likely to raise an eyebrow would be David's family and I doubt they'd have justification to criticise you after what David did. If you want to tell them anything, tell them the truth – that you're visiting your sister in New York. It's just what you need and it'd be a wonderful experience. You'd be able to take things easy on the ship, participate in anything you fancied and they'd put you on a table in the restaurant with other people, so you wouldn't be alone all the time. I've heard there's scores of single men and women on cruises and they often have singles' clubs where you can meet other people who are travelling alone. You'd enjoy it. Forget about what other folk might think or say. It's your life. Go for it!'

'I don't know what to do. It's a big step to take on my own but whatever I decide, I intend to return to work a week on Monday. The ship sails in a couple of days and takes six days to sail over to New York. I'd spend a few days with Bryony, time enough to see the major highlights before flying back and I'd be home in time to come into work on the Monday. It's very tempting.'

'What's there to think about? In your position, I wouldn't hesitate. I can manage by myself here for a few more weeks so don't worry about this place. You need a break, a time to relax to come to terms with everything that's happened over recent weeks. Get it booked before they sell out. If you need any holiday stuff, I've plenty. What about eveningwear? You'll need that for the restaurant.'

'I'm definitely short of eveningwear. I have a few cocktail dresses that would be alright but very little formal wear. I haven't bought any new dresses for ages and as I've lost weight over recent months due to all the stress, they might not fit me now. Maybe I should go home first and have a look what I've got before rushing into anything.'

'Pack it in! You're just looking for excuses. I've a wardrobe full of stuff. Go and book while you still can and we'll attend to the clothes tomorrow. Just imagine Robyn....a nice relaxing cruise on the QE2. I bet it'll be fabulous....all the pampering and silver service. I wish I were coming with you,' she sighed longingly.

'You must be joking! You wouldn't leave Gerald behind would you?'

With a faraway look in her eyes, Abbie smiled. 'I suppose not, especially when everything's going so well. Yes, I'd be a fool to rock the boat now.'

'I'm happy for you Abbie. You deserve a decent guy like Gerald in your life and I hope it works out for both of you. When are you seeing him again?'

'We haven't arranged anything further. He might just turn up at my place tonight, who knows? He's promised to ring me later. It's strange you know....I feel like a silly infatuated teenager again and at my age too! How ridiculous does that sound?'

Robyn laughed heartily. 'Just make the most of it. You're obviously in love. Right I'm going now. I'll nip back to the Travel Agent and see if the cruise is still available. I'll call you later and let you know.'

'Thanks for the butties!' Abbie called after her.

'Thanks for the advice!' Robyn called back.

By the time Robyn arrived in the High Street, she was having second thoughts about the trip. What on earth had she been thinking about? It was a stupid idea to go off on her own....and all that way. What if she hated sailing? What if she couldn't face going into the restaurant alone? What if she didn't like the people she had to share the table with? What if she were sea-sick? Who would take care of her?

The palms of her hands were sweating profusely and she shuddered. She had never been on holiday without David. How could she possibly do it alone? It was unthinkable.

She turned the key in the ignition and raced away, knowing Abbie would be disappointed in her but it was her choice....her decision. She wasn't worldly like Abbie nor was she as street-wise. Abbie would board a plane or ship on her own without giving it a second thought and she would make lots of friends during the first few hours but that was Abbie. Look how she had daringly propositioned Gerald, the day they had visited his office.

With tears streaming down her face, she parked in a lay-by to regain her composure. David was once again in her thoughts and she missed him so much. She dreaded the thought of returning to her empty house....to the empty life she now faced alone. Full of self-pity, she sobbed quietly and recalled happier times.

Walking towards her was a young couple pushing a pram and they looked so full of joy as they gazed at their child. That could so easily have been them if only....

She dried her eyes and stared ahead silently. She had lost everything that had been meaningful to her, the husband she loved and the prospect of bearing a child....David's child. As Robyn's life had virtually ended, Abbie's was just beginning with Gerald and she envied Abbie her new found happiness. If only Bryony lived closer....Bryony, who was always the one to turn the other cheek and bounce back like the proverbial Kelly doll. *She* would have been coming to terms with her grief by now had their roles been reversed.

It was at that moment she made a decision, not so much on impulse, as based on balanced judgement. She had her own life to lead now and so she *would* visit Bryony and to hell with what anybody thought or said. All she had to do was climb aboard a ship. How difficult was that?

Before she could change her mind, she started up the car and checked her rear-view mirror. The road was clear as she made a U-turn and sped back in the direction of town.

She felt elated as she returned home after booking the cruise though still apprehensive about travelling alone. The more she thought about it however, the more she began to realise there would be others in her position....other widows!

What a dreadful word that was she thought, as she conjured up in her mind's eye a picture of wrinkled elderly women who had lost their life-long partners. She was twenty-six and had lost the love of her life. No man could ever take David's place. She would be alone forever. It was a most depressing outlook.

The top item on her agenda was to call her sister who was overjoyed that Robyn was finally making a visit and she promised to take a few days off work to show her the tourist attractions. She made a note of Robyn's arrival details and arranged to meet her at the docks.

'You'll be able to meet my friends,' she told her. 'I know you'll love them.'

'I'm looking forward to that. If I feel out of place because I'm alone on the ship I can always stay in my cabin and read a book.'

'Don't be ridiculous!' Bryony said tersely. 'I fly all over the world on my own. Get out on deck and enjoy yourself. You wouldn't catch me hiding away in my cabin on such a fabulous ship. There's loads of things to do and you'll find lots of people to talk to. Everyone's very friendly so you're sure to make new friends and you'll have a fabulous time.'

Robyn laughed. 'Alright you've convinced me. If it shuts you up, I'll make an effort to join in and I'll see you next week. Despite some reservations about coming, I'm sure I made the right decision but time will tell.'

Almost immediately, Abbie called her. 'Have you managed to book?' she questioned hopefully.

'Yes, I have. It's booked and paid for, so there's no turning back now. I've called Bryony and she's delighted I'm going but I'm still a bit anxious. I just hope I don't live to regret this.'

'Trust me, you won't. It's exactly what you need right now. A nice relaxing holiday, together with a change of environment, will make you feel so much better. You'll enjoy every minute, I'm telling you.'

'I hope you're right. It's a big step to take on my own. I've never done anything like this before.'

'I know but you can't keep sitting about staring at four walls and wallowing in sentimentality. You're far too young to be doing that. You've got to find a way to move forward and this is the perfect way to begin. None of us can change the past, so we have to look to the future. Just keep telling yourself that you've nothing to feel guilty about. Don't lose sight of the fact that David made a conscious decision to leave you. *David* left *you*. This might sound callous but you'd lost him the moment he wrote that letter, not when he was killed. He was making a new life for himself without you and you must do the same.'

'I know you're right but I can't get him out of my thoughts. Whatever I do, he's there with me. I think of him night and day, Abbie. I miss him so much.'

'Time is a great healer. It'll get better, I promise. So, are you calling round tomorrow to look through my wardrobe?'

'If you're sure it's alright. There seems little point in buying clothes I'll probably never wear again.'

'Come around six then and we'll see what we can find. I'll rustle something up for our tea. I'm really going to miss having you around,' she sighed.

'I doubt that now you have Gerald. I'm sure he'll be in touch before long with another nice surprise.'

'He already has. Just after you'd left, I received a dozen red roses, so it's a positive sign that he's still interested I'm pleased to say. I like him a lot. I like the way he talks to me and he listens to what I have to say. He's totally different from other blokes I've ever been involved with. It's hard to explain and it probably sounds daft when I say this but he makes me feel important....special. No man has ever made me feel like that before.'

With furrowed brow, she said earnestly, 'Oh dear, it sounds to me like you're *definitely* in love.'

'Do you reckon?' she asked on a trail of laughter. 'I wouldn't know love if it smacked me in the face! Right, someone's come in. I have to go. I'll see you tomorrow.'

Robyn sighed with diverse sentiments of joy and envy. Those feelings Abbie held for Gerald....those emotions of exhilaration and anticipation, mirrored what she had felt for David and she recalled how he had returned from the office unexpectedly early the day before he had left her, and he had made love to her with a special tenderness and passion that had been absent from their marriage for some time.

On reflection, *that* had been his final farewell to the woman he truly loved.

David was in her thoughts for the rest of the day and in the contemplative moments before she cried herself to sleep that night, Robyn recalled the heart-rending and most memorable words of Alfred Lord Tennyson; ' *'Tis better to have loved and lost than never to have loved at all....*'

4

'That's more than enough Abbie! I've packed three carrier-bags already!' Robyn protested. 'If I borrow anything else, I won't be able to lift my travel bag.'

'What about swimsuits? You haven't even looked at them and they'll not take up too much room. You want to look sexy don't you when you're posing on a sun-lounger?' Abbie said, removing a selection of swimwear from the drawer and piling it on the bed.

'I wasn't planning on *posing* thank you!' Robyn retorted contemptuously with a look that could kill. 'In case you've forgotten already, I recently lost my husband!'

'No, I haven't forgotten, but it doesn't mean you have to dress like Widow Twankey!' Abbie argued. 'There *is* a happy medium!'

Her remark brought a faint smile to Robyn's lips. 'Alright, let's have a look then but I'm not going to wear anything I feel is inappropriate.'

There was a sudden knock at the door and Abbie looked up in surprise. 'I can't think who that is. I'm not expecting anyone.'

'Well, if you don't go and answer the door, you'll never know,' was her glib response.

As Abbie disappeared, Robyn swiftly returned the revealing swimsuits to the drawer and stuffed three conservative ones into her overflowing carrier bags.

Abbie still hadn't returned when she went downstairs where she found her locked in Gerald's arms.

Looking embarrassed he quickly released his hold and took a step back. 'Hi Robyn! I didn't know you were here,' he said apologetically. 'I ought to have telephoned first.'

'It's alright. I was just about to leave,' she replied with a wry smile.

'Oh no....please....don't leave on my account. It's my fault. As I said, I ought to have telephoned first but I just happened to be in the neighbourhood,' he remarked feebly and when Abbie laughed, he added with an embarrassed smile, in the knowledge he'd been caught out, 'Well....er, what I really *meant* to say was, I was in the area when I arrived. Oh, what the hell....the simple truth is I can't keep away....so there you have it!'

'Good for you!' Robyn declared. 'Make the most of it Gerald because you never know what's round the corner. That's definitely a stark lesson I've had to learn the hard way, speaking of which, have you heard anything more?'

'Yes, I received a call earlier. The Inquest should be opened next week.'

'Oh no! I won't be here!' she cried. 'I'm going to visit my sister in New York.'

'Don't worry about it. You don't have to attend. Nothing's going to happen until after the trial of the accused driver. The Coroner will merely open and adjourn the Inquest. He'll need to have the verdict to hand to proceed and that could take months. I'll also need to have a word with your Car Insurance Company. I understand your car's a 'write-off' and so I'll need details of the accused driver's Insurance Company as I'll be submitting a claim for damages from them.'

'Gerald, no amount of money will ever bring my husband back.'

'I'm well aware of that but there's your future to think about. I'll do my utmost to handle everything sensitively but we have to proceed along the right course. Have you eaten yet?' he queried, changing the subject.

'No, we were just about to make something when you arrived,' Abbie answered.

'In that case, why don't I escort my two favourite young ladies to dinner?' he asked optimistically.

'I'll pass! I've loads to do and I wouldn't want to play gooseberry,' Robyn replied with a wink of the eye. 'You two lovebirds go and enjoy yourselves.'

'But I insist!' he said.

'My mind's made up. I'm leaving tomorrow and I've still a hundred and one things to do before I go but thank you Gerald and I hope you have a lovely evening. I'll catch up with you tomorrow Abbie and thanks for these.'

Robyn looked around in amazement as she stepped aboard the QE2 and an array of superlatives sprang to mind. It was magnificent....totally exceeding her expectations for a ship that had been in service for almost thirty years.

Immediately, she was greeted by a smartly attired officer who briefly glanced at her paperwork before directing her to her stateroom.

When she appeared somewhat bewildered, with a heartening smile he enquired, 'Is this your first time aboard Madam?'

'Er....yes it is,' she answered hesitantly. 'I don't want to get lost. It's a much bigger ship than I ever imagined, in fact this is my first ever trip aboard a cruise ship.'

'In that case, do you prefer to be escorted to your stateroom Madam? It can be a little daunting at first until you've got your bearings.'

'I don't want to put you to any trouble,' she stated apologetically, though at the same time appreciative of the offer. 'I'm sure I'd find my way eventually.'

With a hand gesture, the young man indicated the way forward. 'It's no trouble whatsoever, in fact I'll take you there myself and if at any time you can't find your way, don't worry; we've never once lost a passenger,' he assured her on a friendly smile. 'I'm sure you'll have a wonderful trip and please speak to a member of staff for anything you require. Here we are,' he announced a few minutes later as they arrived at her door.

'Thank you very much. I would never have found my way without your help.' She pressed a couple of dollars into his hand appreciatively.

'Thank *you* Madam and I hope you enjoy the rest of your day.'

Her bags were already in her stateroom when she entered and for that she was grateful. She unlocked her large case, expecting to find everything creased but was pleasantly surprised to find her clothes just as she had packed them. After hanging her evening and day dresses in the wardrobe, she found ample storage space for her remaining items. She was very pleased with her accommodation. It was a spacious, bright and well-designed room and she was equally pleased with her furnished balcony as she slid back the door to deeply inhale the bracing sea air.

Before leaving her stateroom to explore the ship, she removed her outdoor clothes and slipped into a pair of white slacks and a pale blue jumper.

As she made her way down the seemingly never-ending corridors, she smiled at the confounded and bewildered expressions on the faces of new arrivals as they scrutinised the stateroom numbers, grateful that she had enlisted the help of an escort and when an elderly lady requested her help, she was only too happy to assist. 'It's tricky isn't it?' she said. 'Tell me what number you're looking for and we'll try to find it together.'

'Do you know, I've forgotten,' she laughed. 'I'm a silly old fool aren't I? Let me see....I know I have it somewhere,' she said, ferreting through her hand-bag. 'My husband's wandered off to look for some-one. We've already walked the entire length of this corridor and believe me, it's a very long walk.'

It transpired she was on the wrong side of the ship but they quickly found their way across to the other side and as they located the stateroom, her husband arrived too, accompanied by a steward.

'Remember that odd numbers are on this side and even numbers are on the other side,' Robyn advised her. 'That should make it a bit easier next time.'

'Don't worry my dear; I won't make *that* mistake again. It's a jolly good thing you were here.'

'Well, all's well that ends well as they say. I hope you and your husband enjoy your trip.'

'Thank you so much for your kindness and I hope you and *your* husband do too.'

Those innocently spoken words cut Robyn to the quick and without another word she hurried away, barely able to contain her distress. David was at the forefront of her thoughts, David, her soul-mate who had been snatched from her so calculatingly by that evil woman who had shown no concern for anyone but herself. He would never enjoy anything again; he was gone forever and without his presence, she was an empty soul, merely surviving day to day in an endless void with nothing to cling to but painful memories of the husband she had lost and a future she would have to face without him.

She was already beginning to wish she had stayed at home....or at least taken a flight to New York to see Bryony. All this felt so wrong and disrespectful to David's memory. Despite Abbie's assertions that it didn't matter what other people thought, what *she* thought mattered and *she* believed she had made an ill-conceived and foolhardy decision.

For some considerable time, she walked back and forth along the corridor, debating whether or not to return to her room to spend the duration of her trip there. After all, she had her balcony; she had a good selection of books and she could call room-service for anything she needed. There was really no need to mix with other people....to feel guilty....but then why *should* she feel guilty? What had *she* ever done wrong to feel guilty about? She wasn't responsible for David's death....nor was she responsible for any of the causes leading up to his death. If anyone was to blame, it was Leanne who had contrived to take him away from her. David should have been talking to his wife about his concerns, not to Leanne, so he had not been blameless either and now she was the widow, left to pick up the pieces to try and rebuild her life and also likely to be subjected to the wrath of his family for choosing to take this short trip.

With that in mind, she decided to make the most of her time and when she reached the next opening, she took a lift to a higher deck where she stumbled across an exit door.

Once outside, she ascended a flight of steps to the upper deck, where several passengers were already re-positioning sun-loungers in the best sun-traps.

Robyn was about to follow suit when she caught sight of people meandering towards her with plates of food. Feeling a little peckish, she wandered past them and returned indoors where she discovered the Lido Buffet. Weaving her way through the various food stations to view what was on offer, she joined the queue for the hot counter. The large juicy roast ham the Chef was carving into thick slices looked very appetizing. A nice slice of that with the crusty bread she had seen at another station would sustain her very well until it was time for dinner. En route to the dining area, she couldn't resist adding a fresh cream trifle and some fresh fruit as she passed the dessert station.

After finding an empty table by the window, she flopped down and began to enjoy her delicious slice of ham, her earlier distressing thoughts temporarily transferred to the back of her mind.

As more new arrivals crowded into the buffet area searching for vacant tables, she felt guilty that she was occupying a table for four and she finished her trifle speedily before collecting her bag and moving away.

As she was passing the buffet stations on her way out she spotted a cold drinks' dispenser. She waited her turn behind a young man carrying a holdall that he repeatedly and ineffectively tried to haul onto his shoulder. When he turned to walk away, holding a full glass of orange juice, yet again his bag slipped from his shoulder, causing his arm to jolt abruptly. Although Robyn tried to leap away, she became the recipient of the entire contents of his glass and her clothes were completely saturated.

'I am *so* sorry,' he spluttered, throwing down his holdall and staring in amazement at the state of her clothes. 'Please….let me help,' he added, grabbing hold of a paper napkin with which he proceeded to pat her chest to soak up the liquid.

'*Take your hands off me*!' she bellowed angrily. '*What do you think you're doing*?'

'Er….I don't know. Please forgive me. I'm sorry. I was...er....just trying to help.'

'I think you've done enough damage already. I'm absolutely soaked through,' she complained crossly as she rushed away close to tears.

She could feel the sticky wet juice on her flesh as it penetrated her clothes; her new white slacks were dripping wet and to further compound matters, she was unable to find her way back to her stateroom. Whichever route she chose, she couldn't locate the aft of the ship and by the time she found a steward, she was already in tears.

'Would you please direct me to my cabin? I can't find my way,' she asked desperately.

He smiled. 'Don't worry Madam; you're in safe hands. Come with me and I'll explain the layout of the ship to you.'

He directed her to the lift and pointed to a plan of the ship. 'If you're lost and there's no one around to ask, find a lift and study the plan to find where you are but be sure to remember that not all lifts serve all deck areas. This for example is of no use to you, but if you go down to the next one, *that* serves the aft where your stateroom's located. Always look at the plan to see where you are until you've familiarised yourself with the ship. Everybody gets lost and confused at first....even the staff.'

Within minutes, she was safely in her room and at that moment, the way she felt, she didn't care if she remained there until the time came to disembark. It had been an idiotic idea to try to put on a brave face and make such a trip when she felt so downhearted. What had she been thinking about? How could she ever expect to enjoy a holiday without David when she missed him so desperately and how would she ever be able to get through the remaining days? Her mind was in turmoil.

After stripping off her clothes, she tossed them in the shower tray and turned on the cold water, using the spray to slowly dilute the intense orange stream that persisted to flow. She pummelled and squeezed her clothes until the water began to run clearer and then filled the wash-basin where she put everything to soak before taking a shower to remove the sweet sticky juice from her skin.

After stepping from the shower she slipped on her bathrobe and lay on top of the bed. 'This was a big mistake!' she sobbed. 'I should never have come on this trip,' and for the second time in recent days she cried herself to sleep.

Later in the afternoon when she awoke, she was deeply ashamed of her earlier outburst. It had been nothing more than an unfortunate accident and the young man had shown genuine concern. He hadn't been groping her! He had been attempting to wipe the sticky juice from her clothes, that's all, yet she had drawn everyone's attention to the slight mishap that would undoubtedly have passed off unnoticed but for her disgraceful conduct. Moreover she could offer no apology to the young man as she wouldn't recognise him again. She had behaved as if he were a serial rapist and he must have felt very humiliated when everyone around was listening and watching. What on earth had she been thinking of to conduct herself in such a vulgar, unrefined manner? What a start to a holiday!

Robyn was escorted to her seat at a circular table in the restaurant where six places had been set. When she took her place, five people were already seated and they smiled at her warmly to acknowledge her presence.

Soon, everyone was involved in conversation and Robyn learned that two of the five were making the trip to New York with their daughter, who appeared to be about fifteen years old. During the subsequent conversation, it transpired that Ellie, as the daughter was called, was in fact twenty-one years old though her manner of dress would certainly have suggested otherwise. Without any trace of make-up and with a child-like hairstyle, scraped back from her face with cheap plastic hair-slides, she looked much younger. Furthermore, no fashion-conscious twenty-one year old would have been seen dead in the dress she was wearing. It was positively vile!

Her rather loud mother who, from the outset, was intent on monopolising the entire conversation, lost no time in enlightening everybody that her daughter had been born with Spina Bifida but fortunately, as her condition hadn't been of a very serious nature, surgery had corrected her *problem*, as she called it.

Robyn was of the opinion that Ellie's mother kept her wrapped in cotton wool and over-protected her. She had to admit that Ellie did look a little frail but she felt nevertheless *that* was more likely due to her mother's relentless supervision and her assumption was confirmed when the waiter arrived to take their order.

'Ellie doesn't want a starter,' her middle-aged and overweight mother proclaimed noisily to the waiter. 'She'll have chicken fillet if you please and without any trace of sauce. Ellie doesn't eat much red meat and not too large a fillet, mind you. We have to be careful not to overface her with massive portions of food. It does no good whatsoever to overload one's stomach. It can create insurmountable problems in

106

later years,' she added, heaving her huge bosom off the edge of the table as the perplexed foreign waiter stood to attention, patiently awaiting the end of her incomprehensible monologue.

Ellie appeared embarrassed, in the knowledge that everyone around the table had overheard and it was apparent to Robyn that the other couple at the table shared her feelings of revulsion at the way the poor girl's mother had humiliated her. Not only had Ellie been forced to endure the degradation of having her medical history broadcast around the table, she had had to face added embarrassment when her mother had selected and ordered her food for her as if she were a small child.

As Robyn studied Ellie's facial characteristics, it was obvious she had the potential to be an attractive young woman whose rich golden hair would have curled naturally around her slender face had it not been fastened back so severely. Her expressive blue oval-shaped eyes bore a sad and pained expression and instantly brought to mind in Robyn, the image of a scolded puppy. She barely uttered a word other than to answer her mother in reply to a question.

'Are you looking forward to your cruise?' Robyn enquired in an attempt to get her to open up to her but before Ellie had chance to respond, her mother intervened.

'Yes, Ellie's really looking forward to visiting the ship's library. She reads lots of books, non-fiction mind you. She likes to read, in fact she'd spend all her time reading if I allowed her to, isn't that right dear?'

'Yes Mum,' she mumbled softly without looking up, her hands twisting her serviette nervously.

'Don't fidget with your napkin dear,' her mother said and Ellie stopped instantly.

Robyn glanced across at the other couple, who in turn caught her eye. The woman held up her napkin to her face but Robyn had already seen her lips curl as she tried to contain her amusement.

What a terrible woman, Robyn reflected, allowing her thoughts to turn to her own mother with whom she'd had many a confrontation during her teenage years but this one she likened to Cruella de Ville.... an absolute monster.

There was an awkward silence for a few moments before Ellie's mother declared, 'She reads because she doesn't like to sunbathe you see.'

Before anything could be added to that disclosure, Robyn asked, 'Why is that Ellie? Does the sun not agree with you?'

'No!' her mother remarked abruptly before Ellie had chance to open her mouth. 'You see, she's very fair skinned and we have to be particularly careful. Exposure to the sun can be very dangerous and we wouldn't want her to get burnt. You hear such tales about people who spend too much time in the sun.'

Robyn offered no response but her thoughts were that Ellie's mother should be burnt....at the stake, for it had become clear after only a few minutes in Ellie's company that the poor girl had no social life outside her mother's austere control and Robyn felt the need to bite her tongue to avoid saying anything confrontational.

She attempted no further conversation with Ellie at that time, content to remain silent as she listened disinterestedly to the nonstop ramblings of the rude, domineering woman whose jowls flapped like sails in the wind with each fresh breath she took.

As Robyn and the other diners continued to enjoy their meal it quickly became evident, when Robyn made eye contact with the other couple sharing the table, that they held views akin to hers....a fact that was eagerly confirmed the very next evening when they took their seats a short while before Ellie and her parents arrived.

The woman who had suppressed her laughter the previous evening greeted Robyn warmly.

'Hello again. I'm Jennifer and this is my husband Mark.'

'And I'm Robyn. Pleased to meet you....officially. Have you enjoyed your day?' she asked politely.

'Very much. This is our first cruise,' Mark said.

Robyn nodded in acquiescence. 'It's my first too. It's very relaxing isn't it?'

Jennifer grinned. 'I didn't find it very relaxing at dinner last night. I thought I was going to burst out laughing when I looked up and caught your eye. It was *so* embarrassing. I didn't dare look up again.'

'I know just what you mean. Isn't she awful....the mother?' Robyn said. 'The poor girl. I could hardly believe she was twenty-one! Her mother treats her like a baby.'

'Yes, she certainly goes too far and she's a pretty young girl. It's ever such a shame. If my mum had spoken to me like that....well I'd have....'

'I think we'd best change the subject. They're on their way over,' Robyn whispered through clenched teeth before smiling agreeably at the family as they approached the table.

'Has anyone looked at the menu?' Ellie's mother grunted in general terms without looking at anyone in particular and before she had even taken her seat. 'I was hoping there might be fish tonight for Ellie.'

Robyn couldn't resist the urge to ask, 'Oh, do you like fish Ellie?'

She was surprised when Ellie managed to answer before her mother cut in, 'No, not very much.'

Argumentatively her mother contradicted, 'Don't be a silly girl Ellie....of course you do. You eat fish at least twice a week when we're at home. It's very good for you. It's very nutritious.'

'I only eat it because you *make* me have fish,' she replied cautiously.

Ellie's mother guffawed, 'Did you ever hear such nonsense? I never make you do *anything* you don't want to do. Of course you like fish. It's one of your favourites.'

Ellie merely bowed her head and didn't reply and when the waiter arrived, her mother ordered fish for her with no starter and which she barely touched.

Robyn hadn't heard Ellie's father speak aloud and she therefore assumed he must be under the thumb too, although he had been permitted to mumble his preference to the waiter.

After the meal, Robyn went for a walk around the ship. There were still many decks and locations she hadn't visited. From a lower deck, she had noticed several shops the previous evening and she wanted to check them out. Maybe she would see something suitable for Abbie, some small gift as a token of her appreciation for her most invaluable help. She also wanted to buy a souvenir for Bryony.

As Robyn leisurely wandered through the various lounges, she stopped to admire the many paintings on display, some of which were for sale, but when a group of people were seen walking hurriedly in her direction, she exited the gallery and tagged along at the rear to find where they were heading. She was led towards the theatre where the late show was just about to start and she managed to find a single seat although the theatre was almost filled to capacity.

Following an enjoyable concert, presented by the ship's crew, she was pleased to have discovered the theatre and decided to make a point of attending the show each night for the rest of the journey, having felt much less conspicuous and consequently more at ease there as a lone traveller.

When she left the theatre, she stopped for a while to listen to a talented young woman competing in a Karaoke contest. At the end of her song, there was tumultuous applause and another contestant eagerly took over the microphone. It seemed a friendly bar and Robyn wandered in, finding an empty table in a corner.

Immediately, a bar waiter arrived by her side and placing a coaster on the table, asked with a pleasant smile, 'Would you care for a drink Madam?'

'Er....yes please. I'd like a gin and tonic with ice and lemon.'

'Thank you Madam,' he answered and continued to wait at her side.

Robyn was embarrassed and looked away but still he continued to wait.

After several moments had elapsed he cleared his throat and asked, 'May I have your ID card please?'

She regarded him with a confused expression and spluttered, 'Er....sorry....my what?'

'The small plastic card you were given when you boarded the ship Madam. I need to charge the drink to your account.'

Since boarding the ship, this was the first time she had been asked for proof of identity and blankly she stared at him as he continued to wait, conscious of hot colour rising vividly in her cheeks.

'Allow me,' a male voice alongside interrupted as he handed his card to the waiter.

'Excuse me! I don't think so!' Robyn protested as the waiter hovered uncomfortably.

'Please let me buy you a drink by way of apology and then I'll leave,' the young man said. 'I promise not to throw it all over you this time.'

'Oh, it's you! I'm sorry, I didn't recognise you,' she confessed remorsefully for her further outburst.

The young man nodded to the waiter who wasted no time in beating a hasty retreat.

'I'm not usually so ill-mannered,' she apologised once more. 'I think you and I have got off to a very bad start on the couple of occasions we've bumped into each other, metaphorically and literally speaking. I immediately jumped to the wrong conclusion when you offered the waiter your card and I'm very sorry. For a moment I believed you were attempting to....er....'

Though Robyn halted mid-sentence, he couldn't resist the temptation to add to the fascinating young woman's embarrassment and on a short shrill burst of laughter quipped, 'Pick you up? Most definitely not! I simply wanted to say how sorry I was for my inexcusable clumsiness the other day. Do you mind if I sit down until the waiter returns with my card? If you're going to castigate me again, I'll feel rather less conspicuous if I'm not in the public eye.'

At that she smiled warmly. 'Please do and it is I who should be saying sorry to you. I should never have behaved in such a way. It was an unfortunate accident and I shrieked at you in front of everyone. You must have felt so humiliated.'

'Not at all,' he replied with a friendly smile.

'I'm quite sure that's not true and I most certainly humiliated myself. My outrage was totally uncalled for and I apologise.'

'Well, let's put it behind us now,' he said, trying to bring the matter to a conclusion. 'Honestly, it's forgotten and I hope your clothes weren't ruined.'

'No, they're alright thank you,' she assured him with a kindly glance.

There was an awkward silence for a few moments before he asked, 'What did you think of the theatre show?'

'I thought it was excellent. I really enjoyed it. Did you see it too?'

'I did and I thought everyone worked very hard. I was sitting directly behind you so I took the liberty of following you when it was over to apologise for the other day.'

'There was really no need but at least it's given us the opportunity to clear the air.'

The waiter returned with Robyn's drink together with the bar slip which the young man signed and returned to the waiter with an added tip.

'Thank you for the drink,' she said.

'Don't mention it, and now, if you'll excuse me, I'm off to my room. I've had rather an active day. I enjoy playing deck sports and I think I've overdone things today so I'll say goodnight.' He stood up and smiled. 'No doubt we'll bump into each other again before too long, *metaphorically* speaking of course. I hope you enjoy the rest of your evening.'

'Thank you and goodnight,' she rejoined with an equally amiable smile.

She watched him walk away, thankful that she'd had the opportunity to clear the air.


It was particularly hot and sunny the next day and Robyn, who had just enjoyed a hearty breakfast in the Lido restaurant, was leaning against the rails on the sun deck when Ellie and her parents approached and stopped to pass the time of day.

'A very good morning,' Ellie's mother announced in her all too recognisable resonant voice. 'Isn't it a beautiful day?'

'Good morning,' Robyn replied. 'It most certainly is here with the sun on my face.'

'You must be very careful. I was just telling Ellie, the sun can be very harmful. I insisted she cover up well before we left for our constitutional around the deck. Are you enjoying the trip?' she enquired.

'Oh I am, very much so,' Robyn responded, at the same time attempting to contain her amusement as her eyes were drawn towards Ellie, dressed in laced boots and heavy jeans, together with a long-sleeved pullover which hung to her knees. Her huge floppy-brimmed denim hat shaded her face completely and she held her head low as if attempting to avoid eye contact with Robyn.

Addressing Ellie, Robyn enquired, 'What do *you* have planned for today?'

'Nothing! We take each day as it comes don't we Ellie?' her mother replied on her behalf.

'Well in that case, would you permit Ellie to take a short stroll around the decks with me? There's an art auction later and I'd very much like to view the paintings on display. I also wanted to call in at the library and I'm sure Ellie would enjoy that. She'll be quite alright with me and I would appreciate the company as I'm travelling alone.'

'Well er...I don't know about that. I like to know where Ellie is and what she's doing. I suppose it'd be alright if only for a short while. What do you say Bill? Do *you* think Ellie should be allowed to go off with this young woman?'

Before he could voice one monosyllable in reply she added, 'Alright, but be sure to bring her back in half an hour or I'll begin to worry and you mustn't forget to keep yourself covered Ellie. You mustn't let the sun see your fair skin. Keep in the shade. Do you hear me?'

'Yes mum,' she agreed with an irritable sigh.

Gradually, Ellie became more talkative during the short period of time they spent together and Robyn was able to confirm her earlier suspicions that she was rarely out of her mother's sight.

'Were you unable to attend school because of the Spina Bifida?' Robyn enquired.

'I was perfectly alright. I always went to school. I wasn't supposed to do sports but I did them anyway and as luck would have it, mum was never aware I was doing them. Mine was the meningocele variant of Spina Bifida and although it can be quite serious, mine wasn't, luckily. I made a total recovery without adverse after effects. Mum won't let me apply for a job though. She thinks I'm not well enough to hold a job down.'

'And what do *you* think Ellie?'

'I'd love to go to work. I feel totally dependent on my parents. Everything mum does involves me too. I have to go everywhere with her and it can be very frustrating at times. I'd give anything to spend time with people my own age. I was surprised when she let me go off with you, because I'm not allowed to go anywhere alone, so I miss out on the things that other young people do,' she revealed sadly.

'Have you never tried talking to your mum about how unhappy it makes you feel? When all said and done, you're twenty-one....you're not a young child anymore. I understand your mother's apprehension but at the end of the day it's *your* life not *hers* and you're entitled to some social life. There'll come a day when your parents aren't around. What then?'

116

She sighed heavily. 'She never listens to anything I have to say. It'd just be a complete waste of time and I wouldn't want to end up falling out with her about it.'

'Right, listen to me Ellie because the way I see it, *you* are your own worst enemy. I'm the last person to create a barrier between mother and daughter but you must make a stand. If you're ever going to gain your independence, you have to start by telling her you want to go to work. That will get you out of the house and you'll have the opportunity to mix with other people. You don't have to raise your voice or be angry....just talk to her quietly and if she tries to talk you down, be persistent. Don't be afraid to air your point of view. She probably feels, because you are so quiet and withdrawn, that you're not capable of holding your own in the workplace. You are the only person who can show her she's wrong. Do you have any qualifications?'

She laughed scornfully. 'Oh yes, I have plenty of qualifications. All I've ever done is study. It was a means of escape from mum's clutches. She always left me alone if my head was buried in a book and that's what I find so frustrating. She encouraged me to do well at school but for what purpose when she won't let me apply for a job? I have twelve GCSEs and four 'A' levels, all good grades. I speak fluent French and I've also done a correspondence course in accountancy. I actually got a distinction in that. I liked maths at school and I'd set my heart on being an accountant and running my own business some-day.'

'Then *do* something about it for heaven's sake or she'll carry on mollycoddling you forever. You've got to be firm! Like I said, as long as she believes you're dependent on her, she'll never change. Why not try to get your dad on your side first? He never seems to intervene.'

'That's because mum always gets her own way so he doesn't get involved. I wish I could be like you. You're stunning; your clothes are lovely and you're so confident. I bet you're not much older than I am but mum chooses all my clothes and she's very old-fashioned so I don't have anything suitable for my age.'

'Well, from what I've seen, I can't argue with you on that score! Gosh, have you seen the time? We'd better head back or I'll be in trouble for leading you astray.'

They hastily made their way back to the sun-deck but when they arrived, Ellie's parents were nowhere in sight.

'I wouldn't mind betting they've gone off to look for me,' she told Robyn. 'I expect I'll be in trouble now. It's a wonder she hasn't had my name shouted over the ship's tannoy.'

Just then a familiar voice boomed, 'Oh, there you are! I *said* only half an hour Ellie and you've been missing for over forty-five minutes. How could you worry me like that?'

'I needed to go to the toilet and I wasn't *missing* at all mum. I knew precisely where I was. It wasn't Robyn's fault we were late back. We had a terrific time, didn't we Robyn?'

'Yes we did and I can assure you Ellie was quite safe with me Mrs er.....?'

'Flora Johnstone and my husband's name is Bill,' she stated brusquely. 'Well, thank you for spending time with Ellie. One can't be too careful these days, especially on a cruise-ship. One hears such dreadful tales about all the goings on! It doesn't bear thinking about.'

'Quite!' Robyn responded though she had no idea what Flora was talking about. 'I'm off to the buffet for a snack now. I don't suppose you'd permit Ellie to join me? It's not very nice eating alone. There's an excellent selection of chicken and fish dishes to choose from.'

'We were just about to go down to the restaurant. I really don't know....'

'Oh please....you and dad go to the restaurant. I'd rather go with Robyn to the buffet.'

Flora's bosom rose and fell as she sighed heavily. 'Very well then but I want to see you back here at two o'clock....and not a moment later. Is that understood Ellie?'

'Yes mum. Thanks. I'll definitely be back by two o'clock. You have my word.'

'You said that earlier and your father was frantic, weren't you?' she asked but he offered no response. 'Off you go then but be sure not to eat anything you shouldn't.'

Ellie skipped away with a grin stretching from ear to ear. 'Thanks for that Robyn,' she said as soon as they were out of earshot. 'I can't remember the last time I picked what I wanted to eat. I'm telling you now, I definitely *won't* be having chicken or fish,' she chuckled impishly. 'I'm sick and tired of being pampered. Have we time to nip to my room and I'll change out of these hideous clothes? I look like one of the Bisto kids dressed like this.'

'Hey....don't you go insulting the Bisto kids!' she laughed. 'Come on then. Let's see what else you've got in that wardrobe of yours.'

When Ellie stepped out of the bathroom, wearing a pair of blue light-weight trousers with a blue and white striped cotton blouse with the sleeves turned up to her elbows, she looked nothing like the dreary person who had entered the room moments earlier.

'Remember to roll down your sleeves before your mum sees you,' Robyn warned her. 'Have you any trainers or sandals?'

'I have a pair of white sandals.'

'Wear those then. They'll be perfect. Hurry up or there'll be no tables left.'

Ellie selected several items from the buffet, none of which consisted of chicken or fish and she ended her lunch with a generous helping of sticky toffee pudding.

'Mm....that was delicious,' she remarked, licking her fingers. 'Can I ask something personal Robyn? It's not that I'm trying to pry or anything but why are you travelling alone?'

'I'm visiting my sister for a few days. She lives in New York and I haven't seen her for a while. She's been nagging me for ages to go, so I decided to take up her offer and I thought this would be a good way to travel as I'd never set foot on a ship before.'

'How lovely. I wish I had a sister. I get really fed up at times with only mum to talk to.'

'Don't you have any friends?'

'No, I was never allowed to go out on my own, so the girls I knew at school were simply friends in the classroom.'

'So you don't have a boyfriend then?'

Her face turned crimson with embarrassment and she stuttered, 'I....I've never really associated with boys but mum says it's for the best because I'm not like other girls.'

'Not like other girls? I don't know about that! I'd say, from the little I've seen of you, that you were a healthy young woman and I'm not patronising you. You appear to have no physical disfigurement and you're very pretty so I can't think what your mother means by that remark.'

'Well I don't think I am. Anyway, boys poke fun at me because of the way I dress. Mum buys all my clothes and I look ridiculous.'

'Don't undervalue yourself Ellie. You've a lovely face, your hair's beautiful and you look very pretty in the clothes you're wearing now. I'm sure there'd be plenty of young men who'd be delighted to take you out, given half a chance.'

'Hi there,' someone called out and Robyn turned to see the young man who had bought her the drink the previous night. 'Do you and your friend mind if I join you? I can't seem to find an empty table.'

Robyn pulled a chair towards him. 'Please, be my guest. This is my friend Ellie and I'm Robyn.'

'Raine,' he introduced himself.

Robyn looked confused. 'I'm sorry, I didn't catch that.'

'Raine,' he repeated on a laugh. 'It's rather wetter than orange juice though obviously not as messy, as I discovered to my cost a few days ago! My mother chose that name for me because it was raining cats and dogs the night I was born though my name has 'E' at the end. It could have been worse I suppose. It could have been snowing and I might have ended up being called Snowflake.'

Robyn chuckled and went on to describe to Ellie how Raine had first introduced himself by throwing a glass of orange juice all over her.

Raine felt an explanation was called for. 'It was a clumsy accident Ellie and truly, I could have curled up and died when I saw the state of her clothes. She was soaked to the skin. I certainly wouldn't advise you try it. She was *very* annoyed and that's putting it mildly,' he grimaced.

'As I've apologised twice for my rude behaviour, how about we forget it?' Robyn suggested politely but with a critical frown.

'That suits me fine. So how are you both enjoying yourselves?'

'It's terrific,' Ellie said. 'It's my first ever cruise and I'm enjoying every minute.'

'I didn't realise you were travelling with a friend Robyn.'

'Actually I'm not. I'm travelling alone. Ellie and I are on the same table in the restaurant so we spend a little leisure time together.'

'So are you on your own too?' he asked Ellie.

'No, I'm here with my parents....more's the pity,' she added as an afterthought. 'Are you with anyone Raine?'

'No, I'm on my own as well. My in-laws live in a suburb of New York and my son has been staying with them since they returned home after spending Christmas and New Year with my wife and me. I'm bringing him back home next week. He's four years old and quite a handful, so I'm sure they'll be more than happy to hand him back,' he grinned.

'So is your wife at home then?' Ellie questioned.

'Yes,' he replied without qualification.

Robyn thought it strange that Raine's wife was in England and that he had chosen to sail to New York when it would have been cheaper and quicker to fly but she felt it wasn't her place to question the issue. Ellie had discovered more about Raine in the space of a few minutes than she had discovered about this intriguing young man during three meetings.

'Well, fancy bumping into you!' Flora Johnstone bellowed in a tone of condemnation. 'I would have imagined you'd be gone from here by now Ellie. I trust you selected your food carefully, particularly when you know how certain things don't agree with you. I suppose I should have insisted that you come to the restaurant with your father and me.'

Raine immediately jumped up and offered her his seat.

'*Sit down young man. I'm not staying*,' she said to him abruptly.

Robyn was in no doubt that this meeting had been deliberately orchestrated by Ellie's mother to check on her and also the company she was keeping and she was furious, particularly as she was humiliating her daughter in the presence of other people and it didn't end there.

'Good gracious! You've been back to your room to change your clothes! Whatever possessed you to do such a thing child?' she hollered dictatorially as Ellie rolled down her sleeves nervously, aware that everyone close by was listening.

'I spilled a glass of water on my jeans so I had to hurry back to my room to get changed,' she replied, appreciative of the orange juice revelation that had saved the day by providing her with a satisfactory answer.

'What a careless child you are! Have you finished your lunch?'

'Yes, I had chicken and fish, just like you told me to and it was lovely.'

'If you'll excuse us then, we'll be on our way and we'll leave you to enjoy the company of this young man,' Flora stated with a toss of the head, directing a brief but censorious glance in Robyn's direction. 'Hurry up and move yourself Ellie! You know how your father doesn't like to be kept waiting.'

'Thanks for everything Robyn. I had a really nice time,' Ellie murmured politely as she hurried after her mother.

'Me too and I'll catch up with you later no doubt. Enjoy the rest of your day,' she called after her.

As Ellie disappeared from view Raine said, 'Who the hell was that? Devil woman? What a nauseating piece of work she is! How old is her daughter?'

'How old do you think?'

With an irreverent grunt he remarked, 'The way her mother talked down to her, I'd have to guess at about thirteen or fourteen.'

'She's twenty-one!' she informed him. 'I'd gladly swing for that evil monster if she were *my* mother. She's insufferable. Just imagine having to contend with that day in day out. The poor girl doesn't have any social life; she doesn't have a single friend and she's only permitted to go out if her hideous mother accompanies her.'

'What a shame and she's a pretty young girl. Why is her mother so over-protective do you suppose?'

'Ellie was rather ill when she was a baby and so her mother is afraid to let her out of her sight,' she explained without going into detail. 'So, what have you been doing today? Have you been playing your deck sports?'

'No, I've been down to the gym to work out. It's very well-equipped. Have you tried it?'

'I haven't been on that deck yet. I'm still having some difficulty in finding my way round the ship. I only found the theatre by chance but I think I'll go again tonight after dinner. I enjoy the shows and it said in the news-sheet that the one tonight is based on musicals so that should be good. Besides, I don't feel as conspicuous in the theatre when I'm on my own.'

'I know. It feels odd wandering into some places unaccompanied.'

'Tell me about it! It's even worse when you're a woman. At least *you* can stroll into one of the bars without everyone staring at you. I felt conspicuous last night when I walked in that Karaoke bar and I hadn't a clue what the waiter wanted when he asked for my ID card. I didn't know it was the card I open my stateroom door with. I felt really stupid when I realised. It was in my bag all the time but there's so much going on when you're boarding that I hadn't realised what it was for. I hadn't been in a position where I'd had to use it prior to last night but I know now so I won't make that mistake again. Thanks for bailing me out Raine. It was very kind of you.'

There was an awkward silence for some moments as they thought of another topic of conversation and then they spoke simultaneously and laughed.

'You first,' Robyn said.

'No, after you,' he insisted with a smile.

'I was wondering why your wife hadn't come too when you're visiting her parents. Does cruising not appeal to her?'

'I'm sure she'd have enjoyed it had she been able to join me but my wife's ill.'

'I'm so sorry. What a shame for her to miss such a lovely trip. I hope she's soon better.'

He hung his head and replied, 'Yes well, we can only hope and pray for a miracle. My wife's been in a coma for more than two years. Tragically, something went badly wrong during childbirth when our second child was born. She suffered a haemorrhage, which in turn caused a massive stroke and despite the medical team's frantic efforts, they were unable to bring her round and she's been unconscious ever since.'

As Raine raised his head, she recognised a look of despair in his eyes and her heart went out to him.

'How awful; that is so tragic,' she said in barely a whisper.

'Yes, it is. She was only twenty-five at the time. Unless you've personally experienced a tragedy of such magnitude, it's hard to imagine what it's like. We were so excited about the new baby and then in a matter of a few moments our lives were shattered so unexpectedly. I love her so much and it pains me that she can't hear me when I tell her. I'm sorry....I suppose I'm feeling guilty for leaving her for a few days but I really needed a break. It's a very stressful situation. I just needed some time alone.'

'I'm pleased you told me. Sometimes it helps to talk to someone. You must feel very lonely.'

'The word is *helpless*. I feel so bloody helpless,' he told her and his eyes filled with tears. 'Forgive me please. You're here to enjoy the cruise and here I am pouring out all my sorrows and spoiling your pleasure. Let's have a change of topic. What made *you* choose this trip?'

'I'm visiting my sister for a few days. She lives in New York.'

'That's nice. Have you been before?'

'No, it's my first time and I'm looking forward to taking in the sights though I doubt I'll have time to see everything. I only have three days there.'

'Where does she live?'

'Manhattan.'

'That's the nucleus of New York. You'll love it.' As he stood up to leave, he smiled at her cordially.

'It's been nice talking to you Robyn and doubtless our paths will cross again. Enjoy your day.'

'I shall do my very best. You too.'

As she strolled around the decks she was recalling Raine's words and the sadness in his eyes. She had deliberately omitted to tell him about David's death and as she compared her tragic loss to his suffering, she felt his was probably much worse. In her case, she could seek closure because there was a certain finality about death. It brought its own kind of pain and grief but could she have coped had David been returned to her in a coma when each new day would have brought a new challenge, a new hope or a new disappointment? Raine must have a horrendous life, she thought. Though she wasn't aware if the second child had survived he definitely had one for whom he was totally responsible.

She studied other passengers as they sauntered by and wondered what secrets they concealed. She had lost David but she would be eternally thankful for the years they had enjoyed together and though no other man would ever fill the emptiness created by his departure, there were other things in life that she could do. He had given her financial security and so she would realise her childhood dream, for now she had the means to work with and be among animals, and that would be her future life when she returned to England.

'Who was that young fellow sitting at your table at lunchtime with you and that friend of yours?' Flora asked, bursting with curiosity.

'Just someone Robyn met on the ship a couple of days ago.'

'Well, I think it's disgraceful. Did you not notice she was wearing a wedding ring? The nerve of the woman! There she was, laughing and joking as bold as brass with another man.'

'They were only talking mum. He was wandering about trying to find somewhere to sit down when he noticed her. He accidentally threw a glass of orange juice over her the first time they met.'

'Ugh! Accidentally on purpose if you ask me. It never ceases to amaze me the lengths men will go in order to make a conquest. I don't like the thought of you associating with a married woman. Where's her husband? He should be here with her instead of allowing her to go gallivanting on holiday without him. I think it's absolutely scandalous. He ought to have put his foot down to show who was boss! It's asking for trouble if you want my opinion. Fancy, a married woman travelling alone on such a holiday! It beggars belief. Some people have no morals.'

'Yes mum,' she replied, barely unable to contain her laughter at the thoughts of her father putting *his* foot down. 'Robyn's a very nice person and we get along well together.'

'Be that as it may, I'm not having it! You'll have to see her at mealtimes....I can't do anything to stop that unfortunately but for the rest of the trip, I won't allow you to associate with her. Do you understand me Ellie?'

'I understand perfectly *mother*,' she retorted, with special emphasis on the word mother. 'I understand a lot of things! I understand that I am a woman, not a small child. Despite the fact that I am twenty-one years old, you still persist in making my decisions for me but that has to stop right now. I can't accuse you of picking my friends because I don't have any and when I do manage to find someone with whom I enjoy spending some time, you forbid it! If Robyn wants to see me again, although I very much doubt she will after the way you behaved, then I shall see her. I'm sick of being treated like an invalid. I'm a human being not a pet animal and there's simply no justification for the way you pamper me and follow me around all the time. You embarrass me in front of people; everybody you meet has to be told about my Spina Bifida. It's *cured* mother! It's been cured for twenty years and if I *did* have a life-threatening illness, wouldn't it be preferable for me to enjoy the time I had remaining, rather than being fastened to your apron strings day in day out? I have to learn to stand on my own two feet, so tell me how I can do that when you won't allow me any leeway? I think the world of you and I appreciate everything you've done for me but it's time I began to fend for myself. I won't be treated like an invalid anymore, and the minute we're home, I intend to look for a job. I've had enough of being mollycoddled and please don't stare at me like that because I mean it. I have plenty of qualifications I aim to put to good use and I want to go to work like everyone else does but first and foremost I want to be treated like an adult.'

Flora's jaw dropped open and she clutched at her chest with both hands. 'I can't believe what's come over you Ellie. Please go to your room immediately and we'll discuss this later.'

'There's nothing to discuss. I *will* go to my room but only to put on my swimsuit. Yes, I'm going for a swim. I learnt to swim at school and I love it. I've wasted far too much of my life already so now I'm going to start enjoying myself, with or without your permission,' she announced with a flourish and she strutted away, leaving her mother speechless.

Bill felt he ought to intervene for once. 'The girl's growing up Flora and I have to agree with much of what she says. She's a young woman now and she's missed out on such a lot. You shouldn't be too hard on her. She sees other young women doing things and it's only natural she wants to spread her wings and do the same things....'

'Just keep quiet if you can't be supportive!' Flora interrupted. 'If it were left to you, she'd go off the rails. What do you know?' she asked caustically.

'I know what *you* were like at twenty-one. I recall *you* were a wild-cat at her age!' he exclaimed.

'Yes, well, I didn't have a debilitating illness and for the record, I was definitely *not* a wild-cat. I just liked having fun.'

'And that's all Ellie wants....to have a little fun in her life. What's wrong with that? Give her a break Flora. I seldom interfere because I know you mean well but you really do go too far. Ellie's on holiday. It'll be over in a few days so let her enjoy herself. When all said and done, she was only having lunch with her friend. From what I could see they weren't doing anything wrong. It's good for Ellie to have a friend. She'll not see her again once we disembark. Just let her be, for pity's sake.'

'Be it on your head then Bill Johnstone if she gets herself into trouble. I'll not interfere again. I won't say another word....not one word.'

'You go and get ready dear and I'll go and see if I can find her. If she's not down in her room, I'll see if she's in the pool. Trust me Flora; she'll be fine. You just try not to worry about her. She'll never let you down.'

Ellie *was* fine and she was having the time of her life. It felt invigorating to splash about and swim in the pool and she had joined in a game with several young children who were playing with a ball.

'Throw it to me,' one boy called as Ellie dived for the ball and when some of the others tried to take it from her, she used her height to keep it from their reach before returning it to the first boy. Bill stood silently by the side of the pool, happy to watch her as she laughed and darted dexterously between the children. He was aware that Flora had Ellie's best interests at heart but the time had come for Flora to release her hold. He had known for some time that his daughter would finally become rebellious about his wife's over-protective control and he supported Ellie wholeheartedly though he knew it would be a rocky road. Flora did not take kindly to having her authority usurped. Flora was accustomed to getting her own way and heaven help anyone who stood in her path.

Ellie caught a glimpse of her father and waved to him. 'It's great. The water's lovely and warm,' she made known as she climbed out of the pool with a warm glow. 'I suppose you're angry with me too?'

'No darling I'm not. I agree it's time you enjoyed yourself but give your mum time to get used to the idea. You know she means well. You've said your piece now and I believe things will start to improve from now on. She was quite shocked that you spoke back to her.'

'Oh dear, I'd better apologise then.'

'*No*, you can't do *that*! That would be tantamount to an admission you were out of order for speaking up for yourself. She'll give your comments a great deal of thought and I don't believe she'll try again to prevent you from spending time with that young woman. You've shown you can stand your corner and that's a giant step, believe me. I'm very proud of you.'

'Thanks dad.' She slipped a towelling smock over her swimsuit and picked up her bag. 'We'd best get back or we'll be late for dinner. I have to wash my hair.'

Flora was dressed and waiting when Bill returned and he related how much Ellie had enjoyed herself playing in the pool with some youngsters. 'She's a good lass, thanks to your upbringing Flora. She has to learn by her mistakes though. Give her a chance.' He kissed her on the cheek. 'She's making her own way to the restaurant this evening and she'd like to order her own meal so I told her that would be fine. I'm sure she'll be sensible.'

Although incensed, she merely stared into space without offering a single word of reply.

133

Ellie took her seat in the restaurant soon after the others had arrived.

'Good evening,' she declared confidently, pulling her chair close to Robyn's.

Robyn looked up in amazement when she noticed Ellie's pale pink fingernails and there was a golden glow to her skin not previously seen.

Flora was about to make a derisive remark when Bill prevented her by interrupting, 'Don't you look pretty this evening Ellie? I see you've painted your fingernails. Very becoming.'

Ellie smiled and glanced at her mother who stared ahead poker-faced.

When the waiter returned to take their orders, he hovered uneasily at Flora's side after she placed her order, awaiting her customary order for Ellie. Flora inhaled deeply, causing her oversized bosom to pop open a button on her dress as she returned her menu to him in silence.

After making his way around the table, the waiter arrived at Ellie's side.

'I'd like Cream of Broccoli soup please followed by Roast Duck à l'orange.'

'Thank you Madam,' he said, relieving her of her menu.

Turning to Robyn and in earshot of everyone she announced, 'I'm ravenous. I've been swimming in the pool and I seem to have worked up an appetite. I'm really looking forward to my dinner. I could eat a horse.'

Jennifer and Mark listened in utter disbelief to the only real dialogue to have escaped Ellie's lips since their initial introduction and a brief sideways glance at Flora by Jennifer revealed her discontent.

There followed an uncomfortable quiet before the conversation around the table recommenced when Jennifer broke the silence. 'Did any of you go to the show last night?'

'Yes I did,' Robyn replied. 'It was great. Shortly after I'd left the restaurant, I saw a crowd of people heading towards the theatre so I followed them. I'm still not too good at finding my way around. Everyone worked really hard I thought.'

'I thought so too,' Jennifer said. 'Tonight's show is based on popular musicals so I think there'll be a packed house.'

Ellie's ears pricked up. 'Why don't we go mum? You know you love that kind of music.'

'Well....er....I suppose it wouldn't do any harm to give it a try for once. It'd certainly make a change from playing Scrabble. Having said that, it doesn't end too late does it?'

'About elevenish I think,' Jennifer told her.

'That's alright then. I don't want Ellie....'

'Don't worry about me,' Ellie interrupted before she could be humiliated once again. 'If you and dad feel tired, you can go to bed. I can find all kinds of things to do to keep myself amused.'

Flora was quick to realise that Ellie was making yet another stand and she chose to say nothing that might provoke an argument at the table. That awful young woman with the bird name had undoubtedly put her up to this and Flora didn't wish to play into their hands. In any event, she feared she might lose as Ellie now had an ally in her father and Flora was livid about that. Wild-cat indeed! How dare he say such a thing? Bill certainly hadn't heard the last of that remark!

The theatre was almost filled to capacity when the three of them arrived and Flora carefully scrutinised all seating blocks for three vacant seats together.

She was on the verge of suggesting they return to the games room for a game of Scrabble when Ellie announced, 'Robyn's over there mum. She's saved me a seat so I'll go and sit with her and there's two together there for you and dad.'

Before Flora could object, she scampered away to join Robyn.

'I was hoping you'd see me,' Robyn said. 'Come on, tell me everything that's happened. It's obvious there's been an altercation of some sort but I didn't dare mention anything at dinner. Your mum hardly took her eyes off me all through the meal so I guess I'm in the dog-house! Am I right?'

'Yes you are,' she screeched with laughter. 'She believes you're a very bad influence on me.'

Robyn laughed too and asked, 'And is that what you think?'

'Of course not! You merely confirmed everything I already knew. I couldn't carry on like that....being humiliated in front of everyone. I needed a helping hand and you were there for me. I needed someone to give me a nudge and boost my confidence.'

The theatre lights slowly dimmed and the variety show commenced so nothing further was discussed about the matter.

As everybody made for the exit at the end of the show, Flora and Bill waited in the corridor for Ellie to appear.

'Hello,' Robyn said cheerily. 'Have you enjoyed the show?'

Distantly, Flora answered, 'Yes thank you. It was very entertaining.'

'I'm off to watch the Karaoke now with Robyn,' Ellie told her mother. 'I won't be too late.'

'I guess we'll see you in the morning then,' Flora replied frostily, briefly casting her eyes in Robyn's direction. 'Make sure you behave yourself!'

'I'll see she does,' Robyn answered on her behalf. 'I'll take good care of her.'

'Ugh!' Flora grunted. 'Come along Bill. It's time for bed.'

'How are my two favourite young ladies tonight?' a familiar voice piped up as they entered the bar.

'Hi Raine. We're both great thanks. What about you? Have you had a good day?' Robyn enquired.

'Couldn't be better now you've arrived. May I get you a drink? I was keeping my fingers crossed that you'd both turn up here.'

'I'm buying,' Robyn said. 'What would you like to drink Ellie?'

'Orange and soda please.'

'Raine?'

'I'll have a Budweiser please. It was another good show wasn't it?'

'Oh yes, it was brilliant. I love musicals. I like to sing along to the music though I couldn't do that in the theatre,' Ellie giggled.

'Er....does your mother know where you are?' he asked jokingly.

She tittered. 'She'd die if she knew I was in a bar but she and dad have gone to bed now. I retaliated earlier so she's stormed off in a huff but I can't say I'm bothered.'

'Good for you! So what about you Robyn? Have you enjoyed your day?'

'I fell asleep on my balcony so I've had too much sun and my arms are burning. Apart from that, one could say it's been rather an entertaining day,' she answered, casting a sideways glance at Ellie.

Raine ordered a further round of drinks and they continued to enjoy interesting conversation. 'Would you like to go dancing?' he enquired optimistically. 'There's a steel band on the upper deck.'

'No thanks. I've had enough. I'm tired so I'm off to my bed when I've finished this drink,' Ellie said. 'You'll go dancing with Raine won't you Robyn?'

'No, it's well past midnight and I'm tired as well. I can hardly keep my eyes open but thanks for the offer Raine. I'll walk you back to your room Ellie. Don't forget I promised your mother I'd take good care of you. I don't want you running off with one of the stewards whilst my back's turned.'

'And who'll take care of you Robyn when you're wandering along the corridors at this unearthly time of night? There's only one thing for it. I'll have to walk both of you back,' Raine said, swallowing the remains of his drink.

'That won't be necessary,' Robyn said.

'Oh, but I insist,' he replied with a boyish grin.

Having ensured that Ellie was safely locked in her room Robyn and Raine caught the lift to the higher deck where Robyn's stateroom was situated.

'Wow....this is impressive! I'm not wallowing in luxury on a posh aristocratic deck like this, rubbing shoulders with the genteel folk. Mine is a *very* basic room in the bowels with the hoi polloi,' he told her humorously and with a wink of eye.

She laughed at his descriptive comment. 'Well, I only booked at the last minute so I had to take what was on offer but I have to say it's a bonus, having a private balcony where you can sit quietly with your thoughts.'

'You're very serious Robyn. Is something wrong? I'm a good listener if you want to talk to someone.'

'What? Oh no; I'm fine,' she lied. 'I don't know why I said that. Ignore me.'

'Are your arms bothering you? I assume you used plenty of cooling lotion after you got burnt?'

'No, I didn't. I didn't bring any. It never entered my head when I was hurrying to pack. Having said that, I never intended getting burnt but I'll check if they sell it in one of the shops tomorrow if it's still bothering me. I didn't have time today.'

'I've got some in my room. Would you like me to nip back for it? It won't take many minutes. It's no trouble.'

'No, I'll be alright, really. It'll probably feel a lot better in the morning but thanks for offering. Right, here we are. This is my stateroom.'

As she searched for her key, Raine hovered. 'I've enjoyed talking to you Robyn. I so rarely have the opportunity to enjoy any female company. My time is completely committed to caring for my wife and children. I employ both a nurse and a nanny during the day but I spend many a lonely evening simply sitting with my wife, holding her hand and talking to her. I used to believe she could hear me and that I might say something which would prompt her to open her eyes but now I'm learning to be realistic. As the months come and go without any indication of change in her condition it's not likely to happen but then you can't give up hope can you? You still have to believe there's a remote possibility that one day there'll be a miraculous recovery.'

'You're right Raine. You can never give up hope. You must remain positive and miracles do happen every now and then. I've actually read about people like your wife who have been in a coma for several years and who have unexpectedly recovered, so it's not beyond the realms of possibility that she might too. I'm sorry you're having such a hard time. Did the doctors give any indication that your wife might make a full recovery?'

'I was informed it was very unlikely but possible. As you quite rightly said, you do occasionally hear of someone who unexpectedly awakes from a coma after many years and apart from temporary physical impairment that can be rectified by physiotherapy, psychologically they're usually fine. It's not as if I had many choices in the matter. All I had to decide was whether to leave her where she was or have her brought home....that was it....and so I chose to bring her home. That way, I could guarantee she received the best possible care and it gave both the children and me so much more time to spend with her.'

Robyn fought to restrain tears of compassion and pity, while conscious of an overwhelming desire to throw her arms around him to comfort him and tell him how much she understood his suffering.

Having experienced a recent tragedy of her own, it was very easy to feel empathy with this sensitive young man who had openly revealed his innermost thoughts to her. His life was slowly ebbing away as was hers but then was it compassion she felt or was it something else, something much more profound? During the past weeks since David's death, she had learned the meaning of loneliness and despondency, facing each day as if it were her last with nothing in the world to look forward to but further despair and solitude.

When she suddenly became aware she was gazing deeply into his troubled eyes, she looked away, at the same time resisting her earlier urge to take him in her arms and instead she kissed him hurriedly on the cheek and unlocked the door to her room.

Turning to face him once more, tears scorched her eyes....tears of distress for Raine mingled with tears of longing for her beloved David.

He smiled sensitively at her. 'Thanks for listening Robyn. It really does help to talk to someone about it. I didn't mean to cause you any distress and I'm sorry; I just got carried away. Right, I'd best be on my way now. Goodnight,' he whispered.

'Goodnight Raine,' she said and as she closed the door behind her, she leaned against it silently for a few moments with tears coursing down her cheeks once more.

Raine returned to his room with restless feelings. Robyn was in his thoughts and he couldn't rid her from his mind. She was a beautiful young woman and at one point he had come very close to making a move but thankfully he had found the willpower to resist the temptation yet for one special moment, he was sure he had sensed from her body language that she might have been a willing recipient of his advances.

After he undressed he climbed into bed but found sleep to be an unattainable longing. His mind raced with thoughts....thoughts he shouldn't be having but that he found impossible to lay to rest. He pictured his wife whom he loved dearly but the apparition of Robyn remained at the very forefront of his mind, Robyn who was so vivacious and stimulating. Why did he feel this way? Never before had he so much as looked at another woman nor had he wanted any other woman but there was something electrifying about Robyn, something he found totally irresistible and he wanted her so desperately but would Robyn want him too or was he mistaken in his belief that he had observed, if only for a split second, a certain hunger for him in her eyes? Had it been so or was it nothing more than a figment of his imagination? He had to know.

He leapt from his bed and paced backwards and forwards for several minutes before changing into his jeans and as he fastened his shirt his heart was pounding.

On his way out, Raine collected the cooling lotion from the bathroom and swiftly made his way to her stateroom, stepping up his pace as he strode along the final corridor.

Barely able to contain his emotions, he knocked assertively on her door.

Robyn awoke with a start and jumped out of bed. After slipping on her bathrobe, she opened the door and showed no surprise to see Raine standing there with the cooling lotion in his hand.

His dark soul-searching eyes penetrated hers and no words were exchanged before Robyn opened the door fully to allow him to enter.

Breathlessly he whispered, 'Robyn,' and as they fell into each other's arms, the one and only sound to interrupt the silence was that of the door closing behind them.

5

Raine was the first to awake the next morning. He leaned towards Robyn and kissed her lips tenderly, causing her to stir.

She opened her eyes and smiled. 'Good morning,' she murmured sleepily.

He returned her smile. 'Good morning to you too. Did you sleep okay?'

'Mmm....very well thank you. What about you?'

He grinned. 'I went out like a light. Thank you for last night Robyn. It was amazing.'

'Yes it was Raine but it was also a crazy thing for us to do.'

'Does that mean you're sorry?'

'No, that's not the word I'd use. I'm ashamed that I slept with a married man. I do have a conscience. I've never done anything like this before.'

'I'm married in name only Robyn. Yes, I love my wife and I've made no secret of that but I was also attracted to you from the first moment we met when I threw my orange juice all over you,' he said with a solemn expression, causing her to laugh aloud.

'Liar,' she grinned.

'It's true! I think it must have been your hot fiery temper or your vitality. There was something about you that really turned me on.'

'Get lost,' she jeered. 'I've heard some one-liners in my time but that takes the biscuit!'

'Alright, you believe what you want to believe. I know it's true but in all honesty, I didn't believe it would culminate in this. I never planned any of this, truly, but I had to come back last night. I was going out of my mind. The question now is where do we go from here?'

Robyn was shocked. 'Nowhere Raine! We don't go *anywhere* from here....we *can't*,' she answered bluntly. 'We both had a need....we acted on impulse in the heat of the moment but this has to end, right here....right now.'

He stared at her in disbelief. 'You can't possibly mean that….not now....not after all those things we said to each other last night….unless you're telling me you're involved with someone else. Are you?'

'Not in the way you mean but you have to forget about the things we said last night.'

'I can't forget; I don't want to forget and I don't want it to end. Surely we can continue to be friends and keep in touch? Don't tell me we have to go our separate ways and....'

'I'm sorry,' she cut in. 'Please don't be difficult. The last thing I want is to hurt you. Let's just say I have my reasons. That's really all I can say, so let's leave it at that.'

'I can't Robyn. Is it something I've said or done? You have to tell me. I don't want it to end like this. It can't. Last night, you gave me something that's been missing from my life for two years and I don't mean sex....I mean a new reason for living.'

Caringly, she looked into his eyes. 'I'm sorry. It's nothing *you've* done. It's personal.'

'Then talk to me about it, *please* Robyn. Share it with me. I'm sure we can resolve matters if you'll only open up to me. Answer me this; did last night mean nothing at all to you because it certainly did to me?'

'Yes, it meant a lot Raine....more than you'll ever know. You're a decent and sensitive guy but when I leave this ship, the cruise ends and so does this. It has to. In any case, you're married so it'd be wrong to continue.'

'I can't hurt my wife Robyn but you can provide me with some sanity.'

She threw back her head and laughed scornfully. 'Yes, right! As your bit on the side? I don't think so Raine.'

Furiously he countered, 'Don't make what we had last night feel cheap. You and I both know it wasn't like that.'

'You're right, it wasn't but don't you see it would be were we to continue? There could be no future in it for either of us and apart from that, it's not what I want.'

'So tell me Robyn, what is it that you want?'

'What exactly do you want Raine. Be honest.'

'Did you ever see Pretty Woman?'

'Didn't everyone?'

'I want exactly what she wanted. I want the whole fairytale. I want you,' he said passionately.

'Now you're being absurd! We've only just met. You know absolutely nothing about me and you're unavailable Raine and for that matter, so am I. I'm not looking to become involved with anybody and if I were, I wouldn't opt to add more of a burden on someone who has the problems you already have. I wouldn't be helping your cause. I'd just be adding

146

to your problems, creeping around, trying not to be seen by anyone who knows us. I'm going to have a shower now and I trust when I come out that you'll have left. Believe me Raine; it really is for the best that we end it here and now. If I could offer you an explanation then I would but I can't.'

When Robyn returned to the bedroom, Raine had dressed and left. She threw herself down on the bed with her head in her hands and cried, 'Despite what you did to me David, I could never do that to you. I'll love you forever and I could never leave you for anyone else.'


'Good morning Mrs. Johnstone,' Robyn greeted as she caught sight of her entering the deck where she was sunbathing. Isn't it a lovely day again?'

'It certainly is,' she replied coolly.

'Isn't Ellie with you?'

'No, I haven't seen her this morning but then that doesn't surprise me. She seems to spend all her free time in your company,' she retorted acidly.

Robyn allowed the remark to pass unchallenged. 'I'll check the Lido Buffet and the Library to see if she's there. Where will you be?'

'We're staying right here, assuming we can find somewhere to sit down, that is! I do declare I don't know what's come over that daughter of mine since she met you. She's nothing like she used to be. She was a sweet kind-hearted child until you turned her into an absolute monster!'

Robyn laughed. 'I think that's rather excessive. I haven't done anything to turn her against you. Ellie

147

is *still* a sweet-natured girl who's simply trying to enjoy her holiday.'

'Ugh! Is that so? So what time did she go to bed last night?'

'Not long after you. I walked back with her to her room. Don't worry; I'll have a look round for her. I'll find her.'

Robyn made her way to the Lido Buffet but Ellie wasn't there. From there, she methodically searched every deck without success and she was becoming increasingly concerned as she scrutinised a plan of the ship to find a place she might have missed. The only remaining possibility was the gym, though she doubted she'd be there. Still, it was worth a try.

The receptionist greeted her with a pleasant smile. 'Good morning. What can I interest you in today?'

'Nothing thanks. I'm just looking for someone. I can't find my friend so I wondered if she might be here.'

'Please….take a look round. Try the pool too.'

'Thanks,' Robyn said as she hurried inside.

As she approached the pool area, a familiar voice called out, 'Hi Robyn,' and she turned to see Raine exiting the changing room.

He gave her a beaming smile. 'Were you looking for me, by any stroke of good luck?' he questioned optimistically. 'You're obviously looking for someone. Are you joining me for a swim?'

'As a matter of fact, I'm trying to find Ellie. She's missing and I've looked everywhere for her. I can't think of any other places to look. You haven't seen her have you?' she asked worriedly.

'Actually I have but it'll cost you a kiss if I'm to tell you where she is,' he grinned.

Feasting her eyes on his sun-tanned body, she felt weak at the knees but speedily recovering her self-control, with furrowed brow she demanded, 'Stop it Raine and tell me at once.'

'No, I won't….not until I get a kiss,' he repeated, his eyes glinting with mischief.

She moved towards him, dispassionately planting a quick peck on his lips. 'Right, now tell me where she is. I've given you what you wanted.'

'That wasn't a kiss! You did a lot better than that last night. Just one proper meaningful kiss, please,' he requested seductively. 'Do it for old time's sake if nothing else or you'll never find her in a million years.'

She shrugged her shoulders. 'Alright if you insist but understand it *won't* mean anything,' she let him know impatiently.

'It will to me. Please Robyn….I don't want you to be angry with me.'

'I'm *not* angry with you Raine. I have no regrets about what happened. What we had last night was very special,' she said softly and when he took her in his arms she made no attempt to resist when he kissed her with passion.

'Thank you Robyn and I could feel that *did* mean something to you.'

'Maybe….but it doesn't change anything, so will you tell me now please?'

'Ellie's in the Spa. It's a formal night tonight and she wants to look her best. She was about to leave the pool when I arrived and we had quite a lengthy conversation.'

'You didn't tell her about us Raine....about what happened last night? Please tell me you....'

'Hush!' he said placing a finger over her lips. 'It's our secret. I'd never breathe a word to anyone. Go and find Ellie before she disappears again.'

She expelled a huge sigh of relief. 'Thanks Raine. I've no doubt I'll see you around the ship later.'

'I can guarantee it. We only have today,' he said and before she could turn away, he pressed his lips to hers once more and when she didn't resist for a second time, he held her close for several moments before releasing her.

Robyn hurried away feeling flustered. It had been an unexpected although certainly not an unpleasant encounter. She couldn't understand the feelings that Raine aroused in her. There was something magical about the way he touched her, yet she loved David but then Raine loved his wife and she aroused *him* likewise. It was inexplicable.

Robyn turned up at the Spa as Ellie was about to leave, thankful at having finally found her.

'I've trailed all over the ship, looking everywhere for you and your mother's been up and down looking for you too.'

'Well let's hope she's too breathless to hassle me when she sees me then,' Ellie smirked. 'I've had a wonderful time being pampered. I've had a relaxing massage, followed by a manicure and pedicure and that's not all; I'm going back again before dinner to have my hair done. I've decided to have it trimmed and re-styled. I felt I wanted a complete change so I looked at some pictures and chose a new style.'

'So you're going to be the belle of the ball tonight then?'

'Hardly! Not when I'll be wearing that repulsive frock my mother packed for me as formal wear. It's positively obnoxious. Mum chose it! I think it's one of Elma Flintstone's cast-offs she stumbled across in one of the charity caves at Bedrock or then again it might have fallen off Steptoe and Son's rag cart.'

Robyn howled with laughter. 'Well, I must admit I'm not overly enamoured with your mum's choice of evening wear, hers as well as yours. She's somewhat out of touch with the current fashion scene but I'm sure she means well. Listen, I have an idea. Do you have any decent evening shoes with you?'

'I have a pair of high-heeled silver evening shoes and a matching evening bag. I bought them at one of the shops onboard. I *was* going to buy myself a new dress too, just to make a point, that was until I looked at the prices on the labels! I couldn't believe how expensive they were.'

'When we go back to our rooms, you can borrow one of my dresses. I'm sure mine will fit you. You can make a grand entrance with me. I'm sure I can manage to keep out of your mother's way until we dock tomorrow,' she giggled.

'You're fantastic Robyn. I've never had a friend like you before. Do you think we can keep in touch when we're back home?'

'Of course, I'd love to hear how you're going on. I'll give you my number....remind me later.'

'This is the best holiday I've ever had in my life. I've met you and I've met Raine and you're both so kind. I saw Raine a short while ago when I was at the pool. He's such a nice person.'

'Yes, he's a sweet guy. I saw him too and he told me where to find you.'

'I'm looking forward to this evening. I can't wait to dress up in something decent and flounce into the restaurant in front of my mother. I can only imagine what her reaction will be.'

'Speaking of which, we'd better look for her right away. She'll be frantic.'

'You won't mention anything about what I'll be wearing tonight will you?'

'You *are* joking! Notwithstanding that I wouldn't dare, I wouldn't spoil that for *anything*. I can hardly wait to see the look on her face when you strut in to dinner. Remember to hold your head high. Don't be a shrinking violet. Remember too that your mum's unlikely to make it common knowledge that you're wearing one of *my* dresses so do your utmost to act self-assured.'

'You bet I will,' she laughed. 'This is going to be the best evening of my life, without a doubt.'


'Oh, there you are!' Flora remarked sarcastically as Ellie appeared in view on the upper deck. 'It's good of you to join us. I was starting to think you might have fallen overboard.'

With equal sarcasm she rejoined, 'Well, I'm *very* disappointed in you mother. Here you are, casually sipping a cocktail and you thought I'd drowned.'

'You know exactly what I mean Ellie. It was just a figure of speech! I couldn't find you anywhere on the ship. Where were you?'

'I went to the gym and then I went for a swim in the pool. It was lovely. There was nobody there but me when I arrived so I had it all to myself.'

'Oh, good gracious me, you could have drowned! You see what Ellie does when she's left to her own devices?' Flora admonished critically, directing her remarks at Robyn.

'Oh mum, you're obsessed about drowning. I'm a very good swimmer and there are plenty of people about to keep an eye on everything. Don't you want me to enjoy my holiday?'

'Of course I do Ellie but I like to know where you are. You've taken to going off heaven knows where all by yourself and nobody has any idea where you are. Don't you realise that all this anxiety is bad for my heart?'

'There's nothing at all wrong with your heart. It's just you being paranoid and melodramatic like you always are. I'm more than capable of taking care of myself as I've told you a hundred or more times.'

Try as she might, Robyn was unable to suppress her laughter any longer. 'Daughters and mums,' she chuckled.

'Er....excuse me....do you have children Robyn?' Flora asked pointedly.

'No I don't Mrs. Johnstone.'

'Then be kind enough to allow me to be the better judge of what's best for my daughter and when *you* have children of your own, perhaps then you'll be able to understand a mother's concern. Until then, I'll thank you not to interfere.'

Completely ignoring her mother's outburst, Ellie remarked, 'I'm off for a glass of orange and soda so do you want me to get you one Robyn?'

'Yes, that would be nice thank you. I'll stay here with your mum if you can manage to carry two.'

As Ellie left, Robyn remarked, 'I know you think I'm a bad influence on Ellie but you have to believe it isn't my intent to cause ill-feeling between you. Ellie's a wonderful young woman and it's thanks to you but you can't clip her wings forever. She needs her own space. She knows right from wrong. You taught her that. I've tried to encourage her to have more confidence in herself, that's all, because you won't be around forever and she has to learn about independence.'

Flora was infuriated. 'How dare you even *think* of lecturing me about my own daughter's welfare and needs?' she snapped. 'Why, you're little more than a slip of a girl yourself so what could *you* possibly know about life at your age?'

'You'd be surprised,' she countered distantly.

'The thing that surprises me is that your husband sanctions your gallivanting on holiday without him and I find that quite disturbing but I imagine that's the way young people of your generation carry on nowadays. One reads about such things all the time and I certainly don't want that kind of behaviour to influence *my* daughter, thank you very much. I've noticed you're wearing a wedding ring, so it's quite obvious you have no shame and for what it's worth, if you want my opinion, I say your husband should be here with you!'

'I couldn't agree more and how I wish that were possible. It's Tuesday today Mrs. Johnstone. Would you like to know what I was doing last Tuesday? I was burying my husband who'd been killed in a car crash. Does that brief explanation satisfy your idle curiosity? The reason I am *gallivanting* as you put it, is because I'm going to visit my sister who lives in New York and who I haven't seen for more than eighteen months. I chose this means of travel since I wanted to relax peacefully with all my thoughts. I needed to flee from the loneliness as I tried to come to terms with my grief. David my husband, wasn't even thirty when he died so you should reflect very carefully before voicing your insulting remarks and airing your vicious condemnations at other people you know nothing whatsoever about. Yes, I wear a wedding ring. I will always wear David's ring. He was my life and I lost him tragically. I was happy to find friendship with your daughter on this trip and I made a point of reassuring her how much you care about her, that you're only trying to protect her, but she's twenty-one years old with a mind of her own. Ellie wants to express herself and do all the things other young women of her age do. She's neither a child nor is she an invalid and should be allowed to live her own life. Nobody can second-guess what's lurking around the corner. Four weeks ago, I would never have imagined I'd be a widow at twenty-six years old, so I *do* know a lot about life....and about death as well Mrs. Johnstone.'

Flora was mortified and stumbled over her words. 'I….I am so sorry my dear….do please forgive me. I had no idea and I'd never have said such dreadful things to you had I known. Ellie didn't tell me that you'd lost your husband recently.'

'That's because Ellie doesn't know. She's so full of life and enthusiasm and she'd like to spread her wings a little. Please don't deny her that. That's all she's asking of you….a little understanding. Just try to meet her half way Mrs. Johnstone. She loves and respects you very much and I know she won't ever let you down.'

Flora sighed. 'When Ellie was born, I thought we would lose her. She was so poorly. I broke my heart as they wheeled her away for surgery….I even said goodbye,' she revealed as she wiped a tear from her cheek. 'I never expected her to make it through the operation, let alone make a full recovery and when she did, I vowed I would always be there to protect her. It's so hard to let go Robyn. I've told myself a hundred times what you told me earlier and I knew this day would come when she would rebel against my control, so I shouldn't have blamed you. It was bound to happen sooner or later. Bill has repeatedly warned me of the consequences of my actions but I wouldn't listen because I'm an awkward domineering woman who never listens to reason.'

Robin smiled. 'No you're not. What you did, you did with good intent. You had your reasons and it's never too late to make amends. There's something else I must tell you before Ellie reappears. I'm not supposed to breathe a word about this but suffice to say she has a surprise planned for later. I'm saying no more but you'll know when it happens so please be happy for her and show her your approval. It'll mean so much to her.'

With tears only a blink away she said falteringly, 'I'm not a bad person Robyn, believe me. I've tried to be a good mother to Ellie. All I ever wanted was what was best for her and when, as a baby, the good Lord spared her I vowed to protect her and raise her as a decent human being.'

'And you have, but surely it's time to loosen the reins a little now she's twenty-one? I know you're a good mother but more importantly so does Ellie. I apologise if I've said or done anything to offend but you don't want to drive her away. She's happy and if you need any convincing of that she's on her way back with the drinks now. Just look at the contented smile on her face.'

'Sorry, there was a long queue as they've opened the buffet now. Are you ready to eat yet Robyn? I know I am,' Ellie said eagerly.

'Hungry? I'm starving!'

'You and me both! I swam about thirty lengths in the pool earlier. By the way, I've just bumped into Raine. He was off to his room for a quick shower. He'd been jogging round the deck but he's coming back for the buffet afterwards, so he said he'd look out for us. He'll be about twenty minutes.'

'Who's Raine?' Flora enquired. 'Is he that young man I saw you with the other day?'

'Yes, he's really nice Mum. He's on his own too so we hang out together when we meet up.'

'Well, be careful Ellie. You never know....'

'Raine's a married man, Mrs. Johnstone. He's on his way to New York to collect his son who's been staying with his grandparents in New York. Raine's wife isn't here because she's been unconscious for over two years. He has a very stressful life and this is his first break since his wife had a serious stroke when their second child was born.'

'The poor boy! I'm very sorry. How awful,' Flora exclaimed.

'Yes, it is,' Ellie agreed sympathetically.

'You should make the most of your life since you never know what's about to happen from one day to the next,' Robyn remarked pensively, followed by a huge sigh.

'I couldn't agree more,' Flora nodded. 'And he is such a well-mannered young man too. Did you see how he jumped up to offer me his seat? You won't find many young men like that around nowadays.'

'We each have problems but we have to learn to come to terms with them. Please don't mention to Raine that I discussed his wife Ellie. I wouldn't like people to repeat things to others that I'd divulged in confidence,' she said, looking at Flora who nodded in acknowledgement that her hidden message was understood. 'Right Ellie, shall we make our way to the buffet now?'

'Yes, I think we'd better or there'll be nowhere to sit.'

'Enjoy your lunch,' Flora called after them.

'We will,' Ellie called back. 'I wonder what's got into her,' she added to Robyn. 'That remark almost sounded like a vote of approval. Maybe she's taken note of what I said to her.'

Robyn merely smiled smugly but said nothing.

The two of them shot off in different directions at the crowded food stations to make their choices and when they met up to find an unoccupied table, Ellie covered her plate with her free hand when she saw Robyn's plate contained a mere fraction of what she had selected.

'You glutton Ellie! You'll never eat all that food! I can't imagine what your mother would say if she caught you with that lot,' Robyn shrieked when she caught sight of it. 'You'll be sick if you eat all that.'

'Don't put money on it,' she quipped with a broad grin. 'Anyway, I have to make the most of it while I can. I'll be back on a diet of chicken and fish once I get home.'

'I wouldn't be too sure about that. Just talk to her Ellie. She'll see your point of view if you explain to her without losing your cool. I'm pretty sure she's had an eye opener over the past few days.'

She smiled. 'If she hasn't, she most certainly will this evening. I can hardly wait to see her face when I walk in the restaurant.'

'Nor can I but remember that winning the battle is one thing but you don't want to lose the war in the process. Think before you open your mouth and try not to appear as if you're gloating.'

'I'll try my best! Look, Raine's on his way over.'

Raine arrived with a plate in each hand and as he approached the table, he pretended to trip, causing Robyn to jump out of the way.

'Don't you dare,' she threatened him.

As Ellie laughed, he said, 'I couldn't resist doing that. You're so cute when you're grumpy.'

'I would have been a lot more than grumpy with that lot in my lap,' she commented dryly.

'I'm going back for a coffee. Would either of you like one?' he asked and Ellie shook her head.

'I would please,' Robyn said. 'Can you manage to carry two?'

'I can but there's no guarantee I won't tip one all over you. It wouldn't be the first time would it?' he reminded her as he ambled over to the coffee point, grinning from ear to ear.

'How old do you reckon he is?' Ellie asked.

'Raine? Between thirty and thirty-five I'd guess, maybe nearer to thirty. He might look older than he is because of the strain he's under. It's hard to say.'

'I'd have said about that too. He's very handsome and well-mannered isn't he? There's a certain suave sophistication about him and he speaks nicely too. He sounds like a well-educated guy. Do you know what he does for a living?'

'No and I don't want to get involved in personal issues. It's nothing to do with me and I don't want Raine quizzing me about my personal life so I don't ask any questions,' she said sharply.

She found that to be an odd response but it wasn't her place to probe. 'It's such an awful tragedy about his poor wife isn't it? I feel so sorry for him. Would *you* say Raine was good looking?'

'Er....yes, I suppose he is although I can't say I've taken that much notice,' she said, concentrating on her plate of food as the colour began to rise in her cheeks.

'And how old are you?'

'Twenty-six but I won't be for much longer. It's my birthday tomorrow on the eighth of April.'

'No, tomorrow's the *ninth*. It's the eighth *today*,' Ellie corrected her.

'No it isn't. We disembark on the eighth,' Robyn contradicted. 'Er....what's today's date Raine?' she asked as he returned with the coffees.

'I've lost all track of time....er....it'll be the eighth today....why?'

'Because it's Robyn's birthday and she thought it was tomorrow,' Ellie answered. 'Fancy anyone not knowing it was their birthday!'

'I could have sworn it was the eighth tomorrow!' Robyn said. 'How stupid of me!'

'Happy birthday Robyn. I wish I'd known,' Ellie said, walking round the table to give her a hug.

'Yes, happy birthday darling,' Raine whispered as he drew his chair close and kissed her affectionately on the cheek.

Her face flushed with embarrassment for a second time and she spluttered, 'Th....thank you. Can you believe it? It's my birthday and I hadn't a clue. Am I crazy or what?'

'I'll pass on that if you don't mind,' Raine stated and Ellie laughed. 'Actually, we can have a bit of a celebration. I was just about to tell you that there's a party on the upper deck tonight. How about we go up there and give the theatre a miss as it's our last night together? That steel band's playing again and they're very good. It should be fun so what do you say?'

Excitedly Ellie gushed, 'Oh yes, I'd like that.'

'Good, that's settled then. We'll go to the party,' he declared, avoiding Robyn's eye.

'I have to pack. I've done nothing yet. We need to have our bags outside our doors by midnight,' she reminded him.

'We all have to pack Robyn! Throw everything in this afternoon and then you'll only need to pack the clothes you've worn tonight. We won't have to be too late though. We have to be up early tomorrow. I think breakfast opens around six o'clock. Right, so that's all sorted because we aren't taking *no* for an answer are we Ellie?'

'Certainly not! I've never been to a party before except for a family party.'

'And your mother would never allow me to escort you alone without a chaperone would she?'

'Most definitely not!'

'Okay, you've made your point....you win! We'll all go together,' Robyn agreed, conceding defeat.

'I'm going to make a start on my packing straight after lunch,' Ellie told them.

'First things first. We need to decide what we're wearing tonight when we've had our lunch,' Robyn reminded her.

'I'll be in my monkey suit,' Raine declared, 'So I can pack everything else.'

'You'll look a plonker wearing your monkey suit to breakfast and around the docks in the morning if you've packed everything else,' Robyn pointed out and Ellie burst out laughing at the ridiculous vision in her mind's eye.

'Now you see how reliant I am on a good woman Ellie. I never gave that a moment's thought.'

'Hurry up Ellie. You've eaten more than enough now. You'll not find anything to fit you if you don't stop shovelling food in your mouth. Come on, let's rummage through my evening dresses and you can choose something to wear tonight. We'll catch up with you later Raine.'

Optimistically he asked, 'Will you both be going for afternoon tea at four o'clock?'

'More than likely, that's assuming we've finished the bulk of our packing in time.'

'Then I'll look out for you in the lounge. See you later.'

As Robyn walked away, Ellie scampered towards Raine and whispered, 'Would you meet me by the shops at three o'clock? I want to buy something for Robyn's birthday and I haven't a clue what to get.'

'Right, I'll be there and I'll buy her something too but keep schtum about that. I'll give her mine later.'

'I can't believe how many long evening dresses you brought. I only brought one,' Ellie sighed, fingering through Robyn's wardrobe.

'I wasn't sure what people would be wearing. I'm wearing this one so you can pick any of the others you like but nothing too revealing though!' Robyn cautioned her.

'I love this,' she murmured, taking hold of a pale blue satin gown. 'That's not too revealing is it?'

163

'No and it's a very flattering style. Try a few and I'll tell you which suits your colouring best.'

After trying on four dresses, Ellie decided to stick with her first choice and when Robyn had provided her with matching accessories, she led her towards the full-length mirror.

'Wow!' she shrieked to see her reflection. 'I can't believe that's me.'

'Then imagine what you'll look like when you've had you hair re-styled and done your make-up. That will make a big difference too.'

'Do you think I could come here to get dressed? Mum might come to my room and I don't want her to see anything.'

'I don't see why not and don't forget to have your shower before going to have your hair done and be here by seven-forty-five at the very latest. Dinner's at eight-thirty. What time's your hair appointment?'

'Four forty-five so I haven't much time.'

'Right, I'm throwing you out now. I need to pack. It's turned two and I've loads to do. Hopefully, I'll see you in the lounge at four for afternoon tea.'

'I'm so excited,' Ellie squealed as she left.

Raine was already waiting for her when she arrived breathless at the shops.

'I'm sorry I'm a bit late. My packing took longer than I thought it would but I've finished it all now. It's surprising how much more stuff you appear to have when you're packing it all up at the end of the holiday. My bag was full before I'd even started on the drawers.'

'Well you're here now so let's see what's on offer for Robyn. Have you any suggestions Ellie? Do you know what she likes?'

'No but it would be nice to find a memento of her holiday but I'm going to choose my card first.'

'Me too,' he said and quickly found one that said, 'To Someone Very Special'. When he opened it, he found the inside to be blank, thus allowing him to compose his own words.

'Right. I've chosen mine now,' Ellie said.

'Me too but I've no idea what kind of gift to buy. It might have to be perfume unless something else strikes me as suitable as we walk round. I'm not too good at choosing presents.'

'What about jewellery?' she suggested.

'I don't know her taste,' he said, carefully perusing the display counters before noticing a fine gold chain with a spherical multi-faceted crystal pendant that reflected the light in a myriad of colours.

'I think this fits the bill very nicely,' he laughed. 'Look, doesn't it remind you of an orange, with all those tiny facets? You remember how we met when I spilled juice all over her clothes?'

'Yes, I know all about that. That's perfect. She'll love it and she'll no doubt appreciate the reason for your choice. Now I have to find a suitable gift but I must hurry.'

'Would you like that Sir?' the assistant asked.

'Yes, I would and would you please gift-wrap it for me?'

'Certainly Sir....I won't keep you a moment. We carry a matching bracelet too but without the crystal drop if you're interested,' he said, trying to procure an additional sale.

'Could I see it please?' Ellie interrupted. 'Oh yes, that's pretty,' she added when the assistant returned with it. 'Why don't I buy that and the matching set will remind Robyn of both of us?'

'Good idea! Please wrap them separately,' Raine requested.

As soon as they'd collected their purchases, they hurriedly made their way to the lounge to look for Robyn where Raine made a point of sitting directly opposite her and she quickly became aware that he never once took his eyes off her.

This caused Robyn grave concern. The last thing she wanted was for Ellie to deduce that there was or had been anything between them and she felt very uncomfortable on each occasion she raised her head and caught his gaze.

'Have you finished your packing yet Raine?' she asked, providing legitimate cause for him to stare.

'Not yet,' he replied, his dark eyes fixed fervently on her face. 'I've made a start.'

Noisily replacing her empty teacup in her saucer, Ellie interrupted, 'Will you excuse me now please? I'm off to my room. I've still got one or two things to sort out and I also have an appointment with the hairdresser.'

'Alright, I'll see you later,' Robyn said and when Ellie was out of sight, she glared critically at Raine. 'You're not being at all discreet. I'm sure Ellie has beaten a hasty retreat out of embarrassment. While she might be a tad naïve, she's most certainly not a dim-wit. She's intelligent enough to see what's going on under her nose. You should try to exercise a little more control over your emotions.'

'I know and I apologise but I can't help myself. I can't believe I'm never going to see you again. It's driving me crazy.'

'Let's not keep going over old ground. This is just as difficult for me too.'

'Then make it *easy*. Tell me why you won't keep in touch! Come back to my room where we can talk in private. If only I could see you from time to time, I could be satisfied with that. I can't put into words the effect you have on me. Please darling, just talk to me. Don't end things like this. I'm going out of my mind here. Promise you won't walk out on me now.'

'Raine, you know nothing at all about me. This is just a holiday romance and you'll feel differently in a few days' time when you're back home with your family. You have enough to contend with, without me as an added complication in your difficult life. It's the right decision Raine and I'm trying hard to be strong for both our sakes so help me, please. My mind is made up and I won't change it so will you try to accept that?'

'Then look me in the eye and tell me that you feel nothing for me and be honest for once. Tell me you can just walk away from this without any regrets or lasting memories.'

She stood up. 'I have to go. I've things to do.'

'*Tell me dammit!*' he demanded furiously; then he laughed scornfully. 'You can't can you?'

'No Raine, you're right. I can't and I won't lie to you. Are you satisfied now?'

In a subdued voice he answered, 'No, I feel worse now. At least let me have your phone number then, so I can call you from time to time. I'd like to get to know you properly. I know so little about you.'

'That's the way I want it to be Raine. Please don't pressure me. I'm sorry I can't give you my number nor can I give you any explanation but you have to accept that it's over between us.'

'I'll never believe that Robyn.'

'Then you must try harder. I never set out to hurt you. *You* pursued *me* don't forget but I should have been stronger. I should have sent you away. We're equally to blame for what's happened but we can't turn back the clock. What's done is done so let's try to end things in a dignified manner, please. I don't want us to quarrel. I'll see you later.' She picked up her bag and walked away without another word.

Robyn returned to her room to finish her packing where bewildering thoughts flitted back and forth in her mind about David and Raine.

David had been the first and only man in her life, that was until yesterday, and she was stricken with remorse for her behaviour. Why had she slept with Raine when she loved David? Could it be that she had seen something of David in Raine? Had David sent Raine to comfort her? Would those feelings for Raine, dear sensitive Raine, diminish when she was home or would she live to regret her decision to end their liaison now? She had none of the answers but told herself repeatedly that she was making the only decision possible. While trying to rebuild her empty shattered life she needed no further complications.

David had turned to someone else for consolation and it had cost him his life and that was what Raine had been to her....her solace as she had been his. It had been nothing more....

Only after she had taken her shower did she feel able to face the evening ahead.

Raine had returned to his room feeling downcast and dejected. He had given a great deal of thought to the words he should write on Robyn's card, yet when he picked up his pen, his words flowed easily from the heart.

*You brought sunshine to my life,*
*You brought peace where there was strife.*
*Your laughter took away my tears,*
*You gave me strength to face my fears.*
*I know that soon we'll have to part*
*But you'll remain, locked in my heart.*
*Happy Birthday Darling Robyn and grateful thanks*
*for making the time we spent together very special.*
*I'll never forget you. With deep affection, Raine xx*

He sealed the envelope and placed it by Robyn's gift before heading to the nearest bar to drown his sorrows.

Bursting with excitement, Ellie scurried to Robyn's room at seven forty-five and banged impatiently on her door.

'Wow, your hair looks terrific!' Robyn exclaimed when she opened the door. 'I hardly recognised the new you.'

Ellie spun round to reveal the soft curls that hung around her shoulders.

'I love the way she's arranged the curls at the top. You're as tall as I am now and you look really chic and sophisticated.'

Ellie giggled. 'I can't imagine what it'll look like tomorrow but I don't care. I'm just so happy it'll be nice tonight. I haven't done my make-up yet as I'm not sure what to do. Will you have time to show me please?'

'Come on then, sit down. We haven't long and I haven't done my own make-up yet. You won't need any foundation. You have beautiful skin but a touch of blusher will highlight your cheekbones.'

'Oh....I don't have any blusher.'

'Right, use mine. This will tone nicely,' she said, brushing a little on her face. 'See what a difference that makes and silver shadow will complement and emphasise your eyes....see like this,' she advised as she graduated the density at the outer corners of her eyes. 'Perfect! Now the mascara. Brown will look a lot better than black with your fair hair, but you'll have to do that yourself. I'll have it everywhere if I try. Carefully brush upwards and outwards, then do the other. Give it a moment or two to dry and return to the first and do them both again. You have lovely long lashes so mascara will make a huge difference to your appearance.'

Robyn watched while Ellie carefully followed her instructions. 'Well done....now go over them again, slowly and carefully and try not to blink or sneeze or it'll be all over your face....and by the way, you don't need to stick your tongue out like that while you're doing it.'

Ellie giggled. 'It helps me concentrate. Mum will have a fit when I walk in the restaurant! She won't even recognise me but I bet she'll have something derogatory to say once she does.'

'You might be pleasantly surprised. I think she's starting to realise that she has to stop being critical and confrontational but you mustn't rock the boat.'

'That's a good pun!' she chuckled. 'I like that.'

'Get dressed and *step* into your evening gown so you don't spoil your hair, then put your lipstick on and finally your jewellery and shoes. I'm going to the bathroom to get changed now. Remember not to sit down or you'll crease your dress. There's a price to pay for elegance. Help yourself to my perfume if you have none of your own but try not to overdo it. You only need a tiny spray. You don't want to spoil everyone's meal. Why not take all your stuff back to your room while you're waiting for me?'

'Good idea. I'll drop it off and hurry back before mum sees me. I'll take your key to get back in.'

Robyn closed the bathroom door behind her and proceeded to finish her make up.

After brushing her hair and tidying her make-up away she rushed from the bathroom in her skimpy underwear almost into the arms of Raine who had knocked on the door during her absence. She yelled when she saw him and crossed her arms across her chest.

'I'm so sorry Robyn,' Ellie squealed in horror. 'I thought you'd be dressed when you came out.'

171

'Don't mind me, I've seen it all before,' he stated with a broad grin and in reply to Robyn's shocked expression he went on, 'When you wore that bikini a couple of days ago....you remember....that's what I was referring to.'

She was about to say, 'But I don't have a bikini,' when he winked at her and grinned.

She was furious. 'Would you mind waiting on the balcony please?' she asked curtly, flashing a black look.

'Of course,' he replied with a further meaningful smile....his having thoroughly enjoyed that startling though provocative treat.

Ellie followed him to the balcony and remarked, 'You're very smart tonight; you look like a younger version of Sean Connery.'

'Why thank you Ellie. It is Ellie isn't it? You're not her older, prettier and more sophisticated sister, are you?' he teased.

She gave him a beaming smile. 'Actually, this is one of Robyn's dresses. She's lent it to me. She has some gorgeous clothes in her wardrobe. The one I was supposed to wear, that mum packed for me, is drab and old-fashioned so I'm dying to see her face when she sees me in this. Do you think it suits me?' she asked, giving him a twirl.

'Yes I do. It suits you perfectly. You look divine and the colour matches your eyes. You'll turn quite a few heads this evening and I think your mum will be more than a little surprised too.'

'Give me a hand will you Ellie?' Robyn called to her. 'I need you to fasten my zip please.'

Ellie excused herself and went to Robyn's aid.

'Wow! What a beautiful dress,' she gasped. 'You look like a fairy princess.'

'Thank you Ellie. Let's have a look at you now. Yes, you look perfect! You'll stand out in a crowd tonight,' she told her as she stepped into her shoes and collected her evening purse. 'Your jewellery is lovely too. You can keep the dress and shawl. It fits you much better than it fits me. I'm not planning on taking any more cruises so I won't have a need for it anymore.'

'Oh, thank you Robyn,' she cried. 'Are you really sure?'

She smiled at her enthusiastic response. 'Yes I'm really sure. Right, we're ready now,' she called out to Raine.

As Raine walked in from the balcony and caught sight of Robyn he stopped suddenly and caught his breath. 'You look amazing,' he whispered, looking intently into her eyes. Then, turning his attention to Ellie he continued, 'I'll definitely be the envy of all the men on the ship this evening when I escort two such beautiful ladies to dinner.'

'And we'll be the envy of every woman,' Robyn made known with an evocative smile. 'I agree Ellie. Raine *does* look like Sean Connery. Right, if you're both ready, let's get this show on the road, as they say. I can't wait to watch your mum's palpitations.' With a quick flourish of taffeta, she hurried through the door followed by Ellie and Raine.

'I'm starting to feel scared now and my tummy's full of butterflies,' Ellie confessed. 'I hope I haven't

173

overstepped the mark. I'll die if mum causes a big uproar at the table when I walk in the restaurant.'

'Trust me Ellie, she won't,' Robyn reassured her.

When they stepped from the lift, Raine led them in the opposite direction, away from the restaurant.

'We're going the wrong way,' Ellie pointed out. 'The restaurant's the other way.'

'Ah yes, but we're not going to the restaurant, not yet anyway.'

Robyn looked surprised. 'So, where are we going then?'

'I've decided to have my photograph taken with the two most beautiful women on the ship.'

'Great!' Ellie exclaimed, hurrying ahead of them.

As Robyn was about to protest, Raine whispered, 'Don't begrudge me a photograph Robyn....please, above all when you've refused me everything else.'

Seeing the poignant, beseeching look in his eyes, she relented. 'Alright....I don't suppose there's any harm in that and it would be the ideal memento for Ellie to take home too.'

As they waited in line, Raine tried to take hold of her hand but she immediately stepped aside, afraid of allowing her emotions to get the better of her for a second time.

On a couple of occasions as they stood in silence she glanced at him. How easy it would be to fall in love with him, she reflected but how irresponsible it would be. It could lead nowhere and it would only cause further heartbreak. After all, she loved David and she could never experience such deep feelings for any other man.

All of a sudden, the line of people ahead of them dispersed and the photographer beckoned them to move into position in front of the backdrop.

'Sir, would you stand at an angle behind the dark-haired lady and place your hands on her shoulders? Will the other young lady stand in front at the same angle please? That's perfect,' he said, checking his viewfinder. 'Move in a little closer now please and I'll take another.'

'With pleasure,' Raine whispered in Robyn's ear and she felt his firm body against hers.

'Smile...thank you! Now if we could have the two ladies together and....'

'Will you take them individually as well?' Raine interrupted.

'Of course Sir.'

When the photographer had finished, he informed them their photographs should be on display within a couple of hours.

'I can't wait to see mine in this gorgeous dress,' Ellie said as they approached the restaurant. 'Look, everybody's gone in already. I'm having butterflies again.' Feeling uneasy, she began to fiddle with the curls around her shoulders. 'Am I sweating? I feel as if I am. Is my hair still alright?'

'You look beautiful Ellie. Stop worrying,' Raine told her. 'I'll escort you to your table if I may.'

'Thank you,' she said with a worried smile.

When they arrived at the table, Flora was in deep discussion with Jennifer and Mark, unaware of her daughter's presence....that was until Jennifer's concentration was unexpectedly diverted, to behold the incredible image before her eyes. Clearly surprised, her mouth fell open.

Flora then turned to seek the cause of such great interest to Jennifer.

Bowing his head slightly, Raine said, 'May I wish everyone a very good evening and I'll call back to collect you after dinner, ladies,' he added, directing his final remark to Robyn and Ellie.

For what appeared to Ellie an eternity, Flora was thunderstruck as she gazed at her daughter, blinking her eyes rapidly as she tried to contain her tears and then suddenly she spoke in a faltering voice.

'Oh darling, you look so beautiful and your hair looks lovely. I hardly recognised you. Doesn't she look the perfect lady Bill?' she beamed with pride.

'She certainly does,' he agreed with a broad grin, winking at his daughter. 'Your friend looks equally stunning,' he added, eyeing them both from head to toe at the same time smiling at Robyn, undoubtedly responsible for the transformation in his daughter's appearance.

'Thank you Mr. Johnstone,' she said courteously, taking her seat beside Ellie.

Flora whispered, 'I'm very proud of you. I wish I were twenty-one again.'

Overhearing her remark Bill jokingly commented, 'Well *I* don't. If you recall, when *you* were Ellie's age, you were a wild-cat....a real handful! I'd never keep up with you now!'

'Oh Bill, what a tale,' she chuckled, nudging him playfully and Ellie smiled happily at her parents in the knowledge that not only had she won the battle, she had won the war too! Finally she was free and she could never thank Robyn enough for that.

Towards the end of the delightful meal, the lights in the restaurant were dimmed before the conventional 'Baked Alaska Parade' began, but the darkness was soon illuminated by a mass of candles and flashing cameras as the chefs flocked past the diners in their scores while everyone applauded.

When the lights were turned up at the end of the parade, Ellie reached into her bag. 'Happy birthday Robyn,' she said with a beaming smile as she gave her the card and gift.

'Why, thank you Ellie. You're very kind.'

'Is it your birthday today Robyn?' Flora enquired and when Robyn nodded she added, 'You ought to have mentioned it to me Ellie. This calls for a bottle of Champagne. Bill, please summon the sommelier immediately.'

She turned to Jennifer and Mark. 'You'll join us too in a celebratory toast to Robyn won't you? I've enjoyed your company so much.'

'Yes, of course and thank you,' Mark replied.

'I'll certainly join you,' Ellie giggled.

'Well, maybe just a small glass for you dear,' she replied, winking at her daughter.

As soon as the waiter had filled everyone's glass, Bill stood up to propose a toast and when they were about to raise their glasses in response to his good wishes, Raine suddenly appeared on the scene.

'*Sit down young man*!' Flora commanded in her usual imperious manner. '*Fetch a chair over here.*'

Somewhat startled by her demeanour, he speedily took hold of a chair from an adjacent table and sat down to await what he expected to be some kind of admonishment from Ellie's mother.

'You're going to have a glass of Champagne with us,' she advised him. 'It's Robyn's birthday today. Waiter....another glass please!'

Robyn thanked them for their good wishes before each dispersed to enjoy the final evening.

'So where are we going first?' Ellie asked Raine eagerly.

'To look at the photographs of course. I'm hoping there's a nice one of my two favourite young ladies that I may have as a keepsake.'

'If there's a good one of me, I'm going to have it framed when I get back home,' Ellie made known as they made their way along the seemingly endless corridor. 'I'm glad you suggested we went to have our photographs taken.'

'Right, we're almost there now,' he said. 'Come on Robyn....try to keep up.'

'My shoes are pinching my toes,' she whispered.

'Pride must abide, though I never will understand why women wear shoes that contort their feet,' he laughed.

'We wear them because they *look* nice,' she told him. 'Don't you think it improves the appearance of a girl's legs when she wears high-heeled shoes?'

'I can think of nothing that would improve *your* legs darling,' he murmured.

'Stop it Raine!'

'I won't!' he declared petulantly. 'Look for your

178

photographs. There are scores on display. Let's take a section each or we'll be here all night.'

Robyn was delighted with her photographs when she found them. 'He's very good at his job! They're all excellent,' she said as the three of them studied the full selection.

'I have to agree, although he's only as good as his subject and camera permit,' Raine said. 'You look as good as any photographic model on your portrait Ellie. It's perfect.'

'I'm definitely having that one and look, they've printed three copies of the one with the three of us together so we can each have one.'

Looking disappointed, Robyn queried, 'Didn't he take one of you on your own Raine?'

'Yes, I have it here.'

'I'd like that if you don't want it,' she told Raine. Then, feeling some explanation was warranted, she turned to Ellie. 'Purely as a memento, of course.'

He nodded in accord. 'Okay, we'll do a swap then and I'll have yours. How's that?'

'That's worked out very well, hasn't it? We've all got exactly what we wanted,' Ellie remarked as she hastily joined the lengthy queue at the desk to pay for hers.

Raine leaned towards to Robyn, their faces close. 'I haven't got what *I* wanted and if you don't have a change of heart in the next few hours I never will.'

'Please don't start that again Raine. Let's pay for our photographs and join the party. I don't want to be miserable on our last night. We've only an hour or so left so let's do our best to enjoy it.'

It was heaving when they reached the upper deck. A live band was playing Caribbean music and more would be participants than could be accommodated zealously elbowed their way to the dance area.

'There looks to be a grand buffet. Are you hungry girls?'

'You're joking,' Robyn remarked. 'I doubt I'll eat anything for days following the huge meal I ate this evening. I couldn't manage a morsel but I'll wander past and take a few photos. It definitely looks very appetizing and there's some rather spectacular ice-carvings on display. You're not hungry are you?'

'Only for you darling,' he murmured tenderly.

Robyn let the remark pass unchecked as she felt the same. In just a few short hours, Raine would be out of her life forever but she reminded herself once more that she was making the right decision.

Ellie was standing close to the dance area with a radiant smile on her face, tapping her feet in time to the music and watching everyone.

'Just look at her Raine. Look how she's changed. She hasn't a care in the world anymore. She's such a sweet, innocent girl,' Robyn sighed heavily. 'I'm delighted things have worked out with her parents. She must feel as free as a bird now.'

'Do you intend keeping in contact with her?' he asked furtively in the hope he might feather his own nest were she to answer in the affirmative. He could easily persuade Ellie to keep in touch with him and thereby remain informed about Robyn, he believed.

'Yes, I want to be sure she doesn't slide back into her old ways once she's home. I've worked far too hard over the past day or two to have all my efforts wasted.'

'I have to agree you've done an amazing job. She definitely has more self-confidence now, though I'll never understand how you succeeded in converting her ill-mannered overbearing mother to your way of thinking.'

He laughed before continuing, 'When she ordered me to sit down in the restaurant, I was expecting a strong reprimand, to put it in polite terms, although for the life of me I couldn't imagine what *I'd* done wrong and I was gobsmacked when she offered me a glass of Champagne. Maybe the old bird's not as bad as I gave her credit for. Maybe she's got a heart after all.'

'Well, they say there's good in everyone. What's that familiar expression about never judging a book by its cover?'

'I guess you're right but I don't want to spend my last evening discussing Mrs. whatever she's called. I want to talk about you. I want to know everything about you Robyn and I want you to reconsider your decision to abandon me.'

When she answered his question by flashing him a withering look, he smiled. 'You can't blame a guy for trying and I won't stop harassing you until you change your mind.'

'It won't make any difference Raine. I've already told you a dozen times....this is the way it has to be and I'm sorry if you read more into it.'

Motivated by a fierce and burning desire to hold her in his arms once more, he stared deeply into her eyes and whispered softly, 'Will you dance with me please?'

'Where?' she laughed. 'They're so tightly packed they're like sardines. Nobody's moving.'

'Exactly! I want to get a grip of you Robyn and it seems this is my only opportunity. I'm going crazy here. Come on,' he said, pulling her into the crowd. 'It's only a dance and you wouldn't refuse a dying man his last wish would you?'

'You're only making matters worse.'

'They couldn't *be* any worse. I'm simply trying to make you see sense.'

She sighed heavily. 'I wish you'd understand. I'm the one who *is* being sensible. You have to believe that Raine.'

'Shut up,' he whispered as he enfolded her in his arms and held her close and Robyn was happy to be near to him. If only they had met in another place at another time, things might have been different, she reflected as she moved even closer. She could hear the beat of his heart and feel his hot breath against her cheek and she wanted to be with him just as he wanted to be with her at that moment in time but it could never be.

He moved his head from her cheek and rested his forehead against hers momentarily; then as he drew back she recognised both sadness and passion in his eyes.

'Spend the night with me Robyn,' he whispered, searching her eyes. 'Please darling. Don't say no.'

Her heart was pounding rapidly but she found an inner strength to reply, 'I can't. Please don't ask.'

Ignoring her answer he repeated, 'Spend the night with me, please Robyn. I want to spend every last moment with you now. I know you want that too if you speak the truth.'

This time Robyn didn't respond but her heart was breaking for the hurt she had caused him and when the music stopped, she released her hold and began to walk away.

Ellie watched them return and she fought her way through the crowd to join them. 'It's a terrific band isn't it?' she chirped cheerily. 'Don't forget Raine; you promised me a dance.'

'Well, there's no time like the present,' he replied trying to force a smile and glancing despondently in Robyn's direction before taking Ellie's hand.

'I don't know how to dance so I'll probably tread on your toes,' she told him.

'Better mine than somebody else's then,' he said with a congenial smile as the music struck up again. 'You'll have to give me your number Ellie and we can keep in touch.'

'Oh yes, I'd like that very much,' she stated with a beaming smile. 'I'll write it down after this dance and don't forget to let me have yours as well. Oops, there I go again....I'm really sorry,' she apologised for standing on his foot for a second time.

Raine felt better in the belief that all hope wasn't lost as they exchanged numbers. A miniscule spark of hope was better than no hope whatsoever. Robyn had feelings for him. The chemistry between them proved that and hadn't she clung on to him tightly during the dance? He couldn't understand how she could simply walk away as if nothing had happened and close the door on what they had. He had been truthful from the start that he was married and that he loved his wife so it wasn't that. Had Robyn been hurt before he wondered? Whatever her motive, it was something more powerful than the feelings she had displayed for him and he would have given his right arm to understand what was driving her away from him.

Suddenly Ellie declared, 'Gosh, it's almost twelve o'clock and I haven't put my bags out yet.'

'Me neither. We'd better be on our way,' Robyn said. 'We have an early start tomorrow. Is someone meeting you at the docks Raine?'

Dispassionately he responded, 'Yes, my father-in-law's driving over to collect me. He's bringing my son with him. Are you being met?'

'My sister's coming for me. You must be looking forward to seeing your little boy again after all this time.'

'I most certainly am. Although I talk to him two or three times a week on the phone it's not the same as having him at home with me. I've really missed him and his brother has as well. So, are we heading down now?'

'Yes, I think we'd better,' Robyn replied. 'I don't relish the thoughts of humping my own luggage if I were to miss the final collection and I've still a fair amount of stuff to pack yet. I'll be lucky to have it outside my door by midnight.'

'Right, come on then. We'll take you first Ellie,' Raine said, taking charge.

Ellie sighed dolefully. 'I've had a lovely time and I'll never forget meeting the two of you. I wish we could have had more time together. I'm sorry it has to end.'

'I am too,' Raine cut in before Robyn could reply.

The emotion in those three words was electrifying and Robyn was close to tears as they made the rest of their way in total silence.

'We'd better say our goodbyes here Ellie,' Raine said sadly. 'I might not see you in the morning. It's been such a pleasure to watch your transformation into a beautiful swan.'

'From an ugly duckling!' she giggled.

He smiled affectionately. 'No, you were never an ugly duckling Ellie. All you needed....or rather, all your mother needed was a gentle push....'

'By Robyn,' she interrupted, ending his sentence. 'She's fabulous isn't she?'

'She certainly is,' he agreed, gazing lovingly into Robyn's eyes. 'Enjoy the rest of your holiday and I wish you a safe journey home. Give me a hug. It's been a great honour to meet such a fine young lady. Take care of yourself Ellie.'

'Come here you!' Robyn said emotionally. 'I've enjoyed your friendship so much. Remember not to quarrel with your mum. Count up to ten before you open your mouth. A discussion is always the better option when trying to prove your point. I hope you don't forget me. I certainly won't forget you.'

'Never,' Ellie replied as she burst into tears. 'I'm really going to miss you and thank you once again for the beautiful dress and shawl.'

'You're most welcome. Goodbye and God bless, Ellie,' she murmured, kissing her cheek. 'Do please convey my fondest regards to your parents.'

Raine took Robyn's hand in his as they leisurely strolled down the corridor and they continued their journey to her room in deep thought. 'May I come in for a moment to give you your birthday present?' he asked in a faltering voice.

'Yes, if you promise you'll leave afterwards.'

'I promise, if that's what you really want.'

Robyn didn't answer. In her mind, that was what she wanted but in her heart, more than anything she wanted him to stay....to spend a final blissful night with him but she refused to be ruled by her heart.

'I've still got your cooling lotion,' she reminded him calmly as she unlocked the door. 'I'll just get it for you.'

When she stepped from the bathroom, he handed her the card and gift. 'Happy birthday darling. May I kiss you one last time?'

She was too overwhelmed with sadness to refuse him as she closed her arms around his neck, resting her head against his breast. 'It's been a pleasure and a privilege to know you Raine and I sincerely hope everything works out well at home,' she murmured softly.

She raised her head and kissed him gently on the lips. 'You're a very fine man and I only wish things could have been different,' she sobbed.

'Please don't cry darling. I can't bear it,' he said with tears gathering in his eyes. 'You never know, maybe somewhere, someday we'll meet again. I'll never forget you as long as I live,' he added with a watery smile.

'And I won't forget you either,' she said tearfully, releasing her hold.

As he reached the door, he turned and grinned. 'It was the nearest thing I could find to an orange.'

'What?'

'I'm pretty sure you'll work it out. You're quite intuitive. Goodnight Robyn. I won't say goodbye. I hope you enjoy New York.'

Without speaking another word or turning back to look at her, Raine opened the door and walked from the room and at that moment she thought her heart would break.

She perched on her bed and taking the card from the envelope, she first read his handwritten note.

'*My Dearest Robyn, Should you ever need me, I've written my number on the back of the photograph, with deep affection, Raine. P.S. I'm no poet but the words are my own and are straight from the heart.*'

Opening the card with quivering fingers, she read the tender, sincere words he had written and unable to contain her sorrow a moment longer, she sobbed like a child. She was still weeping when she carried her packed bags into the corridor.

Once in bed, she removed the wrapping from the gift and lifting the lid from the box, she peered inside. Carefully, she removed the pendant, mesmerised by the swaying crystal, glinting and sparkling like a diamond on its gold chain. Raine was at the very forefront of her thoughts yet again as she held it to her lips and kissed it lovingly. 'Thank you so much. It's a truly beautiful gift. I'll treasure it and always wear it with pride.'

When Robyn's alarm awakened her at six o'clock and after she had checked that her luggage had been removed from the corridor, she took a shower and dressed.

She stuffed the few remaining items in her carry-on bag and checked her watch. As Bryony wouldn't be arriving for at least another two hours there was sufficient time to get a cup of coffee before she had to join the queue at the disembarkation point.

Taking a final fond look round her stateroom, she closed the door and headed for the lift, praying that she wouldn't bump into Raine or Ellie for it would have been apparent she had spent most of the night in tears and there would have been no satisfactory explanation to offer them.

All meeting areas were swarming with passengers so she proceeded to the fore of the ship where self-service coffee was on tap all day. There was hardly anyone about as she sat by a window, gazing in awe at the majestic sky-scrapers that appeared to fill the sky. The sun was beginning to rise and it produced an unbelievable sight as its rays flickered and shone on the multitude of windows as far as the eye could see.

She sipped her coffee leisurely while reflecting on her six eventful days aboard the ship. It seemed an eternity since Raine had spilled his orange juice all over her. Dearest Raine....he had fought desperately to hide his emotion at the point they had exchanged their final goodbyes....but then Raine had refused to say goodbye, clinging to the aspiration that at some point they might meet again but what would be the likelihood of that ever happening?

Her thoughts transferred to Ellie who had moved mountains over the past few days and finally there was Ellie's mother who had at first appeared to be an abominable woman but who, it later transpired, had simply been a concerned mother, watching over the daughter she adored.

In those few days, she had learned so much about other people.

Robyn checked the time once again and found she still had half an hour to wait before disembarkation commenced.

The limited trickle of passengers at the fore of the ship had come to an end as each one had made his or her way to the exit point and Robyn continued in solitude to observe the diverse activities along the hectic dockside.

'I'm very sorry to trouble you my dear. I appear to have lost my bearings. Could you possibly direct me to the Purser's Office?' a frail and elderly lady enquired of her. 'I'm unable to find my way around this ship. I seem to get lost everywhere I go. It's so confusing and I don't even know if I'm on the right deck.'

With a sympathetic smile, Robyn agreed. 'You're right; it is very confusing. I'm forever getting lost as well. You are on the right deck but I'm afraid it's quite a long walk from here. It's at the other end of the ship. Let me take that holdall and I'll carry it for you. I was just about ready to make my way to the disembarkation point so I'll be happy to show you which way to go.'

'Well, if you're sure it's no trouble dear. I do feel such a nuisance having to keep asking other people which way to go. I used to come on this ship every year with my husband but he died last year. He was very good at finding his way around so I never took much notice. You've no idea what it's like to lose your soul-mate. In the early months it's so difficult. You lose the will to carry on but soon, you learn to pick up the pieces and start to rebuild what's left of your life. I think it was a mistake though....making this trip on my own and I doubt I'll ever be coming back again. We'd been married for fifty-eight years and we always did everything together. I miss him so very much but then I expect we'll be meeting up again quite soon,' she sighed thoughtfully. 'It'll be my eighty-fourth birthday in August and let me tell you, it only seems like yesterday that I was a young woman like you with everything to look forward to. Life passes by so quickly.'

Robyn smiled pensively. 'What's your name?'

'Ethel, dear.'

'Well Ethel, I hope I look as good as you do when I'm eighty-three and I think you're very courageous to come on a cruise on your own at your age. That's quite an achievement.'

'There are always plenty of people to talk to. I've made several new friends on this trip and I intend to keep in touch with all of them. You can't have too many friends dear and when you're a lonely widow like me and you meet someone special, you should hold on to that person. A loyal friend can be of such comfort, especially to a silly old fool like me.'

'You're not a fool. You're a very wise lady Ethel and don't ever let anyone tell you otherwise. Here's the Purser's Office and now if you'll excuse me, I have to dash. I've something very urgent to attend to. Goodbye Ethel,' she called as she started to run swiftly down the corridor.

Robyn knew what she had to do and there wasn't a moment to spare. She had to find Raine before he left the ship. She had to tell him she was sorry and that she felt for him what he felt for her but it had to be said now before the window of opportunity was lost forever, because if she didn't find him now, it would be too late.

Frantically, she searched the waiting areas but he was nowhere to be found and she retraced her steps, diligently scrutinising the long lines of passengers who were waiting to disembark but he wasn't there either, nor was he in any of the lounges.

Despondently, she took her place at the end of the queue, which by then had been whittled down to a dozen or so passengers.

On her arrival at the baggage hall Robyn retrieved her suitcase and via the Customs Hall, she made her way to the street.

'*Daddy*!' she overheard a child cry out and when she cast her eyes in the direction of the call, in the distance, she watched as a young man picked up his son and she continued to stare intently as he threw the small boy high into the sky and caught him before twirling him round and round. The two of them were laughing joyfully and then the father hugged and kissed his son affectionately as he held him in his arms.

'Oh Raine,' she cried. 'I've been such a fool,' and she wept uncontrollably to see Raine and his family climb into the taxi that sped away and disappeared from view. 'I've lost you forever now.'

6

'Will you call him when you arrive home?' Bryony queried after Robyn had sworn her sister to secrecy before pouring out her story.

'No, I should have made the right decision when I had the opportunity. It's too late now. I treated him very badly.'

'Maybe you *did* make the right decision Robyn. It sounds as if the guy has more than his fair share of problems already. It was probably the kindest thing to do in the circumstances, besides which, you need to look carefully at the long-term consequences of such actions. Did you ever stop to think what would happen if his wife recovered? It *has* been known to happen. He would then have been put in a position where he had to choose, so think about that because you wouldn't have wanted to share him, nor would you have allowed him to leave his wife and so your heart would have been broken yet again. Just try to forget him,' Bryony said compassionately, handing her a box of tissues to dry her tear-stained face. 'It's the better option in the long run.'

'Then why do I feel so miserable if I've made the right decision?'

'Just listen to me. It's less than three weeks since David was killed. You were feeling abandoned and lonely and in need of some love and attention, like the guy you met on the ship and you just happened to hit it off. You must know that almost all holiday romances come to an abrupt end immediately after the lights have gone down when you're back in the land of stark reality. The guy will be alright now he has his family around him and you'll get over him in no time at all. You're still grieving for David and it's a slow healing process. Your emotions are still in tatters and you were understandably vulnerable. On reflection, you must have believed it was wrong or you would never have turned him away, so don't let your heart rule your head Robyn. My advice is to stand by your original decision, your gut instinct. Try to rid him from your thoughts now. For all you know, he could have forgotten about you already.'

'But he cried, Bryony. I've never seen a man cry before and he pleaded with me. I'll never forget the look on his face when he walked out of my room. I watched and waited for him to turn round one final time but he couldn't even look back at me so don't tell me he's forgotten me already because I know it isn't true.'

'Promise me something Robyn. Give it the test of time....say three months and then if you still feel the same, give him a call then but tread very carefully,' she cautioned her wisely. 'Your feelings have to be mutual and he might not feel the same about you in three months' time as he does now. Make small talk at first and see where it leads but please, do nothing at all for three months. I don't want you to get hurt. Try to be sensible like you've been up to now. I've no doubt you'll still be very lonely in another three months but don't make that an excuse to be drawn into anything you might later regret. Remember, *he* has a wife and family to go back home to after your clandestine meetings draw to a close but you don't have that luxury. Surely you can do better than that for yourself?'

'If I had that luxury, I wouldn't want anyone else would I? I just can't get Raine out of my thoughts. Three months is a very long time to wait.'

'Exactly, which gives both of you time to reassess the situation. If you really love each other then your feelings will stand the test of time. Will you do that for me?'

'I suppose so. I know you're right because you're always right. I'm not even sure of my own feelings anymore. I don't know whether I feel need or love. I didn't tell him I loved him.'

'Did he tell you?'

'No, I don't think he did in so many words. It was kind of....er....implied.'

'That's not good enough. You wait three months and there must be no contact at all during that time! Agreed?'

'Agreed!' she replied reluctantly.

'Right, sort yourself out; get your bags unpacked and then we're hitting the town big style! You're in New York now and a load of my mates are coming over later tonight and they're all dying to meet you. What's in the large brown envelope?'

'It's a photograph of Raine.'

'May I?' she asked and Robyn nodded.

Bryony took the photograph out of the envelope. 'Wow, I can see now what you mean. He's one cute guy....very handsome! I could just do with one who looks like that! Unfortunately they're rather thin on the ground in New York.'

'I don't believe that. What about all the business tycoons?' she asked, blowing her nose noisily.

'They tend to live out in the suburbs. Some of the guys I know are cute but the vast majority are just dropouts. They're great fun though. They scrounge, beg and live on their wits from day to day but then I guess you'd find that type of guy all over the States if not all over the world. They're certainly not the kind of guy you'd want to settle down with.'

'Is there nobody at work you fancy?'

She shrieked with laughter 'Will you get *real*? I work with British Civil Servants. Can you honestly imagine me making it with one of them? How gross is that? I'd rather die celibate!'

Bryony's remark brought a trace of a smile to her lips. 'Right....and pigs might fly if you expect me to believe that,' was her slick rejoinder.


The time Robyn spent in New York was amazing. Central Park was within easy walking distance and Times Square at night was stupendous. The fashion outlets were to die for but the highlight of her short stay was a surprise helicopter trip with Bryony over New York City. That had been a truly remarkable experience and one she would never forget.

When it was time to leave, Robyn felt sad. 'I've had a great time Bryony,' she sighed. 'I only wish I could have stayed a while longer. I'd love to come again. It's been a real eye-opener and nothing like I imagined it'd be. I can't believe how hospitable the American people are. Everyone wants to talk to you and they want to know everything about you, your

196

ancestry, where you were raised, where you went to school et cetera and they know more about England than I do and I live there. They certainly go out of their way to make you feel welcome here.'

'That's because you're British. They love to hear you talk; they like to listen to the tone of your voice because it's different but you're right; in the main, they *are* polite and hospitable. It's a pity we can't take a leaf out of their book back home where some folk are too rude to give you the time of day. Your observations are a mirror image of the ones I had as soon as I arrived here. I too found them to be very helpful and obliging.'

'Have the powers that be given any indication of how long you'll be in New York or where you'll be sent next?'

'Not yet but then I could be moved at very short notice. If or when that happens, you'll have to visit me there. I soon settle wherever I am, I don't have a problem making friends, so it doesn't bother me too much where they post me. As long as the pay goes in my bank account each month, I'm happy.'

'It's been great to see you again and you've even succeeded in raising a laugh out of me and believe me, that's some achievement considering what I've had to contend with over the past few weeks.'

'I'm sorry I couldn't make it to David's funeral. I probably could have taken a couple of days off but definitely no more and it's a heck of a long way to come for two days. I'd rather shoot over later when you're feeling more settled and we can go out and do girly things together. How does that sound?'

'It sounds great....like the advice about Raine but then you always were the level-headed one where I was the scatterbrained romantic who fell madly in love while I was still at school.'

'Yes, but who got the better qualifications? I was always too busy arguing the facts with my teachers. I believe I would have re-written history had I not been kept on a very tight leash. I was never an easy pupil to control.'

'That was because you were very strong-minded and innovative. In *your* eyes, everything had to be black or white. There could never be any grey area with you but you've done well in your job and you get to see the world. Thousands would swap places with you given half a chance.'

'Maybe, but I can't find myself a decent guy!' she sighed. 'I envied you and David because I miss that togetherness the two of you shared.'

'That's rich! I manage to find them but then I lose them one way or another. Believe me, that's a heck of a sight worse.'

'I guess we're all different. Take the two of us for example. We're nothing at all like sisters. We're as different as chalk and cheese. Anyway, who knows what the future holds in store for us? Perhaps I'll let lucky and find a nutty professor with megabucks!' she laughed. 'It's time you were on your way to the airport or you might be late for your flight and it's also time to say goodbye to our over-easy eggs and streaky bacon, with buttery pancakes and oodles of maple syrup all on the same plate....not to mention the corrupted English language we speak!'

'And which *you've* also picked up! Shame on you Bryony.'

'I know but you've heard the expression, *when in Rome, do as the Romans do*! Your cab's here,' she made known, glancing out of the window. 'It'll be around thirty bucks and he'll expect a five-buck tip on top of that. Do you have enough cash? I think I can rustle up a few bucks if you're short.'

'I've plenty. It's one thing David made provision for, my future financial security, so I've no worries whatsoever on that score. Don't leave it long before you come for a visit. Mum misses you so much and so do I. I hate this part now. I hate goodbyes. Give me a hug and thanks again for everything. I really enjoyed meeting your friends. I've had a great time and I really do wish I could have stayed for another few days,' she sniffled.

'Stop that now....and don't you dare start skriking again! It's been great for me too. Give me a bell as soon as you get home and pass on my best wishes to everyone. Enjoy your flight. Love you!'

'Me too. Take care Bryony.'

En route to the airport, Robyn chuckled at Bryony's final remark, doubtful that the word *skrike* existed in the American vocabulary or indeed in the Oxford English Dictionary but it was a descriptive word, no doubt of local origin and accurately expressing the action of noisy, squawking tears. She had certainly done more than her fair share of skriking during the past few weeks and there was no doubt in her mind there would be plenty more tears to come.

Reflecting on her nine action-packed days, it was abundantly clear that her trip had not turned out as initially expected.

Instead of the anticipated tranquil, uncomplicated and leisurely break, it had been a most invigorating experience, filled with emotion and drama that she could never have anticipated in her wildest dreams, and no matter what the eventual outcome might be, she would neither forget nor would she ever regret one single moment of her whirlwind and passionate affair with Raine.

7

Robyn turned her key in the lock and stepped into *the land of stark reality* as expressed by her sister. How different her house appeared from what it had been just a few weeks ago. The decor looked faded and uninteresting; in fact everything that caught her eye seemed to be dated and drab. It was no longer a home like the one that had been filled with laughter until two or three months ago. Now it was simply a building in which to live, nothing more than a roof over her head.

After stacking her travel bags at the bottom of the stairs she shivered and rubbed the goosebumps that covered her arms, mindful of an incomprehensible eerie silence not experienced before. She turned on the gas fire, flexing her fingers before the flickering flames and her eyes were instantly drawn towards the photograph on the small hexagonal table beside the fireplace....their wedding photograph.

She took it from the table and smiled longingly. 'I miss you so very much,' she said. She continued to stare at David's handsome smiling face for several minutes until she could no longer focus through her tears, before returning her favourite photograph to the table.

She drew her chair close to the fire and picked up the telephone to call Abbie who answered instantly. 'Hi, it's me, Robyn! I thought I'd better give you a quick call to let you know I'm back. I've just got in and I'm shattered. I know what folk mean about jet-lag now.'

'Tell me about it! It took me about three weeks to get over it the last time I went to America. I wasn't expecting to hear from you until much later today. So how did it go?' she enquired cheerily.

'I enjoyed the cruise very much. The ship was an absolute dream and New York is fabulous. I would definitely go back again. It was great to see Bryony and in addition to the customary tourist attractions you can visit free of charge, Bryony had booked us a helicopter trip over the city. That was incredible! I'd never been in a helicopter before so that was an experience I won't ever forget.'

'How was Bryony?'

'She was very well like she always is but she was grumbling as usual about not having a regular boy-friend. She was overjoyed to see me, although she said I looked a little peaky. I was also introduced to quite a few of her friends who we went out with in the evening. They were a friendly bunch who made me very welcome.'

'English or American?'

'Both, and there were also two Mexican girls and an African American guy. New York's like London in a lot of ways. It's very cosmopolitan. My sister loves it there.'

'And what about you? Are you feeling any better after your break or are you still a bit weepy?'

'I'm very weepy; in fact I've just had a good cry. As soon as I walked in, the first thing to catch my eye was David's photograph so that set me off but I guess it's only to be expected. I still find it hard to accept that I'll never see him again. I keep thinking he'll walk through the door. It's early days yet. It'll take time to readjust won't it?'

Abbie sighed. 'Yes, it *will* take time Robyn. Did you make any friends on the ship?'

'Yes, they were a good crowd and I met up with a girl who was travelling with her parents so we hung out together most of the time. How's it progressing between you and Gerald?'

'Everything's fine! We went down to London last Saturday and saw a show in the West End and he'd booked us in overnight at a very exclusive hotel off Park Lane where we had dinner before we left for the show. Things are going really well between us. He treats me like royalty. I've never known a guy as considerate as Gerald before and we have such a laugh. He can be so witty. There's a lot more to him beneath that hard exterior he portrays.'

'I'm delighted for you Abbie. Has there been any more news about the Inquest?'

'Not that I'm aware of but I'll tell Gerald you're back and if there is anything, I'll ask him to get in touch with you. He's coming over later for dinner. Why don't you join us and you can tell us about the holiday?'

'Thanks but I haven't unpacked yet and I've loads of washing to do, besides which I'm tired out so I'll probably have a quick bite to eat and take a nap for an hour or so. Incidentally the evening dresses were a great success. If I don't get chance to speak to you before, I'll see you in the morning.'

'Are you sure you're up to it? You don't have to rush back to work you know. Why don't you take a few more days to sort yourself out? We're not very busy so I can manage on my own a bit longer.'

'I'm sure you can but I must get out of this house. I can't just sit here twenty-four hours a day staring at four walls. I'll go mad. I've only been back five minutes and that's five minutes too long.'

'Suit yourself. I'll be glad of the company if you do come in so I'll see you tomorrow hopefully and you can fill me in on the details of your trip.'

No sooner had she replaced the receiver than her telephone rang again and she was surprised to hear Ellie's excited voice.

'Is that you Robyn? I couldn't remember whether you were back today or tomorrow.'

'Ellie! How lovely to hear your voice. I've only just walked in. When did you get home?'

'Yesterday. I looked all over the ship for you on the last morning but I couldn't find you anywhere. I bumped into Raine on my travels. He was looking for you too.'

Her heart missed a beat. 'Why was he looking for me? Did he say?'

'I think he just wanted to say goodbye to you. He went to your room and the steward told you you'd already left. I take it he didn't find you then?'

'No, he didn't. I went for a walk as I'd plenty of time to kill. We were probably following each other round the decks. I didn't bother going for breakfast. I suppose I was too excited at the thought of seeing my sister,' she lied. 'I went to the coffee point and sat by the window overlooking the docks. It wasn't busy at that end of the ship and I wanted to escape from the hustle and bustle and the long queues I'd seen earlier. When I disembarked, only a handful of passengers remained, so I was able to walk straight off the ship.'

'It's a shame you missed each other. He appeared anxious to see you. He asked if I had your number but I lied. I said you hadn't given it to me but that you'd got mine. Did I do the right thing?'

'Yes you did and please don't give my number to him if he happens to call you.'

'Is something wrong Robyn? Did you and Raine quarrel?'

'Of course not,' she laughed. 'He's a married man and I don't want any further contact with him now. He's a nice guy and he was good fun on holiday but that's over now.'

'So shall I tell him that if he calls me?'

'Heavens no! I wouldn't want to hurt his feelings. Just tell him I don't like to give my number to anyone. I'm sure he'll understand. Don't give him my address either.'

'That'd be tricky. I don't know it!'

Robyn decided to leave it that way. If Ellie didn't have her address, then she couldn't be persuaded to give it to Raine should he ask.

'How was he when you left him? I expect he was excited to be seeing his little boy?'

'I imagine he was though he didn't say very much and I thought he was rather subdued. We left before he did as he was on a lower deck, so he had to wait to be called. I really enjoyed his company. How did you like the necklace he bought you?'

Robyn was shocked to learn that Ellie knew about the gift from Raine. 'It....it's beautiful but how did you know he'd bought me a gift? I never showed it to you as he only gave it to me when he walked me to my room.'

'I was there with him when he chose it. I got you the matching bracelet. Raine loved that pendant as soon as he saw the shape of it. He said it reminded him of an orange because of all the tiny facets and he thought it would amuse you after what happened when you first met.'

'He's a very considerate young man,' she replied as the significance of the pendant suddenly became apparent and she twisted the crystal droplet around in her fingers as they continued to speak. 'Actually I'm wearing Raine's necklace now *and* your lovely bracelet Ellie. Thank you again for your thoughtful gift. How are your parents?'

'They're both alright thanks. Dad's still the same, but mum's really altered now and she's told me at least three times how much she likes you.'

'My word, she really *has* changed. She was very caustic towards me one day. She bellowed at me at the top of her voice and accused me of leading you astray, amongst lots of other things. Where do you live Ellie? If it's not too far, perhaps we could meet up and have lunch one day. It'd be great to see you and your family again.'

'Oh yes Robyn! I'd like that too. We live in North Staffordshire. Where are you?'

'I live in South Cheshire so we're not what you'd call a million miles apart. Do you drive?'

Ellie sniggered. 'You're a right comedian aren't you? Drive a car….me? I can't even ride a bike. As you can no doubt imagine, mum was always afraid I'd fall off and end up under a truck but that's about to change!'

'What….you're going to learn to ride a bike?' she screeched with laughter.

'No!' she said, joining in the laughter. 'I'm going to learn to drive a car. Dad said he would teach me because he's the only person in the family who can drive. I'm looking forward to my first lesson.'

'So is he going to teach your mum to drive too?'

'You'd better be joking! Not if I'm a passenger. Besides, you can't teach an old dog new tricks,' she giggled.

'She'll *old dog* you if she overhears you speaking about her like that!' she replied on a laugh. 'Listen I have to go. I've got stacks of washing to do but I'll call you soon. I promise.'

'It's great to talk to you again. You can tell me all about New York next time and we'll compare notes about the places we visited.'

'We will. Take care Ellie.'

Robyn removed Raine's holiday photograph from the envelope and looked at it affectionately. He was certainly a handsome guy and the photographer had captured his warm smile perfectly. He seemed to be looking into her eyes as she spoke to him from the heart. 'I'm so sorry I missed you Raine. I did try to find you, truly. Three months isn't very long to wait and if we both feel the same then, we'll work something out….I promise. I never thought I'd say this to another man but I love you and miss you so much. I think of you all the time.'

She held up his photograph to her face and kissed his lips.

As the days and weeks went by, Robyn readjusted to her revised daily routine although she found the lonely nights and weekends extremely stressful and her thoughts constantly turned to Raine. In addition, the Crown Court hearing, just two weeks away, was constantly praying on her mind though she believed once that was behind her, she would be in a better position to get on with the rest of her life.

She became very tense as the date for the hearing drew closer and she dreaded that day. Almost three months had elapsed since her return from America and three times, she had overcome a burning desire to call Raine when she had felt particularly low.

Although she had maintained regular contact with Ellie, there had been no recent news of Raine when she had briefly enquired but she had discovered that Ellie had told him that her telephone number could be disclosed to no one and after that conversation, Raine hadn't contacted Ellie again.

Maybe he'd finally given up on her, she thought, not that she could blame him if that were true. If he had felt as miserable as she had during the past few weeks, he'd have had justification to believe there was little prospect of reconciliation, particularly as he had no means of communicating with her.

Nevertheless, she was determined to wait out the full three months, especially as there were only two more weeks to wait. She had given her word to her sister in all sincerity and she would therefore abide by that decision.

The next day at the office, Robyn felt below par. 'It's because I'm uptight about the Court case,' she told Abbie. 'It's on my mind every minute of every day. I can't stop thinking about it. I know I'm going to be listening to all the terrible things I don't want to hear again and I just want it to be over and done with. I keep wondering how I'm going to feel when I come face to face with the driver who's ruined my life and Leanne's name will crop up as well, in fact I imagine her family will be there too. There never appears to be any end in sight and I'm churning up inside. I'm tossing and turning all night and so I'm not getting a decent night's sleep. Added to that I'm not eating properly because I've no appetite either.'

'Have you talked to Gerald about the Court case?'

'Only briefly. He's told me there's nothing I need worry about but I can imagine what it's going to be like and I'm absolutely dreading it. I'll just be glad when it's over.'

'Why don't you make an appointment to see the doctor? Go and have a word with her. She might be able to prescribe a mild sedative or tonic. You need something to help you calm down, otherwise you're going to be really ill. You've been through so much over recent months and there's no shame in talking about the way you feel. She'll understand. It's her job. Doctors are used to dealing with such matters. They do it all the time.'

'No, I can't be bothered with doctors. I'll see how I feel after the Court hearing and if I'm no better by then, I'll call the surgery. I'm certain it's just nerves and that I'll be fine after it's over.'

By the end of the week, Robyn was feeling much worse. She was still neither sleeping nor eating and her nerves were completely shattered. At times she would burst into tears in the office for no apparent reason. Reluctantly, after a further lecture by Abbie, she telephoned the surgery to make an appointment.

Dr. Hamilton carried out a thorough examination, took urine and blood samples and talked to Robyn sensitively about the grieving process.

'I can give you something to help you sleep and that should also allay your anxiety about the Court case that's causing you some concern but I'm afraid that won't resolve all your problems. Grief is a very personal issue and affects people in different ways. I can prescribe nothing to speed up the process. It's something you have to come to terms with in your own way and in your own time. Let's just wait for the test results. They should be back in about seven days and then we can look at the bigger picture. In the meantime, try not to worry as that doesn't help matters. The tests might show that a mild infection is responsible for your lethargy. I'm quite sure it's nothing serious. I suggest you take a day or two off work and try to get some rest.'

When Robyn returned to the surgery a week later, nothing could have prepared her for the bombshell delivered by Dr. Hamilton, following receipt of the test results.

'I'm sure you'll be pleased to hear there's nothing at all to worry about, in fact your lethargy is merely symptomatic of your condition Mrs. Ainsley,' she told her with a beaming smile. 'You're pregnant.'

Robyn stared at her blankly for several moments before saying, 'But I can't be. I can't have children. David and I had been having fertility treatment for the best part of two years and that didn't work and there had been several failed IVF procedures. There has to be some mistake.'

'Believe me, there's no mistake. There's no doubt whatsoever. You're definitely pregnant.'

'I can't believe this. How many weeks?'

'It's difficult to be precise without an ultra-sound scan but from physical examination, I'd say around three months. I was pretty sure when you came last week but I didn't want to give you false hope until the test results confirmed my diagnosis, especially after all the failed IVF treatments. I'm delighted for you. Congratulations! I would like you to attend the ante-natal clinic as soon as possible. They'll be able to give you a more accurate date. Had you no idea?'

'No, I often felt ill following IVF treatment and it messed up my cycle so it never entered my mind I might be pregnant, particularly after I'd lost David three months ago.'

'Yes and it's sad he can't be here to share in your joy after all you've been through. Should you need to speak to a counsellor, I can arrange that. Nobody would criticise you if you believed you couldn't go through with it alone but....'

'I wouldn't even consider a termination after what I've gone through to become pregnant and I find it very offensive to believe that *you*, as a supposedly responsible person would advocate such an option,' Robyn interrupted irately.

'If you would let me finish, I'm very pleased you mean to proceed with your pregnancy. I was merely informing you that your counsellor might help you reach an informed decision. There's a great deal of help available to single parents, so you wouldn't be expected to cope on your own. That was the point I was trying to put forward before you jumped down my throat,' she rejoined with a perfunctory smile. 'I wasn't advocating any kind of option.'

'I'm sorry. I'm still in shock and I shouldn't have jumped to conclusions. I can't believe I'm pregnant after all this time so please forgive my outburst. I'm a bag of nerves. That's why I came to see you in the first place. I just thought I'd be leaving here with a prescription for a mild sedative, certainly not news like this.'

'I suggest you go home now, sit down quietly and think everything through and meanwhile, I'll make arrangements for the ultra-sound scan and someone will call you with a date and time. If you do decide you'd like to speak to a counsellor, call the surgery for an appointment to be made.'

'Thank you,' Robyn replied, still reeling from the shock of the revelation. 'Once again, I'm sorry.'

'We're going to have a baby,' Robyn sobbed as she held Raine's photograph in her quivering fingers. 'I want to thank you so much. I could never put into words what this means to me. I'll never tell a living soul, I promise. I would never do anything to hurt

212

you. I'll deal with it and I'll love your child just as I love you.'

She raised the photograph to her face and kissed his lips tenderly to say goodbye. 'We came so very close but this has changed everything. Goodbye my darling. I realise now how much I love you and I'll never forget you as long as I live but I could never burden you with this,' she cried.

She returned his photograph to the envelope and sealed down the flap before hiding it in a cardboard box on top of her wardrobe.

That night, she cried herself to sleep, concurrently shedding tears of happiness for the embryonic life within her and tears of anguish for Raine who was gone from her life forever and who would never see his child.


'You're looking much brighter this morning. How did it go at the doctor's yesterday?' Abbie enquired as soon as Robyn walked in and before she'd even had chance to sit down.

'Alright, but you're never going to believe what I have to say! Relax, take a deep breath and prepare yourself for the biggest shock of your life. Are you ready? I'm pregnant!'

Abbie was astounded. 'You're *pregnant*? Tell me you're joking! After all that time trying, it's finally happened? I'm so sorry Robyn.'

'Well, I'm not. I'm ecstatic.'

'I meant what rotten timing.'

'I know. That's exactly what I thought when the doctor told me. I didn't call you last night because I was very distressed when I got home. David would have been so happy and now he'll never be able to see or hold his child.'

'Listen to me! You have to forget the past and try to focus on the positive. When are you due?'

'The doctor wants an ultra-sound scan to confirm her estimate but she thinks I'm about three months. It was obviously David's parting gift before he left me. Some legacy!'

'Are you bitter?'

'I'm sad. I want David to share in my joy but he can't. He wanted to leave me well-provided for but he certainly couldn't have envisaged that he'd left me *with child* too.'

'Well, it's fantastic news. You must tell Gerald as soon as possible.'

'Why?'

'Because it will affect the claim against the other driver's Insurer. Gerald will have to contact them. There'll be a child to provide for as well now. That will really push up the payout.'

'I wouldn't want that, in fact I'd rather it wasn't mentioned,' she stated earnestly, fidgeting with her pen.

'Don't talk wet. Why are you concerned about the Insurance Company? They don't give a damn about the victim when they're trying to wheedle their way out of coughing up the cash for a legitimate claim. You should take them for whatever you can get out of them. They're liable. It costs tens of thousands of pounds to bring up a child nowadays. Anyway, you won't have any say in the matter when Gerald finds out and it's definitely not something you can keep quiet about. You'll look like a house-end in another few months.'

Robyn grimaced. 'Gee thanks, Abbie! You don't half know how to make a girl feel good.'

Nothing more was mentioned about the additional Insurance claim but later that evening, when Robyn reflected, she was very concerned. It was one thing to pass off Raine's child as David's but fraud was another matter....a very serious matter. Had Raine been a free man, then she would have rushed to him with open arms but this news would tear him apart if it were to become public knowledge. Raine was a sensitive guy who loved his wife and family and the knowledge of his having fathered her child would be too much of a burden. He could never know.

The following week, Ellie called to arrange their long overdue meeting. They hadn't seen each other since their holiday though they had talked regularly on the telephone. She was excited at the prospect of seeing Robyn again and could hardly wait for it to happen.

'How about Saturday? Dad reckons it's only forty minutes by car from where you live. We could look round the shops for a while and then have our lunch somewhere,' she said eagerly.

'Alright then, I yield to your demands! Shall I call for you about ten o'clock?'

'Brilliant! I'm thrilled you're coming and mum's looking forward to seeing you again.'

Robyn deliberately didn't ask about Raine and as Ellie had made no reference to him, it was apparent he'd made no recent contact with her or she'd have mentioned that.

Saturday turned out to be a hot sunny day and that delighted Robyn as it provided an excuse to wear a loose-fitting sundress. She was conscious of a slight bulge which Ellie was unlikely to notice but she felt Flora might be more perceptive and she didn't want to chance her seeing it. Soon, she would have to tell everybody and she wondered what David's parents would have to say about the news.

Robyn ensured that she had sufficient time to find Ellie's address and she arrived with fifteen minutes to spare. Holding her bag in front of her to conceal her small bump, she rang the doorbell and Ellie ran to the door to welcome her.

'Come in. You look fantastic as usual,' Ellie cried as she opened the door. 'That's a lovely dress. You look really pretty and summery.'

'Thanks,' she said, smiling sweetly at her.

As she stepped in, Flora appeared in the hall with a broad smile stretching from ear to ear. 'I'm happy you were able to come. Ellie might stop squawking for a while now. She's been so excited about your visit. I'm just making a nice pot of tea and Ellie has baked us a large custard tart.'

'That sounds very tempting Mrs. Johnstone.'

'Do call me Flora. I feel ancient when you call me Mrs. Johnstone.'

'I'll just run upstairs for my photos,' Ellie said. 'I won't be two minutes.'

'I'll fetch the tea-tray and we can all look at them together,' Flora stated. 'I'm dying to hear what you

216

thought of New York. Isn't it a wonderful place? It was our first time and there was so much to see and do. We could have done with a few more days.'

'I know; I said the very same thing to my sister. I enjoyed every minute of it and it was lovely to see Bryony again. I'm definitely planning another visit to see all the things I supposedly missed last time, though the way my sister rushed me around, I can't imagine I missed much. I even took the helicopter trip over the city.'

'Wasn't that incredible? We did that too. I hadn't been in a helicopter before so I was nervous at first but we thoroughly enjoyed it and the commentary was very good too....very clear.'

Before Flora left the room, Robyn asked, 'How's Ellie? Is she becoming a handful?'

'Surprisingly not,' she replied in a barely audible whisper. 'We're getting on very much better these days, all thanks to your intervention. She's having driving lessons now you know. She has a great deal more confidence now. Yes, Ellie's grown up a lot.'

'I wasn't aware she'd already started her driving lessons but I'm sure she would have told me today. I'm pleased everything's working out well. Mothers and daughters rarely see eye to eye about anything. I had more than my fair share of squabbles with my parents, especially my mother. I was still at school when David and I met and she was distraught when I wouldn't go to University because I didn't want to leave him. You'd never believe the rows it caused.'

'Oh, the fights *we* had at home when I was young, but mine were with my father! He used to chase the boys away from the front of the house,' she laughed heartily.

'Well I did hear it said that you were a bit wild!' Robyn made known with a wry smile.

'I was more than a *bit* wild dear but that's another story,' she whispered. 'I'll get the tea.'

When Ellie reappeared with the photographs, they passed them round and recalled happy memories of their trip, reliving all those special moments they'd enjoyed.

'Look, there's a lovely one of you Robyn in your polka dot sun-dress and here's a really good one of Raine. Doesn't he have an infectious smile? He's so handsome isn't he? He's joining us later for lunch,' she announced matter-of-factly.

As Robyn strove to maintain her composure at the shock revelation, Ellie explained, 'I *was* intending to surprise you but I wasn't able to keep it to myself any longer. It will be just like old times....the three of us together. He called me earlier in the week and when I told him you were coming today, he said it would be nice for all three of us to meet for lunch, assuming he could get a sitter for his children. I told him where we were going and he called back later to say he'd be there too so we're seeing him around two o'clock. Isn't that great? I was ever so thrilled Raine could make it as well. I bet you're surprised aren't you?'

'Yes I am but that means we won't get very much shopping done,' she struggled to reply indifferently while inwardly, she was anxious about the feelings such a meeting might evoke.

'Robyn, you're not eating your custard pie,' Flora remarked.

'Sorry, I was totally absorbed in the photographs. It's delicious.'

'It's Bill's favourite. He has a very sweet....'

'It's my favourite as well,' Ellie interjected, 'Now that I'm allowed to eat it, that is!'

'I was merely being cautious Ellie. Everything I said or did was with good intent. Maybe I *did* go a little overboard at times.'

'Mum....you drowned!' she replied on a laugh. 'I eat pretty-well anything now and nothing seems to disagree with me.'

'I shall if you don't stop your lip Madam!' Flora warned her. 'That was the door. It'll be Bill.'

Following the usual pleasantries between Bill and Robyn, the two girls left for the town centre where they scoured the shops until the time came to meet up with Raine for lunch.

Robyn felt apprehensive as she fixed her make-up and brushed her long hair. Standing sideways, she looked at her reflection in the full-length mirror to ensure there were no tell-tale signs before returning to Ellie. She felt nauseous at the thought that in just a few moments, Raine would be sitting only inches away from his unborn child and he could never be allowed to know her secret.

'I'm famished,' Ellie grumbled, glancing towards the door. 'I wish he'd hurry up. I do hope he hasn't forgotten. I was looking forward to seeing him.'

'Perhaps he couldn't get a sitter after all,' Robyn answered optimistically.

At two fifteen Raine appeared in view and Robyn suddenly felt very tearful. He walked towards them, holding his gaze on Robyn's face until he arrived at their table. 'Ellie! How lovely is this?' he declared, hugging her tightly and kissing her on both cheeks. 'I'm so pleased to see you again.'

Then, turning his attention to Robyn he remarked frostily, 'What can I say? This rendezvous was so unexpected that I couldn't possibly have ignored an opportunity to speak to you. Incidentally, I have to say you look radiant, as usual.'

He made no attempt to hug her nor did he kiss her before taking his seat. 'I apologise for my tardiness. There was an accident on the motorway and a lane had to be closed. Isn't that tiresome? I was hoping I wouldn't miss you again,' he said looking pointedly at Robyn who recognized an unambiguous element of sarcasm in his voice.

Robyn wanted to cry out, 'But I searched for you Raine...I searched for you everywhere. I wanted to find you....I wanted to say I was sorry....I wanted to make everything right between us.'

Robyn's thoughts were abruptly curtailed by Ellie who smiled and chirped jovially, 'It doesn't matter Raine. I know you had quite a distance to travel and we haven't been here very long. It's not a problem is it Robyn?'

'Of course not,' she answered, her head buried in the menu to avoid Raine's piercing stare.

'Can we order now?' Ellie asked. 'I'm ravenous. I think I'm having the roast beef. What do you fancy Raine?'

Again, he stared intently at Robyn. 'Now there's a question,' he said cynically without even opening his menu. 'I'll have the same Ellie.'

'Me too,' Robyn added, turning away.

'Order mine for me please and I'd like a glass of white wine too. I want to wash my hands before we eat,' Ellie said.

Ever the gentleman, Raine stood up as Ellie arose and scraping his chair along the floor noisily, he sat down again as she left.

Several seconds elapsed before Raine spoke. 'Tell me why, Robyn! Just tell me....why?'

'Why what? I don't understand what you mean,' she prevaricated, mindful of the colour rising in her cheeks.

'Don't treat me like an idiot. You know perfectly well what I mean. Why did you leave the ship without saying goodbye?'

'Please don't do this Raine. It wasn't like that at all,' she replied, twisting her crystal pendant around in her fingers as she was accustomed to doing when feeling distressed or nervous.

'Answer me this then. When did you learn I'd be here today?'

'An hour or so ago when I first arrived at Ellie's.'

'Would you have come today had you known?'

'I'm here, aren't I?'

'I only asked because you're wearing the pendant I bought you. Tell me, were you wearing that when you left home or did you purposely put it on when you found out I'd be here, just to appease me?' he enquired with sarcasm ringing in his voice.

221

'I never take it off. I've worn it from the day you gave it to me. It's beautiful....and so was your card.'

'But nevertheless you left the ship without saying goodbye to me.'

'I know you won't believe this but I *did* look for you and I couldn't find you. That's the truth.'

He sneered contemptuously. 'I was standing near the disembarkation point for ages so you didn't try very hard did you?'

'Yes, I did. You must have left just before I did. I saw you in the distance. I saw you with your son in your arms, then you climbed into a taxi and left.'

'You broke my heart Robyn. I thought we meant more to each other than a one-night-stand but I was so wrong.'

'I can't explain it to you here Raine. Ellie will be back shortly but you deserve a proper explanation and then, maybe you'll understand my reasons for doing what I did.'

'It doesn't matter now. It's over so forget about it. The reason I came today was to give you a piece of my mind. Do you know how much it hurt me when Ellie said you wouldn't permit her to give me your phone number?'

'It wasn't like that. I asked her not to give *anyone* my number.'

'Oh, credit me with some intelligence for Christ's sake. Don't patronise me as if I were some half-wit. Who the hell else would Ellie give your number to? She doesn't know anybody else who knows you! If you can't be honest with me Robyn, I might as well leave now. I'm already starting to believe it would have been better had I not bothered to come today. You have the unhappy knack of bringing the worst out in me. I should have had more sense and stayed away.'

'Please don't leave Raine. I'll tell Ellie I have to leave at four o'clock, and I'll meet you back here at four-thirty and we'll discuss everything when we're alone. You can at least let me explain. You owe me that.'

'From where I'm sitting, I owe you nothing at all, but out of idle curiosity, if nothing else, I *will* listen to what you have to say as I've nothing better to do with my time. When all said and done, it's not as if I have an overflowing social diary, so four-thirty it is then.'

'Ellie has been looking forward to this reunion so much Raine. Please don't say or do anything to ruin it for her. This is our argument, not hers.'

Robyn detected a slight grunt. 'Alright, for Ellie's sake I'll try my best but don't expect too much. All I wanted was a civil goodbye from you and you hid yourself away.'

'You're right; I did. At first I couldn't bear to see you but then I really did try to find you.'

The waiter arrived with his notepad. 'Would you care to order Sir?'

'Yes, we'd all like the roast beef please and may I also order one glass of white wine, half a lager and what would you like Robyn?'

'Water please,' she advised the waiter.

As the waiter left, Ellie returned. 'Have I missed anything interesting?' she asked.

'No, not a thing. We were making small talk until you returned,' Raine answered. 'So how have you been Ellie? Are you keeping well?'

'Yes, I'm very well thank you. I've been having driving lessons with my dad.'

'Good for you. How's it going? I don't think I'd like to be learning to drive again these days.'

'I don't seem to have enough hands and feet,' she giggled.

'How's the job-hunting progressing? Is there anything that takes your fancy yet?' Robyn asked.

'I've been to sign on but they haven't been able to find me anything. There's not much work available where we live and until I can drive, it's difficult to find a job but mum's been teaching me how to cook and I enjoy that. I'd made that custard tart we had when you arrived,' she announced proudly.

'And it was delicious too,' Robyn told her.

'Well, food's the best way to a man's heart Ellie,' Raine informed her. 'You'll make some young man a good wife before too long. If I weren't married, I might well proposition you myself. You are also a beautiful young woman *and* dependable I dare say, which is more than can be said about many young women these days!' he added, glaring at Robyn.

Ellie's face was scarlet and she giggled, covering her face with her serviette.

'Pack it in Raine. You're embarrassing the poor girl,' Robyn chastised. 'Take no notice of him Ellie and there are hundreds of much younger and much better-looking men than Raine to choose from when that time comes.'

Raine burst into laughter at her remark. 'Robyn's right I'm afraid and I'm far too serious for my own good. Where's that food we ordered?' he said, looking around. 'I'm famished. I've had nothing to eat yet today.'

'He's coming over now,' Ellie told him and after the waiter had placed each of the plates before them she added, 'Bon appétit!'

'Multi-lingual too! Is there no end to your talents Ellie?' he asked.

'Shut up Raine,' she muttered on another giggle.

Raine glanced at his watch at the end of the meal and made his excuses to leave. It was three-thirty. 'I have to get back for the children,' he told Ellie who looked disappointed at the proclamation of his early departure. 'We must be sure to do this again....soon. I've enjoyed it very much. Moreover, I'm depriving you of valuable shopping time and that would never do would it?'

'I've eaten far too much to even think about more shopping,' Robyn remarked. 'I shall be leaving too very shortly but it's been great. I'd like to avoid the rush hour traffic. We'll definitely do it again,' she advised Ellie.

Raine summoned the waiter for the bill which he promptly settled with his plastic.

'Close your purse Ellie. This is on me. I might not be the best-looking man in the world, though that's only Robyn's opinion *and* debatable,' he remarked light-heartedly, 'but I was taught from a very early age how to behave properly and old habits die hard, at least with me they do.'

His remark was lost on Ellie but Robyn was quick to realise it was yet one more snipe at her when she caught his eye.

'Goodbye Ellie....or I should say *au revoir*? I'll be in touch soon,' he said, leaning over and kissing her on the cheek. 'You take good care of yourself and I wish you good luck with the job-hunting. Please be sure to pass on my regards to your parents.'

Turning to Robyn, he added coldly, 'Robyn, what can I say? It's been a pleasure,' and he stretched out his arm to shake her hand.

Though she felt insulted and enraged by his most insensitive gesture, she bit her tongue and, smiling nicely, she ignored his hand and merely responded, 'Goodbye Raine and thank you for lunch.'

Raine turned on his heels and left the restaurant, leaving Robyn with a feeling of total rejection. She collected her bags and said, 'Come on. I'll drop you off at home Ellie.'

'There's no need. A bus stops outside which takes me right to the door.'

'Are you sure?'

'I'm positive. It doesn't take many minutes and it will give you an earlier start on the road. I've really enjoyed our reunion. It was great for the three of us to meet up again. It revived happy memories of our trip. Raine's lovely isn't he?'

'Yes he is,' she replied unemotionally. 'I'll give you a call next week Ellie. Take care.'

She walked briskly towards the car park, feeling hurt and humiliated. It was blatantly obvious to her that Raine would now be on his way home. He had never had any intention of meeting her later to hear what she had to say to him. He had turned up at the restaurant for one reason and one reason alone. This had been pay-back time.

She loaded her shopping into the boot of her car and slammed down the lid heavily. On the verge of tears she stood silently for a few minutes, breathing heavily. How dare he expect her to shake his hand? She was carrying his child and he had acted totally without compassion *and* he'd had the effrontery to claim *he* knew how to behave! She had offered to provide him with the explanation he so rightly deserved and yet he had both shunned and humiliated her in Ellie's presence.

A hot trickle ran down her cheeks as tears flowed from her eyes and she began to sob so hard that she heard nothing until Raine appeared behind her and wrapped his arms around her.

'Robyn, I'm so very sorry. Forgive me please,' he pleaded with troubled eyes. 'I hate myself for those awful things I said to you in the restaurant. The fact I was hurt is no excuse. I've behaved abominably. I've no idea what you're hiding from me but I think it's time you told me. For both our sakes we have to talk Robyn. I need you to explain everything to me because this is tearing me apart.'

'I know I've hurt you Raine but my pain is just as bad as, if not worse than yours,' she sobbed. 'I only did what I believed was right and I believed that a clean break was best for both of us and when I read the words in your card I knew it was right to have sent you away that night as I wouldn't have had the fortitude or courage to have done so the next day. I had the same feelings for you.'

She removed a tissue from a pack in her bag and blew her nose. 'That was one of the most difficult things I'd ever had to do. I was in agony too Raine. I had feelings for you that I had no right to have. I was bewildered, I was scared and above all I didn't want to hurt you, truly I didn't. Hand on heart, I'm speaking the truth.'

'You aren't making any sense to me. Why don't you start from the beginning? I'm not in any hurry to leave. My car's parked over there. Let's at least be comfortable.'

She wiped her tear-stained face as he escorted her to his car.

'Promise to let me explain everything without any interruption,' she said. 'This is very difficult for me and there's a lot to explain and above all I need you to understand my reasons for doing what I did.'

'I promise. Just take your time,' Raine murmured with a warm comforting smile as they sat down side by side in his car.

Robyn took a deep breath. 'When I was eighteen, I married a boy I loved passionately. We were soulmates, and as time went by, the only thing missing from our lives was a child. David, my husband was anxious to start a family as soon as possible. He had nephews he adored and wanted a child of his own, in fact both of us did. There was nothing clinically wrong with either one of us, yet for some unknown reason, it just never happened. A year or two later, we travelled the rocky road of IVF treatment; each time that failed too. David was desperate for a child and so the repetitive failures had a somewhat prejudicial effect on our marriage, mainly because I was ready to abandon the treatment. We still loved each other very much but my health due to the treatment, was driving me to despair and I believed that David could have been more supportive in my corner as I was the one feeling so wretched, so that led to one or two minor arguments and he began to stay late at the office, clearly to avoid anything confrontational at home.'

She glanced at Raine and without uttering a word he gave her a reassuring smile and nodded his head for her to continue.

'I wasn't aware at the time, but my husband had confided in a woman at the office about the habitual IVF failures and she, to her own advantage used his distress as a means of taking him from me and they embarked on an affair which was merely an outlet for David's frustration....just a temporary diversion. When he eventually came to his senses and tried to end the liaison, that devious woman tricked David into believing she was pregnant with his child and he was devastated as he didn't want to abandon his child, nor did he want me to suffer as a result of his infidelity.'

Raine took Robyn's hand in his and held it tight.

'David wrote me a letter explaining everything in detail. He wrote that he loved me and that to spare my feelings, he was leaving me,' she sniffled as she wiped away the tears that flowed from her eyes. 'I discovered the letter a matter of hours after he had left with the other woman and a little while after the police had arrived at my home to tell me that David and his female passenger had both been killed in a road traffic accident earlier that afternoon. That was the first I knew of the affair. I was unable to contain my grief as I truly believed that had David confided in me, we'd have been able to work things out.'

She took a deep breath and dried her eyes before continuing. 'The funeral was agonizing and it later emerged there was to be a criminal trial as a drunk-driver had allegedly been responsible for the tragic accident. I just found everything too much to bear so I decided to visit my sister for a few days in New York. I needed to get right away from everyone and following the funeral on the Tuesday, I boarded the QE2 for New York on the Friday and you know the rest. That's how I came to meet you Raine....just a few days after my husband's funeral. We were both vulnerable because you had horrendous problems at home and I'd just lost my husband. After we spent the night together, I couldn't defend what I'd done. On reflection it seemed so immoral and that's why I called a halt to any further involvement but I knew in my heart I had feelings for you - strong feelings; it was incomprehensible. I wasn't ready for another man in my life; I would never be ready for that, or so I believed, besides which, you weren't available. I'd been on the receiving end of the consequences of an extra-marital affair; I loathed that woman responsible for David's death, yet I was no better. I'd slept with you, a married man, and my mind was in turmoil. To end it right there was the only course of action to follow, I told myself. So there you have it, my explanation for my behaviour on the ship.'

'My poor darling. Why on earth didn't you talk to me about it?'

'Everything between us happened so quickly and unexpectedly. You'd told me about your wife and I suppose I felt we shared a common ground but had I stopped to think for a moment, I would have realised I didn't want another man; I wanted *my* man; I wanted David,' she sighed. 'Afterwards, I couldn't figure out my emotions because then I wanted you too and it scared me. I never wanted to hurt you but I felt so guilty at having betrayed my husband that I tried to rid you from my thoughts....but I couldn't. That final morning when I left my room, I hid like a coward at the front of the ship. I knew you'd come looking for me and I couldn't bear to see the pained expression on your face that I'd seen the previous night but later, I knew I had to find you and I tried so hard but you'd already left ahead of me. When I finally found you, you were too far away. You were tossing your son in the air and twirling round with him in your arms and you looked radiantly happy. It broke my heart to watch you drive away because I thought I'd never see you again.'

'But you had my phone number. You could have given me a call. I had no means of contacting you or I would have done.'

'I know but I thought it would have been too late then. Besides, as soon as I got to my sister's place, I burst into tears and told her what had happened and she made me promise not to make contact with you for three months so I'd be sure of my true feelings. I even marked the date on my calendar as soon as I arrived home because I knew I'd still feel the same then. The date was the ninth of July.'

'That was several days ago so why didn't you call me?'

'I haven't felt very well recently and on the fourth of July I went to see my doctor. I'm sorry....there's no easy way to say this. I'm pregnant with David's child.'

Raine's mouth fell open in total disbelief before he rested his head in his hands and sighed. 'Christ, I don't believe what I'm hearing. Are you absolutely certain? Are you sure there can be no mistake?'

'Am I sure it's David's baby? Yes, I'm certain,' she lied. 'The dates don't fit for us.'

'I didn't mean that. I meant, is there a possibility you're not pregnant? Christ, I don't know what I'm saying because I don't know what I mean anymore. I'm clutching at straws here. Say something to help me out Robyn.'

'I can't Raine but let's consider the facts. Perhaps everything has turned out for the best, considering your circumstances too though it's rather ironical it should happen at this point in time, especially after all the years we were trying but at least we can say goodbye properly now without ill-feeling. I'll never forget you and I wish you every happiness in your future life.'

She turned her head to avoid the grief in his eyes.

He took hold of her hand. 'You have my number so will you give me a call from time to time, just so

I know how you are?' he asked with an optimistic smile.

'No, I can't Raine....one of us needs to be strong. It'll only cause more heartache. We both have very difficult lives ahead.'

He sighed heavily. 'I suppose you're right Robyn. So, if that's the end of us, then I'd like to wish you a long and happy life. Take care of your baby and I hope he or she brings you great joy. Children are so precious and I hope your baby becomes heir to your very special qualities. You're amazing Robyn and I won't ever forget you. May I please have one final kiss of friendship?' he questioned longingly.

She smiled through her tears as he took her in his arms and savoured the moment as he kissed her lips gently before releasing her.

'This really is a final goodbye Robyn,' he said in a faltering voice.

Fighting back the tears she murmured quietly, 'It is, I'm afraid. Goodbye Raine.' With a watery smile she left and hurried to her car.

Barely three months had passed by since David's death and another significant chapter in her life had come to an abrupt end. Would there ever be an end to her anguish though? Would she ever again be the happy, carefree young woman she had been until a few short months ago? Only time would tell.

8

'Well, if you ask me, I think it's a ludicrous idea,' Abbie told her. 'So does Gerald. He's all for private enterprise but the project you're about to embark on could only be described as crazy and ill-conceived, considering your present circumstances. I think you should get your head examined.'

Robyn glared at her. 'I *didn't* ask you so *butt out*,' she said heatedly. 'If and when I want your opinion I'll ask for it. It isn't a spur of the moment decision. I've been considering it for weeks.'

'Well, I wish you'd given *me* some consideration as well. How am I going to run the business without you there?'

Robyn sighed with irritation. 'Everything doesn't revolve around you Abbie. In case you've forgotten there are *two* partners in the business, you and *me,* and this is about what *I* want and I want out! Your future life with Gerald is mapped out whereas mine isn't and I'm slowly trying to rebuild my shattered life by doing something I want to do. How on earth could I come to work every day with a young baby? You can't answer that, can you? Just be reasonable Abbie. Martha Pipper is ideal to take my place and more than capable of running the management side of the business. She's done that kind of work all her life. Believe me, what she doesn't know isn't worth knowing and she outshone all other applicants.'

'Well you've hit the nail on the head there, *all her life*! Why, she must be fifty if she's a day *and* she's a boring old f....'

'Actually, Martha's forty-five, single and likely to remain so,' Robyn cut in sharply. 'That's the reason I gave her the job, so less of the bad language. I'm quite sure you'd prefer someone reliable as opposed to some fly-by-night who'll spend most of her time off sick following drunken nights out. You'd never find anyone who's more reliable and conscientious. Once you get to know her properly, like I do, you'll thank me for taking her on.'

'Right, well answer me this. Why did she have to leave her previous post where she'd been employed for donkey's years when rated as indispensable?'

'Alright I'll tell you but you mustn't let it slip that you know. I gave her my word. It was nothing to do with her work. When her previous manager retired, she didn't get on with the new bloke. He was one of those ghastly touchy-feely guys who was constantly grabbing hold of her.'

Abbie collapsed in hysterical laughter. 'Get real! Tell me you're having me on! What was his guide dog called?'

'Don't be mean. She can't help how she looks.'

'When I learned her surname was Pipper, I nearly wet myself because she puts me in mind of a small pipistrelle bat with her petite stature, widely-spaced dark beady eyes and that horrible chestnut-coloured tufty hair.'

Robyn grinned. 'I suppose I can't argue with you there. She definitely wasn't on the front row when looks were dished out but she's thrifty and was in a position to provide the finance for a partnership if required. You never know, if she's suitable following her trial period and when Gerald gets around to popping the question, Martha might want to buy out your half too. She's obviously worth a few bob and you certainly won't want to carry on working once you're married to Gerald. It could be a good move for you.'

'Huh, by the time *he* pops the question, I reckon Martha will be six feet under and I'll doubtless be drawing my pension. I'm not holding my breath for Gerald's proposal. It's still a question of once bitten twice shy with him I think. I'm really going to miss you Robyn. Things will never be the same again at the office. I can see why you have to move forward with your life and I'm not trying to pick a fight with you. I'm thinking about you and the baby, living in total isolation. It's nothing at all to do with Martha Pipper. Alright, I won't be able to enjoy the smutty giggles with her like I do with you but I know she'll be fine. I'm simply clutching at straws because I'd hate you to make an error of judgment.'

Sighing with exasperation she said, 'For goodness sake will you drop it? It's not as if I'm going to the moon.'

Abbie was determined to prolong the discussion. 'You might as well be and what sort of place will it be for a small child? She has no say in the matter. She'll have no friends to play with. It'll be a terrible life for a kid. Have you given *any* serious thought to your child's welfare?'

'Well you got that bit right. She's *my* child, so I'll decide what's in her best interests until she's of an age to make her own choices.'

236

'She's not even born yet so what are you going to do when you go into labour and you're stuck in the middle of a muddy field, miles from anywhere?'

'I'll do exactly the same as everyone else! I'll use the telephone! I've wanted to do something like this as long as I can remember so now I have the chance to fulfil my dream, I intend doing that and no one is going to talk me out of it, especially you and Gerald so save your breath. David never showed the slightest interest in my dream but he's no longer here, so I'll do as I please and for your information Abbie, not that I have to justify my actions to you, it's less than a mile to the nearest village, only a few miles from Kidsgrove and there's a farmhouse right next door, so there might be children there. Other people do it and they manage alright.'

'They're brought up to it. They're hardy. Think of the winters!'

'I've considered *every* aspect. I love animals and it's my choice. If things don't work out as planned I can sell it. You've never given me a single word of support since I first mentioned it to you. I spent two days there to get the feel of the place and I enjoyed every second.'

'A whole two days? Wow!' she scorned in irony. 'Then you're very easily satisfied....that's all I can say.'

'Thank heaven for that. I thought you were going to carry on badgering me all day.'

Abbie laughed. 'You're such an aggravating b....'

'Hush....not in front of the baby,' she interrupted, patting her bump.

237

'I can't imagine what David would have to say if he were here.'

'If David were here, we wouldn't be having this conversation because I wouldn't be doing it would I? Anyway it'll be fun, running Boarding Kennels and a Cattery.'

'*Fun*? Seventy dogs and seventy cats barking and squawking? You'll never sleep a wink! Think of all the exercise the dogs will need every day, the food they'll all eat and the owners too-ing and fro-ing all the time. You'll never have a minute's peace….and who's going to do all the cleaning up after them?'

'As you're well aware, there's a full quota of staff and they're all staying on. Besides, what other kind of option would I have as a single parent? *I* want to take care of my child. I'd never consider putting her in a nursery, so I needed to find a suitable business where I could raise a child.'

'You don't need to work. You can afford to be at home taking care of your baby. David left you well provided for. You're a wealthy woman and only the other day, Gerald was telling me that the Insurance Company….'

Angrily she interrupted, 'Gerald has no right to be discussing any of my financial affairs with you. I'm his client!'

'We're your *friends* Robyn. We're merely trying to look out for you.'

'Then why don't you help me instead of throwing obstacles in my way all the time? You're not going to change my mind so try to be constructive instead of being negative every time you open your mouth.'

238

Abbie decided she had said enough on the matter. Robyn was determined to go ahead and nothing she said would dissuade her. Moreover, she didn't want to jeopardise their friendship.

They continued to separate the rubbish from the items to be packed and when Abbie removed a box from the top of Robyn's wardrobe and asked, 'Are you keeping this?' she was quick to reply, 'Oh yes, don't throw that out. Put it over there with the other boxes please.'

Robyn hadn't looked inside the box since she had sealed Raine's photograph in its envelope and put it away with his birthday card. She wondered how he was managing at home and whether his demanding lifestyle had improved in any way. At least she was in a position where she could move on and make a fresh start.

When the ultra-sound scan had revealed she was having a girl, Robyn was at first disappointed. She had prayed for a boy who would be the image of his father but when she gave the matter further thought, she then realised that with a daughter, no one would ever suspect that David wasn't the father. That fact could never be disclosed to a living soul, especially when the additional insurance claim for her child's future financial needs had been instantly submitted by Gerald, following the trial.

The day of sentencing had been a harrowing day of mixed feelings for her. The young fellow in the dock had expressed deep remorse with tears in his eyes. He had come across as an honest, respectable young man and when he was sentenced to six years imprisonment, his wife and parents broke down and wept.

The loathing she had earlier felt towards him had melted away when he looked at her with deep sadness and regret in his eyes. He had been barely over the alcohol limit and Robyn wondered whether the fatal accident would still have occurred had he been sober. His defence had rested on the fact that when he had pulled out to overtake another car, David's car had been in the blind spot of his mirror but the judge had been relentless in his sentencing, stating he had cost two people their lives, bringing untold anguish to their families and the custodial sentence would serve as a serious warning to all drivers that drink-driving laws must be respected and adhered to by everyone.

The Inquest that ensued was no more than a paper exercise by the County Coroner who had followed the Crown Court's findings and so at last, Robyn's nightmare was drawing to a close as Gerald awaited the final payout from both Insurance Companies.

From David's insurer, she had already received a more than adequate interim payment, enabling her to property-hunt for a suitable business. It had also provided the means to negotiate a lesser price as a cash buyer for the business she agreed to buy from an elderly couple, anxious for early completion and who were retiring to Spain.

Gerald had ensured that all requisite licensing and additional legal requirements were satisfied before giving her the all clear to proceed and the transfer of the property took place within a couple of weeks.

Remarkably, her house had been sold to the first viewers, a young couple and who were cash buyers.

As the completion date approached, Robyn felt a certain sadness as she made her final preparations to depart from the house she and David had shared but that chapter of her life had ended and she had to move on. Clinging to past memories was no longer an option that appealed to her.

She was approaching the seventh month into her pregnancy when the move to Staffordshire finally took place.

Very soon, she would be giving birth to Raine's daughter and she hoped and prayed the baby would arrive a couple of weeks early. A late arrival would undoubtedly give rise to suspicion since David had been killed almost three weeks before the baby had been conceived. The date of birth had to be credible when weighed against all other factors.

Robyn had been thrust into this situation, not by choice, but rather by Gerald's persistence that she *take the Insurer to the cleaners*, something that she hadn't wanted to do. For her to utter a deliberate lie to Raine, her family and her friends when passing off her unborn child as David's was a terrible thing, but to commit serious fraud was a different matter. There and then, she vowed that once this was over she would never again speak a lie and she would do everything in her power to make sure that her child would likewise be truthful and honest, despite what the consequences might be. Her baby's given name would be *Verity*, a forename Robyn had especially selected meaning *truth*, and she would be advised and encouraged from an early age to live up to her important forename and make her way through life with integrity and honesty.

Once again, her mother's all too familiar dictum was at the very forefront of her thoughts. '*Oh what a tangled web we weave....*'

9

Verity Elizabeth Ainsley arrived on Christmas day nineteen-ninety-seven, weighing in at eight pounds exactly and she was a beautiful baby.

Abbie was in attendance during the final stages of the birth which occurred just a few minutes before midnight, making it the one and only arrival on the maternity unit that day and she rushed out excitedly to tell Gerald who was pacing the floor anxiously as he awaited news in the reception area.

'Come on Gerald....you're allowed in now to see Verity and she's absolutely gorgeous,' she told him breathlessly. 'She weighed eight pounds. Can you believe that?'

He grinned as Abbie tugged at his hand excitedly. 'That's wonderful news and on Christmas Day too. Are mother and baby both doing well, as the saying goes?'

'Perfect,' she gabbled. 'Come on, she's waiting to show off her new baby to you.'

'Hang on! Before we go in, have you told Robyn *our* news yet? I don't want to let the cat out of the bag.'

'No, I haven't found the right moment but I'll tell her soon. Keep it under wraps for the time being.'

Gerald beamed with delight on entering the room to see Robyn with her baby in her arms. He studied the tiny miracle and sighed, 'She's delightful. She's perfect in every way. How do you feel Robyn?'

Wiping beads of perspiration from her brow, she laughed. 'I feel much better than I did ten minutes ago when I was convinced somebody was trying to turn me inside out! No one tells you things like that at the ante-natal clinic.'

'Good heavens, are you serious? Was it really as bad as that?' Abbie questioned with concern.

'Er....what's with the pained expression? Is there something you're not telling me? Come on....spit it out. Don't keep me in suspense.'

'You might as well get her told!' Gerald laughed. 'You know she reads you like a book so she'll drag it out of you!'

Abbie didn't need to speak the words. The broad grin on her face answered Robyn's question.

Robyn was delighted. 'Oh Abbie, Gerald....I'm so thrilled for you both. How long have you known?'

'Only three weeks. I wanted to give it a bit longer before mentioning it to anyone,' she replied with an even broader smile.

'Well I'm surprised at you Gerald,' Robyn teased. 'You're always so pernickety about every detail but you've got this the wrong way round haven't you? You're supposed to get married first and *then* have the baby, so when's the happy day?' she asked him, winking at Abbie.

He shuffled his feet uncomfortably. 'Er....I don't know. We haven't discussed it yet,' he said, staring at the floor. 'There are many things to consider. It's a tricky question to ask without due consideration.'

'What's difficult about that? It's only four words Gerald,' Robyn retorted scathingly. 'What I've just gone through was a hell of a sight harder than that and you spend more time at Abbie's house than you do at yours so for God's sake, what's the problem? Just stop behaving like a useless wimp and get her asked. You don't pussy-foot about when you're in Court; you get straight to the point. You know you want to marry her. You've told *me* often enough so tell Abbie and stop procrastinating, especially now she's pregnant.'

There were still several staff members present and each waited for his response with bated breath.

In the realisation that everyone was attentive, he cleared his throat and taking hold of Abbie's hand, he asked soberly, 'Abbie, would you please do me the honour of becoming my wife?'

'Oh, I will Gerald. There's nothing I want more,' she screeched as she threw herself into his arms and kissed him lovingly.

Everyone in the delivery room gave a loud cheer and applauded heartily except for baby Verity who was content to sleep serenely in her mother's arms.

'I'd like you to know that I *would* have got round to asking you in due course,' he assured her. 'It was merely a matter of selecting an appropriate time and venue, conducive to the formality of the occasion,' he added with an earnest expression.

'Oh shut up,' Abbie said and Robyn howled with laughter. 'Can't you step outside the courtroom for a single moment? I don't want to be subjected to all your pretentious legal verbosity and litigious terminology. I simply want to hear you say you love me and that you'd like us to get hitched.'

He smiled affectionately at her and then, turning his attention to Robyn he winked. 'Okay, let's have a go then though I'm not very good at this. I'm nuts about you Babe and I wanna tie the knot. How are you fixed? Does that dig you?'

Laughter tears sparkled brightly in her eyes. 'On second thoughts, I believe I *do* prefer the stiff and starchy version of Gerald Dunne,' she giggled and Robyn nodded to show her wholehearted agreement as Abbie continued, 'and a hospital delivery ward is as equally romantic and fitting as any other venue Gerald, no matter how the proposal is worded.'

With an austere air he cleared his throat. 'I have to say however that the wedding won't be for some time. I have an exceptionally demanding workload at present.'

When Abbie replied with a withering glance, he promptly rejoined, 'Well, perhaps not *too* long, in fact I have a suggestion....why don't the two of you arrange everything? Send me a fax with the details and I'll nip out of Court for ten minutes.'

'I'm going to kill him when we get out of here,' she told Robyn.

He pondered thoughtfully before replying, 'Come to think of it, that might be the better option, since I've just been brow-beaten into my being formally institutionalised for the remainder of my days.'

'Ouch!' Robyn cut in and tittered. 'I'm quite sure you'll live to regret saying that Gerald.'

'Oh, he will!' Abbie verified. 'He definitely will!'

Gerald expelled a short burst of laughter. 'I think that's my cue to leave. Come on Abbie; let's be on our way. It's well past midnight and Robyn needs to rest now.' Turning to Robyn he said, 'You have a delightful daughter and you'll make a wonderful mother. We're both very happy for you.'

'And you'll make a wonderful husband. Thanks for everything you've both done for me and I'd like to apologise for ruining your Christmas!'

'Don't talk so daft!' Abbie exclaimed. 'What on earth could have been better than this on Christmas Day? It's a day I'll never forget....a beautiful baby for you and a proposal of marriage for me. We can have a turkey dinner any day of the week.'

Robyn reflected on Abbie's parting remark as she cradled her baby lovingly. She was right. Nothing in the whole world could have been better than this on Christmas Day.

She closed her tearful eyes, trying to bring forth an image of Raine in her mind before whispering, 'Thank you darling for your truly amazing gift and on Christmas Day too. I'm so sorry you can't share in my joy but you'll remain in my thoughts forever. I hope you and your boys enjoy Christmas too.'

Over the following few weeks, Robyn developed a workable routine around Verity.

She had handed the general management duties to Andrew Williamson, a university student, who was taking a gap year to raise fees for the accountancy course he was planning to take, following his recent graduation in Business Studies and who had proved an invaluable asset to the business.

He was methodical and thorough, thus affording Robyn the necessary time to devote to Verity at that very demanding time and for that she was grateful.

Verity was a placid and happy-natured baby who rarely cried or sought attention and Robyn believed she was well and truly blessed to have given birth to such a perfect little girl who filled the void in her otherwise empty life.

David's parents had fallen in love with her from the first moment they saw her and in many respects, she had compensated for the loss of their son.

'Look Robyn, she has David's eyes,' his mother had announced and Robyn had felt obliged to direct her gaze elsewhere because of her guilt at the cruel deception though as the weeks passed by, she began to believe that the lie was, to a great extent, justifiable for the joy Verity had brought into their lives, though she felt sorrow for Raine who would never be acquainted with his daughter.

Earlier that week, Ellie had telephoned to say she had passed her driving test and she wanted to drive over to see Verity, who she had last seen when she was just two days old.

'If you're not doing anything on your birthday, I could come then,' she suggested. 'It'll only take me fifteen minutes to drive to your place, dad says.'

Robyn was thrilled at the prospect of seeing Ellie and there might also be news about Raine she could coax out of her were she to structure her questions carefully. Enthusiastically she cried, 'Yes, it would be terrific to see you again. We can catch up on all the news. Be sure to miss the potholes in the lane. I keep meaning to get them seen to. You'll see a big change in Verity; she's altered a lot since your last visit. Try to be here in time for lunch. If I look carefully, I'll be sure to find some chicken or fish in the freezer,' she laughed.

'Very funny! As a matter of fact, I'd like chicken for a change. Mum rarely gives it me anymore since we had the big bust up on the ship. She's gone from one extreme to the other.'

Robyn found that hilarious. 'How is your mum?'

'She's fine, though she gets a bit worked up when I take the car out alone and she's a right pain in the butt when we're out together. She's the proverbial back-seat-driver. She assumes I can't see the traffic lights or the vehicles that are overtaking me! By the way, on the subject of mum, she was asking when you were going to bring Verity to see her.'

'I will in a week or two. Meanwhile, please give my fond regards to both your parents and I'll look forward to seeing you on Wednesday.'

Ellie turned up on the Wednesday looking flustered and apologised for being late. 'I took a wrong turn and got lost and when I turned the car round, I went wrong again and the track simply disappeared. Had it not been for a young man walking some dogs, I wouldn't have been here yet. I was so embarrassed because the dogs became irritable when he stopped to help me. They twisted their leads around both his legs and he almost fell over and it was all my fault.'

'I wouldn't worry about it. You're here now and you'll know next time, so give me your coat and go through to the living room. Verity's sound asleep in her cot so please try not to wake her and we can eat our lunch in peace while you tell me all your news.'

Ellie was peering into the small crib when Robyn returned. 'I can't believe how much Verity's grown over the past few weeks,' she remarked. 'She looks like a little girl now, not a little baby. Happy birthday Robyn,' she added, handing her a parcel and a card.

'Thank you Ellie,' Robyn replied, tearing off the wrapping paper. 'How beautiful,' she gasped as she removed a pretty silk scarf and draped it around her neck. 'I love the feel of a silk scarf. I have a few but I don't have one in these lovely colours.'

'Do you recall last year's birthday when we were on the QE2? You had the dates mixed up and you thought your birthday fell on the next day.'

'How could I forget that?' she replied with hidden thoughts as she twisted the crystal pendant between her fingers while bringing to mind the man who had given it to her. 'I don't suppose you've heard from Raine since the three of us went out for lunch?' she enquired casually.

'He called four or five weeks ago but I didn't like to mention it in front of mum when I was talking to you. He asked about you and he wanted to know if your baby had been born, so I *can* be discreet when I need to be.'

'I'm sure I don't know what you're insinuating by that remark,' Robyn stated defensively, her face red as fire.

'Come on Robyn, I might be a little naïve but I'm not stupid. I've seen the way he looks at you. Why do you think I did a disappearing act when we went out for lunch? It was obvious to a blind man there was something between you. When we were on the ship, he never took his eyes off you.'

'He's married Ellie. I told him I wouldn't see him again and that's why he was looking for me on the last morning, to try to change my mind but it would have been wrong. The very last thing I wanted was to cause him any pain.'

Cautiously she asked, 'Is Verity Raine's baby?'

Robyn was horror-struck. 'That's absolutely preposterous! *David* is Verity's father. I can't believe you even thought it, let alone asked the question.'

'I'm sorry but Raine's so sad when he talks about you and he has such a rotten life.'

Without giving due thought to her next statement she said, 'Well don't *ever* give him cause to believe he's Verity's father. We were just friends.'

'Huh! That's certainly a contradiction of terms if ever I heard one,' she scorned. 'If you were merely friends how could he possibly imagine he was the father? Whilst I might have no hands-on experience of human reproduction I am indeed well acquainted with the text-book exposé of the birds and bees so I don't need you to insult my intelligence Robyn.'

'Okay, I'm sorry. We *were* more than friends but I needed to end it for his sake.'

'So *is* he the father?'

'*No he isn't*! I understood you were pretty good at maths. Work it out for yourself if you don't believe me.'

'I'm sorry Robyn. It's none of my business anyway. I don't know what I was thinking. I shouldn't have asked such a personal question.'

'No, you shouldn't! I know you're fond of Raine but there won't ever be any reconciliation between us Ellie. Raine has his wife and children to care for and I have Verity. It was simply a holiday romance that got a bit out of hand and only *once* if you must know and if he asks you anything about me, please keep your information to an absolute minimum. He has to forget about me. I've already forgotten about him in that respect,' she stated guiltily. 'Right, let's enjoy our lunch now. I'm starving. I assume you're ready for yours too?'

'Yes I am. I had an early breakfast.'

The dust quickly settled on their earlier argument and they enjoyed a pleasant time together without further mention of Raine.

'Do you have time to let me look at the animals?' please?' Ellie asked.

'Yes, I was going to suggest that. Are you fond of animals?'

'I love them. When I was little, I always wanted a dog but suffice to say mum would never allow me to have one because she thought I might be allergic to them.'

With an uncontrollable cackle of laughter, Robyn nodded her head. 'That sounds about right, coming from your mum....forever the worrier or ought I to say warrior! *Come in*!' she called when she heard a sudden sharp knock at the door.

'I'm sorry to disturb you Mrs. Ainsley but some friends have called to see you. Would you like me to show them in?'

'Thank you Andrew. Yes, send them in please.'

Recognising the voice of the speaker, Ellie turned her head and quickly turned away again, appearing embarrassed.

As he closed the door behind him she whispered, 'That was the young man I told you about....the one who got tangled up with the dogs.'

'That's my assistant, Andrew Williamson. He's a University student who's been here a few weeks. I don't know how I ever ran the place before Andrew arrived on the scene. He's invaluable to me and as you've already met, I'll ask if he has time to show you round the kennels and cattery. I think I can hear Gerald's dulcet tone.'

Andrew returned at once with Gerald and Abbie. 'Happy birthday. My word, you're catching me up,' Abbie chuckled, hugging her friend.

'Never in a million years!' Robyn quipped good-humouredly before turning her attention to Andrew. 'Do you happen to have half an hour or so to spare? This is my friend Ellie and she'd like to see all the animals if you have the time.'

'We've already met....rather clumsily in the lane,' he answered with a cordial smile. 'I'd be more than happy to show you round Ellie. Are you ready to go now?'

'Oh, yes please,' she said, hurrying after him.

As Ellie and Andrew left the room, Abbie began to cough, holding her hand to her mouth.

Deliberately ignoring what was staring her in the face, Robyn remarked, 'That's quite a nasty cough you have there. Would you like a drink of water?'

Before Abbie could answer, she turned to Gerald,

253

and winking at him amusingly to make known that the huge rock on her finger had not gone unnoticed, she suggested to him that Abbie should perhaps see a doctor as soon as possible.

'Alright! You can stop playing games you two!' Abbie retorted. 'I know you've seen it Robyn!'

'Seen it? It's little wonder it hasn't fractured your wrist! Congratulations, I'm so thrilled for you both. Let's have a proper look now,' she said, inspecting the biggest diamond she'd ever seen. 'It's *gorgeous* Abbie. When did this happen?'

'Last Saturday. During the evening Gerald passed me what I believed to be a glass of white wine and when I put it to my lips, the ring was in the bottom of the glass, which turned out to be a glass of water. Just imagine, had I not been paying proper attention to what I was doing, I could have swallowed it and choked to death.'

'Get real Abbie....everyone knows you have a big gob but even *you* couldn't swallow that!'

'Charming! Did you hear that Gerald?'

Gerald expelled an ear-splitting guffaw. 'Robyn speaks it as she sees it darling,' he told her.

'And whose side are you on, might I ask?'

'Me? I'm totally impartial,' he responded with a dry smile.

'I don't think I'm going to give you your present now young lady, after that offensive comment. Big gob indeed!'

'Is everything sorted for the wedding?'

'Yes and I hope I make it in time,' she remarked patting her rather large bump. 'You wouldn't think

I was only five months pregnant would you? I must be double the size you were. I'll be huge in another four months if I carry on increasing at this rate. It's a good job I packed up work last week.'

'So how's Martha coping? Are you pleased with her now?'

'My little pipistrelle bat? She's utterly brilliant so I have to hold my hand up to you. She was a really good choice Robyn. She moves as fast as a bat too. She leaves me standing. Currently, she's trying to raise funds to buy me out. From what she tells me, she's not that much short and she's quite taken with the idea of running the place single-handedly. She's outstanding and once you get to know her properly, she has quite a droll sense of humour too.'

'I'm glad because I didn't like leaving you in the lurch like that.'

Abbie smiled. 'I had a few reservations at first I must admit. I thought I'd miss you but as it turned out, I didn't, not one bit!'

'Charming!'

Gerald roared with laughter. 'I believe that's one back for the *big gob* remark Robyn.'

'I think you're probably right. So Abbie, are you fit enough to be going on honeymoon?'

'Yes I'll be fine; anyway it's booked now.'

'Is it a secret?'

'No, not at all. We're off to the West Indies.'

'How fantastic! And how about you Gerald since you'll be giving up your independence quite soon. Are you nervous?'

'Absolutely petrified!' he confessed with a phony

smile. 'I keep asking myself how I got brow-beaten into this predicament by the two of you. Give me a bad session in Court any day. Okay I'm joking!' he added when he spotted Abbie's shocked expression. 'By the way, before I forget, the Motor Insurer has requested a paternity test on Verity. It's nothing to be concerned about. It's standard procedure where there's a posthumous child. If you call the surgery and explain what it's for, you'll be able to arrange it with your GP. I intended to bring the letter with me but I forgot to pick it up so I'll fax it over to you in the morning. That's the only outstanding item now, so the sooner you arrange the test, the sooner you'll receive payment. The Insurer will pay for the test.'

Robyn was horrified beyond belief. Nothing to be concerned about had Gerald stated as her entire life flashed before her eyes in an instant? The paternity test would reveal that Verity wasn't David's child and how would she explain that? *Everybody* would find out about the deception and of her association with another man before David was even cold in his grave. Nothing could cause more concern than that. At that moment, Robyn hated Gerald for his dogged resolve to proceed with the further claim.

Although Robyn tried to appear unruffled by the shock revelation, it was clear she hadn't succeeded when Abbie asked, 'Do you feel alright? You look as if you're about to pass out. You're as white as a sheet.'

'Er...yes I'm okay. It's just that I don't fancy the idea of the doctor sticking a needle in Verity. She's just a tiny baby and she won't know what's going on,' she answered convincingly. 'She's bound to be very distressed.'

Gerald took hold of her hand. 'Stop worrying. It's nothing. It's a simple procedure and she'll be fine.'

'Yes, forget about it for now and open your birthday present,' Abbie said. 'Try to take your mind off the test until it happens. Like Gerald said, she'll be fine. We spent ages trying to choose something we both felt appropriate so we hope you like it.'

Robyn carefully removed the Lladro figurine of a baby girl from the box. 'Oh, it's beautiful! I adore Lladro. David and I always used to buy each other a small memento when we spent a holiday in Spain. I passed many a happy hour wandering around every Lladro shop I could find. Thank you very much. It's really lovely and I'll treasure it always.'

Gerald smiled. 'You're very welcome. That's *two* babies you have now though I guarantee this will be much quieter than the real one.'

'I don't know about that. I wouldn't bet money on it Gerald. She's a sweet-natured and mild-tempered baby. I hardly know I have her.'

'Come off it Robyn! Everyone knows that there's no such thing as a quiet baby,' he argued. 'Where is she anyway?'

'Right there beside you in her cot,' she smiled. 'I rest my case.'

'Well, I'll be damned! Er....can *we* order one like that Abbie?'

'Sorry, it's too late now. The order's already been placed; it'll be delivered shortly and sadly, there's a "no returns" policy.'

The light-hearted repartee had, for the time being allowed Robyn to place the matter of the paternity test to the back of her mind.

When Gerald and Abbie were preparing to leave, Ellie returned from her tour. Robyn introduced her to her friends, at the same time explaining she was the young lady she'd met on the ship.

'I really enjoyed that Robyn. Aren't they lovely? All the dogs were so friendly. I'd love to work with animals,' Ellie sighed.

'I'd better bear that in mind then,' Robyn replied meditatively in the knowledge that Andrew would be leaving in a few months' time. Ellie was good at maths and she would make an ideal replacement for Andrew.

Abbie interrupted, 'Sorry, we really have to be on our way. Are you sorted for a sitter next Saturday?'

'No, not yet. David's mother's still got bronchitis so I'm trying to come up with a suitable alternative in case she's not well enough to come over here.'

'Can I be of any help?' Ellie asked. 'I'd be happy to look after Verity anytime.'

'What a brilliant idea Ellie! Yes, I could trust you with Verity. We'll settle down with a cup of coffee and discuss it as soon as I've seen my friends off.'

'My word, *you're* honoured....that's more than *we* were offered!' Abbie made known. 'Still, with my big gob, I suppose *I* could have asked for one had I really wanted one.'

Robyn looked flustered. 'I'm sorry Abbie. I never gave it a thought. We'd only just finished our lunch and I....'

'Shut up....I'm joking! I don't know what's come over you of late. You seem to have completely lost your sense of humour. Be honest with me Robyn; is this business too much for you to handle now you have Verity? There's no shame in admitting you've made a mistake if you've taken on too much.'

'The business is fine and I love it. To be honest, I was concerned I wouldn't be able to find a sitter for next Saturday but Ellie's now kindly volunteered to step in and save the day. I didn't want to miss your wedding. That's what's been on my mind.'

Much to Robyn's relief, Abbie appeared satisfied with that and nothing further was said as they made their way to the door.

'Good luck for Saturday Gerald and try not to be too nervous. Get a few stiff drinks down your throat before you set off for church.'

'I might just do that,' he laughed.

She hugged Abbie affectionately. 'I can't wait to see your wedding dress and I'll be taking hundreds of photos. It's an excellent weather forecast for next weekend, so let's hope they've got it right. Thanks again for the lovely present. I'll call you during the week. Drive carefully,' she gabbled verbosely.

Robyn was relieved to close the door behind them and lingered in the foyer for several minutes, recalling the revelations of the past half-hour.

She couldn't imagine how she would survive the following few weeks and there was no one in whom she could confide....not one person with whom she could ever share her secret....her burden of guilt and above all her shame....and still the lies continued to ripple off her tongue so effortlessly, day after day. She was absolutely disgusted with herself.

Robyn didn't get one wink of sleep that night. She had suffered a terrible birthday last year, following her decision to end her brief relationship with Raine but yesterday's had been very much worse. With no solution to her predicament, she didn't know which way to turn for were she to refuse the paternity test, Gerald would guess the reason why, yet if she went ahead with it, her deception would be revealed. She could even end up in Court if charges of attempted fraud were brought against her and what if the story ended up in the newspapers? Raine might see it and then he would know he was Verity's father. A story such as that was bound to be splashed all over the papers or even broadcast on national television. She was gripped with fear.

Once again, she recalled her mother's expression, '*Oh what a tangled web we weave....*'

Unable to remain in bed a moment longer, Robyn jumped up, slipped on her housecoat and made her way downstairs with Verity. It was barely dawn and even the dogs were quiet at that unearthly hour.

After placing Verity in the living room cradle, she went to the kitchen to make a strong cup of tea and sighed heavily at her dilemma.

Eventually, after much deliberation, she decided on the best course of action for damage limitation. She would proceed with the paternity test and when it revealed that David wasn't the father, she would tearfully confess to her having spent the night with some guy she'd met in a bar after consuming a few drinks to drown her sorrows. She would say that it hadn't crossed her mind when the claim was filed. No investigating officer could prove otherwise. She would argue that had she believed anyone else was the father, she wouldn't have filed the claim for fear of being exposed as an immoral woman, especially as she was aware there would be a paternity test. It was just a simple mistake, she would maintain....but would anybody believe her? Of course they would, she told herself repeatedly and the date of Verity's birth would add credibility to her misguided belief that Verity was indeed David's child. It wouldn't be possible for anyone to prove attempted fraud. Why should *she* care what David's family thought about *her* morals? At least *she* had been single when she had slept with someone else, unlike David, so what justification could they have for passing judgement on her for doing what David had done? This was all down to Gerald....Gerald who never once missed an opportunity to go for the kill. Why did he not listen to her when she begged him not to make that final claim?

Her head was spinning. She felt queasy and dizzy and she remembered nothing further until Andrew came in and helped her up from the floor where she had fainted.

'I'm calling the doctor Mrs. Ainsley,' he told her. 'You just sit quietly and I'll make you a nice cup of tea in a moment when I've made the call. Don't try to stand up.' He picked up the telephone to dial the number.

'No Andrew,' she protested. 'Please don't call the doctor. I'll be fine, really. I had a restless night with Verity. I didn't get much sleep and I woke up with a banging headache. Did you check to see if Verity was alright?'

'She's fine. She's fast asleep and I'll keep an eye on her while you're resting. I'm still of the opinion I should call the doctor though.'

'I've told you Andrew, I'm alright now. I've been doing too much, that's all. I'm just overtired.'

'Then promise you'll call me immediately if you need anything.'

'I will,' she assured him.

She had, by now, resigned herself to the fact she would soon be exposed and she wanted to expel the paternity issue from her mind, at least for the short term, if only that were possible. Gerald would help. He wouldn't judge her too harshly for a moment's weakness, especially as she had been in shock over David's tragic death and Abbie would definitely be supportive. Nobody else mattered except Ellie who would have to be told never to inform Raine he was Verity's father, when the truth finally emerged.

Andrew called in periodically to check on Robyn and was pleased to find her much improved. 'You do too much,' he chastised her. 'I hope you manage to find a baby-sitter for Saturday so you can relax at your friends' wedding. A break from this place will do you a power of good if just for a few hours. You never seem to go anywhere.'

'It's all arranged. Ellie's offered and she's agreed to stay over so I don't have to rush back.'

'Oh right,' he remarked pensively. 'Does she live locally then?'

'I'd say about four miles away.'

'I don't suppose you happen to know whether she has a boyfriend?'

'I don't think she has. Why do you ask? Are you interested?'

Andrew's face lit up, displaying a broad grin. 'Ah you never know! I might be.'

'In that case, a word of warning. Please tread very carefully with Ellie. She's a little naïve where men are concerned and I wouldn't want her to get hurt.'

'Nor would I. I'll take things slowly but I'd like to get to know her better.'

'Well, I'm quite sure you'll find her as charming as everyone else does. She's very sweet and she's also very innocent. There's only one drawback and that's Ellie's mother, so be forewarned,' Robyn told him gravely. 'She watches her like a hawk. Having said that, her bark is worse than her bite but she can be rather overbearing and that's putting it mildly.'


The anticipated fax arrived from Gerald later in the day and Robyn immediately telephoned the surgery to arrange for the test to be carried out. The sooner it was done, the sooner she could start to rebuild her life which, she believed, would soon be in tatters.

The following Monday brought further emotional feelings to bear when the post arrived. When Robyn opened a re-directed item of mail from her previous address, she was taken aback to find a birthday card from Raine. Inside, it merely said, '*Happy birthday darling. You are forever in my thoughts, with much love, Raine.'*

The envelope was addressed to Mrs. R. Ainsley at her former address yet she had divulged neither her surname nor address to him; in fact she had made it perfectly clear from the outset that apart from their Christian names, no further personal details were to be exchanged.

There was only one person who could have given her surname and previous address to Raine and that was Ellie but she couldn't believe she would have done so willingly. Undoubtedly, Raine had used his sweet-talking powers of persuasion to wheedle the information from her. Robyn was only too aware of how persuasive he could be and was convinced that Ellie was responsible.

As she was replacing the card in its envelope, she came across a folded sheet of paper. It was a hand-written letter from Raine.

Her fingers quivered as she opened it and several times she had to blink the tears from her eyes as she read his words.

*'My dearest Robyn, Please don't be angry with me. I've complied with most of your requests and I have never tried to make contact with you but because of what happened to my wife in childbirth, I was very concerned about you until Ellie advised me you had given birth to a beautiful healthy baby girl and that you were both well. It's exactly a year today since that memorable night and in my mind, I've relived those few short hours lots of times. I took the liberty of visiting your room around midnight the following*

264

*night to copy your name and address from the label
on your bag that you'd left outside your door. How
I found the willpower to return to my room without
hammering on your door I shall never know. It was
wonderful to see you again with Ellie, reviving for
me such enjoyable memories. You will remain in my
thoughts forever. Much love, Raine.'*

'Thank you Raine,' she sighed. 'Never a day goes
by but what I think about you too, above all when I
look at our beautiful daughter, so how could I ever
be angry with you for thinking about me? There's
nothing I'd like better than to see you and hold you
but I can't and it hurts so much.'

She took the card upstairs and placed it in the box
with Raine's photograph but only after removing it
from the envelope and kissing his lips.

10

'It's a perfect day for Abbie and Gerald's wedding and you look stunning. You definitely know how to choose the right clothes for the occasion,' Ellie said admiringly.

'Thank you. Now what did I do with my bag? I'm going to be late if I don't get a move on. Remember everything I told you, won't you? Just help yourself to anything you need. You know where everything is and there's loads of food in the fridge. There's a loaf and some bread rolls in the white bread bin on the kitchen worktop and please....*please* be sure to keep a very close eye on Verity.'

'Robyn....will you stop flapping and calm down? Your bag's over there on that chair and yes, I *have* remembered all your instructions. Just *go* now and forget about this place for a few hours. Verity and I will be fine. Have a fantastic time and remember to give Abbie and Gerald my best wishes.'

'I will.'

As Robyn reached the door she hesitated, looked round and rushed back in towards Verity. 'You be a good little girl for Auntie Ellie. I'm really going to miss you darling.'

Ellie heaved a huge sigh. 'For heaven's sake will you *go*?'

'Alright, I'm going this time. See you later.'

Ellie settled down on the sofa with a magazine as Verity gurgled happily in her cot and moments later when she checked, Verity was on the verge of sleep with her favourite teddy in her arms.

She didn't wake up again until it was time for her midday feed and she certainly appeared to enjoy her lamb dinner which she took from the spoon eagerly. She also gobbled up the creamy chocolate pudding that followed.

'Would you like to see the puppy-dogs and pussy-cats later?' Ellie cooed affectionately. 'Would you like to take a little walk when I've changed you?'

Later, when she made her way through the office, Andrew was hard at work and his face lit up when he saw her.

'Hi Ellie. How's it going? Are you managing to keep everything under control?'

'It's going fine thanks. Verity's just had her lunch and now we're off to look at the animals.'

He jumped up and opened the door leading to the kennels and cattery. 'See you shortly,' he said with a glowing smile.

By the time Ellie had strolled around the kennels, Verity had fallen asleep in her arms.

'She's so cute,' Andrew said as she made her way back through the office. 'Do you know something? You're a natural Ellie. You'll make a fine mother.'

She could feel the colour rising in her cheeks and Andrew was furious with himself for making such an embarrassing and dim-witted remark but to add anything further would only serve to compound his former stupidity.

'Here, let me get the door,' he said, leaping to his feet and Ellie shot past without raising her head or uttering a single word in response.

It had been an awkward moment for both of them.

At six o'clock, following Verity's bath, she made herself comfortable and turned on the TV, keeping the volume low. Once Verity was sleeping soundly, she would look for something to eat from the fridge where Robyn had left a selection of cold meats and salad.

Andrew tapped quietly on the door. 'I'm sorry to disturb you,' he whispered. 'I've quite a bit of work to finish off so I've just phoned for a pizza. It'll be here in about thirty minutes but it'll be far too much for me to eat on my own so I was wondering if you would care to share it with me, that's if you haven't already eaten?'

Her cheeks were turning pink once again but she turned to face him, attempting to act undaunted by his suggestion and replied, 'Thank you Andrew. I'd like that. I was going to make a few sandwiches as soon as Verity fell asleep. Maybe I'll make a salad to go with the pizza if you'd like that?'

'Terrific! That's worked out alright then,' he said, looking pleased with himself. 'So is it okay for me to fetch it in here when it arrives?'

'Yes, I'll find two plates and some cutlery.'

As she frantically searched the kitchen cupboards for plates, she was becoming increasingly flustered.

'Calm down,' she told herself. 'It isn't a proposal of marriage! It's only a slice of pizza! Pull yourself together.'

By the time he turned up half an hour later, Ellie was feeling more settled and quite hungry.

'I think we'd better slice it in the kitchen. I don't want to be in trouble because I've dropped anything on the carpet. Sharp knife?' he murmured, looking around.

'Here,' Ellie said, handing him a carving knife. 'It looks delicious and doesn't it smell good too? I like Italian food.'

'Me too. Have you tried that new place in town?'

'Oh, you mean that Bella something or other? No, but we got a leaflet through the door about it and it was advertised in the paper. They appear to have an extensive menu. Is it any good?'

'It's *very* good,' and before he could stop himself he'd said, 'I'll take you one evening if you like.'

Although startled by his invitation she spluttered, 'Th...thank you Andrew. I'd like that,' and she gave him a beaming smile.

'Terrific,' he grinned. 'Come on....get your plate and let's get stuck in before it goes cold. I'll get the salad.'

No sooner had they sat down, than he jumped up again. 'Hang on a tick. I almost forgot....'

He rushed from the room, returning seconds later with a bottle of red wine clutched in his hand.

She grinned at him. 'It's surprising what you can order from a take-away these days isn't it?'

'*Hoist by my own petard* but then I always was a lousy liar!' he confessed with vermillion cheeks as he joined in the laughter with Ellie. 'Chianti? After all, you can't eat an authentic Italian pizza without a decent bottle of wine!'

Enthusiastically she said, 'Oh, yes please.'

The scene had been set for an enjoyable evening and they found they had much in common.

Later in the evening, when Ellie had given Verity her final bottle, she took her upstairs to the nursery where she fell asleep almost at once. She checked that the intercom was switched on and crept downstairs quietly.

They finished their bottle of wine while watching a film on TV and just after midnight, when Robyn returned, she was more than a little surprised to find Ellie curled up on the sofa, fast asleep in Andrew's arms.

'Verity's fine,' Andrew whispered. 'She's been as good as gold. She's fast asleep.'

'I'll say goodnight then,' Robyn said. 'Thanks for staying.'

'My pleasure!' he replied bashfully. 'So, did you enjoy the wedding?'

'I did; it was superb but I'll tell you all about it in the morning.'

'Well, I have to say *that* obviously went extremely well!' Robyn declared when Ellie appeared the next morning.

Wide-eyed she responded, 'The wedding?'

'You know perfectly well what I'm talking about young lady!'

She giggled. 'I must admit, it was an unexpected pleasure. It certainly wasn't planned, if that's what you're suggesting....not by me at any rate. We had a very nice evening.'

'Good! So, are you an item now?'

'Slow down a bit,' she laughed. 'Having said that, he's taking me out on Friday. We're going to a new

Italian restaurant so we'll have to wait and see what happens.'

'He's a sound guy and he definitely has his head screwed on. That young man will go a long way in life. He practically runs this place single-handedly and he has a great personality.'

'I thought so too. I'm surprised he's not involved with anyone.'

'That's because his studies are very important to him. I believe he's trying to circumvent any conflict of interest. I know he doesn't have much of a social life because of the unsocial hours he works here. He diplomatically fought off two of the girls who work here but he seems keen enough on you. It must be a tricky balancing act I suppose when you're working long shifts and studying simultaneously. In addition to that, Andrew's trying to save for his next course when he goes back to University in October for another year.'

'Maybe he'll do the same with me then, fight me off, besides which, I wouldn't want to compromise his studies. That's a heck of a sight more important. So, how was the wedding?'

'Oh, it was lovely. It was such a beautiful day in every respect.'

'And how was Gerald?' she laughed.

'*Very* nervous! For such a self-assured man who can face up to the opposition in Court, have the jury hanging on his every word and walk out at the end with his head held high following another victory, he was very subdued....that was until we arrived at the reception hall, by which time he was fine, once he'd had a drink. It's amazing how a wedding can reduce a guy to a snivelling wreck,' she chuckled.

'I think most men are like that on their wedding day but then it's more of a girl thing isn't it, all that pomp and circumstance? The men are expected to fall in line with what the women have planned and they're probably afraid to put a foot wrong in front of everyone. Given the option, I think the majority of men would opt for a Registry Office wedding.'

'You're probably right. Still, it was a wonderful day and Abbie looked fabulous, the only downside being that it brought back memories of *my* wedding day so I felt very emotional. I took loads of photos though. I take it everything ran smoothly here with Verity?'

'Everything was fine. I'll look after her anytime if you've somewhere to go.'

'Thank you. I'll be sure to take you up on that if the need ever arises though I don't have much of a social life anymore.'

'Well you should. Other single parents manage to raise a child and have a social life as well.'

'Well *I* don't and I'm quite happy as I am, thank you,' she snapped irritably at what she believed was a critical and censorious remark by Ellie.

Ellie decided to let the matter drop. Robyn could be so pig-headed at times and when she was in one of her moods, it was pointless trying to reason with her. She was no longer the vibrant and lively person she had been when they had first met.

Ellie packed her overnight bag, came downstairs and poked her head round the door to the accounts

272

office to find Robyn poring over a heap of invoices. 'I'm off now,' she told her.

'Thanks a million Ellie. You're a star and I'm so appreciative of your help. Enjoy your evening with Andrew and be sure to let me know all about it.'

Ellie gave her a beaming smile. 'I'll call you next Saturday.'

Robyn threw the invoices back into her tray and rested her head in her hands as she wondered what the postman would deliver the next day. Surely she would be receiving a communication soon from the Insurance Company about the paternity test.

Her nerves were in shreds and she believed if she had to wait much longer, she'd go out of her mind. She felt remorseful about her off-handed behaviour towards Ellie who had just been trying to help but how could she enjoy any kind of social life with all that worry to contend with?

The next week came and went, still with no news and she decided to speak to Gerald on the Monday following his return from honeymoon. There might well be a letter behind his office door, awaiting his return.

By Sunday, she had worried herself into a frenzy. Perhaps Gerald had called at the office on his way home from the airport to pick up his mail and listen to his answerphone messages? If he had, he would already know about her deception.

For some time, she deliberated about whether to give Abbie a call on the pretext of enquiring about their honeymoon in the West Indies when she could casually bring the test results into the conversation.

She paced up and down the floor repeatedly until she could contain her anxiety no longer and picked up the telephone. One way or the other, she had to know. The problem she had created had to be faced sooner or later so it might as well be now.

With trembling hands she dialled the number and when Abbie answered, she coughed nervously and cleared her throat before speaking.

'It's only me. I was just checking to see if you'd got back yet,' she managed to splutter and for some time, she listened unenthusiastically to Abbie, who happily related details of the memorable places they had visited, while Robyn responded robotically and monosyllabically at appropriate intermissions as her animated account directed.

She made no reference to the Insurance Company and Robyn was starting to have some doubts about raising the matter. By asking, she showed concern and that might well be deemed to be an admission of guilt she felt. She was still trying to make up her mind what to say or do when Abbie interrupted her thoughts.

'Oh, by the way, I almost forgot. Gerald needs to talk to you urgently. He's received a letter from the Insurance Company. He's just nipped to the garage for some petrol but he shouldn't be long. Shall I ask him to give you a call when he gets back?'

'What's it about?' she almost cried, experiencing a rush of adrenaline throughout her trembling body.

'Search me. He'll call you as soon as he comes in. Listen, I've loads to do so I'm going. I'll talk to you through the week. I'm still trying to unpack all our stuff and I've got masses of washing to do. It feels nice to be home though. We've brought something back for Verity. You'll love it,' she said excitedly.

Without making any grateful response to that, she replied, 'Yes, and would you please ask Gerald to give me a call as soon as he gets home Abbie?'

Her hands still quaking, she clumsily replaced the receiver and burst into tears. Finally, it was the day of reckoning and she recalled those fear-provoking words from the New Testament she had listened to so often in church as a young child....*the day at the end of time following Armageddon, when God will decree the fates of all individual humans according to the good and evil of their earthly lives....*

With her heart pounding, her whole body clammy with perspiration and filled with dread, for fifteen long minutes she awaited Gerald's call. It was the longest fifteen minutes of her entire life to date.

She snatched at the handset before it had finished ringing the first tone.

'You were quick off the mark,' Gerald remarked. 'How's Verity?'

'Fine thanks,' she answered abruptly, wishing he would get straight to the point.

'I gather Abbie has been boring you to death with all the details of the holiday? Well, all I want to add to that is that we had a fantastic time and no doubt she'll be boring you to death before too long again with all the photographs.'

'I'm pleased you enjoyed it,' she said, twitching nervously, then clearing her throat, took the bull by the horns. 'I understand you've had word from the

Insurance Company? Abbie mentioned it when we spoke earlier.'

There was a moment or two's silence prior to his reply. 'Er....yes I have....so maybe you could drive over to the office tomorrow, say about two o'clock and we can sit down quietly and discuss the....'

'I'd rather you told me now,' she interrupted.

She was sure she heard a sigh. 'If it's all the same to you Robyn, I'd much prefer *not* to discuss it over the telephone. It's concerning the additional claim I submitted for Verity and I must provide some legal advice for you to consider very carefully before you give me your answer. What you tell me could have an enormous impact on the eventual outcome but it needs to be *your* decision. I can merely advise you, that's all,' he said matter-of-factly. 'So, would two o'clock tomorrow be convenient for you or do you prefer the next day at eleven?'

A cold shiver ran down her spine. This was worse than she'd imagined. Gerald wouldn't even discuss the contents of the letter over the telephone and she was terrified. If she were to make a bad decision, or say the wrong thing she might end up in prison and she'd never set out to trick the Insurance Company. What would become of Verity should she be given a custodial sentence? She could even be taken into Social Services' care. Her pain was unbearable.

She was about to cry out, 'I never intended to do anything wrong. I felt trapped. I was only trying to protect my daughter,' but before she had chance to explain, he said, 'Choosing the most advantageous kind of investment is always difficult. There are so

276

many factors to consider, for instance, Verity might be better provided for were we to create a Trust but you need to understand what that means and decide how you would like it to be administered and who the Trustees should be et cetera. That's why I don't want to discuss it over the telephone. We need to sit down quietly and consider all the options. Now that everything has been agreed, there seems little point in letting the grass grow! The sooner the funds are invested, the sooner she'll begin to earn interest.'

Adrenaline surged through her body. 'Er, hang on while I get my head around this. Are you telling me everything has been settled with the claim, Gerald?'

'To coin a phrase, everything's signed, sealed and delivered so you can put it behind you now and get on with the rest of your life. Heaven knows you've waited long enough.'

'I can't believe it's finally over,' she sighed with relief as tears trickled down her face. 'Is this really the end of everything? Didn't they make reference to the paternity test?'

'Only by way of acknowledgement in their letter. Why do you ask?'

That was a damn fool question to have asked, she chastised herself. 'Well er....I suppose I expected it would take several weeks,' she lied convincingly as she had become accustomed to so doing during the last twenty-one months.

'It's been a complex issue from the outset but it's all over and done with now so you can relax. We'll talk about the investment options available in more detail when I see you.'

'Thanks Gerald. I really appreciate all your help,' she said graciously. Weak at the knees, she flopped down on the sofa and again burst into tears but this time tears of total relief.

The *deception* would never be over and done with though, to use Gerald's words. Despite her victory, the fact remained that Verity was Raine's daughter and there could be only one feasible explanation for her success with the deception....that both men were of the same blood group. She had given no thought to such a possibility before, but not being medically qualified, she had been unaware of how the test was conducted. Gerald had advised her it was a simple test and nothing to be concerned about and had they not advised them at the fertility clinic that she and David were also of the same blood type? It had to be a common blood group, she concluded. That was presumably why no query had been raised, she told herself, though it did nothing to ease her guilt at the deception that would remain with her for the rest of her days. Never in a million years would she eradicate such guilt and disgrace from her mind. She had betrayed everybody's trust and she despised herself. What kind of example was that for a mother to set for her daughter in years to come, when everything she made known about her father would be veiled in lies and deception? Verity would go through life believing her father to be dead, when indeed he was very much alive. Yes....she despised herself.

11

It was early December. Ellie had been working for Robyn for three months since taking over Andrew's job when he returned to University to study for his accountancy qualification.

'Your accountancy course came in handy,' Robyn told her. 'I have to say I was becoming more than a little concerned as the time approached for Andrew to leave but I needn't have worried. You're equally efficient.'

'Thank you Robyn and in case you hadn't noticed I'm a very trustworthy baby-sitter too. I'll lay odds you still haven't done your Christmas shopping.'

With an exasperated sigh Robyn nodded her head. 'You're right. I've only managed to get a few of the things on my extensive list but it's so hard trying to shop with a buggy.'

'Then leave her with *me*!' she exclaimed. 'You're worse than mum for being over-protective!'

Robyn laughed. 'I suppose I am, or at least I'm as bad. I've often thought about the things I said to her when she was persistently criticising you and ordering your food like you were a small child and I still recall how scathing she was about my interference. She told me that when I had children of my own, I would understand a mother's concern and I have to hold up my hand; she was right about that. She was so annoyed that day and accused me of being a bad influence on you.'

'I know. She told me about that,' and with a shrill laugh added, 'She made reference to you as....er....

*that awful young woman with the bird name.* I said nothing to you at the time but she actually tried to ban me from seeing you.'

'Did she really?' she screeched with laughter.

Apologetically Ellie spluttered, 'She doesn't think badly of you now. She really likes you so it turned out to be a good thing. It brought it all to a head.'

'On reflection, I think her remarks were justified. Who did I think I was to criticise your mother? I'm probably worse with Verity than she was with you.'

'Well, you could be a bit more flexible. I used to feel I'd like someone else apart from mum around. You don't want Verity to grow up feeling like that. She enjoys playing with the staff. She's not a china doll....she won't break!'

'You're right. I am possessive but that's because I'm a single parent.'

'And likely to remain so. You never go anywhere or do anything other than work. Abbie's invited you to dinner lots of times but you always refuse. She's been a good friend to you, so has Gerald, and you should try to make the effort and get away from this place for a few hours.'

'I've invited Abbie and Gerald *here* for Christmas dinner so it's not as if I'm trying to avoid them.'

'That's hardly the same thing, the problem being that *you* won't go *there* because you refuse to leave Verity, if you speak the truth. You could even take her with you but no, you refuse to alter her routine. Does it never occur to you that she might appreciate a change of environment....to be in the company of other people occasionally?'

'Have you finished the month-end accounts yet?' Robyn asked frostily, changing the subject.

Ellie realised it was the end of the discussion. Her employer had the knack of bringing a conversation to an abrupt end if she were getting out of her depth in an argument, though Ellie knew she would sidle away and reflect on what had been discussed as she always did.

Ellie was proved right once more when, a while later, Robyn returned dressed to go out.

'Would you keep an eye on Verity for a couple of hours while I go shopping?'

Ellie smiled. 'I'd be delighted.'

'I meant to ask you earlier; have you and Andrew made any plans yet for Christmas Day?'

'We haven't decided on anything yet. Mum wants us to go for dinner there but the last thing I want is to ruin his Christmas Day,' she chuckled. 'His mum has invited us too so we have to make sure we don't offend anyone because we can't be in two places at once. We'll talk about it when he comes home and decide then.'

'Why don't you spend Christmas Day here? I'm ordering a large tree this afternoon and I'm going to make it a special day as it's Verity's first birthday. You could tell both sets of parents you didn't want to offend either of them so you've decided to come here instead.'

'I'd love to but I need to check first with Andrew. I haven't dared take him to meet mum and dad yet, especially after what happened when he and I were baby-sitting Verity when you went to the wedding.'

'Tell me that again. I've forgotten but I remember I had a good laugh at the time.'

'It's something *I'll* never forget as long as I live! When I explained to mum about Andrew turning up with the pizza, I told her we'd had an amazing time and that I'd fallen asleep afterwards and needless to say she assumed the worst. She bellowed at the top of her voice, "*I hope you aren't saying what I think you're saying Ellie,*" and I was so embarrassed and red-faced that she wouldn't believe me when I told her nothing like that had happened so I made up my mind there and then to keep him right out of mum's way. She'd scare him witless!'

Robyn howled with laughter. 'I do remember now and I wouldn't mind betting that my name featured as a bad influence again for leading you astray.'

'No, I don't think it did. Anyway she knew you'd gone to the wedding so it would hardly have been your fault had it been true. Besides, as I've already told you, she likes you now. She thinks you're very sensible and level-headed.'

'I'm glad about that. I'd rather have your mum as a friend than an enemy any day. Right, I'm off now or there'll be little point in going. I'll see you later.'

When Robyn returned loaded with shopping bags, Ellie informed her that Andrew had called and was thrilled with the invitation to spend Christmas Day there. 'He offered to put your tree up this weekend and help you hang all the decorations too. He also mentioned that if you were struggling for staff over the Christmas period, he'll help in the kennels. He's a bit strapped for cash with it being Christmas. He's had a few presents to buy, speaking of which, have you managed to do all your Christmas shopping?'

'More or less and I've ordered the food. I'll finish writing my Christmas cards this evening and that's another job out of the way. I'm looking forward to Christmas this year. I felt I'd missed it last year in one respect, although I received the best Christmas present ever, didn't I my precious?' Robyn said as she took Verity in her arms. 'I wonder what Father Christmas will be bringing you?'

Ellie smiled warmly at the child's happy face and touched her hand. 'You're a gorgeous little creature aren't you?' she murmured tenderly, blowing her a kiss. 'I'm off now Robyn. I still have some presents to buy and I want to get something for Abbie's little girl now we're coming here on Christmas Day. I'm looking forward to seeing her again. I'll be in early tomorrow as I've a lot of paperwork to do.'

Robyn kept out of everyone's way, committing the entire day to her remaining Christmas preparations on the penultimate Friday before Christmas.

The large tree that Andrew had decorated earlier with Ellie's assistance was magnificent and Verity was bewitched by the sparkling coloured baubles as she regularly crawled over to them, removing what she could from the lower branches as fast as Robyn could replace them.

She had become quite a handful and Robyn knew she would soon be taking her very first steps.

Each day was a new adventure for a child of that age and also a new headache for Robyn who had to watch her constantly to keep her from harm's way but she provided much joy.

As Robyn reorganized her dining room furniture to accommodate all her Christmas Day guests, her thoughts turned to Raine. She wondered what kind of Christmas he might have with a seriously ill wife to attend to and young children to entertain. Robyn had planned a wide assortment of party games for her guests. It was to be a fun-filled time but there'd be little fun for Raine and his children, she thought and she felt deep sadness for his pain. His daughter Verity would be a year old in just a few more days and he was unaware of her existence, as his child.

She resisted a powerful urge to call Raine to wish him a happy Christmas in the belief matters would probably be best left as they were but she couldn't remove him from her thoughts for the remainder of the day. She had the strangest feeling he was crying out to her and willing her to make contact with him. It was inexplicable. Eighteen months had passed by since their last meeting; she had never experienced such feelings before so why was it happening now?

Towards the end of the arduous day she sat down to wrap her last few presents after pouring herself a gin and tonic.

As she slowly savoured her most welcome drink, the door bell rang. Robyn rarely received visitors in the evening; she wasn't expecting anyone and was therefore surprised.

The night assistant answered the door and Robyn heard muffled voices in the hall before Ellie ran in sobbing.

'Ellie, what's happened?' Robyn asked, searching her weeping eyes as she awaited an explanation for the cause of her distress.

'Oh Robyn, I've had some terrible news. Raine's just called and his wife's died. He was in a dreadful state and he was breaking his heart. He could barely speak. He phoned me because he didn't know who else to turn to, he said. I didn't want to tell you over the phone.'

Robyn was shocked by the news. 'Poor Raine! He must be totally devastated. I can't begin to express my sorrow Ellie because I know better than anyone what he's going through. He never abandoned hope of a recovery. Did she die today?'

'No, it happened a few days ago. Today was the funeral and everybody's left now and he's all alone. His parents have taken the children home with them for a couple of days. I think he'd been drinking and he was very depressed. I couldn't think of anything constructive to say other than how very sorry I felt. Please would you call him? I know he'd appreciate hearing from you.'

'I suppose I should do but it might revive painful memories. Did he mention me at all?'

'Yes but only briefly. He said I should tell you he fully understands now and he's sorry. I didn't know what he meant but I'm sure you do.'

'Yes I do. Raine couldn't understand why I ended things but it was partly because David had recently died. He probably feels guilty now. When someone dies, you look for someone to blame and if there's nobody else, you end up blaming yourself and you harvest all kinds of thoughts from the past. It's very strange trying to understand why certain memories keep flooding back....memories that some time later mean little or nothing but yet at the time appear so important, so relevant. It's all part and parcel of the grieving process but you don't understand it at the time. His bitter feelings and guilt will quickly pass. Rebuilding his life will be the hardest part but thank God he has his children. It won't be easy but he'll survive, as I did.'

'I hope so. I like Raine very much.'

'I know that and I loved him. Fortunately, I loved him enough to give him up because I didn't want to complicate his difficult life further.'

Hesitantly Ellie enquired, 'Do you still love him, Robyn?'

She deliberated for a while before answering and then with a faraway look in her eyes, she smiled. 'I do love him Ellie and I always will. Raine's a very special man.'

'Then please call him Robyn; talk to him. He's so lonely and miserable and I know it'd mean a lot to him to hear your voice.'

'I'll have to give that some careful thought. I've never called him since the holiday. I must consider first whether it would be the right and proper thing to do. *He's* vulnerable now, just as I was then and I wouldn't want him to misinterpret my concern.'

'Yes, he's most definitely vulnerable....he was in pieces. I couldn't tell it was him at first. Right, I've done what I came here to do so I'd better leave you to your thoughts. I've every confidence you'll make the right decision and should you want to talk, you know where I am. I'll see you soon. Goodnight and I'm sorry to be the bearer of such tragic news.'

Robyn poured another drink and gave thought to what she should do. She knew she should offer her condolences, primarily because it would look very bad if she didn't but how would he interpret her call in his present state of mind? Nothing had changed regarding her feelings for him but she hadn't been honest with Raine neither had she been honest with Ellie. The reason for ending their brief liaison was a secret she'd take to her grave. Verity was his child and that fact could never be disclosed.

Maybe she should call Raine if only to restore his confidence that things would improve with time but would he believe her if she did? She never believed anyone who tried to comfort and reassure her at the time of her tragic loss. Her mind was in turmoil. He was Verity's father so she couldn't turn her back on him when he was experiencing such anguish. What kind of person would she be were she to behave in such a callous manner? Of course she must call him to try and ease his suffering.

She went to find the number he'd scribbled on the back of his photograph and for a few moments she stared nostalgically at his smiling face, recalling the wild night of passion they had shared, those stolen moments she would always remember...not merely for the consequences of their actions, their beautiful daughter but also for the profound love she still felt for Raine, a love that could never be....for even the death of his wife changed nothing.

Robyn reflected on the people she had deceived; Abbie and Gerald; David's parents and family; her own family; the driver's Motor Insurance Company from whom she had received an unbelievable award for Verity's future upkeep and last but by no means least, Raine who she had betrayed most. Moreover, there remained a notable question at the forefront of her mind that someday she would have to address. Should she tell Verity the truth?

That important question had prayed on her mind from the day she had discovered she was pregnant. It was one thing to betray her family and friends but what of her child? Had she not the right to know the identity of her natural father? There was no bond to destroy between Verity and David but if she knew, what would she do with such information? Would she be satisfied to do as Robyn had done and keep such knowledge secret....or would she want contact with her father? *Her father*....the mere utterance of those words brought a shiver to her spine for Raine could never be told the truth.

After returning the photograph to its envelope she went downstairs to call him and though apprehensive of making the call, of hearing his gentle voice, she had to go ahead. She owed him that.

Twice she began to dial the number and twice she hung up after losing her nerve. While reconsidering for the umpteenth time whether she was doing the right thing, she swallowed the contents of her glass hurriedly and then redialled his number.

Following a lengthy pause before he answered he impassively said, 'Hello.'

She gulped on her words timorously and in barely a whisper stated, 'It's Robyn. I'm calling to express my deep sorrow for your tragic loss, Raine. I am so distressed about how you must feel.'

There was silence for a moment before he spoke. 'Thank you for calling. It's very much appreciated Robyn. My wife's death wasn't totally unexpected,' he responded rationally. 'Pneumonia took Victoria away at the end.'

The mention of his wife's name sent shock waves through her body as *Victoria* quickly became a real individual in her imagination, as opposed to a frail comatose being whom Raine had adored and nursed for the past few years.

'How are you feeling?' she asked, unable to think of anything more fitting to say.

'Totally drained. I've barely had time to evaluate everything that's happened until this evening. I've been alone for a few hours and I'm now beginning to realize that my entire life has suddenly changed. Nothing will ever be the same again.'

'I know Raine.'

'Of course you do Robyn. That's why I'm happy to hear from you. I was hoping you'd call after I'd spoken to Ellie and I'm so grateful. I wanted to talk to someone who understood....a true friend. We are still friends aren't we?'

'Of course we're friends Raine and we'll always be friends.'

'The thing I'm finding so hard to come to terms with is my feeling of guilt. I despise myself but not because of us, I hasten to add. I never regretted that and I don't now. I feel guilty because I'm relieved it's over for Victoria and I have my sons' emotions to consider as well. It wasn't as bad somehow when they were younger because they didn't understand, but as they became older, I started to be concerned about the long term consequences of their having a comatose mother with whom they couldn't communicate. Oh, ignore me Robyn. I haven't a clue what I'm trying to say. I can't explain what I mean. I've had a few drinks to try and drown my sorrows but all it seems to have done is impede my speech and reasoning. Let's start again. What I'm trying to say is that I never wanted to lose Victoria. I wanted her to come back from wherever she was as the loving wife who'd been absent from my life and yet at the same time, I was unable to face an indefinite future as we were, if that makes any sense to you.'

'I understand Raine and you have no cause to feel guilty. I felt the same when David died yet I wasn't the perpetrator of his death. You're in shock and it takes time to work through your system and whilst that's taking its course, you'll experience all kinds of thoughts, both good and bad but that's a normal reaction. The only thing I can promise is that it *will* get better. I know you don't believe that now but it *will* and please don't bury your head in a bottle. It's definitely not the answer. You have responsibilities; you have to be there for your children. Believe me, you'll work everything out in time.'

'Thank you. I can't explain how much it's helped, talking to you….to someone who understands. Will you call me again?'

'Of course I will, if that's what you want and if it helps a little.'

Hesitantly Raine said, 'Er....I don't suppose you'd give me your number so I could call you?'

She considered his request and answered, 'I *will* give you my number but only if you promise to use it for the right reasons.'

'I will, I promise.'

He noted her number and then remarked, 'That's not a Cheshire number.'

'You're right. I moved last year. I needed a fresh start away from all the memories.'

Tentatively he said, 'I suppose you're wondering how I knew you lived in Cheshire?'

'No, I had my mail redirected from the previous address so I received your card, thank you.'

'I'm sorry for the invasion of your privacy. I had to know where you were. It made me feel closer to you. Where are you living now?'

'I live in Staffordshire.'

'Well that's a coincidence. So do I. We could be within a few miles of each other, so near and yet so far,' he sighed.

'Don't do this Raine. Please don't make me wish I'd never called you.'

'Sorry. Are you with someone now....a guy?'

'No, there's never been anyone since you. I have to go now.'

'Please don't hang up. I'm very sorry. I've upset you. I shouldn't have asked that. I'm confused and I don't know what I'm saying so please try to make allowance for that. Don't be angry with me Robyn.'

'I'm not angry....truly I'm not. Try to get a good night's sleep and I'll call you again soon.'

'Alright, I'll try. Goodnight Robyn and thanks for calling me. I really appreciate it.'

'You're welcome. Goodnight and God bless.'

She couldn't sleep that night. By sharing Raine's distress she had rekindled memories of the anguish she had borne during the months following David's death. For several hours she lay awake before going downstairs to make herself a hot milky drink in the hope it might help her sleep. She finally returned to bed at four o'clock and was abruptly awakened by the telephone a few hours later.

'It's me....Raine. I've just called to thank you for last night. I've given a great deal of thought to what you said and I feel much better already. I realise it must have been difficult for you to call me so I had to say thank you for that and for your kind words.'

'I'm pleased it helped and when your children are back home, your time will be occupied and that will help you too. Be strong for them Raine. Be thankful for what you had with your wife and the legacy she left you. You have a duty to your children now.'

'I'd like to see you Robyn. I need to....'

'*No* Raine,' she interrupted.

'Why not? What harm can it do?'

'The time wasn't right then when I'd just lost my husband and the time isn't right now when you've just lost your wife. I went to hell and back after I'd lost David and then you, so I would never consider putting you through that.'

'Isn't that *my* decision to make?'

'No, I'm making it mine for your protection. You are grieving and your seeing me is definitely not the answer.'

Argumentatively he said, 'Well I happen to think it is.'

'In that case, we'll just have to agree to disagree on that point.'

'Alright, I'll make a deal with you,' he persisted. 'If you tell me you don't still love me, in return, I'll give you my word here and now that I'll never ever contact you again.'

'I never told you I did.'

'And neither did I because there was never a need to speak the words. The chemistry was there Robyn and we both knew what we felt for each other. You can't deny that.'

Robyn was being backed into a corner and needed to escape. Brusquely she responded, 'I can't believe you're saying this on the day following your wife's funeral!'

He was incensed at her reply and bellowed down the phone, '*You've* got some nerve to criticize me! *You* went to bed with me only one week after your husband's funeral. *I'm* only talking for God's sake. I'm trying my damnedest to come to terms with my emotions and understand what's going on inside my head. What gives *you* the right to censure *me* after what you did?'

'I'll tell you what gives me the right,' she replied quietly but curtly. 'I've had to live with what I did and I'm still paying the price to this day. Does that answer your question?'

He laughed scornfully. 'We're getting somewhere now! You should have been honest with me about your regrets Robyn. I mistakenly believed we both felt the same. I didn't have any regrets then when I was cheating on my wife because I knew I couldn't hurt her and now that she's gone I can't hurt her. I devoted my entire marriage to her well-being, both before *and* after she suffered her stroke. That means I've nothing to reproach myself for and regardless of my feelings for you, I would never have left her but she's gone now and that's the reality. Now you, on the other hand have regrets for what we did after David, who, let me remind you, had been cheating on you and had left you for another woman. Let me tell you this; I find your sense of loyalty admirable Robyn,' he added mockingly.

Defensively she cried out, 'It's not the same. You don't understand. David loved me very much.'

'And Victoria and I loved each other very much so I do understand. I understand you are clinging to a memory....an intangible recollection of what you once had but that has gone. You told me last night to look to the future and not dwell on the past. You should try taking your own advice Robyn or you'll end up a bitter, withered and miserable old woman. You won't always have David's child tied to your apron strings. One day that particular bird will fly the nest and then where will you be? I'm trying to be positive. Granted, I've had some years to come to terms with what could happen but it still doesn't lessen the trauma when it becomes reality. Do you know, I felt utter relief when Victoria exhaled her dying breath? That's the reason I felt guilty. I felt I had willed it to happen because my concern was for our children but I realised later that I had nothing to feel guilty about. I did everything a man could have done for his wife. *That's* what I called to tell you. I just called to say thank you, because you helped me put everything into perspective but I won't ever call you again.'

There was no goodbye before Robyn heard Raine slam down the receiver.

'Oh Raine,' she cried. 'If only you knew the truth you wouldn't despise me so....or would you? I only did what I truly believed I had to do.'

Robyn kept herself busy for the remainder of the day but her thoughts repeatedly returned to Raine. Were she to call him back, it would either result in further insults or all would be forgiven and then he would beg to see her again and she would have to reject him for a second time.

She suddenly realised she had become a younger version of Flora Johnstone and was horror-struck to think that Verity might grow up hating her. She had only wanted what was best for her daughter....but hadn't Flora said the self-same thing when warning her about *a mother's concern*?

That evening, when he had calmed down, Raine was giving further thought to his earlier behaviour. His vehement outburst had been totally uncalled for and more than anything he wanted to make amends but to call Robyn back would be a mistake. She had to see in his eyes that he truly regretted his words, that he was filled with remorse for the cruel, bitter things he had said to her. Somehow, he had to find her to say he was sorry. He couldn't leave things as they were.

Passionately, he fingered through the pages of his telephone directory but there was no listing for her name. He was aware Ellie would never divulge her address and when Directory Enquiries were unable to assist him, he turned to the business pages of his directory, hoping she might be working from home but the only company listed was, 'Ainsley Boarding Kennels and Cattery.'

When he checked the number alongside, although the area code was the same, the remaining numbers were different from those Robyn had given him.

It was certainly worth a try, he concluded and he gave them a call, choosing his words carefully as he spoke to the receptionist.

'Hello! Could you tell me where your kennels are situated please? I'm looking for somewhere in the area to board my dog for several days towards the end of January.'

Raine took down the particulars and asked, 'Has the business recently changed hands or is it still run by Robyn Ainsley?'

'Actually it changed hands last year. That's when Mrs. Ainsley bought it from the former owners who were retiring,' she advised him.

'Oh right, I see! I must have got my wires crossed somehow. Mrs. Ainsley is in charge of the business *now*....Mrs. *Robyn* Ainsley?'

'Yes, that's correct. Mrs. Ainsley is the proprietor now. As the kennels are often fully booked, would you like me to check whether the dates you require are available? It will only take a moment or two if you can hold.'

'I'm not sure of the dates yet. I'm still waiting for confirmation,' he lied. 'I'll call you back as soon as I have the information. Thank you so much for your help.'

He checked his watch. He could be there in half-an-hour and if she were going out, he could maybe take up five minutes or so of her time....enough to apologise for his earlier behaviour. At least it would be a move in the right direction towards reconciliation. It was certainly worth a try.

He ran upstairs, washed his hands and face, had a quick shave and brushed his dishevelled hair before hurrying to his car, hoping that the roads would be sufficiently quiet for a speedy journey. He couldn't leave matters as they were any longer. He needed to make amends at once before the window of opportunity was lost forever.

Along the final country track, Raine slowed down to manoeuvre his way between the bumpy potholes before swinging his car into the car park.

As he hurried towards the main entrance, he felt apprehensive and his heart was pounding rapidly by the time he reached the reception area where he had to press a security buzzer before proceeding further. He ran his fingers through his hair whilst anxiously waiting for someone to answer.

There was a grating crackle when the receptionist turned on the intercom. 'Good evening. May I help you?' she enquired.

Raine cleared his throat nervously before saying, 'I'm here to see Mrs. Ainsley please.'

'Is she expecting you?'

'Er....no,' he replied hesitantly. 'I'm a friend and I was in the area so I've called on the off-chance she might be in.'

He waited for the door to be released but instead, she asked, 'May I have your name and I'll call Mrs. Ainsley to inform her you're here.'

Not having anticipated that question, he stuttered, 'Er....tell her it's Doctor Quinlan.'

'Doctor Quinlan,' she repeated. 'Thank you. I'll try not to keep you waiting too long. I'll just speak to Mrs. Ainsley.'

When Robyn picked up her extension, she stated, 'Mrs. Ainsley, there's a Doctor Quinlan here to see you but I haven't unlocked the door. He said he was a friend of yours.'

'Doctor who?'

'No,' she giggled audibly. 'Doctor Quinlan!'

'Alright Hannah! Very funny! Doctor Quinlan did you say? I don't know anyone of that name. Please don't release the door. I'll come through and speak to him via the intercom first. Please inform him that I'll attend to him in a moment.'

'Doctor Quinlan?' she murmured to herself as she checked her face in the mirror and straightened her hair. 'Who on earth can that be? I've never heard of the man.'

When Robyn appeared by the front desk, Hannah asked apprehensively, 'Would you like me to fetch one of the Rottweilers through to reception?'

She laughed heartily, envisaging a potential client being viciously savaged by a large dog, merely for ringing her door-bell. 'I'm quite sure that won't be necessary Hannah. I'll talk to him first through the intercom to try and find out who he is.' Switching it on, she greeted him politely. 'Good evening Doctor Quinlan. I'm Mrs. Ainsley. How may I help you?'

'Robyn?' Raine asked.

'Yes....who's that please?'

'It's me, Raine. Please don't be angry with me. I need to talk to you. We can't leave things like this. Don't hang up on me. I'm sorry about the things I said earlier. I didn't mean any of it. Please, just give me a chance to explain and apologise.'

'How did you find me?'

'Let me in and I'll tell you. Please darling....just give me a few minutes of your time.'

Hannah was listening attentively to every word of the conversation and when Robyn turned to ask her to release the security door, she was grinning from ear to ear.

Robyn was infuriated by such an invasion of her privacy and irritably she snapped at her, 'Have you nothing to do Hannah?'

Sheepishly she answered, 'Er, yes Mrs. Ainsley,' as she pressed the release button, thus allowing the caller to enter.

Hannah eyed the ostensible Doctor Quinlan from head to toe as he appeared in view. There could be no argument that he was a handsome guy, standing almost six feet tall and with a perfect smile that he revealed as he thanked her for her assistance, before

Robyn took his arm and ushered him through to the living quarter.

Hannah would be the most popular staff member for days when she held everybody's attention with this tit-bit of information and which she had every intention of embellishing to the utmost degree. That would be the main topic of conversation for weeks. Mrs. Ainsley was entertaining a mysterious evening gentleman caller who had called her *darling*! Who could ever dream of such a thing happening to the starchy and short-tempered Mrs. Ainsley?

After leading him into the sitting room she glared at him disparagingly. 'I can't believe you've turned up at my home uninvited and more importantly as we're on the subject, would you be good enough to explain how you found me?'

'Grouchy and annoyed, exactly as I predicted I'd find you,' he replied with a boyish grin. 'Don't let's quarrel Robyn. I know you hate it as much as I do. I'm here to beg your forgiveness and then I'll be on my way.'

'Do you believe you deserve my forgiveness after the cruel things you said to me?'

'Probably not but I'm hoping you'll attribute my outburst to my state of mind. I don't usually behave in such a high-handed egotistical manner and I *am* truly repentant.'

'Then I suppose I ought to be hospitable and offer you a drink,' she stated dispassionately. 'Please sit down Raine. You have a propensity to unnerve me when you're towering above me and I don't like to feel I'm at a disadvantage. Are you having a drink?'

'Thanks but only a small one and will you cut the crap? I once forgave your outburst due to your state of mind so I think it's fair that you reciprocate. I'm trying my best to apologise.'

Frostily she responded, 'I have no recollection of any outburst on my part.'

'I believe you have. You bellowed at me in front of everyone on the ship when I inadvertently spilled juice on you.'

'Oh that outburst! Yes, you're quite right, I did. I stand corrected but as I recall I apologised for that didn't I?'

'Yes and that's all I want to do. What's happened to us Robyn?'

'Are you saying I should I be grateful that you've tricked your way into my home?'

'*You* released the door and *invited* me in,' Raine protested. 'So I didn't trick my way in. I managed to track you down courtesy of the Yellow Pages if you must know. I needed to apologise face to face so you could see how genuinely sorry I was for my earlier outburst. I should never have lost my temper and I'm sorry.'

She neither agreed nor refused to accept Raine's apology but turning to look him in the eye she said, 'And what was that phony name all about? *Doctor Quinlan* for heaven's sake! It sounds like a TV soap opera. Was that the best you could come up with?'

'I was taken aback. I didn't expect to be asked for my name and I had no intention of standing behind a locked door yelling out *Raine*. You were the one who insisted on confidentiality. I could have chosen

301

*Horatio Burlington-Smythe*, but whatever name I'd have given, you would have been no wiser as to my true identity and I didn't want you to turn me away. Anyway, what's so comical about Doctor Quinlan? I happen to think that's a very fine name. It rolls off the tongue; it positively reeks of class *and* it got me through the front door!' he hooted with laughter.

Unable to contain her amusement, Robyn giggled. 'Stop it. I'm supposed to be annoyed with you,' she said, handing him his drink.

'That's better,' he said affectionately. 'I really am sorry. You know I'd never say or do a thing to hurt you but your comments touched a nerve so we were equally to blame.'

'You've still not told me the truth about how you managed to find me. Did you prise my address out of Ellie?'

'You know I wouldn't put Ellie in that position. Like I told you, you're listed in the Yellow Pages as Boarding Kennels and I called and asked if you ran the place. It was a lucky break,' he confessed. 'Ask the girl on reception if you don't believe me. I only called her half-an-hour ago so she'll remember me. I feel so much better now I've seen you. It's a smart outfit you have here and I hope it's doing well. You keep pretty busy according to your receptionist.'

'It does very well but I'm sure you haven't driven here to talk about dogs and cats. Why are you here Raine?'

'Firstly to apologise, which I've already done and secondly to ask what I asked before. Your eyes will answer my question. I want to know if you still love

302

me and please don't look away when you answer,' he said, taking hold of her hand.

As Robyn lifted her head there were tears in her eyes.

'I knew you did,' he whispered tenderly. 'What's this wedge that you persist in driving between us? Maybe I could help if you'd give me a chance.'

'There are certain things I haven't told you Raine, things I could never tell you. I'm not the person you think I am. I'm underhand, deceitful and I'm a liar,' she sobbed.

'Don't be ridiculous. You're open and honest and those are the special qualities I love about you. You are a fine young woman.'

'No, those are your qualities, not mine. I'm just a cheap criminal....so there, I've said it now. I never intended telling anyone. Now will you please leave me alone to get on with the rest of my life? I don't deserve anyone like you.'

'I'm going nowhere until you tell me what you've done. If I'm to walk away for ever, I think I deserve to know why. Why won't you confide in me?'

'Just drop it Raine. The truth would hurt you very much. I'm asking you nicely....so would you please just leave me in peace?'

'Not until you tell me. Please darling, don't keep punishing yourself. Just let me share the secret with you. I'm sure there was reasonable cause for you to do whatever you did.'

At that, Robyn burst into tears. 'There was Raine. Everything underhand I did was to protect you and my daughter.'

'I don't understand. Protect us from what?'

'Oh God!' she cried out. 'Why did you come here tonight? She's *your* daughter Raine....not David's. I couldn't bring myself to tell you. I did want to but you have to understand why I couldn't place such a burden at your door. I didn't want to cause further pain, not when you had so much to contend with at home so I allowed everybody to believe that I was carrying David's child. No one had reason to think otherwise but my deception didn't end there. When my solicitor discovered I was pregnant, he claimed thousands of pounds for her future upkeep from the driver's Motor Insurer. David and I couldn't have children naturally. We'd undergone IVF treatment several times and that had proved unsuccessful too. It started off as a simple untruth when I found out I was pregnant and it escalated out of all proportion from there. I knew you had a legal and moral right to be involved but I believed it would have torn you apart to learn you had fathered my child when you could make no commitment to me. I didn't want to hurt anyone. I've never stopped loving you for one moment and our daughter is a constant reminder of what we had but also of the lies I told. I named her Verity which means truth and I vowed I would raise her as a child of true integrity. I'm not a bad person Raine. I was simply trying to do the right thing for everyone,' she sobbed.

Raine didn't interrupt throughout Robyn's tearful account and when she reached the end, he made no criticism of her behaviour.

'May I see her?' he asked.

'Of course you may. She's a delightful little girl. She's so affectionate, like you. I don't expect your forgiveness but I hope and pray that someday you'll be able to understand why I felt it necessary to do such a terrible thing.'

'I do understand. We all have to make decisions every single day of our lives and from time to time we make mistakes. I made an enormous one when I allowed you to walk away. It was what *you* wanted but it certainly wasn't what I wanted though having listened to what you've told me, I fail to understand how you managed to get away with such deception when dealing with an Insurance Company. Didn't they require a paternity test? I'd have thought that would be routine in such circumstances, especially when they are reputed to leave no stone unturned if there's any means of escaping their liability to pay a claim.'

'Yes, they did request the test and I was terrified when my solicitor informed me but as it turned out, yours and David's blood type are evidently alike as they didn't question a thing. I was going out of my mind until I learned everything had been finalised. It was my solicitor who insisted on filing the claim for Verity when I was well into my pregnancy and there was no way I could wriggle my way out of it then....well not without exposing myself as a bare-faced liar. I didn't want to ruin your life, neither did I want anyone to know I'd slept with another man so soon after David's death so I had to proceed with the lie. I had David's parents and family to consider too. Furthermore, I didn't want Verity to discover

305

how she'd been conceived, to grow up in the belief she was nothing more than an unplanned accidental consequence of a grubby one-night-stand. What we had was so special but other people wouldn't have known that. I was in an unenviable predicament and none of it was Verity's fault so I made the decision to lose you in order to protect both of you and I had to stand by that decision once it had been made.'

'You should have told me. It was wrong of you to keep an issue of such magnitude to yourself. I could have helped if only you had confided in me. If you believed I was the father, didn't you think I had a right to know?'

'Yes, you definitely had a right to know but I've already explained that I'd made my decision back then and I can't undo the past Raine. Even now I'm worried that the Insurance Company will discover what I've done and if that day ever dawns, I'll have to face the consequences of my actions. Have you any idea how that makes me feel? There's never a day goes by but what I think about what I've done but having said that I'd do it all again to protect you and Verity. Come upstairs; I'll take you to see her.' Taking Raine's hand she led him to the nursery.

After turning on the lamp by her cot, she reached in, lifted Verity out and passed her to him, feeling a strong pang of remorse that caused her to burst into tears.

'Don't wake her,' he whispered as he cradled the sleeping child in his arms.

He walked towards the light and studied her face. 'She's a beautiful child,' he told Robyn. 'She's got your colouring and your cute turned-up nose. We'd have loved a little girl, Victoria and I, but they were both boys. Would you put her back now please? I'd hate her to wake in the arms of a stranger.'

Robyn lifted her from Raine's arms and carefully placed her in her cot. 'Goodnight my precious,' she said, leaning over to kiss her.

Raine kissed his fingers and tenderly touched her forehead. 'Sleep tight little girl,' he whispered.

When they returned to the sitting room she asked, 'Would you like another drink?'

'I'd better not. I'm driving and anyway, I have to leave shortly. I'm sure with Christmas looming that you must have a thousand and one things to do and I've already taken up far too much of your valuable time but I would like to talk to you about something first.'

'Well, you don't have to rush off on my account. I've nothing to do that can't be done tomorrow. I'm having another drink. I need one after that. I never intended telling you about Verity but my reasoning was justifiable to me at the time. That's the truth. I didn't want to complicate your life further Raine.'

'I understand. Do you feel better now you've told me?' he asked. 'Has your conscience been eased at all?'

'Somewhat, I believe. I hate deception,' she told him, lowering her head in shame.

'I must admit, I do too and as it's confession time I have something to tell you. I should have told you earlier but I didn't know how because you were so distressed. I needed time to choose my words carefully. When my wife had the stroke, there was hope initially that she might make a complete recovery. The doctor did everything in his power to keep her alive and stop the haemorrhage, while all I could do was watch in horror as she gradually began to drift away but in the end, he was able to stabilise her and more medication was administered to try and revive her from the coma. As I explained, Victoria didn't respond to that medication and remained in a coma but I was told by the Consultant Neurologist that if she were to recover at some future time, it would be out of the question for her to have another child so the following week, I booked myself into a private treatment centre for a vasectomy. I couldn't run the risk that she might become pregnant again. Do you understand what I'm saying Robyn?' he questioned, taking hold of her whilst staring intensely into her troubled eyes. 'Verity really *is* David's child.'

For a moment she said nothing. She looked at him aghast, the colour draining from her face. Shocked and confused, she shook her head repeatedly as she continued to stare at him, unable to believe what he was saying. '*No....no*! That's not *possible*. It's not *possible* I tell you. I've already told you; David and I couldn't *have* children. We'd tried *everything*.'

'Right, just calm down and answer me this. Were you specifically told by *anybody* that you couldn't have children....that it wouldn't be possible?'

'Well....er....no, we weren't. As a matter of fact, we were advised there was no medical reason why I couldn't conceive. That applied to David too. It was fairly common, they said. We weren't alone. There were many couples in the same position, where, for reasons unknown, it simply didn't happen.'

'I know this is hard for you to understand but I'm *not* Verity's father. Having said that, nothing would give me greater pleasure if I were. Can you believe I would have put you at risk of becoming pregnant after saying I could make no commitment to you? I told you I was married soon after we met. I'm not dishonest. I loved you then and I still love you now. That's the reason I'm here....to tell you how much you mean to me. I know this must be very difficult to come to terms with but it happens to be the *truth* and on the positive side, you have neither deceived nor lied to anyone. That's the reason the DNA test was never questioned. It's a very reliable test and it confirmed beyond any doubt that David was indeed the father.'

She stared at him uneasily. 'Even if what you say is true, I still lied because I lied to you when I told you I was pregnant with David's child, when I had every reason to believe she was yours.'

'I forgive you! It *was* a lie but I know you said it for the right reasons and I respect you for that but if you'd been honest with me, we'd have discussed it then as we're doing now and you would have saved all those months of heartache.'

'I still can't believe it. David's mother once told me that Verity had David's eyes and I couldn't look her in the face because I felt so ashamed.'

'We should count ourselves lucky, shouldn't we? Victoria gave me two amazing sons and David gave you a perfect daughter. We have a lot to thank them for. The tragedy is that Victoria never got to see our younger son and David never saw his child either.'

'You're right and there's a heartbreaking feeling I have now that Verity has lost her father. I never felt like that when I believed *you* were her father as you were still around, even though I hadn't told you the truth. I looked at your photograph from time to time and contemplated about what might have been had I not become pregnant. I missed you so much and I'll be perfectly honest about this; when I found out I was pregnant, not only did I believe the baby was yours, I *wanted* it to be yours Raine. That really *is* the truth.'

He rapidly blinked the moisture from his eyes and took hold of her hand. 'Thank you Robyn. That has to be the greatest compliment anyone has ever paid me. So….that leads me to ask the same question I asked once before….where do we go from here?'

Without allowing her time to answer, he took her in his arms. 'Please don't say there's no future for us, because you know as well as I do, we'll always be in each other's thoughts, no matter where we are or what we're doing. That's how it's been since the first moment we met. Put me out of my misery and tell me I can call on you again now.'

She smiled lovingly. 'I'd like that very much.'

He held her gently to his body and Robyn didn't resist as they stood in silence, each in deep thought and unified in total and utter relief at finally having resolved their differences.

He was happy just to hold her close, while Robyn was happy to reflect on Raine's startling revelation that had served to exonerate her of all wrongdoing. It had certainly been a bitter-sweet disclosure.

He looked deeply into her eyes. 'Try to relax now and stop worrying. You're shaking like a leaf. It's over darling; it's really over. All your problems are behind you now.'

'Sorry!' she said, forcing a smile. 'I'm all at sixes and sevens. I'm obviously still in shock. I just can't believe what's happened tonight.'

'Same here, but then I was never allowed to know why you wouldn't speak to me.'

'I owe you a debt of gratitude Raine. Thank you for easing my conscience.'

Cautiously he asked, 'May I call you tomorrow?'

'Of course; please do. Are you collecting the boys tomorrow from your parents' house?'

'Yes, I'm picking them up around midday. I can't describe how I've missed having them here but it's been very productive for the two of us and for that I'm so grateful. I'll talk to you soon.' Brushing his lips gently against her cheek he murmured, 'Goodnight Robyn.'

'I'll walk you to the door,' she said and when he ran to his car in the cold wintry air, she experienced a warm and satisfying glow within her as she raised her hand and waved goodnight to him.

Early the next day, Raine called her and when she answered sleepily he said, 'It's only me. I was just wondering how you felt today?'

'A good ten years younger. I feel like a love-sick silly teenager and surprisingly calm too, apart from the occasional collywobbles when I think of you.'

In a petulant tone he rejoined, 'I'm sorry to hear you're only thinking of me occasionally, especially since you haven't escaped my thoughts for a single moment since I left yesterday. I'm disappointed at that because *I* can't wait to see *you* again.'

She laughed. 'Shut up! You know very well what I mean *Doctor Quinlan*. I'm happy we've resolved our differences and it's such a weight off my mind to know I'm not a criminal anymore. My life's been absolute hell for nearly two years. Incidentally, now there's no longer a need for confidentiality, what *is* your real name?'

'Why not stick with Doctor Quinlan? After all, it was due to him that I got my foot through the door last night. You wouldn't have allowed me in otherwise. Besides, I've become quite attached to it now and it isn't such a bad name is it?'

'You're such a clown,' she laughed. 'Alright, you win. I won't argue with you. Doctor Quinlan it can be for the time being but there'll come a point when it backfires on you and I'll be laughing more then. So, how about you? Do you feel any better today?'

'I feel much better knowing I have your support and yes, I'm coming to terms with everything and I'll get there before too long. I'm leaving shortly to collect the boys but I needed to hear your voice and I wanted tell you again that I love you.'

'That's nice and I love you too.'

Raine sighed softly. 'You've no idea how good it feels to hear you speak those words. I've waited for what seems an eternity for that. Listen, have you an hour or so to spare later?'

312

'I've nothing in particular planned and certainly nothing that can't be put off until tomorrow. Why, what did you have in mind?'

'Well, when I've collected the boys, I'm virtually passing your door on my way home and it would be an opportunity for you to meet them. If we were to pop in for a chat, perhaps the boys could see some of the animals, that's if you have enough time. I'm sure they'd enjoy that very much and it would also be an introduction.'

'Do you think it's wise so soon after they've lost their mother? What would you tell them about us?'

'That wouldn't be a problem. I'd introduce you as a friend I've known for some time. There's nothing underhand about that.'

'In that case, I'd love to meet them Raine. What time will you be here?'

'Would around one o'clock be alright?'

'That'd be fine. I'll look forward to it.'

'Me too because I'm missing you. It's ages since I've seen you.'

'Get away with you, you clown! It was only last night,' she hooted with laughter.

12

Hannah Wilkinson, striving to conceal her excitement, gathered the staff together in reception when she hurried into work that morning, assembling the kennel lads and girls first.

'What's up?' Tom, the longest serving employee enquired. 'Are we getting a Christmas bonus or two extra weeks' holiday pay?'

'Huh, you're a right comedian aren't you? When did we ever get owt for nowt?' Hannah responded mockingly. 'Misery guts wouldn't give us the time of day unless we were clocking off a minute or two early. I don't know what's up with her. She walks round all day with a face like thunder like she's lost a quid and found a penny. I feel sorry for that little baby of hers. Imagine having a mother like that! I'd rather be an orphan.'

'Well come on then, tell us why we're here. I've got that fat ugly-faced bulldog to bath and groom. I only did him yesterday and he went and slipped in a sticky wet cow-pat early this morning, the gormless bugger and they're picking him up in another two hours and he's caked in....'

'Alright Tom, you can spare us the details, thank you,' Hannah interrupted quickly. 'The reason I've called you in is to give you a bit of juicy gossip!'

'About who?' Peter Jones, better known as *Pasty-face* Peter asked quizzically and whose fitting nickname had been selected for him when he arrived on the scene a year ago, primarily because of his weird deathly-white complexion but additionally because there was already another Peter who worked in the west-wing kennel and whose nick-name was *Ruddy* Peter.

'About *whom* I think you mean Pasty-face,' Mary Cotteral corrected him snootily while flashing him a critical glance.

'Oh do you now? Well I can't say I've ever heard them dogs complain about bad grammar when I've been feeding 'em, Miss Smarty-Pants and come to think of it, they haven't grumbled when I've forgot to give 'em serviettes to wipe their sloppy chops on when they've done eating.'

Everyone tittered at Peter's sharp comeback.

'Will you lot just shut your big gobs and listen to me,' Hannah said. 'If *she* walks in you'll not get to know anything and trust me you'll be sorry if you don't get to hear what I've got to tell you.'

'Come on then; get on with it,' Ruddy Peter cried out impatiently. 'I can't stand in here all ruddy day waiting. I've all them ruddy dogs to see to.'

Hannah waited until she had everyone's attention and took a deep breath.

'You're never going to believe this,' she revealed wide-eyed. 'Her Ladyship had a visitor last night!'

She nodded her head slowly in confirmation, her eyes bulging with pomposity as she looked at each one individually before continuing quietly, 'It was some bloke! Yes, that's what I said....a bloke,' she repeated in a hoarse whisper. 'He rang the doorbell and when I answered he asked for Her Ladyship by name....said he was a friend of hers....and a *Doctor* would you believe? Needless to say, she cracked on

315

she didn't know who he was when I told her but I could see she'd done her make-up and combed her hair before she came through and then she spoke to him and I heard everything they said. It sounded to me as if they'd had a bit of a tiff earlier on because he was apologising and listen to this....he called her *darling*! She turned round, asking me to release the security lock and I got a right telling off because it was obvious I'd been listening to both of them, but how could I have avoided hearing them when I was standing here behind the desk as they were talking over the intercom? Then this bloke walked in and I could have *died*, I'm telling you. He was absolutely drop-dead *gorgeous*....the most handsome guy I've ever seen and she ushered him through to the living room right away.'

'What happened then?' Mary Cotteral asked.

'Well *I* don't know do I? I left forty minutes later and he was still here then so I don't know what they got up to behind closed doors but it was obvious he hadn't been here before because she asked him how he'd managed to find her.'

'You should have got your ear to the ruddy door. That's what I'd have done if I'd been here. I'd have made it my ruddy business to find out,' Peter said.

'Aye, and you'd have got the ruddy sack if *she'd* caught you ear-wigging at the ruddy door,' Pasty-face advised him in no uncertain terms. 'Aye, you'd have been down that ruddy lane like Emil Zátopek with her boot up your ruddy a....'

'*Enough!*' Mary yelled as the others howled with laughter at his mimicry.

316

'*You're* going the right road for a ruddy thump if you don't watch yourself lad,' he snarled.

'So is that everything you saw then?' Mary asked, looking a bit disappointed. 'I was hoping for much more than that. You didn't catch them in a clinch or anything then?'

'No, more's the pity! But who'd have thought it? Mrs. High and Mighty Ainsley with a bloke?'

'Let's hope he's put a smile on her miserable face for once,' one of the young dog walkers said. 'I get an ear-'ole full every time the old battleaxe looks at me in fact there's only one person here she does get on with and that's Ellie. Ask her if she knows who this chap is when she comes in tomorrow. Happen she knows something we don't. Lady Muck talks to her.'

'I'll do that in fact I might even ring her up later,' Hannah promised them. 'You'd best clear off now. She'll be making her rounds soon and she'll have a fit if she comes in here first and catches us all stood about doing nothing.'

'*Standing* about,' Mary corrected her haughtily. 'I really do wish you'd learn to speak properly.'

'Oh, shut your rip Mary. You've not done so well for yourself for all your airs and graces. You're not employed at Buckingham Palace with the Queen's corgis. You're a bog-standard kennel girl, working here, so go and find some dog muck to sweep up.'

'Make sure you keep us all informed of any fresh developments,' Ruddy Peter called to Hannah as he vanished through the doorway. 'Mrs. Ainsley with a ruddy feller!' he howled with laughter as he made his way back to the kennels. 'That's the best ruddy laugh I've had in a while!'

Robyn's mystery guest was the main topic of conversation for the rest of the morning as further staff members arrived to change shifts with others and as the story was passed on from one to another, it was inevitable that a variety of embellishments came to be added, particularly following her eleven o'clock inspection of the kennels and cattery when she had breezed past everyone full of the joys of spring.

'Excellent Simon!' she remarked, referring to the cattery that was spick and span and he stared at her open-mouthed before spluttering, 'Er....thanks Mrs. Ainsley,' at having been awarded a complimentary remark for the first time ever.

'Isn't it a lovely morning? It's so fresh and sunny that you'd hardly know we were in December. Are you doing anything special over Christmas?'

'Er....no.... just the usual stuff with the family,' he replied, taken aback by her sudden interest in staff welfare.

'Be sure you enjoy it. You've earned your break. You work very hard Simon. Well done!'

As she walked out, he leaned against the handle of his mop, reflecting on their short conversation in disbelief and it transpired later in the day that other staff members had been similarly flabbergasted by her change in spirit and which, they concluded, had to be consequential to the previous evening's clandestine rendezvous with the mystery visitor and the ensuing shenanigans behind closed doors.

13

After bathing and dressing Verity, Robyn hurriedly changed into some fresh clothes and applied a little make-up. Raine would be arriving shortly with the boys and she wanted to make a good impression.

She prepared a platter of assorted sandwiches and with the boys in mind, rummaged in her freezer for a box of small iced cakes and a packet of chocolate rolls.

She was about to relax with a much deserved cup of coffee when Ellie called her.

Without making any reference to a call she'd had earlier from Hannah, she initially made small talk.

'Did you get through your list of jobs yesterday? It seemed to be a bit of a tall order. I can come over and give you a lift this afternoon for an hour or so if you need another pair of hands.'

'Thanks Ellie but I've done everything now. I had a couple of things to finish off but I did those when I got up this morning and I've signed off the VAT returns and they're in the post. I'm pretty-well up to date so I'm going to have a nice quiet relaxing few days now before the onslaught on Christmas Eve.'

It quickly became apparent that Robyn hadn't the slightest intention of discussing her mystery visitor, so Ellie trod carefully to avoid riling her and asked, 'Do you have anything of interest to tell me?'

'No....nothing that springs to mind. Why, what do you mean?'

'Don't play the innocent with me! You know very well what I'm talking about. I'm referring to your mystery guest, the *medical* gentleman who paid you a visit last evening!'

Robyn expelled an embarrassed burst of laughter. 'Is nothing private around here?'

'Excuse me but aren't you the one who constantly reminds the staff to keep their eyes and ears open? Don't criticise them for doing their work efficiently so stop stalling and tell me what's going on. Have you been keeping something from me?'

'Well firstly, he's not a doctor! Secondly, there's no mystery and thirdly he's merely an acquaintance who called round to see me.'

In a sing-song voice she said, 'That's not the way I heard it. Come on, out with it. Everybody's really excited that you have a new boyfriend.'

'I *don't* have a new boyfriend and there's nothing to tell so can we drop the subject please?'

'Alright if you won't tell me I can't make you but you'll not be able to hide him away forever. So are you seeing him again?'

She tittered once more. 'Yes, well….let's just say that's for me to know and you to find out.'

'Oh, I'll do that alright. If I haven't found out by Christmas Day, I'll prise it out of you then in front of Abbie and Gerald. Just answer me this then. Will your new gentleman friend be there for Christmas dinner?'

'Certainly not and shut up about him now or I'll hang up.'

'Is he a client? Is that how you met?'

'I'm telling you nothing at all, so stop asking me questions.'

'Well, whoever he is, I hope it works out for you. You deserve a bit of pleasure after all the tragedy in your life. It's nice to have a diversion. All you ever seem to do is work.'

'That's because I like to work, so please, for the last time, just let it drop,' she replied irritably. 'My private life is my own.'

'Suit yourself but it will all come out eventually. I'll see you tomorrow. Take care.'

Raine and the boys arrived just before one o'clock and he introduced Robyn as a friend he had known for a long time. 'This is Michael who's six and this young rascal is Timmy. He's four.' Addressing his children he told them, 'This lady's name is Robyn.'

'That's a *bird's* name,' Michael scoffed.

As Raine was about to admonish him, Robyn cut in quickly, 'Yes, you're right it is Michael but I'm afraid I can't fly.'

'I can,' Timmy declared, flapping his outstretched arms and running round in circles.

Robyn laughed. 'Well aren't you a clever young man? Tell me Timmy, do you like dogs and cats?'

'*Yes*!' he shouted in reply.

'Don't shout Timmy,' his father scolded.

'He's fine. You have two delightful boys and you must be very proud of them.'

'Yes, I am,' he replied with a modest smile, 'but they can be more than a little exuberant at times.'

'Well, they've been through a lot too don't forget, and you don't have to worry about noise here. It's pandemonium at times with up to seventy barking dogs as you can well imagine though you get used to the cacophony of animal noises after a while.'

Speaking to the boys she asked, 'Are you hungry? Can you eat some sandwiches or better still, would you like a yummy chocolate cake?'

'*Yes....a yummy chocolate cake*!' Timmy yelled.

'Say *please*!' Raine demanded, glaring critically at his young son.

'Please,' Timmy echoed apologetically.

'Let's see what I can find for you then. Take these colouring books and crayons with you to that room right at the end,' she said, handing them a selection of books and pencils.

Turning to Raine, Robyn explained, 'When some clients are booking in their pets, their children can become irritable and mischievous so I have a box of toys in reception to keep them occupied.'

As the boys hurried away, Raine replied, 'You've thought of everything haven't you? You even have toys for the kids. How considerate.'

'It's not that at all. It's what's known as damage limitation. Some of the kids run riot so it stops them wrecking the place,' she grinned. 'I'm a very astute businesswoman. I try to anticipate problems before they arise.'

He leaned towards Robyn and kissed her tenderly, holding her for some moments before releasing her. 'I've been longing to do that since we arrived. You haven't left my thoughts for a single moment since last night and I can't express how happy I am to see you again today. *I've* been like a love-sick teenager *too* since last night. That's what I meant when I told you on the ship that you'd brought something to my life that had been missing for two years, except that it's four years now. You make me feel excited; you also make me feel there's a lot to look forward to in life. There's been so much despair in my life Robyn and you've raised me to a new level of hope. When I think of you I feel happy and it's even better when I see you.'

'I feel the same to see you. I too have had despair coupled with fear in my life for a while and I'm still finding it hard to believe that it's all behind me now and I've been anything but considerate towards my conscientious staff, speaking of which,' she smiled, 'your visit last night raised quite a few eyebrows as well as a great deal of speculation about us. It's not long since Ellie rang, wanting to know all about the good-looking mystery visitor I'd been entertaining. It appears Hannah on reception had told her and so I made sure it didn't happen again today. I sent her home at twelve. We're not busy at the moment so I arranged for all incoming calls to be put through to me. I doubt we'll be interrupted though.'

He flashed a comical smile. 'I'm sorry if I caused any embarrassment. So, what was Ellie's response when you told her about us? Was she shocked?'

'I didn't tell her. I said an acquaintance had called in to see me, that's all. I didn't specify who he was and your name didn't crop up in the conversation. Besides, she thinks my new found friend is a doctor so Hannah, the girl on reception obviously gave her that snippet of information. Ellie would never have imagined him to be you and in the circumstances, I thought it better to keep it quiet for the time being. She sounded a bit peeved but then that's of no consequence since I'm not answerable to my staff.'

'Staff? Why does Ellie work here now?'

'Yes, she's been working here for three months or so. Her boyfriend, Andrew, used to do my accounts but he went back to University in October to study for a further qualification and so Ellie took over his job. She's very efficient too.'

'I *am* behind the times....Ellie having a boyfriend *and* working for you. I bet her mum had something to say about that.'

Robyn smirked. 'She's much better now. I think she's pleased Ellie's working here for me. At least she knows where she goes each day and what she's doing. She accepts it anyway. She's not a bad sort when you get to know her properly. Her heart's in the right place. She was just being over-protective and I can see that now I have a child of my own.'

'Well, I hope you'll be as equally indulgent of my two rowdy lads,' he grinned. 'Believe me, they can be quite a handful so be forewarned. I try very hard to keep them under control but I rarely succeed.'

'Be thankful they're not distressed and withdrawn Raine. Boys will be boys. Try to think back to your own childhood. I'm quite sure they'll have settled down quietly now with their colouring books.'

'I hope you're right. I must confess I was a little surprised by Timmy's behaviour. He's not usually as boisterous as he was today when he meets new people, nor is Michael for that matter. They're very shy as a rule.'

'That's good isn't it? They obviously felt relaxed and at ease. Isn't that what we both want for them? Come on, let's join them before they decide to burn the place down,' she laughed. 'Are you off to your parents' house for Christmas?'

'No, they spend Christmas with friends in warmer climes; in fact they're off to Spain tomorrow. They offered to cancel this time but I told them to go. I'll be okay with the boys and my thoughts. It'll just be a quiet few days but I'll try to make the best of it. I still have many bridges to cross.'

Bringing to mind Ellie's earlier question, Robyn suggested, 'Why don't you and the boys come here for Christmas dinner? We're having a party. Ellie is going to be here with her boyfriend and my friend Abbie is coming with her husband Gerald. He's my solicitor. They have a five-month old baby girl and there'll be Verity as well, so there should be quite a houseful.'

'You're very kind Robyn and I do appreciate your offer but it will be my first Christmas since Victoria died and it wouldn't be....er....appropriate. Believe me, I don't mean to sound ungrateful.'

'I understand what you're saying but think about the boys too. Would Victoria want them to feel sad or would she want them to be happy, enjoying the things other children enjoy at Christmas? A change of environment might be beneficial for all of you so don't just write off the idea.'

'Thank you. I'll give it some thought and let you know. I'm aware I should consider the boys' needs but I don't want to put a damper on things.'

'It's your decision Raine. You must do what you believe is right. You're welcome to come, that's all I'm saying and if you do, we'll be eating at three. If you want to stay over, that's fine too. I have enough rooms for everyone who wants to stay the night and I'm inviting you as my friend, not my lover, so you don't have to feel obligated in any way should you decide to come. I'm sure you know what I mean.'

His cheeks turned pink and he discharged a high-pitched screech of laughter before saying, 'No one could ever accuse you of beating about the bush!'

'I'm trying to be your friend. I'm merely offering options Raine. The rest is up to you.'

Raine kissed her again but this time as a gesture of gratitude, rather than affection. 'You're my very best friend Robyn. I know what you're trying to do for me and thanks. If I appear unappreciative please excuse me. This is a taxing time but I'm trying my best, I really am.'

'I know you are and I also know how much you love Victoria. I still love David but it's a very small heart that can't love more than one person. I would never take advantage of your vulnerability.'

Seriously he questioned, 'As I did yours?'

Distressed by his response, she murmured quietly, 'I didn't mean that at all. You were unaware of my vulnerability.'

'I'm sorry. Why I made such an insensitive retort is beyond credibility. Please forgive me. I seem to spend my entire life at the moment apologising for stupid things I say and do. I should count up to ten each time I'm about to open my tactless mouth.'

He gave her a remorseful hug and looked deeply into her eyes. 'I've a lot to learn yet about grief. I'm annoyed with myself for feeling so happy when my soul is crying out that I shouldn't, but you'd know all about that wouldn't you?'

'It'll pass Raine. It does eventually, once you get things in perspective. Let it take its course. You'll have good days and bad days but the painful feeling of emptiness eases given time, trust me.'

He brushed his lips against her forehead. 'I'm so glad we're friends again,' he whispered.

When they entered the living room, the boys were totally absorbed in their colouring books and didn't even look up.

'See what I mean?' Robyn said. 'They've settled down alright now.'

'It's called a woman's touch and that's something I don't have. I find parenthood awfully challenging at times.'

'You're not alone. It's a very big responsibility. I certainly never imagined it would be so difficult.'

'Look what I've drawn Robyn,' Timmy cried out, holding up a picture. 'It's a....what is it daddy?'

'That's a squirrel, son.'

'It's a screwel Robyn. It eats nuts.'

'*Squirrel*,' Raine corrected him. 'You try saying it properly....*squirr-el*.

'*Screw-el*,' he tried to replicate painstakingly and Robyn burst out laughing.

'Right little guys, are you ready for something to eat now?' she asked.

In unison they replied, 'Yes please.'

'If you like afterwards, I'll take you to see all the dogs. We have many different cats too if you'd like to see those as well.'

Michael beamed with excitement. 'I'd really like to see them Robyn.'

'Me too,' Timmy added eagerly.

Michael glared at his younger brother and grunted indignantly, 'He always copies me!'

'Well now Michael,' Robyn said, kneeling down beside him. 'That's because *you* are his big brother so Timmy looks up to you. You are older and much wiser so when you say something, Timmy knows it must be right. You should feel very proud when he copies what you do as that shows he trusts you and that's *very* important between brothers because you have to look after him when daddy's not around.'

He furrowed his brow. 'I guess you're right.'

Raine put his arm around her waist and pulled her towards him. 'You're amazing Robyn and we *will* be here for Christmas dinner,' he said softly.

At the precise moment Raine kissed her, Michael looked up and gasped, 'Oops!' then quickly turned away to continue with the picture he was colouring.

Raine was shocked to have been caught in the act but laughed heartily when Timmy looked round and asked, 'What?' and when in reply Michael rejoined matter-of-factly, 'You get on with your picture. It's a grown-up thing and I'll tell you all about it when you're older.'

'Precocious little brat,' Raine howled and Robyn rested her head against his shoulder, content to be close to the man she loved.

When they had finished their refreshments, Raine collected up the crockery and followed Robyn into the kitchen.

'This has gone much better than I expected. The boys have really taken to you,' he told her.

'Like father, like son. Come on....let's go see the animals. We'll take Verity too. I can see you're on edge. You can hardly keep still.'

'Only because *you* are driving me crazy,' he said, gazing lovingly into her eyes. 'I'll get the boys. Are you sure you want to do this?'

'Do what?'

'The tour of the animals. Don't you have staff in the kennels and cattery? I was just thinking you'd be starting all the tongues wagging again. Can you cope with that?'

She laughed. 'What's more to the point, can *they* cope with all this intrigue? At least, it will provide an interesting topic of conversation at their surprise Christmas party I've organised for them. Moreover, while they're discussing me, they're leaving someone else alone. Besides, I'm very thick-skinned and after the stress I've had to contend with, I can stand a bit of tittle-tattle if you can.'

'I couldn't care less. It's not me who has to work with them,' he grinned.

The boys thoroughly enjoyed meeting the animals and Verity never tired of seeing them as there were always new breeds to see due to the vast turnover.

Robyn was impressed by Raine's vast knowledge of the various breeds of dog as he explained to his sons the origin of the majority of them.

'You're very knowledgeable,' she complimented him. 'Do you read a lot?'

'Not especially,' he said without any expansion of his reply.

The whole tour took the best part of an hour and when it was over, Raine said it was time to leave.

'Say thank you nicely to Robyn for showing you the animals and for lunch,' he prompted the boys. 'We've had a really nice time haven't we?'

'Thank you Robyn,' they said in chorus.

'Oh, one last thing before you go Raine....would you help me slide an extra leaf in my dining table? It needs to be a bit longer now the three of you are coming too.'

'Certainly, just lead the way.'

'Wow!' Michael exclaimed when they walked in the dining room. 'Just look at that tree dad. That's a *real* Christmas tree. It's a whopper! Can we have a tree please? Me and Timmy can make all the things to hang on it. I know what to do. We've made them at school. Can we dad?'

'Yes, can we daddy?' Timmy echoed, tugging at his father's sleeve.

His brow etched with sadness, he sighed audibly. 'Not this year son. Maybe next year we can have a tree,' he replied, ruffling Timmy's hair and smiling sensitively at the two of them.

Unexpectedly, Timmy remarked, 'Our mummy's gone to Jesus. Will Jesus have a nice Christmas tree daddy?'

Barely able to utter the words, Raine answered, 'I er....I expect so Timmy.'

Robyn's eyes were filled with tears and quick as a flash she turned to the boys and asked, 'How would you like to come here on Christmas Day with your daddy? You never know, perhaps Father Christmas might just leave something under this tree for you. That would be good if he did, wouldn't it, so what do you say?'

The children's eyes lit up instantly. 'Can we dad? Please say we can,' Michael pleaded.

'Yes, can we daddy?' Timmy echoed, jumping up and down excitedly.

'Well, if you're both very good, I think we might do that,' he said with a broad smile, hugging Robyn discreetly. 'I think I'd enjoy it too in fact I'm sure I would.'

Raine swiftly lifted the table leaf in place single-handedly and pushed the table ends together.

'Done! Are you really sure it won't be too much trouble with three more on Christmas Day?'

With a loving smile, she replied, 'Yes, I'm really sure.'

'That's settled then. Thank you very much. I'll be calling you before then,' he told her and as the boys ran off towards the car, he added, 'Thanks for today as well Robyn. I speak for the boys too when I say it all went really well.'

'I thought so too. Drive carefully.'

Robyn checked the time when she went indoors. It was almost six o'clock and that meant it was one o'clock in New York. She hadn't spoken to Bryony in weeks and she decided it was time to give her an update on recent developments, particularly as there was no one else in whom she could confide regarding her new found friendship with Raine.

One o'clock was usually a good time to catch her on a Saturday. Bryony always went out celebrating the end of the working week on a Friday night and rarely returned home before the early hours, so she would sleep in late the following morning and have brunch around two o'clock.

Robyn had recently received a seasonal Christmas card from Bryony that had revived happy memories of Central Park where they had spent time when she had visited New York.

Consulting her notepad for the details, she made herself comfortable prior to calling the number. Her sister eventually answered following several rings and drawled incoherently, 'This infringement of my legal right to sleep had better be a matter of life and death. I'm warning you, whoever you are! You've just woke me up and I'm ripping!'

Apologetically Robyn spluttered, 'I'm very sorry Bryony, it's me.'

'*Robyn*, is that really you?' she screeched, sitting up in bed fully awake. We were only talking about you last night in the bar. Your ears must have been burning for you to call me today.'

'Is this a bad time? I can call you back later if you like, if you'd rather go back to sleep.'

'Don't talk wet. Anyway, I'm wide awake now. I thought it was one of my inconsiderate friends who habitually phone at stupid times. So, bring me up to speed with all the goss. Are you still moping about like a zombie or are you getting a life now?'

She laughed. 'Yes, I'm getting a life at long last and I've loads to tell you. Everything has happened so quickly over the past few days.'

Bryony pricked up her ears. 'Don't tell me you've got yourself a new bloke. You have haven't you? Is he anyone I know? What's he called? Is he dishy? Where did you meet him? Is he single? Well come on; don't keep me in suspense. I'm going mad here. Dish the dirt.'

'If you'll shut up for one second I'll tell you. He isn't a *new* bloke. He's someone I've known for a while, someone I mentioned to you before. It's the guy who....'

'I don't recall anything being said about any guy,' she cut in. 'The only guy you've ever mentioned to me was the one you dumped, you know, that bloke you had a thing with on the QE2....er....what's-his-name....something to do with bad weather....the one with the sick wife.'

'Raine. His name's Raine and yes, that's the guy I'm talking about. That's what I'm trying to tell you if I can get a word in. He's the one.'

'*He's* the one? Tell me you're having me on! So what about his wife?'

'She died not long ago and when I heard I phoned Raine to tell him how sorry I was and he asked if he could come to see me. Needless to say, I refused as I didn't want him turning to me on the rebound but he found out where I live and just turned up out of the blue and it isn't like that. We're just friends and nothing's happened between us yet, but I've made up my mind that I'm not going to walk away from him for a second time. Anyway I just wanted to talk to you and let you know, that's all. I've met his two boys and they're great kids and they're coming here on Christmas Day, all three of them.'

In a tone of frustration she yelled, '*Dammit*! I'm going to miss out on that now but there was no way I could have afforded the astronomical flight price over Christmas. So, does mum know about him?'

'Nobody knows except you and I intend to keep it that way as long as I can for obvious reasons, since Raine has recently lost his wife, so I'd appreciate it if you'd keep it to yourself when you're talking to mum.'

'I won't say a word. I feel really narked that I'm not coming now! I'll be over early in the New Year though so I'll be able to see him then. Flight prices are half the price in January and February and it's also much easier to get time off work when there's less demand for leave. So come on, let's be knowing; what does this gorgeous guy of yours do for a living?'

Robyn laughed. 'You'll think I'm mad when I say this but I don't know. When we met on the ship, we didn't discuss personal issues like that. We had our fling and went our separate ways because that was the way I wanted it. He gave me his phone number but I never used it until I heard about his wife. For all I know he might not have a job but I expect all will be revealed in due course. He's a terrific guy; he's a good father to his kids and that's all I need to know at the moment. He's made his feelings for me clear but neither of us wants to rush into anything.

It's early days for him. Raine's still grieving for his wife and I certainly don't want him to feel the guilt I felt when I became involved with him soon after David's death, so we're just taking things a day at a time. The fact we're back together is enough for me for the time being. For the first time since David's death I feel alive and it's such an amazing feeling. I find myself singing as I'm doing my chores; I feel ten years younger and as for the way my staff look at me now....well let's just say they obviously think I'm off my rocker!'

'Well I'm delighted for you Robyn. Let's hope it works out right for you both this time. God knows you deserve a bit of pleasure and a decent guy after all you've suffered.'

'Thanks Bryony. I hope so too. So tell me, what about *you*?'

'What about *me*?'

'Yes *you*....we haven't talked for ages. Have you got anyone half-decent lined up yet? The last time I spoke to you, you mentioned you were thinking of breaking it off with the IT bloke you were seeing so did you?'

'Oh, there's been one or two since then but I can't really get involved long term with anybody in this job. I never know where I'm going to be posted but suffice to say I really enjoy myself. I go to loads of parties. I'll never get permanently hitched when I'm forever globe-trotting. Anyway, enough about me. I want to know all about my gorgeous little niece. I can't believe she's approaching her first birthday. Is she walking yet?'

'Almost....she will be in a day or two. She's taken a few tentative steps with the help of the furniture and she's demolishing the Christmas tree as fast as I hang the baubles. I bought her a lovely red velvet party frock for Christmas Day so I'll send you some photographs early in the New Year. If I don't have chance to call you again, have a fantastic Christmas and I'll talk to you very soon. Remember me to all your buddies. Wish them a Merry Christmas from me and try to keep sober!'

'I doubt I'll have any option. You ought to see the snow here! I won't be venturing very far in this lot I can tell you. I bet it's two feet deep already and still falling and it's very cold, so, please give my warm wishes to everybody and I wish you the best of luck with your *weatherman*,' she laughed. 'Let's hope it develops into something permanent this time. Tell mum I wish her a Merry Christmas. That'll save me the cost of an expensive phone call as she clacks for England when I'm paying. I wish we could have all been together at Christmas.'

'Me too! I'll pass on your message to mum. Take care of yourself Bryony. I'll keep you posted with developments at this end.'

'You'd better and don't forget, I want a wedding invitation,' she giggled. 'That's a trip I'll definitely make to England, whatever the price of the flight. Wild horses wouldn't keep me away.'

Robyn howled with laughter at that. 'You can rest assured, if it ever comes to that, *you* will be *numero uno* on my guest list; in fact I shall expect you to be chief bridesmaid....or matron of honour if you beat me down the aisle. You never know Bryony, Father Christmas might just pop up with someone special.'

'Huh! There's fat chance of that! I'll look forward to yours though and I *will* be your chief bridesmaid on one condition….if Raine finds me an unattached dishy best man, so have a quiet word in his ear and make sure he does. By the way, don't forget to keep me up to speed with the way things progress in the bedroom department. Bye Robyn….love you.'

Before she could make a fitting response to that, Bryony hung up.


'I need another three place cards,' Robyn said aloud as she rummaged through the drawer, tossing things aside haphazardly in search of a sheet of white card with which to make them.

She had already made out the place cards for the others and as she began to make additional ones for Michael and Timmy she chuckled to herself as she pondered over what she should put on Raine's. 'I'll teach *you* a lesson you won't forget in a hurry!' she mumbled to herself before proceeding to make one out that read *Doctor Quinlan*.

'I'll leave it to *you* to explain your alias to the rest of the guests!' she smirked superciliously. 'Doctor Quinlan indeed!'

14

Robyn jumped out of bed at six in the morning on Christmas Day, aware the twenty-five pound turkey would take hours to cook and she wanted to cook it slowly so it would be done through to the centre.

The turkey was already prepared and in the oven by the time Ellie arrived a little after seven to assist with the food preparation and keep a watchful eye on Verity.

'Andrew should be here in an hour or so. I didn't want him under the feet first thing,' she told Robyn. 'Maybe he could give Verity her breakfast when he arrives and that'd leave us to get on with everything else. What do you think?'

'Good idea because there's a lot to do. Would you make a start on the vegetables please?' she asked, consulting her list. 'Abbie and Gerald should arrive about one and I'd like everything to be finished by then apart from the vegetables which won't take too long to cook. I've prepared a starter that just needs finishing off. We're having home-made cauliflower and cheese soup. So, did your mother agree to your staying over tonight?'

'Yes, she never batted an eyelid in fact I think she was relieved. She didn't like the idea of me driving home in the early hours of the morning on my own in case there were drunks on the road. She's always the same when I'm out alone in my car whether it's night or day but you don't need *me* to enlighten you about how she worries over trivial matters! That'll never end.'

'*Who....your mum*?' Robyn responded quizzically in a high-pitched voice and they both laughed. 'So what about Andrew? Is he staying the night too?'

'We haven't discussed it,' she said, turning pink. 'He could sleep on the sofa I suppose. He'd be able to have a drink then.'

'Ellie I'm not your keeper, neither am I prying. If you want Andrew to stay over with *you*, that's fine. You're old enough to make your own decisions but a word of warning....just make sure you're careful. I don't want there to be any accidents under *my* roof! I've had more than my fair share of grief from your mother already so I definitely don't want any more. You can use the end double room if you like. Abbie and Gerald will be next door to you so do your best to keep the noise down,' she cackled unashamedly and winked at her.

'*Robyn*!' she exclaimed with a bright red face and Robyn decided she'd said enough on the matter.

Ellie was appalled and didn't raise her head again, peeling the potatoes with the skill of a piece-worker on a fast-food production line, merely stopping as required to tip the waste in the bin and replenish her bowl with more potatoes.

'When you've finished those potatoes, I wouldn't say no to a cup of coffee,' Robyn said in an attempt to break the uneasy silence. 'I'm dying for a drink.'

'I'll attend to it in a minute. I've almost finished now and I'm ready for a drink as well. What do you want me to do next?'

'Sprouts and carrots but please cover the potatoes with cold water first or they'll turn brown.'

'Will we be having Christmas pudding and mince pies for dessert?'

'Of course, with brandy sauce *and* I've baked my own mince pies,' she told her smugly. 'I made them a couple of days ago. There's loads of booze in and they smell absolutely delicious. I got a Black Forest gâteau as an alternative in case anyone doesn't like Christmas pudding.'

She had been on the verge of saying that the boys would probably prefer gâteau to Christmas pudding when she managed to stop herself in time.

'I'll just stack a few bottles of wine in the fridge while I remember and then I think we're pretty-well organised for the time being.'

'Have you finished setting the table?'

'More or less so you can bring Verity down now if you like and she can open a few birthday presents whilst we're enjoying our coffee. We can attend to the sprouts and carrots when Andrew arrives to take over.'

As Ellie went upstairs, Raine telephoned to wish Robyn a Merry Christmas.

'Merry Christmas to you too,' Robyn said softly. 'I'm so looking forward to having you and the boys here. I've hardly thought of anything else since you agreed to come.'

'Same here. I know you're busy but I just wanted to hear your voice. Is everything going according to plan?'

'Yes and Ellie's here helping me. She's just gone upstairs to wake Verity.'

'Does she know I'm coming now?'

'No, I haven't breathed a word. I thought it would be nice to surprise her when you arrived although I nearly let the cat out of the bag a few minutes ago when I was about to make a reference to the boys. She'll be thrilled to bits to see you.'

'How are you going to explain my presence to the others?'

'There's only Gerald and Abbie....oh and Ellie's boyfriend Andrew. I'll simply tell them you're my friend and that I've known you for some time. Ellie won't say anything she shouldn't. She's the soul of discretion.'

'But won't she think it odd, my being there with the boys?'

'Ellie's fully aware of what happened between us on the ship Raine, all thanks to you. You made it so obvious that she worked it out and asked me and so I didn't see the point in lying to her. I've told more than my share of lies in the past. You don't need to worry about Ellie. She'll be delighted for us; in fact it was Ellie who begged me to call you when your wife died.'

'Why? Did you need begging?'

'Don't twist my words! You know perfectly well why I was concerned about contacting you. I didn't want to open up old wounds and make matters any worse for you....or me.'

Raine laughed. 'Lighten up darling; I'm winding you up. You'll never know how important that call was to me and what it meant to hear your voice. It was a turning point in my life and brought me back from the brink of insanity, allowing me to take control of my life once more. I'll always be indebted to you for that. That said, I'm not looking forward to being the object of curiosity when I turn up at your place in front of your friends.'

Reassuringly she told him, 'There's no cause for concern. You'll be fine; you'll see. You'll get along well with Gerald and Abbie. They're nice people.'

'The boys are looking forward to coming. Since they called in the other day, they've hardly stopped talking about you.'

'How nice! By the way, did they get a visit from Father Christmas?'

'Oh Gawd, don't remind me, not that I need any reminding. Six o'clock they had me out of bed!' he groaned. 'I'm not joking; the whole house is like a battle ground.'

'I can imagine,' she laughed. 'Isn't it great though when they've reached that age? Verity's too young to understand yet but it's such a magical time for an older child. My sister and I used to get so excited in the run-up to Christmas Eve. Do you have brothers or sisters Raine?'

'No, but why don't we leave all the personal stuff until we can talk properly? Meanwhile, I promise I have no skeletons in my closet. It would be nice if we could go out for dinner one evening and discuss things quietly in a romantic atmosphere. I'm dying to find out everything about you.'

'You're right. Let's save it for the New Year. Are you going to be hungry later?'

'I'm hungry now, for you, that is. I'm glad we're back together again,' he sighed softly.

'You and me both but I must go now before Ellie reappears. I can hear her feet on the landing. What time will you be here?'

'I thought about two if that's alright?'

'That's perfect.'

'I'll bring some wine. See you later. Love you!'

'Happy birthday my darling little girl,' Robyn said when Ellie placed her in her arms. 'Who's a big girl now? Who's one year old today?' she cooed gently over the smiling child. 'Let's sit down and see what we have here.' She tore away the wrapping paper to reveal a huge pink fluffy rabbit. 'Look at that! Isn't that lovely?'

Verity babbled incomprehensibly and tried to put it in her mouth immediately.

'No, you mustn't eat it my precious,' Robyn said, pulling it away and turning to Ellie she chuckled. 'I think this was a big mistake. I should have got her a rubber duck!'

'Why not give her something else to open and I'll move it right out of the way when you've distracted her?' Ellie suggested.

'Good idea and I'll keep it well out of harm's way in the nursery. Why do babies always put things in their mouth I wonder? Right, let's see what's in this one now. Oh, just look at this beautiful dress from Auntie Ellie and Uncle Andrew. It's gorgeous Ellie. Thank you very much. You'll have to try it on later Verity when you've had your nice bubble bath and you can wear it when we go to see grandma. You'll be such a pretty girl in that.'

'It might be a bit too big for her yet but I thought it would be nice for the summer. She'll have grown into it by then. I couldn't resist it when I saw it and mum liked it too. There's another present here from mum. It goes with the dress.'

When Robyn opened it and found it was a matching hat she squealed with delight and flopped it on Verity's head. 'How sweet! Doesn't that look cute? I'll call your mum tomorrow and thank her. There's a few more to open but I think we'll leave them till later. I'd like to have everything ready by the time the guests arrive.'

Just then Andrew walked in with a large bouquet of flowers for Robyn.

'Merry Christmas,' he greeted her and turning his attention towards Ellie he kissed her fondly. 'Merry Christmas sweetheart. You look beautiful.'

'You're joking. I look an absolute wreck. I'm not even washed and changed yet.'

'So? You still look beautiful....and how's Verity?' He leaned over the gurgling child, making a funny face that made her chuckle. Then he gathered her in his arms and gave her a cuddle. 'Are you ready for your breakfast?'

'I'm sure she is,' Robyn answered as she walked towards the kitchen with her flowers to find a large vase. 'I'll get it ready.'

Once Robyn was out of earshot, Ellie whispered, 'Robyn said we could *both* stay over tonight if we wanted but I was too shocked to answer when she mentioned it.'

'What....separate rooms?'

344

'No, silly! That's what caused the embarrassment. She's given us a double, so what do you think?'

'What's there to think about Ellie? Who's being silly now? Too right I'm staying over if we can be together. What brought that about?'

She shrugged her shoulders. 'I don't really know. She's been rather odd lately. She just came straight out with it but she threatened me not to be careless under *her* roof because she wouldn't want another altercation with mum.'

'Good old Robyn. I don't know what's come over her recently either. The kennel staff were telling me only the other day that she's changed from an ogre to a pleasant human being. I must admit though, she was always alright with me. Did you hear that she sent a stack of hot pizzas and half a dozen bottles of wine through to them one day last week? She also bought everyone a Christmas present and told them if they got through their duties quickly, they could pack up and have a Christmas party. Pasty-face told me and he said the pizzas were expensive ones with plenty of topping. They were so shell-shocked that Ruddy Peter blurted out a real swear-word and an extremely bad one at that,' he guffawed raucously. 'Mary Cotteral was absolutely furious and gave him a right telling off, threatening to report him to Mrs. Ainsley if he ever used such language again.'

Ellie chuckled at that. 'I've been off all week so I didn't know about that but you remember I told you she'd had a male visitor the other day? Happen it's something to do with him that's caused her to be all sweetness and light but she refused to say anything

345

when I asked her about him. I'll have another go at her today when we're on our own because I can see a big difference in her too. Something's happened to put a smile on her face so it's bound to come out sooner or later. '

'Some*thing* or some*one's* responsible,' Andrew stated candidly. 'There's no doubt at all about that!'


'Merry Christmas,' everybody called cheerily when Gerald and Abbie arrived.

'Well, look at you,' Robyn said as she took hold of Sophie. 'Aren't you just gorgeous? Are you still a good little girl for your mummy and daddy?'

'She certainly is,' Gerald responded on behalf of both of them with a broad grin. 'Sophie is well and truly daddy's little treasure, aren't you my darling?'

'Are you keeping busy Gerald?' Robyn enquired, handing Sophie to Ellie as she took his coat.

'I'm always busy but I need to be, the way Abbie spends money on Sophie,' he commented dryly. 'I don't think I'm telling lies when I say Sophie hasn't one article of clothing she's worn on more than one occasion.'

'Neither have I Gerald,' Abbie interposed matter-of-factly. 'Maybe you should have married a bloke and adopted a son if you'd wanted to economise.'

'Huh, there's no *maybe* about it. I'm damned sure I should have!' he informed her, winking at Robyn.

Robyn and Ellie laughed at the wordplay between the two of them.

'Excuse me....would you like me to get everyone a drink, Robyn?' Andrew interrupted.

'Please do Andrew and would you also put on the Christmas Carol CD. When you've attended to the guests, perhaps you wouldn't mind having a word with Marianne on reception as well please. If she's not driving home, take her a drink too. Excuse me for a moment. I need to check on the food.'

While Robyn was busy finishing the starter in the kitchen, the telephone extension in the sitting room rang and Ellie answered it.

'Some more guests have arrived Ellie,' Marianne advised her. 'Shall I send them through?'

'Er....just hang on a second. I didn't know anyone else was coming.'

Ellie hurried to the kitchen to speak to Robyn and repeated what she'd been told. 'Marianne wants to know if she should send them straight in.'

'It's alright. I'll attend to them,' she said.

Without any explanation, Robyn walked from the room and reappeared moments later with Raine and his two boys.

Ellie was thunderstruck when she looked up. She yelled, '*Raine*!' at the top of her voice and ran over to hug him, while Abbie and Gerald were bemused at the sight of this unknown young man and his two boys who had presumably been invited to Robyn's home to join everyone for Christmas dinner.

Abbie was already rehearsing a list of questions.

'I bet you're surprised to see me,' Raine laughed as he greeted Ellie with an affectionate kiss on each cheek.

'That has to be the understatement of the decade,' she remarked before turning to Robyn. '*You've* got

347

some explaining to do but at least now I know why you're prancing around with a permanent smile on your face. I supposed I ought to have guessed.'

Demurely, Robyn smiled before announcing, 'I'd like to introduce everyone to my friend Raine and these handsome young boys are his sons, Michael and Timmy. Raine, these are my very good friends, Abbie and Gerald and this is Andrew, Ellie's young man. Ellie of course, needs no introduction.'

'Pleased to meet you,' each replied politely, while with raised eyebrows, Abbie stared questioningly at Robyn, desperately seeking an explanation but none was forthcoming.

Gerald immediately jumped up from his seat and shook Raine's hand vigorously before introducing himself formally. 'Sit here next to me. I'm Gerald Dunne and I'm pleased to make your acquaintance er....'

'Raine Quinlan,' he answered and Robyn froze on the spot when she heard his surname.

'May I introduce my wife, Abbie and this bundle of joy is our daughter, Sophie.'

'I'm delighted to meet you,' Raine said.

Staring into his smiling eyes, Abbie replied, 'The pleasure is all mine and I have to say you've got to be Robyn's best kept secret and I can't wait to hear how you two met.'

When the introductions were drawing to a close, Robyn unbuttoned the boys' coats while Raine, in a child-like voice, told Verity how pretty she looked in her red velvet dress and she gurgled gleefully as if she had understood his most flattering remark.

Andrew wandered across to shake his hand. 'I'm delighted to meet you Raine. Can I get you a drink? Have you travelled far?'

'No, it's only a thirty minute drive from where we live….an easy journey. I wouldn't say no to a lager please if there's one going spare.'

'Make yourselves comfortable and would you get a drink for the boys as well please Andrew. I need to check on something in the kitchen,' Robyn said.

Abbie shot after her like a greyhound coursing a hare. 'So who's the gorgeous hunk, you dark horse? You've certainly kept *him* very quiet.'

'Raine's just a friend,' she said reticently.

Her taciturn reply added to the intrigue, whetting Abbie's appetite for more. 'Hey….this is *me* you're talking to and we never ever keep secrets from each other so tell me, how long has this been going on?'

'I've known him for a couple of years but really, he's just a friend,' she repeated.

'You've known him a couple of years and you've never once thought to mention him to me? Are you sleeping with him?'

Robyn laughed heartily. Her friend always had to know every last detail. 'No Abbie, I'm not sleeping with him.'

Abbie stared at her incredulously. 'Well, if I were single he wouldn't be just a friend. I wouldn't think twice about sleeping with him.'

'Abbie, in my experience *you* would never think twice before sleeping with anyone! I seem to recall how you pulled your dial when you didn't manage to get Gerald between the sheets on your first date.'

'I did nothing of the kind!' she retorted touchily. 'Anyway, don't change the subject. I want to know *everything* about the guy. Where did you find him?'

'We met on the QE2 when I went to visit Bryony. Raine was travelling alone too so he hung out with Ellie and me.'

'Ah!' she said with a sideways glance, her mono-syllabic reply speaking volumes. 'Now I understand why you were exhausted when you got home....jet-lag indeed! Still, who am I to talk? I expect I would have been knackered too with a gorgeous hunk like Raine pandering to my every whim.'

She flashed a scathing look at her friend. 'Have I ever told you you're disgusting?'

Her eyes twinkled with devilry. 'More times than I care to remember but it's water off a duck's back.'

In case you've forgotten Abbie, I'd only just lost my husband when I made that trip. Raine was just a friend. Besides he was married.'

'So? Since when did that stop anybody getting a leg over?' and in response to the further black look flashed back, she apologised. 'Okay I'm sorry, but I wouldn't have to speculate if you told me.'

Robyn smiled submissively. 'Alright, I'll tell you everything when we're alone but I need to get back to my guests now.'

'Tomorrow then! I'll not stand the suspense any longer. Is he still married?....Divorced?' she further quizzed when Robyn remained tight-lipped. 'Won't you even tell me that?'

'I'll tell you about him *tomorrow* and not before!' Robyn called over her shoulder and Abbie returned to the others, the vast majority of her questions still unanswered and dying of curiosity.

'Will you put these presents under the tree please Robyn?' Raine said, handing her a large bag. 'I've brought some wine and a bottle of Champagne too.'

'There's some here from us too,' Abbie said. 'I'll help you carry them in.'

'It's alright, I'll carry them,' Raine offered and he followed Robyn through to the dining room.

As he edged his way past the beautifully adorned table, he caught sight of his place card and laughed. 'Now there's a fine name if ever I saw one,' he said with a twinkle in his eye.

'Oh, shut up Raine. You've spoiled my joke now. Well it's stopping right where it is and I'll leave it to *you* to explain the *Doctor* part.'

'I'm so happy to be here,' he sighed, kissing her affectionately. 'I've waited so long to do that again. I wish we were alone.'

'Yes, but unfortunately we're not,' she reminded him, escaping his hold. 'We'd better get back to the others before all the tongues start wagging. Abbie's already had a go at me. Besides, our dinner's ready now so I'd like to get everyone seated. Maybe you could call them in and show them where to sit? Are you hungry?'

'Like I said earlier, hungry for you Robyn but I'm sure I can manage a little turkey too.'

As the guests took their places, Gerald remarked. 'I see you're a Doctor, Raine. What's your field?'

At that, Robyn pricked up her ears, smugly awaiting his explanation.

'I'm a Veterinary Consultant,' and turning to his hostess he winked triumphantly whilst whispering, 'I'm afraid that's another joke ruined.'

She placed Raine's bowl of soup in front of him, contemplating whether to dribble a few drops down the front of his shirt and muttered through clenched teeth, 'You know I'm going to kill you later, don't you?'

Raine threw back his head and laughed.

'So how's your work different from being a Vet?' Gerald enquired.

'I initially studied for VetMB, Membership of the Royal College of Veterinary Surgeons and pursuant to that, I embarked on in-depth studies in research science. I *am* a Veterinary surgeon but add to that a more diverse expertise in Biomedical Research that interests me a hell of a sight more and that's my job description. So how about you Gerald; I understand you're a solicitor?'

'I am. I went into Law straight from school. Like you, after qualifying, I wanted more. I was eager to learn to broaden my horizons. To this day I'm still learning. It's a minefield. Legislation is constantly changing. There are new and amended laws almost daily.'

'It's the same in science,' Raine agreed. 'There'll always be new techniques; there'll always be more exciting discoveries and breakthroughs. Evolution is a perpetual learning process and I find that very inspirational because you can never know from one week to the next what you or your colleagues will discover next.'

352

'You can say that again!' Robyn grunted. 'I won't argue with that. Merry Christmas everybody. I hope you all enjoy your meal.'

As each responded to the Christmas greeting, she took her place beside Raine.

'That soup was really delicious,' Raine remarked graciously when Robyn collected his bowl. 'Would you like me to carve the turkey?'

'Please, since you appear to be the most apt,' she replied with a smile that he interpreted as less than sincere. He arose and followed her to the kitchen.

'How could you do that to me?' Robyn demanded and he laughed. Wrapping his arms around her he said, 'For want of repeating myself, I don't tell lies. You were the one who ridiculed my name and you were also the one who insisted on secrecy from the moment we met. Anyway, what could be of greater importance than what we knew from the outset? We fell in love with each other, not with our names or professions. Don't forget, you withheld a great deal more from me than I ever did from you. He looked deeply into her eyes and kissed her lovingly and she returned his kiss.

'Where do you want these dishes stacked?' Ellie piped up with a wide beaming smile and Robyn and Raine leaped apart. 'Too late! Caught in the act and not before time. I'm so happy for you both. I didn't know you were a Vet Raine.'

'Didn't you?' Robyn asked innocently.

'I'm sorry. I must have forgotten to mention that,' Raine spluttered. 'Er....shall I get the turkey carved? I'm sure everyone must be starving.'

The brief and embarrassing embrace was quickly forgotten once the main course was served.

Following a delightful Christmas meal, enhanced by pleasant conversation, everyone returned to the living room to relax before opening their Christmas presents, though special consideration was given to Raine's boys who were on tenterhooks to discover whether Father Christmas had remembered to pay a visit there, as Robyn had suggested he might.

'Take them back in and find theirs,' Robyn said quietly to Raine. 'They're wrapped in blue paper. It doesn't seem fair to keep them waiting any longer. Besides, it'll keep them occupied while the rest of us enjoy a few quiet minutes. They were very well behaved at the table and I didn't fail to notice they have impeccable table manners. You should be very proud of yourself.'

The boys scurried back with Raine, their excited eyes glued to the armful of packages they each had to open and everyone's attention was directed to the small hands that ripped frantically at the decorative wrapping paper as it was reduced to shreds.

There were squeals of delight at the contents that kept them occupied for the rest of the afternoon and for some time, Verity was more than happy to play with the wrapping paper.'

There was a humorous episode a little while later when Timmy piped up noisily, '*Robyn*! Look what *Ferret's* doing!'

Raine threw back his head and laughed. 'Timmy, her name's *Verity* not *Ferret*, though I have to say the latter might be more fitting,' he made known to the women. 'She's just removed all the contents of someone's handbag.'

'Oh, you little horror....it's mine,' Abbie chuckled as Robyn hurriedly hoisted Verity into her arms to move her over to where Michael and Timmy were playing with their new toys.

'Sit here and play with the boys,' Robyn scolded her mildly. 'You mustn't empty Aunty Abbie's bag all over the floor.'

'Aw!' Timmy complained in obvious annoyance. 'Does she have to sit with us? I don't like playing with girls.'

'Well you will when you're older, won't he dad?' Michael said, displaying a plausible air of authority. 'I've got a girlfriend at school. Her name's Rebecca and she's nice. She's in my class and she sits on the next desk to me.'

'My God, I don't believe I'm hearing this!' Raine exclaimed as everyone exploded in fits of laughter. 'He's only six!'

When the hilarity had finally subsided, a relaxing peace descended as they opened their presents.

Raine looked round to ensure the coast was clear before whispering to Robyn, 'Save mine until later. I'd like us to be alone when you open it. As soon as you get the opportunity, find a reason to leave the room.'

She awaited an appropriate break in proceedings before excusing herself. 'I'll be back in a jiffy,' she announced to the others. 'I've something to give to the staff who offered to work today and they'll be leaving shortly.'

She picked up two heavy bags containing bottles of wine and Raine jumped up to assist her.

'Here, let me take them,' he volunteered, slipping Robyn's present in one of the bags as he took them from her.

'Can I come?' Timmy yelled boisterously. 'I want to see the animals.'

'No,' Ellie replied. 'You must stay here with me. You can see them later. Andrew wants to show you a magic trick, don't you?'

'Do I?' he questioned.

'*Yes you do*!' she advised him demonstratively, at the same time glancing at Robyn with a wry smile.

When they were well out of audible range, Robyn laughed. 'Everyone knows exactly what's going on! They're not stupid. The only ones we're fooling are ourselves. Like I told you earlier, Abbie's already been quizzing me about you and it's no use trying to pull the wool over her eyes. She'll not rest until she knows everything. That said, I'm beyond caring who knows how much I love you. Why should we have to keep it a secret?'

'My sentiments entirely,' he said, handing her the gift-wrapped package. 'Happy Christmas darling. I hope you like it.'

Robyn removed the wrapping carefully, revealing an orange-juice carton and smiled reflectively at the memory of the unfortunate incident aboard the ship and that had first brought them together.

'Don't worry. The boys drank the juice. I couldn't risk doing that to you again! Please open it,' he said quietly.

Nervously, she twisted her crystal pendant, aware of what she would find when she looked inside and her misted eyes searched his.

'Raine, it's too soon,' she spoke softly as the mist turned to tears. 'It's only two or three weeks since your wife died. You're not ready for this yet.'

Placing a forefinger on her lips to silence her, he asked, 'Were *you* ready when you searched for me on the ship two or three weeks after your husband died?' and then, answering his own question added, 'Yes you were, even when you knew I could make no commitment. Our roles are reversed now; I can also make that commitment to you now and believe me, it's what I want. I want you. *Carpe diem*; seize the day, darling. We've both had unexpected tragedies in our lives and we don't know what else lies lurking. There's no need to rush into anything; I'm not seeking that. I still have many bridges to cross but it'll be all the easier, knowing I have you by my side for support. There'll always be a special place in my heart for Victoria, just as there will in yours for David. That'll never change but the past is the past and life has to go on, so yes Robyn, I *am* ready for this….truly.'

Raine opened the carton and removed the velvet covered box which he opened.

She caught her breath at the sight of the exquisite diamond ring. 'Please say you'll marry me Robyn. I love you so much and I'm not prepared to lose you for a second time.'

She didn't even pause for thought. 'Yes….yes of course I will,' she cried, smiling through tears that

357

scalded her eyes. 'You wouldn't believe how many times I've dreamt of this day but I never believed it possible.'

He slipped the ring on her finger and took her in his arms. Brushing his lips against hers he said, 'I'll be a good father to Verity. I'll love and care for her as if she were my own.' Then, with a faraway look in his eyes Raine smiled reflectively. 'Do you recall I once said I wanted the whole fairytale? Well now I have it.'

She nuzzled his neck affectionately. 'That was *my* fairytale too but I honestly believed it to be beyond reach. I can't even begin to describe how contented I feel. Do you think we should tell the others?'

He cupped her beautiful smiling face in his hands and gazing intensely into her eyes he spoke softly. 'Why stop there? Why not tell the whole world?'